High
Country

Literature of the American West
William Kittredge, General Editor

High Country

A Novel

For Christine,
who knows
the waters

Good
fishing — always

Bill Wyman

Willard Wyman

UNIVERSITY OF OKLAHOMA PRESS : NORMAN

Excerpt from "Time Out" by Robert Frost from *The Poetry of Robert Frost* edited by Edward Connery Lathem. Copyright 1942, copyright 1970 by Lesley Frost Ballantine. © 1969 by Henry Holt and Company. Reprinted by permission of Henry Holt and Company, LLC.

Special thanks to Fiona E. O'Neill for use of her lovely drawings.

Library of Congress Cataloging-in-Publication Data

Wyman, Willard, 1930–
   High Country : a novel / Willard Wyman.
      p. cm. — (Literature of the American West ; v. 15)
   ISBN 978-0-8061-3697-4 (cloth)
   ISBN 978-0-8061-3899-2 (paper)
   1. Sierra Nevada (Calif. and Nev.)—Fiction. 2. Packhorse camping—Fiction. I. Title. II. Series.

PS3623.Y645H54 2005
813'.6—dc22

2005043057

High Country: A Novel is Volume 15 in the Literature of the American West series.

4 5 6 7 8 9 10

In memory of

Irving Howe, Wallace Stegner, and Ian Watt
Different teachers; writers all

It took that pause to make him realize
The mountain he was climbing had the slant
As of a book being held up before his eye
Robert Frost, from "Time Out"

Contents

Book One: The Swan

The Swan Range lifts high above Montana's Swan Valley, its eastern flank spilling its waters down into the South Fork of the Flathead River as it begins its long run for the Columbia. Across the South Fork, other mountains climb up to the China Wall, where all waters change direction and begin their journey to the Missouri.

The million acres draining into the South Fork provide a home for every animal surviving in America's Northwest—and for a few men as well. This wilderness is now called The Bob, for a man who fell in love with it and found a way to preserve it but could never make it his home.

But this story is not so much about the man who found the country as it is about a man the country found. It is about Ty Hardin, who began packing into it when he was fifteen, moving to still higher country when the Swan grew too crowded. It is about his living and dying doing what he loved, his heartbeat in the mountains as surely as other men's are in their work or their art, their families or their women.

It is about the life High Country gave him.

Learning (1937)

"Sometimes in these mountains," Fenton spoke almost gently now, "you find yourself learning more than you got time to think about."

1

Bitterroot

Will Hardin claimed nothing ever had been easy for the Hardin family, that there'd always been a cloud hanging over them. But his son wasn't so sure. From the first Ty could see why his grandfather, old Eban Hardin, had built the barn where he did, the house. Even if the corrals needed patching year in and year out, they were good to work in, had a plan, made sense. Ty thought Eban was probably looking at better things ahead when the big freeze came in and wiped him out.

The big outfit had the Hardin ranch now. They kept Will Hardin on to look after the land his father had homesteaded, live in the house his father had built, teach his sons what the land had taught him. It was a dark picture he painted. Without Mary Hardin around it would have been a darker picture his boys saw. But she had a way of finding light—especially for her boys. She saw that Jimmy understood the big outfit's equipment, could drive it in a straight line and fix it when it broke. She knew Dan had a way with numbers. And it didn't take her long to see that Ty had some of old Eban Hardin in him, had a way with animals—with horses and mules, even with the half-wild range cattle they had to doctor wherever they found them.

Which is how Ty cut open his head and broke his arm. He was heading back to the corrals with a half-frozen calf over his saddle when he hit ice on the same cut bank he'd crossed to rescue the calf, the sun behind the ridge now, the air snapping cold. They went down hard, the filly tumbling over Ty and crashing through the ice before plunging up again, wet and shaking, one hock bloody. Ty waded out to her, knowing something was wrong with his arm and troubled by an odd warmth on his face. He got the calf back over the saddle and washed the blood from the filly's leg. He wiped to clear his eyes and found blood, blotted it with his sleeve as he led the filly out of the draw.

It was almost dark when he came into the corrals, the cow following as though being led. Blood had crusted on his face; the calf hung limp across the saddle. Ty was afraid they would lose it. He was thinking about how to put the mother over an orphaned calf when he heard his father.

"Shit." Will peered at Ty in the failing light. "Got scratched up. Knew I'd have to fire up that damn lantern." Ty heard matches scratching in the shed, saw the lantern take. He led the filly into the broken barn, the light casting outsize shadows behind his father and across old gear, broken and abandoned along the walls.

"Lucky it's still numb." His father probed at the wound. "That'll help when your mother starts in."

"That calf could make it." Ty watched Will ease the calf off the saddle and carry it under the shed, the cow following, too played out to protest. But the filly wasn't played out at all, getting so jumpy when Will came at her that Ty had to calm her himself. He slid the saddle off with his good arm, doctored her leg before following the lantern up to the house.

His mother cleaned his wound, pulling the cut together with tape. She worried over his arm even more, wrapping it and fixing a sling before telling them what to get in Missoula after they saw the doctor.

"Wish them doctors didn't cost so," Will said. "Might save some if we let the damn calves die."

"Better than no doctors. Lucky you grew up at all, Will."

"I was a lot more careful, is what I was. Wouldn't hurt to practice on that." Will got up from the table. "Save money too." He got out the makings for a cigarette, surprised Ty was the one who'd gotten hurt.

They left the next morning before the others saddled and got started for school, needing to get the pickup out while the road was frozen.

Ty was looking forward to a long day in town.

When they left the doctor's office they went to Horace Adams's feed store, Ty with a cast on his arm and shiny white bandages over the stitches. Will had a list of things to do, but Ty knew he'd want to complain to Horace Adams first. Horace supported half the ranchers in that country anyway, never expecting much until folks got their hay in and their calves sold, carrying many even beyond that.

In no time Will and Horace were telling each other how bad things were. Ty drifted off, feeling unsettled not so much because his arm hurt as because he didn't want to hear that kind of talk. He knew ranch people liked to complain, but he also knew this time they were right. There wasn't enough money to do anything *but* complain. Or pretend. Sometimes when he was riding out to check on the cattle he'd start thinking about the crazy schemes his brothers had, and he'd get so blue he'd ride past what he needed to do. It made him even sadder to hear his mother. She was always looking for ways to lighten Will's dour predictions, which was getting harder and harder to do. The big outfit didn't pay much, and they were down to just a handful of cows of their own. And it always seemed their calves that were lost each spring, not the big outfit's.

In one corner of his feed store, Horace kept tack he got from hands down on their luck. Ty went to look at the saddles, dreaming to have his own, one that fit him, that he could rig just the way he wanted. A tall, deep-chested man with the whitest hair Ty had ever seen was holding up a pannier, checking it for weak spots. He brought it down and looked at Ty.

"See you been chased around by one of them grizzlies," he said. "Too bad you wasn't quick enough to step aside."

"No, sir," Ty said, pleased. "I just misread the ground. My horse rolled on me some."

"You think these panniers'll last me two or three seasons if old Horace don't want all my money? They ain't half bad."

"We only use ours to put out salt." Ty thought of the ragged panniers Will kept in a corner of the barn. "They been used pretty hard."

"I believe you have too." The man took in the tattered Levi jacket draped over the cast. "Well, I seen some fellers in worse shape when they *did* get out of the way. Runnin' too fast in my country is near as dangerous as wrestlin' with a damn bear anyhow." He hooked a finger in the ears of the panniers, put them over his shoulder, and went over to barter.

Ty went back to the saddles, thinking his father seemed less discouraged in town.

They had a sandwich at the Elkhorn. "Try this." Will slid a bottle of beer over to Ty. "Ease your ache." He took a pull from his. "Might ease mine too." The beer seemed to perk Will up. He even began kidding with some of the men as they came in.

After their errands they came back to the Elkhorn, using up time before heading for home. Will wanted the meadow frozen solid before he crossed it. He'd had to harness the mules too many times when Mary bogged down in the pickup.

Ty didn't mind. An old-timer got him into a game of checkers. Ty liked the man's stories and the way he laughed when he made a run on the board. He liked seeing his father there too. He wouldn't call Will happy, but with the other men talking about their troubles he didn't seem nearly as low as he'd been on the way to town.

Before long the white-haired man from the feed store came in. He walked directly over to the table where Ty was playing checkers.

"Well, Jasper," he said to the old-timer. "See you found somebody broke up enough so you might win." He looked at the board. "Go easy. This old boy's havin' a hard time. His horse rolled on him, and now you're about to chase him off the board." He took a swallow of Jasper's beer and looked at Ty. "Don't get to bettin' with Jasper Finn. Could hurt worse than rollin' around under your filly." He took another swallow and headed for the bar, where he started right in talking with Will. It seemed to Ty the man had a way of having a conversation with people before they knew they were in one.

"Don't let Fenton scare you," Jasper Finn told him. "I ain't gonna do no bettin'. Save stealin' from colts for when I get old." That made him laugh so hard he began to cough. Ty whacked him on the back until he got his breath. Then he watched him sit up, sip his beer, and solemnly jump every one of Ty's remaining checkers. Ty was so startled, Jasper got to laughing and coughing again, drinking more beer to quiet things down. "Can't beat age and cunnin'," he wagged a finger at Ty, "not with no broke arm."

The bartender came over with a pitcher of beer.

"From Fenton," he said. "He's feelin' unusual generous."

Jasper didn't even offer a thank-you, accepting the beer as though he'd ordered it himself. He told Ty that Fenton Pardee was a packer who packed across the Swan Range all the way to the big divide. Ty didn't know where the Swan Range was, but he didn't let on to Jasper, who was happy explaining that he did a lot of work for Pardee himself, most often as a cook but sometimes as a wrangler. Once as a guide.

"They was pretty thin for guides that year. But I got them fellers some elk. Hell, in them days elk would drift into camp for coffee." He poured a glass, looking disappointed when Ty refused. "Old Fenton gets a lot of folks into tight spots." He drank, watching to make sure Ty was listening. "But he knows mountains. Slickest packer you ever see. All them rough places, and he always got me out. Hardly a scratch. Just frostbit. A little."

On the way home Will told Ty all he knew about Fenton Pardee. And Ty listened almost as though he sensed the part Fenton Pardee would play in his life. He told Ty about Fenton coming up with Tommy Yellowtail to pick up his own father's mules, explaining that after the big freeze Eban Hardin decided on mules, figuring they were tough enough to fight off any winter and he could always sell them to the army. When the army shipped up all the mules they needed from Missouri, Eban was stuck with more than he could handle. He didn't know what he would have done if Fenton hadn't got the Forest Service contract and come to get them.

Will thought about that, rolling a cigarette with one hand, steering with the other, the truck lurching onto the shoulder as he made his smoke. Ty cracked the window a little to keep Will awake. He wanted to hear all of it.

"Pardee's hair black as a raven, then. But he wasn't too young to learn. Your grandfather knew mules. Like you. Got along with all them four-legged bastards, even the cows he kept to remind him of the freeze." He wound down his window, spit, wound it back up.

"One didn't have no ears. The other lamed up till she died. Feelin' never did come back in her leg." He hunched down as though to warm himself.

"It's cold as Canada in here." Will shook himself. "If you're so handy with windows, you drive. That cast don't seem to slow you none."

"Just a little fresh air. I believe it's good for you."

"Not if I'm froze." He slowed. "You drive. I'll crank windows."

Before Will fell asleep he told Ty how Fenton Pardee had trailed the mules, Tommy Yellowtail ahead with a bell mare, down to Missoula, crossing Clark Fork at the University to reach the Blackfoot, then up that to the Clearwater and on to Fenton's meadows below Crippled Elk Lake.

Ty liked hearing about old times, though he was relieved when Will finally slept and he could enjoy the drive up the Bitterroot. He watched the moon on the river and thought about families that had to move into town. He guessed this wasn't as bad as the big freeze. But almost. You didn't have to see your cattle die, just watch as someone took them away.

He'd bounced across the frozen ruts before Will woke. The generator was going, and Mary used the light to make sure they unloaded everything. Then she poured a glass of milk for Will and pushed Ty off to bed.

"Glad he got to relax." She turned back the frayed blanket. "His fretting won't fix anything."

She sounded so resigned Ty got to feeling low himself, even after all the excitement of being in town. And he was surprised to hear her talk that way about his father, about her own fears. He went to sleep thinking about them, their worries blending into his own.

In the night his arm started to throb. The pills were in Will's pocket, and Ty didn't want to wake him. He tried to forget the throbbing by thinking about the summer ahead, which didn't look good. Though they might save that calf he'd brought in, they'd already lost three. And the cattle prices were still going down. The only good thing was they wouldn't have to work the mules so hard. The big outfit had contracted the haying out to a company with all the newest equipment, pulled by their big tractors.

It might cause a lot of racket, but the mules would get a rest.

With his arm in the cast Ty spent most of his time around the barn and the sagging corrals. Will had made repairs over the years, but the corrals still looked tired. Ty guessed old Eban needed things in a hurry when he built. Each spring Ty had helped Will brace a post here or string some wire there. Now he saw places that needed fresh patching—and sections that needed to be torn out and rebuilt. He couldn't do either. All he could do was look, see what ought to be done. There was plenty of that.

Ty did what he could, mostly feeding and some doctoring—when he could do it with one hand. He couldn't remember spending so much time around his mother and father before, or hearing so much talk between them. It seemed like one long conversation, interrupted by what had to be done and then picked up again as though never put down by either. And always the talk was bad. Though the haying contractor would take some burden off the mules, it meant less money from the big outfit. How to get through the summer until the calves were sold gnawed at them, and everyone had a part to play. Jimmy had signed on with the haying contractor. There would be a little money there—unless Jimmy ran off with the Malone girl. And Mary found a job for Dan at the Missouri Bar, sweeping and keeping the ice chest full and making sure the books balanced.

"He'll learn something," Mary told Will. "Not much left to learn here."

Will nodded, rolling a cigarette. The truth was he saw no reason to learn anything about ranching anymore. To him it was a dead-end trail.

c﹒ɔ

A week before the cast was to come off, Ty came into the kitchen with a pail of milk to find his mother and father at it again. It seemed to him all their concerns of the past weeks filled the room. Will went right on talking, but Mary got up and started fussing with the dishes.

"It ain't such a big thing," Will said to her. "Ty knows horses, and the man has that government contract."

"You might as well know your father wrote that man up at Crippled Elk Lake." Mary was wiping her hands on her apron. "Nothing but a bedroll all summer and not much more come winter."

Suddenly the tie on the apron broke. It seemed kind of funny to Ty, but he knew there was nothing to laugh about. Everything seemed to be breaking around the place. Mary kept wiping her hands with the loose apron.

"He thinks you could help with their stock." She looked at him.

"Who does?"

"Why, your father. We haven't heard back from that man Pardee."

It was three more weeks before they did. And Fenton Pardee said all he needed to say on a penny postcard.

> Will—It might work. If he can shoe I can teach him the packing. He will learn the rest soon enough. When school quits send him up.
>
> Fenton

When the day came, Ty put what he needed in his grandfather's old kit bag. He put on his best Levis and his best shirt and jammed his socks and underwear into the old saddlebags Will gave him, deciding to wear Jimmy's outgrown jacket rather than carry it.

Mary looked to see what he'd left and was surprised to see he had about everything he owned with him. She gave him some peanut-butter sandwiches she'd wrapped in brown paper. He put them in the saddlebags with his socks. He'd grown tall, but there was still no weight. He looked much too young to be leaving home.

"You look older." Mary's hands were playing at her apron again. "Be careful. We don't want you coming home in some new cast."

He gave her an awkward hug and she felt his leanness through the jacket, the tightness of his body the only sign he gave her.

She went into the house after their dust settled, thinking she might have a cry. But somehow she couldn't. She took off her apron and found a needle and set about sewing on the tie. It had broken loose again.

Ty felt hollow on the ride into Missoula. He ate one of the sandwiches, feeling a little sad about what was behind him, a little worried about what was ahead. He wasn't nervous about the work; he was just worried that Fenton Pardee wouldn't stand still long enough to answer any questions. And Will wasn't much help. He just drove, concentrating on the road as he smoked. It seemed to Ty his father looked more pessimistic than ever.

His worries grew when they pulled up at the feed store and Horace Adams explained that Pardee was picking up mules north of Hungry Horse and couldn't find anyone to meet Ty.

"Don't you fret." Horace looked at Ty. "I'll ship you out there with the lumberjacks. Won't have to test that bad arm hitching." He looked at Will. "He's growed. Up but not out." His eyes turned back to Ty, the kit bag, and the ragged jacket. "And you got your gear. That's good. Gets cold as a witch tit in that country.

"Fenton will approve of your boy's duffle," Horace said to Will. "What won't snug into them saddlebags he can fit in his pockets." He led Ty over toward the secondhand tack. "Look at the saddles. Fenton needs some bad but claims I'm a robber if I want cash money. You best find one out there that won't cripple you up if you're in it for twenty hours. That'll be one of the short days."

Ty saw that one was a Meana rig, broken in just right. He rubbed a hand along it, tried to focus on it, but his mind drifted. He wondered how far he had to go. How he'd find Pardee when he finally got close.

After awhile Will came over, looking better after talking with Horace.

"Them lumber boys'll get you out there," he said. "Think I'll slip over to the Elkhorn and get a bite before I head back. Wanna come along?"

"I got the sandwiches," Ty said. "Guess I'll wait. Hope I can find Mr. Pardee when I get close."

"You'll find him. Too goddamned big to miss. There ain't a man woman or child up there don't know who he is. Or has had to listen to him talk about his mules. Just don't test that broke arm too soon. And learn the knots, if he'll slow down to where you can see how he ties 'em."

At the Elkhorn Will heard more bad news than he wanted to hear. And spent more money than he meant to spend. It was late when he finally left, so he didn't bother stopping back by the feed store.

By that time Ty had eaten the other two sandwiches. He'd had plenty of opportunity to look at the Meana saddle too, which was rigged almost the way he'd rig one himself. He examined it again and again, looking up every time anyone came in the door.

It turned out the men from the sawmill didn't even come into town until the next day. Ty had to wait three more days before they were ready to go back to work at their mill below Crippled Elk Lake.

He didn't see Will and Mary again until after the big Christmas snow.

2

One Way to Shoe a Mule

The lumberjacks were still drunk when they got to the feed store, which didn't seem to bother Horace. He threw the Meana saddle in the pickup, saying if no one had the money to buy it, Fenton might as well keep it oiled until they did.

"Got somethin' else too." He went back in and came out with a blanket-lined canvas coat.

"Use it." He tossed it to Ty. "I won't be in those mountains anyway. Too busy cheerin' up all the hands outta work."

Ty had spent the last three days at the Adams's house, most of it working with Smoky Girl, Etta Adams's filly. Fenton Pardee had started her under a pack saddle the summer before, and when Etta fell in love with her, he'd traded her to Horace against his feed bill.

Only Smoky Girl hadn't worked out the way Fenton said she would. She was hard to ride right from the start, and over the winter Etta had given her so many sugar cubes and carrots and little sweet apples that getting more was all that interested her. She wouldn't even let Etta get a foot in the stirrup until Ty got hold of her. He made it so she wanted to pay attention, but mostly to Ty, who soon saw she was probably more filly than Etta could handle. He was about to talk with Horace about that when the lumberjacks came, swearing at each other and putting him between them in the cab. The man to Ty's right fell asleep immediately. The driver turned the heater up and started to doze off himself, the smell of beer and stale cigarettes getting so strong Ty felt sick. He was about to ask if he could wind down a window when the driver bolted upright and slapped himself. Ty was startled to see a man hit himself that hard.

"Jesus." The man's cheek was red from the blow. "Another dream about them yellow bears." He wound his window down, stuck his head out into the cold. "Bastards." He pulled his head back in. "Hate that dream."

But the subject kept him awake. From there until Seeley Lake he told Ty stories about the bears and their doings with lumberjacks and Pardee's packers. He was still telling stories when they pulled up at the bar at Seeley Lake. A man with a deep scar on his face was waiting. To Ty he seemed surprisingly good natured, considering the condition of the two lumberjacks.

"A man could get light headed off these fumes," he said, opening the door. "I'll drive. Don't say a goddamned word about why you're late. Those stories lost their excitement for me."

The man who had slapped himself got out and surrendered the keys. Ty climbed out himself, getting into the bed of the truck with the saddle and his kit bag.

"You the guy Fenton thinks can wrangle his mules?" The man with the scar looked at Ty. "Between Fenton and his mules you'll get a compressed education."

"My name is Ty Hardin." Ty was surprised to hear his voice crack. "I look forward to gettin' started."

The man looked at Ty more closely.

"Might as well call me Gus Wilson." He leaned across the bed of the truck, his hand out. "The rest do. Hell, there's Wilsons all over this valley. Won't hurt to know a few." The two lumberjacks were swearing at each other again, this time about who would ride in the middle. "These are some wilted. But they'll repair. They perk right up after a few days at the mill."

Gus Wilson said something persuasive to the men and they piled into the cab. After a few miles Ty dusted off the window and saw that both men had fallen asleep. He settled back, feeling better since the man with the scar had shown up.

He wondered about the scar, thinking it must have come from some scrape with a grizzly. Gus Wilson, he thought, must be the Wilson you could count on if you wanted to get somewhere. And more than anything else, Ty wanted to get somewhere. The more people he met the less sure he was of what he would be doing, even where he was going. The suspense was a lot worse than the work, no matter what that turned out to be.

He buttoned Horace Adams's coat against the wind, watching the high crest of the mountains rising to the east. He had studied this country on Horace's road map and was pretty sure he was looking at the Swan

Range. He didn't know what the name of the range was to the west,
but he saw it was almost as high. Snow was still on the ridges, purplish
looking in the cold and the distance. Beyond the Swan Range was the
mystery. He hadn't seen any roads there until well beyond the Conti-
nental Divide, almost to Great Falls. He wondered what was in between,
what kind of country you would find if you made it over that snow and
rode to where the waters changed direction.

The men woke at the road to Fenton Pardee's, tumbled out of the cab
stomping and spitting. The one who'd slapped himself took a long pee
while Gus Wilson unloaded Ty's gear. They all seemed livelier now that
they were closer to home. Ty liked hearing them call out their warnings
about Pardee and his mules, about the back-country.

He shouldered the saddle and started up the road, wondering what it
would be like to live in the shadow of a sawmill with big saws whining
and skinned logs stacked everywhere. He figured if Gus Wilson worked
there, there'd be some plan, some order to it.

Looking out across a little meadow that opened toward the Swan, he
wondered if there were any order ahead for him. He studied the peaks
lifting above the trees and suddenly had questions about everything. He
was sorry he hadn't learned more from Gus Wilson. He wanted to know
about trails and horseshoeing and schedules, fearing Fenton Pardee
wouldn't provide many answers. It was getting late, but he was held
there, caught by the sunlight slanting through the trees, deep shadows
on the Swan, snow on the ridges beyond.

He was not yet into his sixteenth year, but he already felt a long way
from home. And he was looking at a country that seemed to pull him
still farther. He felt odd, apart from himself, just as he felt apart from his
new height and the strength he was beginning to know, apart from his
family's problems—as far behind him now as the Bitterroot Valley. He
wasn't thinking about what was behind. Everything in him was looking
ahead, up at the Swan Range, across it and into the country beyond.

Fenton didn't have much faith in the way the Conner boys had
stacked the hay, and they'd only tied the bales down with one lash cinch.
He wasn't even sure they'd cinched that tight, which was why he was
creeping along at five miles an hour when he saw the boy staring off into
the woods. He was taller than Fenton remembered but thin as a post,
and Cody Jo's misgivings came back to him. She'd watched him hurry
Buck and Spec out to the barns that morning to shoe the mules. "Strong

as trees," she'd laughed, "and about as inventive. They need perfect directions." Fenton knew she was right. He also knew he wasn't very strong in the direction-giving department.

Which is why he'd sent for Ty, who was supposed to be different. He'd heard from Horace, who picked up things from people in the Bitterroot, that the boy had a lot of his grandfather, old Eban Hardin, in him. That was good enough for Fenton. He thought he might have learned more from Eban Hardin about mules than he'd learned in his forty years of packing, and he hadn't even seen him that often. But what he had seen of Eban made him know what he needed now: someone to quiet the stock, not fight it like Buck. And when Spec slipped off into the woods like the Indian he was, someone to watch the camp, know which way the horses were drifting, when to get wood, water, how to keep the bears away. He needed someone who looked after things rather than let them slide.

In the Elkhorn that night, Will Hardin had finally admitted that Ty was better than good with the stock—gifted somehow. But Will didn't linger on the good. Mostly he talked about how accidents weren't supposed to happen to Ty, who was so careful with his stock he never had wrecks. To Will Ty's accident proved how sour the Hardin luck had gone. He didn't need it verified with a lot of doctor bills.

Fenton thought Will must have been born discouraged. He didn't pay nearly as much attention to Will's complaining as he did to the other, the part that said it wasn't the boy's way to have accidents. Fenton figured that even if Ty had some of that gloominess that kept dragging Will down, he had the right training. He'd done about everything there was to be done on the Hardins' scratchy little ranch. And he had Eban Hardin's blood.

Trouble is, Fenton thought as he slowed the truck, he *is* just a boy, which had been Cody Jo's worry all along. "Boys grow," he'd told her. "I'll take it slow. Make it so he won't get jumpy—bent mean somehow."

Cody Jo had just smiled, saying she doubted it was in him to take things slow.

Maybe I am optimistic, Fenton thought, shoving the hay hooks off the dashboard to stop their rattling. But no serious deaths on my trips . . . and I never had to kill one mule.

Ty was considering what to say to Fenton Pardee when he realized the man was already talking, his hat pushed back on his white hair.

"I see Horace give in and sent me out that Meana saddle. Bet he didn't say a goddamned word about how deep he is in my pocket." Pardee leaned over and opened the door. "Throw in them things and climb up on the bales. It'll ride smoother with some weight up there."

It wasn't until the truck was moving that Ty realized he hadn't said a word to Fenton Pardee since the feed store. But he didn't think about that for long; he was bouncing around so he had to grab the rope to stay put. He supposed the rope was meant to cinch things down, but it was a lot looser than he would have it. The road got rougher and he flattened himself on the bales, holding on to keep from bouncing off.

Fenton was easing the flatbed around a curve when the bales started going. One popped loose from the second layer, then the bale Ty was on started to go, Ty scrambling to keep from going with it. But bales came out from underneath and the whole stack tilted and went, Ty still scrambling but scrambling now to keep from being buried in bales. He hit the ground running, still clutching the rope but inside its loop now and running to stay upright. He fended off bales and got closer to the truck, holding the rope with one hand and pounding on the door with the other.

Fenton hit the brakes, figuring something had gone wrong with his gear box. He was surprised to see bales fly past and bounce up the road. Ty went by as fast as the bales, running until the rope took him down, a final bale knocking out his wind before bouncing on.

Fenton thought he'd seen something go by with the bales and got out to check, thinking maybe the trouble wasn't his gear box after all. He was surprised to find Ty on the side of the road opening and closing his mouth as though he wanted to say something.

"Doubted that rope was tight," Fenton said, looking at the bales scattered along the road. He reached in the truck for the hay hooks. "Well, we ain't got far to go. Lets us load up a few and send Buck and Spec for the rest. Them boys is cut out for this work."

Ty managed to suck in just enough air. "Jesus!" he said, wanting to say more.

"Skip the formalities." Fenton threw him a hay hook. "Climb up and I'll toss up these close ones. And call me Fenton." The first bale was already flying onto the truck bed. "Old Jesus never knew his ass from his elbow when it come to mules."

Horace Adams claimed Fenton Pardee was well into his sixties, but the way the man buried his hay hook into bale after bale and swung them up made Ty wonder. It was all Ty could do to slide one into place before the next one came at him. And somehow Fenton talked the whole time. Ty was finding it harder and harder to heave the bales into place when suddenly Fenton threw him the lash cinch. "Cinch her down some," he said. "Them boys can get the rest. I'm curious how they done with those mules."

He watched Ty cinch down the load. "Hard to beat a tight rope, ain't it?" he said, taking the saddle out of the cab and throwing it on the truck bed with the bales. Ty got in and they drove on to the pack station, which—Ty had learned while Fenton was throwing the bales at him— wasn't even the starting place for their trips into the mountains.

Fenton did most of his packing at the corrals he'd built three miles up the trail at Crippled Elk Lake. Fenton's stock trail converged there with the road, the same that led past the Wilsons' sawmill. The Pardee pack station itself was dominated by a log lodge where Fenton and Cody Jo lived. Cody Jo fed the packers there, making fun of how much they ate but always ready with more. The rest of the pack station consisted of an old barn and some ragged outbuildings Fenton had tacked together for his gear, the outbuildings sprawling along the edge of the big meadow where he wintered his horses.

"Weren't we ambitious?" Fenton stopped the truck and studied the big log building. "Thought those eastern folks couldn't wait to come out here to shoot our elk. But they never. Not like we thought. The way money is now, I doubt they will." He pushed his hat back. "Cody Jo would dance up a storm if I was to up and finish this place." He looked at Ty, amused. "She loves to dance. But you know this packin' business." He eased the truck on toward the barn. "Little time for dancin' and a shit load less for construction."

They'd rigged a little room off the barn for Ty. They threw Ty's things in: Fenton pleased because Buck had done a good job boarding up the broken window and sweeping out a rat's nest. Ty because he'd never had a place all to himself. Dusty tack was hanging in one corner, and he would need to get a bedroll for the cot. But there were shelves under the window and two pack boxes he could store things in. It would clean . . . and it was his.

They saw dust and heard swearing as they went through the barn.

"Bet Buck's got himself crossways with a mule," Fenton said. Ty followed him, jogging now and then to keep up.

Over the top rail of the catch corral they watched a slender, dark-haired man ease a fence pole across a mule's body, levering up the hog-tied legs. Another mule, moving back and forth until she seemed to be trotting in place, was tied to a fence post at the far end of the corral. She had a white bull's-eye on her rump, which was tucked down as though waiting for a blow. A big, flat-nosed man with a torn shirt was lying across the thrown mule's head, swearing and gesturing, a blood-soaked rag wrapped around his hand. The slender man sunk his weight onto the pole and brought the mule's feet up. The mule thrashed, bridging up so violently the big man was thrown into the dirt. The mule jobbed his legs and went all the way over, flopping down heavily on his other side. He lay there panting, his hog-tied legs useless, streaks of sweat darkening his neck. He lifted his head, offering a mournful bray, and the other mule's rump dropped even lower.

"That won't work," Ty said.

"Not too graceful. But we gotta tack the damn shoes on."

"Good shoes on a bad mule's worse than none."

"Hell, that rope ain't hurtin' him." Fenton was a little startled to hear the boy talking at all, much less being contrary.

"His body's not the problem."

Again Fenton was taken aback. The boy had hardly said a word when Fenton tipped him over with the bales. And here he was objecting because they'd had to throw a mule. He grunted and dropped into the corral. "Buck may be gettin' downright inadequate," he said, surprised to see the boy move past him.

Ty bypassed the downed mule and went to the other, whose eyes rolled as she pulled back furiously. He eased himself along the fence, talking quietly, careful not to get trapped against the fence as she swung about. He got his hand on the tie rope, felt her weight hard against it as her rump dropped, almost touching the ground. Ty kept talking, moving along the rope until at last he could touch her, move his hand to brush at her neck, brushing and calming her until she came forward enough for him to loose the rope. He kept the dally as he let the rope out, gave her room as he kept touching her. He stepped away to shuck his Levi jacket, moved back to touch her with it, rub it along her neck and shoulders, waiting for the wild look to leave her eyes.

Finally she calmed, tolerating that steady voice, the hands that kept moving and moving across her neck, her shoulders. Fenton opened the gate, easing it wide and stepping away. Ty loosed the lead and walked the mule in tight circles before taking her through, ready for her when she tried to bolt, holding the rope short and bringing her head around until she was facing where she didn't want to be—the sweat and noise and the downed mule. He turned her again, led her around the corner of the barn and tied her to a bendy limb, rubbed her, talked to her, touched her with his jacket, let her get the smell of him.

"Stick that hand in a badger hole, Buck?" Fenton asked the flat-nosed man. "You was in trouble even if you could convince that mule to hold his feet up. Who was gonna shoe? You couldn't. Not with that hand. And nobody but Cody Jo to set on the mule's head if you was whole." He shook his head. "Cody Jo's never been too keen about sittin' on a mule's head."

"Got skinned some, ropin' that mule." Buck studied his hand. "Got down to me or the damn mule. Looks like that mule's gettin' ahead too. Sure ain't gonna be much help with this fuckin' hand."

"Comes from using that rawhide rope. My people can handle them. Yours can't." The dark-haired man had dropped his pole and was examining Buck's hand. "Didn't lose no fingers. For a minute I thought you might of."

"I was so goddamned mad at him I threw the rope out there. It was more a warning. If I thought I'd of caught him I would of got myself ready."

"I'm sure Spec was cheerin' you on." Fenton looked at the mule, who seemed to be saving his strength for his next protest.

"I'm a hunter, not a damn blacksmith." Spec looked at Buck. "That mule did hit that rope! Dragged you some too."

"It come as a surprise." Buck slapped some dust out of his pants with his good hand. "But I stopped the mule."

"Not till you took the dally on the post, you didn't. Near lost your fingers doin' that." Spec turned to Fenton. "Mule hit that rope so hard old Buck's lucky he's still intact. Got his shirt. Pinched some skin off him too. You and that boy hadn't arrived, that mule might of skinned Buck's upper half."

"Good you picked a seat where you wouldn't miss no details." Fenton handed the long fence pole to Spec. "Let's tack these shoes on while Buck's still alive. Then maybe we can doctor him."

Before they could get started, Ty came back into the corral with his Levi jacket. He hunched over the hog-tied mule, wiped at the dust streaks on his neck, rubbed him with the jacket, working it up toward the mule's head.

"Stretchin' those legs out might help," he said.

Fenton got a lash rope, looped it around the mule's legs, pulling them straight before tying it off to a fence post. The mule struggled, but with nowhere to go he quieted.

Ty kept rubbing the jacket along the mule's neck, across his face. He pulled the sleeves of his jacket through the halter and knotted them, fashioning a blindfold. He rubbed at the mule's ears a little, then lowered himself into the dirt, folding one of the mule's ears over and biting down on it, a good half of the ear in his mouth.

Fenton turned to Spec. "Stick the goddamned pole under them feet and get 'em up. Buck, get me that shoein' kit. Let's get it done."

"Ty," he said, after Buck came back with the shoeing box. "These here are Buck and Spec. You'll be workin' with them."

Ty looked up and nodded a hello, the mule's ear still between his teeth. Fenton began rasping a hoof, fitting a shoe. He looked at the boy from time to time, shaking his head, taking advantage of the quiet.

3

Dancing

After the shoeing Ty went back to the cottontail, working with her until supper time, rubbing her with his jacket until he found a brush, then brushing until she began to like it. She got edgy when he brushed down her legs, but he kept going back to them, getting closer and closer to a hoof before she would fidget, stutter-step away.

They would let Ty try to shoe her his way. They liked the solemn way he talked, laughing at him, asking about his mule magic. But they didn't laugh too hard. There was the practical side. The shoeing had to be done; if his way didn't work, they could still use theirs. And if his way did, they were ahead. Packing these mules would be problem enough.

"Them mules is green broke and then some," the man had told Fenton at Hungry Horse, carving a chew from Buck's plug and counting the money. "Not likely to jump through no hoops. But they could walk through. You show the way." Not owning a saddle horse, he had walked the mules in, leaving the fields he had no reason to plant, the house he had patched into a home, covering the thirteen miles in five hours. Fenton was impressed. The mules' coats were shiny, their bellies full. But there was something driven about the man. Fenton didn't think he'd stopped once on that long, hot walk.

He'd looked at the man's family, waiting in a battered truck loaded with mattresses and buckets and bedsprings. The children, pinched and flat eyed, watched him. Fenton suspected they hadn't eaten as well as the mules, but he knew that wasn't unusual for these country people drifting through, searching for a place they could take hold.

"Not tryin' to make money." The man folded the bills, tucked them in his shirt pocket. "Just get back some of what they took." Fenton's ease seemed to anger him. "The bank's what beat me. Not your damn country."

"New start ain't always a bad thing." As shrewd a trader as Fenton was, he began to wonder if he shouldn't pay the man a little more. "What now? Where you headed?"

"Them mines in Anaconda. They pay a salary. With a paycheck a man might make it." He climbed into the truck, the woman and children looking at Fenton with eyes empty, beyond curious. "I'll try that," he fired the engine, "or some other damn thing."

Fenton watched them leave through the gray-black exhaust. He shook his head and turned to the mules, thinking the Anaconda mines might not be the best place to recover from a hurt.

What was green broke to the man didn't seem like green broke to Buck and Spec. It had taken an hour to load them in the trailer, and though Fenton claimed they'd come right along once he got them on the trail, Buck and Spec weren't convinced. It seemed the longer you fought these mules on one thing the longer you had to fight them on the next, which is why they were happy Ty wanted to shoe the cottontail. They just doubted he could.

Ty worked with her until he heard the bell, only then realizing how hungry he was. He left her tied between two posts in the barn and went to wash up at the sink behind the house. Buck was there, looking blue, his right hand bandaged so it hardly had any definition.

"Wish Angie was here. Cody Jo's got me so wrapped I'd need a third arm to pack." He looked darkly at the bandages. "Spec had to load them bales himself. I could scarcely drive the truck." He threw Ty a towel and they went in through the kitchen door. "Doubt I can handle a dern spoon."

The kitchen was a wide alcove opening onto the biggest room Ty had ever seen in a house. But it seemed only half finished. There were log beams with Indian blankets thrown across them and a stone fireplace with braces, but no mantel. Beyond the fireplace makeshift stairs went up from the unfinished floor. There were no cupboards in the kitchen, just shelves nailed up. Log planks on sawhorses fashioned a long table, benches along either side. At one end was a chair. Five places were set there, with glasses and a big pitcher of something cold. At the far end of the table was a wind-up phonograph, a stack of records next to it. There was a walk-in pantry next to the kitchen. They heard dishes being moved.

"You there, Cody Jo?" Buck's voice seemed different, cautious. "Ty's here. He's been helpin' us get shoes on that mule."

"I bet he's thirsty, poor thing." The voice seemed filled with life. "All that mule hair! Drink some lemonade, Ty. We're having my aunt's recipe. And somewhere . . . ," more dishes rattled, "is what I need to serve it."

Buck poured some lemonade and Ty drank it—cold and tart. Buck poured him more.

"Ain't she somethin'!" Buck said, his voice low. "Full of shit as a Christmas turkey. Watch her dance with Fenton. . . ."

Ty drank the second glass, looking at Buck over the rim, noticing again the flatness of his nose, the bridge wide just where it should have shape.

"Well, Ty." Cody Jo came from the pantry with a big serving dish. "I'm Cody Jo."

She took in his long frame, his hair wet from the washing, the big hat set carefully on the counter. She put her hand out and he was surprised by her grip, long fingers wrapped around his. He was surprised by everything about her. "I didn't think you'd be this tall," she said. "Or such a handsome young man."

She stepped back, pleased. Ty was afraid he might start sweating through his forehead the way he had when Etta Adams praised him about Smoky Girl. He was relieved when she turned away, still talking, as though telling people what they looked like was something she did every day.

She started dishing noodles into the serving dish, adding a cream sauce with lots of meat in it. "Elk Stroganoff," she said. "Spec says it'll win out over beef." She handed Ty the platter. "We'll see. You sit right down next to me and tell us how you knew to bite that mule's ear. What a thing! You'll be the thirstiest packer in these mountains." Ty's attention was on her so completely, he was surprised to see that Fenton and Spec had joined Buck at the table. They watched as Ty brought the platter over, Cody Jo coming behind him with noodles and vegetables in another dish.

Before he knew it he was sitting at the table eating the best food he'd ever tasted and talking much more than he meant to. He'd only taken a bite or two before he found himself saying that he'd actually never bitten a mule's ear before, or any other ear for that matter. But he knew that if you got a mule's attention in one place, the mule might overlook what was happening in another. It was something his grandfather had learned from a Nez Perce, who claimed when nothing else worked, biting an ear would. His grandfather said a strong buck with good teeth could practically hypnotize a mule—if he clamped down hard enough. That was why the Nez Perce could handle the stock they stole so much better than the tribes they stole from, even when they had to sneak in the night and take a horse staked right outside a lodge.

So, Ty explained, when he saw the mule lying there braying and sweating and getting edgier, he figured it was time to try ear biting. He knew the mule was going to fight them until he couldn't fight any more anyway, and he didn't think a mule ready to fight you until he was exhausted would be much good. The blindfold, he confessed, was mostly a diversion, a way to keep the mule from knowing what had him by the ear.

He heard his voice stop, felt sweat on his forehead, saw a faint smile on Cody Jo's face. Suddenly he realized how quiet they all were, hardly eating, just looking at him—as though he might start in speaking again.

Finally Fenton spoke. "Well, I'm damned. If Eban Hardin believed that's the way to get a mule's attention, it likely is." He looked at Spec and Buck. "I've told you boys Eban Hardin forgot more about mules than most get to know. Bitin' that ear today sure as hell quieted things down."

"That's true." The thought seemed to come to Buck suddenly. He changed his fork to his left hand the better to manage it. "That mule was pretty loco until Ty bit the ear. Sure stilled him."

"Could of exhausted himself watchin' you roll in the dirt," Spec said. "Ain't pleasant to see a grown man deposit blood all over a corral."

"Loco wouldn't be a bad name for that mule," Fenton said. "He's likely to earn it trying to recover. What would you name that one you're workin' on?" he asked Ty. "Those folks at Hungry Horse were so discouraged, they never got around to naming their mules."

"Cottontail?" asked Ty, surprised. "Isn't that her name?" "By God, it is now." Fenton started in to eat again. "That concludes the naming. And this is a damn fine way to eat elk, Cody Jo. That Chicago aunt may be walleyed, but she knows food."

"She isn't walleyed. And I still can't get those people out of my mind. Or people like them. No crops worth planting. Cattle prices down to nothing. The banks moving in. What are they going to do?"

"I'd mistrust those mines. If a cave-in or a union man don't get you, a strike breaker will."

"It isn't right." Cody Jo had stopped eating. "Men with good lives one month, homeless the next. Of course they do desperate things." She spoke so intently Ty could feel the words run through him. "Who wouldn't?"

They talked on and on, disagreeing and agreeing about things Ty's parents had never mentioned. Even Buck and Spec chimed in. Ty was taken by it, his embarrassment fading as he watched, listened.

He'd always thought the problem was the cattle prices, which to him centered in the Bitterroot. Now it seemed Will and Mary's problems were only shadows of troubles plaguing people all over. They talked about Roosevelt and the unions and government subsidies. They talked about the drought and the winds and the WPA. They talked about displaced farmers, ranchers, factory workers—arguing about whether the government was helping or ruining them.

"A man should grow what he wants, hunt when he needs to," Buck was saying. "It ain't American to tell a man what to do."

"Farmers shouldn't hunt and hunters shouldn't farm," Spec said. "Mixes things up. Thinkin' you can own the land is where the trouble starts, tearin' away grass that's meant to be grazed." He looked at Buck, getting angry. "Them government people don't know their ass from a moose. If them know-nothings can tell my tribe what to do, why shouldn't they tell you? We can fight the bastards together."

"Each of us has a point if you look at it careful from a certain place." Fenton took his plate into the kitchen. "Truth is it ain't easy to stand up an empty sack."

"You can't," Buck said. "But if you got a little grain left and tie off the neck down where the grain's at, what's left'll stand up pretty good."

"Oh, Buck," Cody Jo said. "There's no grain left for them. Nothing. Not a sack. No string to tie with."

Ty was taking a last bite when Fenton leaned over him. "I believe Buck's been slowin' down ever since that mule flattened his nose down Lost Bird Canyon."

Buck kept chewing, considering Cody Jo's meaning. "Don't you dwell on it, Buck." Fenton took Ty's plate. "There's times Cody Jo leaves me behind too. What we got to do now is teach you to eat with that left hand so we can start with Cody Jo's lesson. Gonna join in? Cody Jo says you and Angie could win a contest."

"Ain't my kind of dancing," Spec said, carrying dishes into the kitchen. "And cleanin' up ain't my line of work. I'm doin' this cause of Cody Jo's elk."

"Just the beginning." Cody Jo was cranking the handle on the phonograph. "We're a team. Keep the elk coming. I'll go to Chicago for recipes. I like their music."

She was humming with the record now, doing a little step as she came into the kitchen. Ty was holding a plate, watching her.

"Try rubbing." She took the towel, dried the plate while he held it, gave him back the towel. "Things go faster."

Ty felt the sweat break out again. He put the dish on the stack and stood with the dish towel, surprised to be working in a kitchen with these men. The Hardin men never did anything in Mary's kitchen.

"You do shoot tasty ones, Spec. Could be you know something I don't." Fenton dried his hands on the towel Ty was holding. "Which I doubt. But if you get Buck to stop being so drear about that hand, I might reconsider."

He looked at Buck's bandaged hand. "Get Angie to perk you up. You'll be drivin' all over hell and gone while we're in the mountains. When Ty here comes to, I'll tell him he has to fill in. Might not know hitches but he knows to tight a rope. And he ain't encumbered by a pillow on his fist."

The day was long. There was still light enough for Ty to grain the mule, get her comfortable with the feed bag, call her Cottontail. He brushed her again, brushing lower and lower on her legs, humming bits of the song.

He kept at it until it was dark and he needed to go back for a lantern. He was surprised to hear the song still playing, Cody Jo and Fenton dancing to it, easy with each other and the music.

The dancing didn't surprise him. Ranch people traveled long distances to go to dances. What surprised him was how much fun Fenton and Cody Jo were having all by themselves. He'd never seen anyone like Cody Jo—the beat of the music seemed to be inside her. He couldn't take his eyes from her and was relieved to realize Fenton liked to watch her just as much as he did.

"More fun with a live partner," Cody Jo told Fenton, letting her long body go out and away so Fenton could pull her back. They came together perfectly as the song ended. "Don't be shy, Ty. Later we'll teach you some steps." She stood there, a little out of breath, looking at him. "But first the packing. With Fenton it's always 'first the packing.'"

"Dancing makes me want to change priorities." Fenton tipped her against him. "You do teach an old dog new tricks."

"You haven't shown me all yours yet." Cody Jo rested her head on his shoulder, looking at Ty. "I'm a little jealous. Leave me here while you go into the mountains and pass them along to Ty."

"There's a ways to go first. Shoes to get on that cottontail."

"Oh yes! Then packs to get on her and on that crazy one." Cody Jo smiled at Ty. "Rest up for tomorrow. Fenton keeps us all on the run."

She hugged Fenton and handed Ty the lantern. "Here. And take my bedroll. It's yours to use."

Ty spread the bedroll on the cot, put barley in the nosebag, and went through the barn to Cottontail. He put the lantern to the side and held out the feed bag. This time she didn't hesitate, nosing deep, wanting it all. She rubbed her head against his jacket as he untied her, led her out to the corral where Loco trotted up, nosed at her, relieved to have some company. Ty held a hand out and watched Loco move to the off side of Cottontail, not trusting him. Not yet.

"Maybe you won't be so loco after awhile." Ty ran his hand along Cottontail's back, letting Loco see it didn't hurt. "You got reasons," he said. "I know you do."

He slid between the blankets of the bedroll, folded and laced so you could undo it and air it out. He imagined that was the way Cody Jo did most things, tidy but without much fuss. He couldn't get her off his mind—her dancing, her laughing, her worries about people losing their homes, drifting with their families in search of what couldn't be found.

He pictured those people gathered in lamp-lit kitchens, knowing they had to move on but not knowing where, how. It unsettled him: lost homes, families hungry, fathers so beaten they couldn't stay—took to the rails, disappeared.

He tossed and worried in the bedroll until the song came to him again, the dancing. That was a relief. He was glad to be here at last, liking these people who treated him as if he'd been here always.

Just before he slept the name of the song came to him. He'd looked at the record there on the kitchen table. "It Don't Mean a Thing," the label read. The bandleader was Fletcher Henderson.

4

Another Way to Shoe a Mule

Ty took the feed bag into the corral, squatted, rattled the barley. Cottontail came closer. He scooped some into his hand, showing her. She nibbled and followed his hand into the nose bag. He waited until she settled before easing it from her, holding it out for Loco, who snorted and danced away. Ty watched him come closer the second time, stretching his neck before his nostrils flared and he slid away again, liking the smell but not the looks of the mysterious bag— the bony boy crouched there holding it.

It took almost an hour to get Loco to nibble barley from his hand, Ty looking away, disassociating himself from the hand, steady and tempting before the big mule. After that it wasn't long before Loco followed that hand into the feed bag, the sides rolled down now, the grain revealed.

He'd been working at it since he'd stumbled from his bedroll, shivering in the first light. Shoeing the cottontail had gnawed at him. But he knew what to do first, considered it as he stuffed his shirt into his pants and pulled on his boots. He wanted those mules married to the feed bag.

And he knew that getting things right now could save hours later. It was a relief when he got a halter on Loco without roping him. He fed him more barley, tied him there, ran his hands along his neck, talked to him as he looked out across the meadow, watched the early mist give way to sun. He could see the rest now, grazing out there, the Swan Range lifting beyond, its bright ridges sparkling in the early sun.

"See you didn't have to rope him." The big voice startled him. "Might depress Buck. He don't feel warmed up till he's gone a round or two with a mule." Fenton was chewing a straw as though he'd been there for an hour. He might have been for all Ty knew.

"Got plans to shoe, you might go light on the romance and heavier on the foot liftin'. That's still where they tack them things on." Fenton threw the straw away and started for the house. "Food could help. We got some."

Jasper Finn hummed as he made pancakes, putting a stack and some bacon on a plate and handing it to Ty. "Eat up, high pockets." He poured coffee into Ty's cup. "Them bones might poke a hole in your britches."

Ty saw Spec was there too.

"Where's Buck?"

"Off with Cody Jo to get the dudes."

"Buck's already forgot about his hand," Fenton said, sitting down with them. "Like a pig in a wallow with that Buick car. I'll fit them saddles before we push everything up to Crippled Elk." He looked at Ty. "You and Spec shoe the cottontail." It seemed to Ty that Fenton poured half the syrup bottle on his pancakes. "One way or the other."

"You watch too," Spec said. "Ty might get kicked from here to Texas." Spec poured syrup over a fried egg. "We got them saddles fit perfect last season."

"What fit Sugar then won't now. Not after this spring feed. She goes up and down like a balloon. And she ain't the worst. Just the greediest."

"Father claims she's had a fix on feed ever since you left her down Lost Bird Canyon," Spec said. "She was abandon."

"She wasn't abandon, goddamn it. Your father may know mountains but he's a liability with history. I did what had to be done." He stood, ending it. "Still packin' her ain't we?"

Ty had sweat through his shirt and his legs were soaked under the shoeing apron, but he had Cottontail's leg up. If he could keep her quiet through this last shoe, he'd have her ready.

"We still got to pack her," Spec reminded him. "That won't be no picnic." Spec kept taut a cotton rope Ty had tied around Cottontail's hind leg and thrown over a rafter. She was tied with two halter ropes, one running to the right, the other to the left. With Spec holding her leg she was pretty much immobilized. But Ty wanted her to think things were her idea. Each time she moved against the rope he had Spec loosen it, held her leg himself, pulled it back up when she was ready, motioning to tighten the rope, talking to the mule, starting in again, patient, steady—dripping sweat.

"If you don't wash away, I believe you'll outlast her," Spec said. "Might beat Buck's system."

"What would that be?"

"He would go at it more direct."

"Throw her right off?"

"Or bulldog her. To Buck commotion equals progress."

"When it cripples him up?"

"That comes with it. If there's no blood, he's inclined to think he ain't done his work."

Ty clenched off the nails. "Makes your tools slippy." He motioned to Spec to let the rope out, lowered the leg to the ground himself. He stood, wiping sweat off his face with his hand, drying it on Cottontail. "Doesn't sound too efficient."

"Efficiency ain't Buck's style."

The rest of the morning they fitted pack saddles, Fenton pleased to see how quickly the boy saw what needed doing. Most were cross bucks, but there were some Deckers too. Ty moved easily from one task to another, loosening a breeching here, a breast collar there. Adjusting the quarter straps, the latigos.

Jasper brought out a jar of peanut butter and a warm loaf of bread. They sat in the shade drinking Cody Jo's lemonade and eating, Fenton and Spec considering the personalities of Cottontail and Loco. Ty was back at work first, easing the Decker saddles onto the mules, adjusting the straps.

"Don't you trust them bastards," Fenton warned. "They'll likely go sky high when we pack."

"Might pack them light the first day," Ty said. "Ease into things."

"No such thing as packin' light on Fenton's first day." Spec was up helping Ty now. "He makes promises, but it don't come to jack shit."

"If these people don't bring a trunk load of clothes we might could," Fenton said. "Though that ain't likely. They bring everything." He seemed resigned. "Never see that a mule's only human."

"See?" Spec jabbed Ty. "Only crazy bastards pack. Don't let him talk you into taking over a string. You'll wind up in a wreck to make you sick."

Horace and Etta Adams pulled up, a horse trailer behind their pickup. The bed of the truck was filled with bedrolls and dunnage bags. Ty saw some saddles under all the gear.

"Came out to make sure you weren't working that boy too hard," Horace said. "And I got some saddles. Cut rate for you."

"We brought Smoky Girl," Etta said. "Horace thinks she needs more time with Ty."

"Sweet Jesus." Fenton looked at the gear in the truck. "We brought this boy out to pack mules, not to teach Etta's horse to go fetch."

Spec went to unload Smoky Girl. She kicked the trailer door as he opened it, scrabbling backward to be free of the trailer before spinning away, Spec barely able to hang on.

"Spunky." Fenton walked around her. "Ain't she ridable?"

"Let's say she's not the rockin' horse you advertised," Horace said. "Even if we could get up on her."

"Be fine if she got rode each day." Fenton admired the spooky little mare. "But dudes like to start off on one that has been, not one that needs to be."

Horace decided to play the rest of his cards. "You can use the saddles for a spell," Horace said. "No one has money to buy 'em. Might get you over the hump while Smoky's gettin' to where she don't object to Etta so much."

"Smoky does know trails." Fenton went over to look at the saddles. "Packed her considerable last season."

"Told Etta you rode her."

"Did." The filly was spinning again, pulling Spec with her. "After she'd been packed some."

"You mean night and day."

"I mean not grained up so she thinks she's hung the moon."

"Optimistic, ain't he?" Spec said to Ty, who came over to help.

"Beats bein' sour all the time." Ty was already calming Smoky.

"That's because he's crazy. Father says he never had a idea he didn't try."

"Must be good ones. He's still here."

"Like to kill everyone tryin' them out too."

"Who'd he kill?"

"Like to," I said. Don't you be the first."

Fenton was looking at the duffle, hoping this was all of it.

"Don't worry. There's more," Horace said. "With Buck."

"Ain't that the way? Always *more*." Fenton held a saddle up. "These could help." He looked at Horace. "We'll see what we can do with the Smoky horse, wound up as she is." He started taking the saddles out of the truck. "Might put Ty back on her."

⌒⌒

Spec and Ty hazed them along the trail to Crippled Elk Lake, the horses farting and kicking after all the spring feed. Ty had a hard time holding Smoky in. He was thankful Spec kept crossing in front of him on his big dun.

Smoky had quieted when Ty got her into the corral, Horace and Etta watching and Fenton coming out of the barn with the Meana saddle.

"Truth is," he said, "Fred Mueller sent me a saddle from Denver. Made for a rancher who died in it. Outlasted him and it'll outlast me. Try this, Ty. Just don't pretend it's yours." Ty didn't think Fenton minded if Horace heard him. "Ole Horace'll have you bareback by sundown."

"Shit." Horace looked at Etta. "He's at it again."

"You hardly get here before you're talking just like Fenton. That language isn't doing Ty any favors."

"That's a truth," Horace said. "Try to do Ty a favor and Fenton grabs it anyway. It's enough to make your minister swear."

Ty hardly heard them. He had the Meana on Smoky and was on her before they settled into their argument. He worked her around the corral, stopped her, backed her, moved her right and left, eased her into a low lope.

"Told you, Etta," Fenton said, watching Ty. "She's like a lamb. And don't that rig fit the boy about right?"

"Hell." Horace pushed Etta back into the pickup. "Let's go before he has the whole damn feed store."

Ty tried to keep track of Cottontail and Loco as they scrambled up the trail, but it was hard to keep Smoky calm. He knew it wasn't doing her much good trailing after skittery horses. She was only partly settled herself. But Fenton wouldn't have it any other way. Working under a saddle was what she needed, he claimed—the sooner started the better finished.

Ty wasn't so sure. He liked calm when he worked a horse. But the temptation of getting back in that Meana saddle had been too much for him. And he wanted to see the corrals at Crippled Elk, the mountains. They would start in the morning, and there was still much to know.

The trail finally merged with the road. They saw Fenton's truck at the corrals, loaded with pack saddles and panniers. Fenton had opened the corral gate and was talking with a worried-looking man in a Forest Service shirt. Smoky wanted to follow the others into the corral, but Ty brought her to the side, stood down to close the gate, surprised to see other horses already there.

"Someone's horses got away," Spec said, watching them back away from all the new commotion. "Bet we're spread out like Cheyenne come dawn."

"Bob Ring is in there with a broke leg," Fenton said to them, as if to verify it. "Horses run out on him. His number one man too, looks like."

"There was no other way to get the horses," the ranger said, his mouth barely moving as he spoke. "If I can borrow a saddle, I'll take them back." He looked exhausted to Ty, his shirt wet with sweat.

"Then we'll have another goddamned broke leg," Fenton said. "You can work with that snow up there, but you can't fight it. It'll be mush by now. You'll drop a horse through sure. We'll wait till morning."

"His daughter is alone with him," the ranger said.

"And he's lucky to have her. We'll wait."

"Shit," Spec said, disgusted. "There goes our sleep."

༄

Bernard Strait was dog tired. He'd been so worried about Ring's leg the night before, he'd hardly rested. That morning he'd moved around their camp in widening circles before he realized the horses had gone up a draw and come high onto the trail, finding sun there as well as the way home.

He hadn't been far behind, finding their droppings still steaming. But he'd seen them only once, high above, looking down before hurrying on. He'd crossed the switchbacks then, trying to come onto the trail ahead of them, dropping his feed bag and his ropes as he swung himself upward. But when he regained the trail, winded and shirt-torn, they were still ahead. He'd started to run then, running until he could run no more, then walking until he could run again, walking and running until he reached the broad snowfield hugging the pass. He'd jogged over the firm sun pockets to the bench where they'd rolled, where he'd heard them, the faint, insistent bell far below, telling him they were going down. Going out.

He'd thought of turning back, doing what he could with the leg, hoping some packer would find them, pull them out. But he knew what Bob Ring would think of that. And the girl.

"Get them," Wilma Ring had said, none of the boy-girl sassiness in her voice. "I'll make him comfortable here."

"If she doesn't fuss me to death she will," Bob Ring had answered, embarrassed and a little worried about Bernard too. "Just track those devils down. I can tell you what to do, even if I'm too damned crippled to help."

Fenton read it all in the way Bernard looked: the Forest Service hat pulled straight across his brow, his face sweat streaked, his ranger shirt dirty and torn—everything about him exhausted and determined. "You done everything you could, Bernard. Get you some rest. We got work to do come first light."

He turned to unload the truck. "You know Spec, Bernard. This other one is Ty. He's new." He handed a saddle to Bernard. "Keep a light handy. Gets pretty dark before dawn."

5

Twice across the Pass

There was moon enough for Ty to see Bernard, stiff and determined as he led Apple, Wilma Ring's little mare. Fenton rode ahead of Bernard. In the open places Ty could see him too, turned almost backward on Easter, watching the long string of Forest Service horses, tail-tied, using the halters Fenton and Ty would bring back. If everything worked.

The first matter was Bob Ring. Ty saw how closely Fenton focused on his task. He'd come back at dusk with food, waking Bernard to make him eat, Fenton himself half-angry and half-amused to tell them that Buck had come back from Missoula without the tents, which needed more patching. Rather than stay to see it done, Buck had picked up the guests and driven back to tell Fenton.

"Maybe he thought I could hold back the rain." Fenton handed Spec a plate. "Your people ever try that? Dance to hold back the rain?"

"We don't fool with what ain't changeable. You shouldn't fool with no ranger's leg. Let the government pull his ass out. They put him in."

"Hell, Spec, you know Bob Ring. You'd pull him out too."

"I ain't pleased with where he gets his paycheck," Spec said. "Which don't help me warm to your plans."

Spec was against it from the first, but Ty didn't see what else Fenton could do. Jasper and Spec would take the guests in over the north pass without tents, while Buck went back to Missoula to get them. Fenton and Ty would take Bernard's horses in to the south, find a way to bring Ring out, then pack up the tents and catch up with Spec.

Fenton guessed they'd be a day and a half behind, that he'd catch them at their second camp. Spec had the kitchen fly if it rained, and

Jasper's good cooking. The only thing missing, as far as Ty could see, was sleep. And Fenton acted as though he'd forgotten what that was.

He'd kept talking and organizing gear until dark, then he'd gone back to the big house to reassure the guests, who were getting edgy about starting without Fenton to tell them what to do. In the middle of the night he'd come back to the corrals, gotten Ty up, caught up the Forest Service horses, and had them all on the trail before Bernard was all the way awake.

Now he hardly stopped Easter for a breather, not until the snowfield. Ty got his first look back at the country from there, Crippled Elk Lake far below, above it spare cliffs, broken rocks and boulders jumbled at their base. He could see the stream they'd crossed and recrossed boiling down, jumping and foaming before settling back into its course.

Fenton stood down and climbed onto the snow, which pitched steeply before easing into the milder grade of the snowfield beyond. There was no wind, just the icebox cold lifting from the snow.

"Slick," he called down. "Hard to stay upright." He slid back and climbed onto Easter. "Gotta get back here before it gets mushy."

Easter was already moving across the snow, the string trailing behind, slipping and skidding but coaxed along by Fenton and Easter as they worked their way up the snowfield.

Ty held Smoky in as Bernard struggled up the bank, his horse slipping and scrambling for footing so vigorously that Bernard dropped Apple's lead and grabbed his saddle horn. Apple turned and bolted, trying to pass Smoky on the low side of the narrow trail. Ty grabbed the lead and managed a dally just as the little mare went knee deep into the scree above the cliffs.

It was all new for Smoky, but she saw nowhere to go but onto the snow, away from the unpleasant drag. She spun Apple back from the cliff's edge, and before Ty knew it they were pulling her up onto the snow.

"Saved, by god!" Fenton had watched it as he angled Easter across the snowfield. "That's why I'll take a mule, boys. A mule never would come that close to suicide. Willie will be thankful."

"Wilma," Bernard spoke up now, the color coming back into his face, "seemed to know everything to do about that broken leg."

"She is a pistol." Fenton looked ahead to find the trail emerging from the snow. "Won't be long now before Bob has to dust off his shotgun."

They saw the smoke as they came into the meadow. They forded the creek and there was Bob Ring, his leg wrapped and elevated, his toes bluish.

"Not sure Wilma's too interested in your circulation, Robert." Fenton dismounted and threw his lead-line toward Ty.

"I knew it." Bob Ring was propped up against a wadded canvas manty. "Break my leg and now I got to listen to you. Don't know which is worse."

"We'll have you out before you decide it's me." Fenton reached into his saddlebag and pulled out a bottle. "Enjoy this while you think on it." He handed Ring the bottle. "I'll loosen up this rescue work."

"I didn't want him to bend it." Wilma came up from the creek with water, tall and thin, her eyes so sharply blue they made Ty look again. "He tosses so." She let Bernard take the bucket.

"You done fine, Willie." Fenton got the first knot undone. "Tidier than what I'd of done. And I been the doctor in here more than I like. Drink up, Robert. Ty'll have things packed before the sun hits the meadow."

Ty wasn't sure Fenton remembered the only thing he'd ever packed was salt, in rotted old panniers with no hitch to tie. He knew enough to balance the loads, which he did as best he could. Fenton kept checking, jamming something deeper into a pannier now and then to give Ty the idea. But he never stopped his conversation with Bob Ring.

"Throbbing might slow if you concentrate on that bottle. Soon as these boys get lined out, I might have a sip myself."

"Time they get lined out it might be gone," Bob Ring wiped at his mouth. "It's some better than your usual."

There were beads of sweat on Ring's face, lines of dampness showing through his shirt.

"Drink lots. We'll get you out. It just ain't gonna be pleasant."

"I'll do that." Ring took another pull on the bottle. "Stop your morbid forecast and I might even save you some."

"Stirrup sip's all I need." Fenton was looking at saddle pads. "Help yourself. I'll ready that leg after we pack."

Fenton packed the first horses so fast Ty couldn't follow it. He just pulled rope where Fenton pointed, watched a perfect diamond appear.

"Pack this last one." He handed Ty a lash cinch. "I'll look at that leg."

Ty tightened the cinches and hung balanced panniers on the cross bucks. He tucked a bedroll over the top and threw a manty over all of it, snugging it tight. That was as far as he could go.

"Can you tie a hitch?" he asked Bernard. "He went too fast for me."

Bernard shook his head. "He was teaching me. I think she knows."

"I know some." The girl looked to see that her father was all right, then pointed at this rope and that, telling them when to pull, how to tighten. She was serious and precise and now and then a little unsure. But when Ty pulled the last rope taut, a lopsided diamond appeared.

"Doubt I could do it again." He tied the rope off, surprised.

"You will. He'll show you. Just make him as careful with my father as he is with his mules." She went to Fenton, crouched over her father's leg.

"Need it straighter before I splint it." Fenton seemed to be speaking as much to himself as to Bob Ring, who held the bottle and watched.

"Doubted you would be so generous with this just for pleasure." Bob Ring looked at his daughter. "Hang on to my upper half while Fenton straightens my lower. That lump doesn't want to be there."

"Ty," Fenton called. "Come hold this leg steady." He touched the bump again. "Save on the bleeding in there if things is more in place."

Bob Ring lifted up into his daughter's arms, sweat dripping from his face. Ty and Bernard held the leg steady as Fenton pulled, Ty queasy as he felt the thigh muscles tense, Ring fighting against Fenton's pull.

"Not sure I got you drunk enough, Robert. You ain't exactly relaxed." Fenton ran his hand across the blue place on the side of Bob Ring's calf, the lump diminished. "It's near in line. Drink more. I'll hustle us up a splint."

He pulled the torn pant leg back down, wrapped the leg in a saddle pad, then opened a length of bark from a lodgepole, fit it over the pad. He tied the bark closed with strips of canvas, padding the top and bottom and making sure the splint locked Ring's foot, stretching the leg. He wrapped a manty around all of it, tied it firmly with canvas strips.

"Drink," he said. "You've rode drunker than this and still got home."

"Not with a leg this fat. Or this broke."

The color had gone from Ring's face. Fenton saw circles of sweat soaking through his shirt. "Don't see how to make it ride better, Bob." Fenton massaged Ring's toes. "It'll bleed in there. But less. It's mostly in place."

"Mostly'll have to do."

"That leg won't kill you. I ain't as confident about the splint."

Ty got Ring to his feet. He saw that the girl was crying.

"Get me on and lead me out." Ring looked at Ty belligerently. "And leave me that goddamned bottle . . . I got plans."

Bob Ring's parents had been Pentecostal preachers. It wasn't long before he began singing hymns. He knew all the verses, each verse more vigorous than the last. He was singing loudly when they climbed onto the snow, Fenton leading with the pack horses and looking back to see if Ty and Ring were all right. The snow was softer now, a worry to Ty. Ring hadn't been all that steady, singing and drinking and flopping around in his saddle, trying to get comfortable. It would be rougher crossing the snow. He looked back at the girl, leading Apple now, her face as white as Ring's when Fenton set the bone. Bernard followed, grim faced as he listened to the hymns.

Fenton circled his string and dismounted.

"Bet we're on ten feet of snow here," he said. "But solid. Good place to have a look at that leg. It won't like the downhill."

"I have no plans to complain." Bob Ring was casting around for what hymn to sing next. "It's not the Christian way."

"The Christian way won't keep you from bleeding all over your saddle if that splint rubs you wrong." Fenton added his kerchief to the padding.

"'The meek shall inherit the fuckin' earth.' That's what He said." Ring offered Fenton the bottle.

"Forget about who's gonna inherit what till we get to the doctors." Fenton saw something was left in the bottle and handed it back. "By the looks of that leg you won't want a meek doc."

They slipped and slid their way down the softening snowfield, finally dropping back onto the trail, Bob Ring rolling around in his saddle more than Ty wanted him to. Ring's face was drained of blood again and Ty heard him begin swearing, quietly at first, then tilting the bottle up, draining it and smashing it onto the rocks.

"Fuck 'em," he shouted. "All of 'em. Fuck 'em all. . . ."

"Oh!" Wilma was off Apple, looking for broken glass. "Oh Father!" Ring's, eyes were glassy. He kept swearing in bursts, Ty finding himself as lost for what to do as the girl, knowing only to keep following Fenton.

He didn't look back much after that, concentrating solely on keeping Ring from being jarred. The trail switched back in long traverses, fording the stream again and again, the final crossing just below the waterfall he'd barely seen as they'd climbed in darkness, the country invisible and unknown. Now he felt it more than saw it, all of him concentrating on Ring.

By the time they came to the corrals the swearing was over. Ty wasn't even sure Ring was conscious. His eyes had been closed for the last mile, and he was slumped in the saddle, the splinted leg, grotesque, protruding like a growth.

Buck was there with the tents, mantied and waiting to be packed. Cody Jo was there too, with two coolers of fresh meat they would pack in for Jasper. Fenton pulled the unconscious Ring from the saddle, holding the wrapped leg steady with his great strength. Ty watched as Cody Jo cut the pant leg off. Blood had soaked through the saddle pad, the splint cutting through the muscle of Ring's thigh.

"Never said a word." Fenton unscrewed the cap on a bottle of peroxide. "Just sang and swore." He poured peroxide into the wound, the foam hissing and whitening. Ty turned away and saw Wilma crying as she dug through the packs looking for something, anything, that would help.

"Make sure that don't infect," Fenton said to Cody Jo. "He'll claw it when he wakes. He's got himself pretty drunk."

"I'll go with him," Cody Jo said. "I'll have Wilma. Buck can drive."

"Willie's done herself proud." Fenton turned and looked at the girl, weeping quietly now in the pile of duffle. "This ain't been no picnic."

After they left Fenton took the truck to get more hay. Ty sponged the sweat marks from Smoky and looked around to see what Spec and Jasper had left them to pack, counting five mules and one pack horse. He pulled his bedroll from the the pile of duffle, spread it out to get some sleep.

But sleep didn't come. He lay there, thinking about his first day of packing. Or was it two days? He wasn't sure knowing was important as he wondered about what was still to come. They would start in soon after Fenton got back, going over the north pass this time and riding steadily until they caught up with Spec. Fenton had said they'd be a day and a half behind. Ty thought it might be longer.

He guessed Spec was right: Fenton was optimistic. But he did what he had to do. Bob Ring had needed him. Ty didn't see how any of it could be helped.

He got out the neat's-foot oil and began to oil the Meana saddle, wondering if Bob Ring and Willie were all right. He wasn't sure if he was more concerned about Bob Ring or the girl, knowing only that he was very tired, that there was a lot of riding still to come.

He was worried about the packing too. Two of the mules Spec had left were Cottontail and Loco.

6

Across the South Fork

The sun was dropping by the time Fenton returned, and still Ty hadn't slept. After oiling the saddle he'd started weighing out panniers and mantying up Decker loads, laying out things for Fenton to change.

But Fenton didn't change anything, just nudged the packs with his foot and began. Ty asked no questions, tightening the ropes Fenton pointed to, hoping answers would surface. They packed the mules with sawbucks first—then Turkey, the only horse Fenton packed. He blew up against his cinch. Fenton jobbed him in the belly and cinched him tight.

"Lazy bastard," he said. "Won't make a move till dinner . . . or when I crank on his latigo."

"Might be scared. You were to tighten my latigo, I'd catch air too."

"Nothin' wrong with a tight cinch." Fenton was amused by Ty's solemn ways. "A tight everything. Start packs riding right, they'll ride all day . . . all night too."

When Turkey was packed, Ty led him away and returned with Cottontail, snubbing her to the post in the middle of the corral. "These here Decker saddles make balancing some easier." Fenton undid the sling ropes, actually explaining something. "Packs gotta balance, of course, but if one side rides up on your Decker, just lower it by loosing up one of these loops. Evens things out." He picked a mantied pack and gave it to Ty. It was so heavy Ty's knees buckled. "These two match." Fenton held the second pack with one hand, gesturing with the other. "Put yours up against the saddle and pull that loop over."

Ty tried to get the pack high enough to brace it, work the loop across. But it was too heavy and came down hard against Cottontail. She jumped, scuttling toward Fenton, who cracked her rump with his free hand. She reversed direction, skittered back. Ty dropped the pack and tried to calm her, but she saw she was astraddle the pack and went up, the tie-rope yanking her back to her knees.

"Keep this up she'll be crazy as Loco." Ty pulled the pack away and skipped free of her hooves.

"No time to romance her." Fenton still held the pack. "And Loco sure won't be an improvement. Never warmed to his shoes at all."

"One crazy mule's enough. Let's put these heavy ones on Loco."

Fenton put the pack down and watched as Ty calmed Cottontail and led her away, tying her out of sight. Fenton had watched Ty shoe a bronc mule, quiet Smoky, pull a runaway off the cliffs, ease Bob Ring down the switchbacks with a gentleness he could hardly manage with Easter. Late as it was, he decided to let Ty do this his way. He wanted him comfortable with the long ride ahead.

Ty snubbed Loco to the post and tied a blindfold on him. Fenton watched as the boy fashioned a bowline around Loco's neck, ran the rope around a hind leg and back through the the bowline collar, pulleying the hoof up until it was almost touching Loco's chest.

"Thought we'd come to that," Fenton said. "Only later—given your tender heart. Now let's pack. You can learn that Decker lesson on the job."

Ty heaved up the heavy pack and gave it to Fenton, who took it effortlessly and turned to Loco. Loco couldn't see what was coming, but he sensed something bad when Fenton got close. He kicked out with his untied leg and spun around the post on three legs until the tied one came free. They watched through the dust as he reared back against the lead-line then tried to charge by the post, the lead yanking him back. He tried again and was spun back, the post cracking this time, then breaking free as Loco backed away, his lead dragging the post through the dust. He turned, ran from it, the post relentless behind him, toppling and rolling as he circled the corral at a run. Finally he backed from it, backed until he was cornered, stood quivering and dripping, the blindfold hanging useless from his halter.

"Lucky we didn't tie this on." Fenton still held the heavy pack. "Would have played hell with my jelly jars."

Ty hardly heard it. He was talking to Loco already, freeing the big mule from the spooky post, touching him, rubbing his legs until the quivering stopped. He led him around the corral in circles, then in figure eights.

"If you can pack him," Ty spoke in the same low voice that had quieted the mule, "I'll hold him. He's gainin' his confidence back."

"He drags you around like that post, it's you who'll need the confidence." Fenton separated the packs so the mule could pass between. Ty led Loco through, turned and led him through again.

"That post didn't help," Ty said quietly. "It might be a spell before he stops trying to uproot every tree we tie him to."

"Better he uproot a goddamned tree than you." Fenton eased a pack against Loco's saddle, kept the weight off the mule until he got the loop across the pack, pulled it tight, and tied it off. Ty held the mule, calmed him as Fenton let the weight down.

When he felt the weight, Loco went up like a shot, front legs striking out as Ty tried to keep him from going over. Fenton managed to release the knot and let the pack drop as Ty was pulled through the dust by the big mule, who fought back from the pack, the big man, even the boy until at last he stood, calmed by the voice, the relentless hands reaching to touch him.

"He quieted," Fenton said, surprised. "And neither of you hurt."

"He'll tire." Ty moved Loco around the corral again, circling it twice before bringing him to the packs.

"If he don't kill you first," Fenton said, readying the packs again.

For an hour the mule fought off the packs—once when Fenton was almost finished with the last knot.

"Maybe Spec's right. We need to build a packing platform." Fenton's shirt was soggy with sweat and dust and mule hair. "He just won't wear down." He moved the packs back into place. "Determined bastard."

Ty thought panicked was more like it. He hated what they were doing—but saw no choice. Again he circled the mule before bringing him back between the packs. Fenton eased the first pack against his side and again Loco went up, pulling Ty beneath the flailing feet. Fenton kicked the pack aside and grabbed the rope to help. Together they fought Loco down only to have him go up even harder, pulling them under him as he staggered backward for balance.

"Let him go." Fenton knocked Ty into the dirt with a sweep of his arm and dropped the lead. With no weight to check him, Loco went all the way over, his head cracking against the broken post, the big body suddenly limp.

"Maybe we killed him," Fenton panted. "Or is he just slowed?"

"Might of killed himself." Ty got up from the dirt.

"Suicide, you mean?"

"No. Suicide takes being thoughtful." Ty walked over to the fallen mule. "Maybe he panicked himself to death."

"Thoughtful folks can panic to death too." Fenton nudged the mule with his boot. "Just more rare."

Ty was trying to figure out what Fenton meant when the mule stirred, rolled to get his feet under him, came partway up, went back down.

"Think he's all right?" Ty asked.

"Maybe. Might be knocked a little walleyed."

Loco was up now, legs splayed, head low, seeking balance.

"Quick." Fenton was already moving. "Let's pack him."

"Pack him? Those packs could knock him back down."

"Could. But he might concentrate so hard on stayin' upright he won't know he's packed." Ty braced himself for the pack Fenton pushed at him. "Hurry—he might improve. Don't want his complete attention."

〜

They crossed the pass in darkness, Loco moving in a trance behind Cottontail, who had caused no trouble after seeing Loco serene under his packs. The climb had been fast, the Mission Range growing purple before dropping into night. Now there was only the crunch of snow, the creak of leather, the click of a shoe on rock as they regained the trail.

The moon lifted and gave Ty a ghostly picture of the country below—the high lakes making darker stains above where the timber began. They rode down, crossing the lake-drainage just as a coyote lifted a cry from high above. Others answered, calling and yipping, making such a racket that the first voice was lost. Ty guessed it was the moon. That's when their calls lifted in the Bitterroot. He doubted these were different. Except that lone coyote who started it. He must have seen something the others didn't.

The Bitterroot was almost forgotten as Ty rode into this new life with these new people. He felt the chill lifting from the stream and shouldered into his Levi jacket, the trail flattening to work its way through wet meadows, dark stands of timber. He liked moving along in quiet, the only sound packs in motion, a horse blowing, coyotes calling intermittently—as though tracing their progress from some wild route above.

He watched Fenton and slowed where he did, easing into darkness, and climbing back into moonlight at the same pace. He led Turkey, who would doze before snorting and farting as Ty yanked him awake. After

Turkey came Cottontail, then Loco. Ty kept watching the big mule, worrying about how he would act when it came to him he was packed.

Toward dawn they skirted a long lake, the trail sometimes dropping to its bank but for the most part staying high, dipping into dark woods to cross drainages, the lake continuing on. There seemed no end to it.

He might have been asleep when he heard hooves on wood, saw Fenton's mules crossing a walkway where a spring surfaced. Smoky and Turkey weren't bothered, but Cottontail paused before bolting forward, yanking Loco onto clattery logs he didn't like. He stepped off, away from the racket, and sank hock-deep in ooze before scrambling back, the sucking sound of his hooves coming free making him crowd the others. They settled as soon as they were back on the trail, but Ty saw Loco was awake, his trance gone.

They dipped into the woods once more. Ty heard water before he saw Fenton's mules on the bridge. They were in shadow, then back into moonlight, the two pack strings almost opposite as Fenton came out of the draw.

"Take it slow!" Fenton called above the water. "It's narrow."

Ty eased Smoky and Turkey onto the bridge. Cottontail hesitated, then hurried onto the planks after them. Loco didn't like the clatter. His rump went down and he scrambled backward just as Turkey heaved forward, snatching Cottontail from the bridge and into the creek. She struggled up only to be pulled down farther, going over again and then again, her packs finally wedging into the V of the stream, her ropes running taut to Turkey and Loco, each struggling to stay upright, eyes flashing white in the moonlight.

"Why don't the damned pigtails give!" Fenton was making his way back to Turkey. "Buck must of used bailing wire." Ty was already in the stream, crawling over Cottontail, his knife out as he reached to find the loop behind the mule's saddle.

"Pigtail's buried!" Fenton yelled. "Cut the lead-line."

Ty sawed through it, watched Loco spring free, fall, struggle to his feet, disappear up the trail. Fenton, somehow managing to unsnap Turkey's line, was suddenly down in the streambed with him.

"Hustle. Mules ain't happy on their backs . . . Any broke legs?"

"She isn't kicking."

"Crawl a tad further. Undo them cinches. She might roll free without the saddle."

Ty pushed across Cottontail's belly to reach the latigos, fearing her hooves but having no other choice.

The mule made no move as Ty struggled with the swollen leather. He got the latigos free and inched himself back, joined Fenton to pull Cottontail's lead, stretching her head back across her body to make her fight them. She kicked up, struggled against them and found she was free of the saddle. She fought it too, fought the packs and the creek bed and came up, testing her legs, scrambling up the bank to the safety of the trail, shaking and blowing.

"Get Loco." Fenton tied Cottontail to a lodgepole and slid back into the creek. "I'll snag her packs. They'll be full of water."

Ty found Loco stopped where the walkway began, unwilling to go farther. He crossed through the mud to head him off, caught the frayed lead, and led him back, Loco nosing at the trail now, more interested in it than the packs on his back. He nosed at Cottontail too, rubbed his neck on her rump, so happy to see her he calmed.

"No damage." Fenton's voice rose above the stream. He had the saddle and packs across the creek. "But I don't like the looks of them clouds." Ty saw darkness to the south, a scrim already crossing the moon. "Bring her over. Let's saddle and scoot. Gotta get those folks under canvas."

Ty didn't know what to do with Loco, but the big mule seemed so happy rubbing at Cottontail he left him there, leading Cottontail back toward to the bridge, which she bolted across.

"She don't want to go in the creek again," Fenton said. "Another story with Loco, unless he gets lonely. Let's stay out of sight while we saddle."

Ty followed Fenton up the trail with Cottontail and began brushing debris from her back. Lightning came suddenly, followed by deep thunder.

"It does like to rain when we camp at White River." Fenton watched Ty saddle. "Tents are on them first two mules." He spoke as though he'd resolved something. "Let's get Loco over that bridge. I'll slip on into camp before this rain. You pack up and follow."

"I don't know where to go." Ty looked at him across Cottontail. "I never been there . . . I never been here."

"You can track, can't you?" Fenton checked Cottontail's cinch.

"Not in the dark, I can't."

"Won't be dark long. I'd worry more about the rain washin' them tracks out. Let's get Loco. Bet he's lonely."

He was right about that. Loco was so anxious to get to Cottontail he hardly noticed the bridge.

Fenton tied him near the packs, tightened Easter's cinch, and mounted. "Your Loco mule might civilize after all."

"I don't know where to go." Ty looked at the packs and then at Fenton. "Without the moon I won't see a track at all."

"No turnoffs before the South Fork. Hit the big river, turn up it four miles. Be light by then. Look for tracks to the river. Good ford. Cross and climb them benches. You're in camp." Fenton started Easter up the trail. "I'll have coffee."

"Rain could wash those tracks away!" It came to Ty why Spec was wary of packing. He felt a little sick.

Fenton stood down and got something from his saddlebag. He came back and handed Ty some strips of jerked elk. Lightning flashed, thunder close behind.

"Sugar here ain't carrying any tents." Fenton untied his last mule. "I'll leave her. Ride up the big river a ways and then put Sugar and Turkey out in front. They'll bring you in."

"How will they know?" It made no sense to Ty.

"Turkey knows where there's grain, and Sugar goes for White River like a homing pigeon. Smart mule and a greedy horse'll bring you in every time."

Fenton watched Ty chew as lightning flashed again.

"Sometimes in these mountains," he said, his voice almost tender, "you find yourself learnin' more than you got time to consider."

Ty bit off more jerky, wondering what he was supposed to consider. He chewed, watching Fenton ride off into darkness.

It seemed to Ty he had horses and mules tied everywhere, but it was Cottontail's packs that worried him. They were so water soaked he could barely lift them, and he was afraid if he got one on it would pull the saddle over before he could get the other in place. He found a high bank down the trail, wrestled one up, tied it off, and rested it there as he fought the other into place.

He lined the string out, Sugar in the rear to encourage Loco. Lightning was almost their only light now. When they left the lake and entered the woods, there was no way he could see at all. He gave Smoky her head and hoped the packs would ride, finally dozing in the saddle until a rumble too steady to be thunder told him they'd found the river. Smoky turned up against it, paralleling the noise, which lifted and faded and lifted again. At dawn he saw they were on a faint trail crossing low benches and going through stands of timber that opened into meadows. Across the meadows he could see the river, swollen and gray with silt.

The rain was starting in as they crossed a bog, the sucking sound of hooves too much for Loco. Ty was thankful Fenton had fashioned a new pigtail. It gave way as Loco fought back, his knotted lead hanging useless as he stood with Sugar, watched Ty cross with the others. Ty tied up and made his way back. He released Sugar, who hurried across to join Turkey, flinging mud on Ty in her haste. Loco wouldn't follow. Ty stroked him, leaned against him, dozed as he talked and calmed him. But it was no good. Each time he led him to the crossing, he balked, set his weight, scrabbled back.

Ty knew Loco wasn't crazy this time, just scared. He also knew he was too tired to fight him. He took the lead-line and slopped his way through the mud to Smoky, mounted her to ride into a country he'd never seen. He'd come back for Loco when he found out where he was, if he ever did.

Turkey and Sugar were free now—both of them unconcerned as Ty led Cottontail and tried to pick up tracks. But the trail was everywhere awash—and he was having trouble staying awake. He stopped when he saw a faint trace leading off toward the river, the animals so tired they made no protest. Turkey drifted off to graze, but Sugar nosed along the trail until she passed him, moved down the trace, and turned through timber toward the river. Ty followed, seeing what they were on hadn't been used for years and knowing he should turn back—if his body would respond. Then Sugar, well ahead now, went belly-deep into the river, quartering upstream against the current. Smoky followed her, the rain settling in hard now but Ty too weary to think about his slicker. He looked back, thankful Turkey was following so closely, and thought he saw something along the bank. There was too much rain to be sure. And he was tired, coming alert only as they pitched steeply out of the river, climbed up and still up again to a broad bench, an opening in the timber. In the clearing was Fenton, standing under the big kitchen fly, the wall tents already up against the rain. Spec and Jasper were there too, all of them looking at him, calling out to him.

He got off Smoky, relieved his legs didn't buckle, tied Cottontail to the log where the saddles were stacked.

"Had to leave Loco." He looked at Fenton, standing under the ridge beam of the cook tent with his coffee. "But we made it. Sugar brought us in."

"You ain't the first to be rescued by a mule." Fenton was smiling.

Ty saw the others were were smiling too. He looked down at the mud on his pants, his shirt—mud everywhere from his struggles in the creek bed and with the packing and through the muddy crossing.

"It ain't the mud," Jasper said. "We was wondering about the waterproofed trousers. Is that to keep you dry when you wade the river?"

Ty looked, saw that the neat's-foot oil had stained and darkened his pants everywhere.

"Guess I oiled too much. Wanted to protect the saddle."

"That oil's done its work," Fenton said. "You have too. Come in here and get you some coffee."

"Gotta unsaddle. Then I'll slip back for Loco."

Spec put his slicker on and went out to help. Fenton held his cup out to Jasper, who was waiting with a steaming cup for Ty. Jasper poured it into Fenton's cup instead.

"Jasper," Fenton said, sipping the hot coffee. "I believe we've found us a packer."

Fenton (1927)

There are some who still say Fenton Pardee is where Ty Hardin really started.

7

The Packer

Fenton Pardee and Cody Jo Taylor were married in 1927. Fenton was fifty-five years old, Cody Jo twenty-six. But their union aroused people's interest for larger reasons. Fenton had enjoyed being single for so many years it was hard to predict what would happen when he wasn't. The mountains always seemed to answer his spiritual needs, The Bar of Justice his physical ones. Though it was clear the tall schoolteacher with the wonderful smile could make even Fenton change his priorities, none predicted she would be the one who did the convincing, not the other way around. Half the bachelors in the valley had vied for her hand. It shocked them to see Fenton wind up with it, looking a little shocked himself.

But it wasn't such a shock to the others. They'd enjoyed watching Cody Jo find such humor in Fenton's doubts, find humor in her efforts to dispel them too. She seemed to take pleasure in his apprehension. They would shake their heads, puzzled over why a man like Fenton Pardee would be skeptical about such a sparkling woman. Some thought it his age, some his general contrariness, others his deep wariness. None saw it had less to do with what they could see than with what they couldn't: Fenton's love of his mountains, his fear that this wonderful girl would keep him from them.

What was clear to all of them from the day Cody Jo arrived was that she made things better, bringing more life to the Swan Valley schoolhouse than it had ever known. Children liked her, mothers believed in her, cowboys and lumberjacks lined up to dance with her at the schoolhouse socials. There wasn't a man not pleased to tip his hat to her, a woman who didn't like to visit with her: the women liking her because she got things done with so little fuss, the men because she kept them so off-balance they couldn't tell whether she was laughing at them or with them. All they knew was that when she was happy, things were livelier. They were thankful for whatever triggered it.

And Fenton made her happy. It was a mystery that only added to one already alive in the Swan: how Fenton Pardee could be the shrewdest, most relentless trader in the country when he was out of the mountains; the most selfless and charitable packer in the range when in them.

But all talk of how frugal Fenton could be, how unconventional the courtship, was put aside for the important day. No banter was exchanged, no jokes delivered by forsaken suitors. And if someone smiled because for once they were seeing Fenton manipulated, no one minded. What interested them most as they drank and laughed at the big wedding on the edge of Fenton's pasture was that they had never seen Fenton Pardee as happy—or as grateful. At least not when he was out of his mountains.

᠎ↄ

They all knew about Fenton, but only Fenton knew about Cody Jo. She had told him everything, looking at him steadily, going through it carefully—as though their future depended on his seeing all of it. As she talked he became so full of admiration for her she could have told him anything. Her candor left him queasy and dry-mouthed, every doubt he had vanishing. It was like jumping off a cliff into a South Fork pool. After you stepped off, you left behind everything that had held you back.

He had met Cody Jo at the fall dance in the schoolhouse. "The tall one," she'd said. "White on top, like your mountains." Then she was off with one of the Wilson brothers, swinging out among the couples on the dance floor. He could see she was a marvelous dancer, liked it that she gave him a wave or a smile as she went by.

He enjoyed watching the young men circling her for their chance, watching them drift outside to drink and talk about everything but the schoolteacher before they came back in to try again. He watched her encourage them too, laugh with them, help even the clumsiest come more alive when they moved around the floor.

"That bell mare the new teacher?" Jasper was beside him, not yet too full of drink to watch the dancers.

"She is," Fenton said.

"She does have them eatin' from her hand." Jasper looked at Fenton as though an idea had just hit him. "Let's get us a drink."

Jasper had some liquor out in his truck, which surprised Fenton. Usually he spent his time angling for someone else's. Out in the lot they found Buck Conner arguing with a cowboy who had danced too long with Angie, the Murphys' new hired girl. Buck's face was getting red, but Fenton stepped in with his big voice and his big body and got them laughing. It was as easy for him as separating two nipping horses. Jasper watched Buck and the cowboy head off together to find Angie and got out his bottle. They warmed there, drinking and talking about Fenton's mountains.

Fenton thought of the schoolteacher off and on during that winter but didn't see her again until spring, when he stopped for coffee at Murphy's all-purpose store, his truck so loaded with gear he wasn't sure he'd unload by dark. Angie got him coffee, and when he turned to leave he almost knocked Cody Jo over. She clutched at her groceries as if to protect them.

"The big one," she laughed, her face coloring. "I remember you because you're the only one I haven't seen at the recitals."

Fenton waited, not knowing how to answer.

"Come now." She enjoyed his confusion. "Culture won't hurt this valley. They even claim you," she tapped him with a long finger, "are a very cultured man." She seemed to like how uncomfortable she made him.

"But you're in luck. There's one more." She shifted her bag to the other arm. "I'll save a seat. Seven tonight. Cookies. Entertainment." She turned and left but poked her head right back in. "I'll hold your ticket."

Fenton, who hadn't been able to think of anything to say while she stood there making fun of him, still couldn't think of anything to say.

"Better go," Dan Murphy advised. "She's got that ticket for you."

"I got gear to unload. . . . You goin'?"

"Yep. Better than hearin' her tell me why I should of." Murphy wiped at his counter. "She arranged a season ticket for me."

There were dark clouds over the Missions by the time Fenton unloaded. He washed up and before he'd thought much about it was back on the road headed for the schoolhouse. The sky was black. He knew a wind would kick up soon, the rain not far behind.

It was blowing hard when he pulled into the lot, the sky so dark he wasn't surprised to see only a few cars. When he was given the little program he saw the reason wasn't just the weather. Four performances were scheduled: a reading of "Invictus," the singing of "My Buddy" accompanied by violin, a recitation of "The Cremation of Sam McGee," and a piano recital of "The Parade of the Wooden Soldiers."

Bump Conner was scheduled to sing "My Buddy," which explained why all the Conners were there, Buck and the Murphys with them. Other parents were there too, but not many. Fenton thought the idea of a ticket must have been one of Cody Jo's amusements.

He found a chair by a screen they'd set up and was listening to people move around behind it when a clap of thunder rifled through and made everyone jump. The lights blinked, held, blinked again, stayed on.

Fenton decided to get his slicker. By the time he got to his truck the rain had started. He put the slicker on and got out a lantern. When he got back to the porch, the rain settled in to stay. He took the slicker off and went back inside, putting it by the wall with his lantern. He heard the rain ease for a minute before starting in even harder.

When the lights began to blink, Cody Jo came from behind the screen, not nearly as cheerful as she'd been that afternoon.

"Might rain," Fenton said.

"You found your seat." Her eyes were wide. "We saved it."

"Have to fight off many people?" Sheets of rain were hitting the windows.

"I have cookies."

"Could sog up in this weather."

The lights blinked and went. Fenton scratched matches and got his lantern going. He held it up, peered around for Buck.

"Should I get them?" Cody Jo's eyes were round in the uncertain light.

"Hard to pass 'em in this dark." Buck appeared in the circle of light.

"Who told me this place has a generator?" Fenton asked him.

"I told you this place has a generator. If someone hasn't thought they knew better, it's right where I set it up in the first place."

"Hope you remember. Not much help out there in that dark."

They went out into the rain, leaving the room in darkness. Cody Jo knew she should do something, but the rain made it hard to think.

Rosie Murphy began to sing "Ten Thousand Goddamned Cattle," about a cowboy whose sweetheart leaves him for "a son-of-a-bitch from Ioway." It was the song Buck's mother sang when she was putting her children to sleep, so all the Conners joined right in. When it ended someone started another. They were on "The Zebra Dun" when the generator kicked in and they had light. They finished the last verse anyway, liking the singing and wishing someone had a bottle so they could keep going.

Fenton and Buck stomped and shook off water on the porch. "Where's your slicker?" Fenton asked. "You could get wet."

"I am wet." Buck looked out at the rain. "I don't see the sense of puttin' a slicker on now so I can keep all this water inside it."

"Which means you didn't bring one in the first place. Trainin' you is like relearnin' a mule." Fenton took Buck's hat and poured the water from the brim. "Let's go listen to that music. I hear they got cookies."

As they left the porch the rain became hail.

Cody Jo had to play chords on the piano to let people know Sue Jamison was going to recite. The hail sounded like hammers across the roof. It was easy to see Sue was scared. Fenton wasn't sure whether she was scared of the hail or of having to stand up and speak.

"Out of the night that covers me." She tried to lift her voice above the sound. Hailstones were hitting the window so hard Fenton was afraid it would break. He stood and flattened his back against the glass to keep it from shattering. The girl smiled as though she finally understood the meaning of the words. "Black as the Pit from pole to pole." Fenton still had his slicker on, which might have kept him from getting cut up when a big hailstone shattered the pane and splashed glass across the room.

"Shit goddamn," Buck said as people and chairs moved this way and that to avoid the glass. Fenton spread his slicker wide and backed into the opening, nodding to the girl to continue.

The hailstones were as big as golf balls now, seeming even bigger to Fenton, who thought some might be giving him bruises. "Under the bludgeoning of chance . . ." The girl smiled at Fenton, her face going blank as she searched for the words.

"My head is bloody . . ." They heard Cody Jo's prompting even above the hail, and everyone laughed. Sue finished with no more trouble, though Fenton had to take that on faith. The hail was hitting his slicker so hard he could only hear a word here and there until "I am the master of my fate: I am the captain of my soul."

"I sure as hell ain't the captain of *my* fate." Dan Murphy was beside him even before the little round of applause ended.

"You mean you didn't arrange this hail?" Fenton was thinking of a way to get free of the window.

"You'll have to bring Cody Jo back. I gotta make tracks. This could wreck my store." Others were getting up now, Buck protesting, saying he wanted to hear Bump sing "My Buddy." Fenton called him over.

"You're still damp." He patted Buck on his soggy shoulder. "Won't hurt to stand here. I gotta fix somethin'."

He had Buck in the window before Buck could think up an argument. Fenton took an old bulletin board, held a geography book over his head and went out through the hail to get a hammer and some nails from his truck. Pushing Buck inside enough to get the board flat, he tacked it over the broken window, then went back inside with the hammer and nails, sure something else would break any minute.

"Them hailstones smart." Buck was dripping water again.

"Which is why you need your slicker." Fenton got him into Bump's, and they found a sheet of plywood, lifted it high over their heads to ferry the Jamisons out to their car. They got others out too, then began covering the most exposed windows, working until the hail began to let up.

Buck went out to check his truck for broken windows, finding some dents but no serious damage. He came back across a yard white with hailstones. Only Fenton and Cody Jo and Bump were left.

"You best get in this," Buck said to his brother, taking off the slicker. "Don't want to ruin your fine tenor voice."

"I'm glad for the hail." Bump took the coat. "Singin' that song wasn't my idea."

"Don't worry." Cody Jo put her hand on Buck's arm, startled by how soaked he was. "You can hear him next time."

"With the violin?" Buck asked. "That violin's important."

"If she can get him to sing," Fenton said, "she'll get the violin to squeak along too."

"I have cookies," Cody Jo said to Buck. "You and Bump must be hungry. . . . And you need dry clothes."

"Don't you worry." Fenton saw that Cody Jo was worn out. "Buck's like a duck. I doubt he knows he's wet."

"I'm bruised some." Buck rubbed at his back.

"Let's shut things down." Fenton looked around. "Won't be all that easy gettin' home through this hail."

Buck and Bump went out and moved their truck so its headlights were on the generator. Fenton got Cody Jo into his truck before crunching across the hail, shutting the generator off. Cody Jo saw his shadow on the schoolhouse growing bigger and more crooked and then he was in the truck beside her, Buck's headlights still on the hail, which looked ghostly in the last misty rain.

"Bring your slicker next time," Fenton called to Buck. "Keep you from gettin' crippled up."

"I ain't crippled. Just stung some." Buck waited until Fenton got his engine started. "I'd repair quicker if Angie could rub me." He wound up his window and headed north toward the Conners.

Fenton eased his truck south toward Murphy's store, the road a strip of white, his headlights making a tunnel of the trees. He drove slowly, hunched forward in his slicker, careful not to get into a slide.

"Glad you brought us some culture." He looked over at Cody Jo. "Don't know how we got by so long without it."

"That wasn't at all what you expected, was it? That poem . . ."

"Didn't know what to expect. I sure didn't think we'd get a storm like this. I believe we'd have done better in my tents."

"You seemed to know just what to do."

"Not that many choices. . . . How many people you roped into these 'cultural' events?" He enjoyed the way she sat so straight on the seat.

She felt his big presence waiting for her to answer.

"Have a cookie," she said, holding out the plate. Somehow she'd gotten the cookies out to the truck without getting them wet or crumbled or even very broken. She handed him one.

"You do beat all." He took a bite. "And they hold right up. Unless I'm so hungry I can't tell. I slid right past dinner tonight."

"No wonder you looked so anxious in that window. Can't be captain of your fate on an empty stomach." She smiled and held up the plate of cookies again. "You were good with little Sue."

"Not a cheerful poem." He took two more. "She needed a little encouragement. Suppose you could make some of these up in the mountains?"

Fenton was always on the lookout for cooks for his pack trips. He couldn't help playing with the idea now, even though he was pretty sure that was the wrong thing for Cody Jo.

"Oh yes. The big packer. That can't be too hard. Put everything on those poor mules and loaf around all summer in the mountains."

"It gets more complicated." He looked at her. She realized again how much there was of him, how focused and uncluttered he was. He was about to say something when Dan Murphy appeared in their headlights. He was waving at them with a shovel, his little Ford tilted almost on its side in the ditch behind him. Rosie Murphy tried to climb out, but the pitch was too steep and she dropped back in.

"See you been practicin' your trick drivin'," Fenton said.

"This stuff is slick." Dan opened Fenton's door. "We was all right until Rosie got edgy. I overcorrected."

Fenton got the lantern going again. "You done fine, Daniel. Hardly anyone else could of tilted her so tidy."

"Buck put them store windows in. Had his eyes on Angie so much I believe he only partly did his work. Bet we're knee deep in hail balls."

The Murphys had hired Angie off a ranch outside of Whitefish. She was the hardest worker they'd ever had, and the spunkiest. Everyone knew Buck was courting her. And everyone knew he wasn't doing very well—not since he'd made a scene at the schoolhouse dance. She'd even refused to come to the recital because she'd heard Buck would be there.

"Buck ain't my problem right now," Fenton said. "You are." He hauled Rosie up out of the Ford and she gave him a little hug.

Fenton rummaged around in the bed of his truck for a lash rope. "Pull you free, maybe you won't charge so much for what you call coffee." Cody Jo was holding the lantern and trying to calm Rosie. Fenton tied the lash rope onto the bumper so fast Dan Murphy didn't realize it was done. He pulled his truck ahead, getting the rope taut.

"Buck just needs to get Angie off his mind when he wants to hit a nail. Pop her into gear, Daniel. Help me snake you out."

The moon came out, reflecting off the white road. Fenton's truck pulled the Ford along in the ditch for a way, the Ford's wheels spinning as it tried for a purchase. Finally the front wheels came up, the car sliding along almost sideways before the rest of it bounced up onto the road. Rosie trotted alongside it the whole way, shouting encouragement as though she were driving a team.

"Damned if them lash ropes don't come in handy," Dan Murphy said. "I been doubtin' you on that."

"Just don't drive so fast we got to tie onto you again. Wet is tough on knots. And we might twang Rosie into next week." Fenton looked at her. "Never told me you was a mule skinner, Rosie."

They decided Cody Jo would go on with the Murphys so Fenton wouldn't have to drive to the store and back out again. Cody Jo got her things and came over to say good-bye, saying that maybe packing was useful, if packers could tie knots like that. She said she was leaving the cookies for him so he could be "captain of his fate."

Fenton drove home and started the fire, doing some chores before eating a cold supper. Then he started in on the cookies, wondering what it was in the schoolteacher's voice that touched him so.

8

Lost Bird Canyon

Fenton saw the schoolteacher only a few more times that year, meeting when they were moving so fast in different directions that he simply avoided thinking about it—as though something were wrong with enjoying that look on her face just before she started to laugh.

Then just before Fenton's big August trip, Jasper nearly severed his thumb with his cleaver and was out for the season. When Rosie Murphy heard Fenton planned to use Buck and Bump as cooks, she threw up her hands and volunteered, if Fenton would keep Buck on as wrangler. She knew Angie would be a lot more help to Dan if Buck were elsewhere.

The next thing she did was talk Cody Jo into helping her. Before he knew it Fenton found himself riding toward the pass with seventeen pack animals, two green cooks, and a lovesick wrangler. He had Tommy Yellowtail to help with the mules, but if Gus Wilson hadn't agreed to come, he didn't know what he would have done. That was before Gus got the big chunk torn from his face. And with the unexpected turn the trip took, Fenton felt lucky to have him.

Three Chicago grain traders had brought their families out to look at the country Fenton had shown them the year before. They'd come for elk, but the country was what won them over, the country and the big packer who handled their horses, kept them fed and dry, found elk for them in the thin light of morning. Now they wanted to show it to their families, acting like old-timers themselves, talking with Fenton about routes, helping saddle, herding their families around as though they'd done this all their lives.

Except for the trouble in Lost Bird Canyon—and nearly drowning Goose in the South Fork—the trip went the way Fenton's trips always did. But there was nothing ordinary about any of it to Cody Jo. It seemed to her she learned something new every step of the way, a matter she wouldn't admit at first, even to Rosie. She insisted on riding her flat saddle, but it took only a day of watching Fenton tie her slicker onto other peoples' saddles to see she'd been wrong. She wouldn't admit that either, just as she wouldn't admit how much she wanted to stay in her bedroll when Rosie prodded her awake the first morning.

"Time to make coffee," Rosie said. "They're saddling."

"What's the matter with them?" Cody Jo looked out at the night. "They can make their own coffee."

"They look for tracks." Rosie nudged her again. "Our job is to send them out happy so they won't be discouraged when there aren't any."

"What?" Cody Jo was up now, shivering. "Will the horses run away?"

"Maybe." Rosie lit the kindling. "But the sooner they find tracks the less likely it is."

An hour later they heard the bells and saw the horses. It was lovely to watch as Fenton and Tommy Yellowtail eased the herd into the meadow so they wouldn't run through and out the other side. Cody Jo watched them feinting and kicking at one another before circling around Gus Wilson, out in the frosty meadow moving among them with a nose bag. She saw Buck and Tommy Yellowtail begin to catch them up, taking the gentle ones first, sometimes moving too quickly and spooking one off. There were over forty head to take care of; it took time.

Rosie took pancakes to the men when they started saddling, Tommy putting his on a log and eating as he saddled. Fenton, troubled by all the talk the night before, came into the cook tent to talk with the traders.

One of the men had convinced everyone they should go down Lost Bird Canyon to the White River camp. Fenton had made it through the canyon years ago, which he'd made the mistake of admitting when he took that same man to the head of the canyon looking for elk the year before. It was the shortest way, that was true. But Fenton couldn't remember how he'd done it then and was pretty sure no one had done it since. What worried him was that he'd enjoyed sipping their bourbon and looking at Cody Jo so much the night before that he might have given the impression he'd try, which in the morning light he knew was a bad idea. There would be undergrowth everywhere, deadfall, and bogs—often the only way through the thick timber—that could play hell with his mules.

He got some coffee and went through it all again, surprised that his reservations made everyone even more interested. If they had to turn back, they said, the adventure would make up for lost time. They felt lucky Fenton knew the canyon. They called it "challenging," trusted Fenton to "meet the challenge." Rosie and Cody Jo just made things worse.

"When do we start?" Rosie asked. "Kitchen's packed and mantied."

"Just the way you said it would be." Cody Jo's smile warmed everyone. "High country under a Montana sky. You the hero." She patted Fenton's arm. "I like you as the hero."

Fenton raised a few more objections before going off to saddle. He felt undone again by Cody Jo. He'd been so taken by her confidence in something she knew nothing about, he'd lost his own. He grabbed a saddle and shook his head, thinking about the way she'd looked in the firelight the night before.

They were well into the canyon by midmorning. Old Babe, the horse he'd ridden before Easter, kept finding the remnants of a trail, but after awhile it didn't seem important. The sky was clear. They moved easily through meadows and open timber, watching game and stopping once to watch a black bear and her cubs scurry up the bluffs, the sow looking them over before disappearing.

They had lunch in a high meadow. Below them the canyon narrowed and flattened, the timber heavy. After that it eased down to the South Fork, across the stream's broad alluvial fan. Fenton knew that part would be easy, a gentle ride through open woods to the South Fork ford. Getting through the heavy timber was the problem. Even watching Cody Jo couldn't keep him from worrying about that.

Tommy Yellowtail rode Pinto ahead to scout out a route while Fenton let the mules graze. He sat with Gus and Buck, apart from the rest, eating and talking about what was ahead. They could hear Rosie and Cody Jo bantering with the children, getting the littlest to help make sandwiches.

After lunch it seemed no time at all before they were at the edge of the deep woods, Fenton deciding to loose-herd his mules. He'd just finished breaking up the strings when Tommy appeared, coming from the other side of the stream and shaking his head.

"Got our full hands. Like bear shit in there. Wet."

Fenton didn't waste any time. He sent Tommy back into the woods to try again, told Rosie and Buck where he'd spotted a likely campsite and sent them back to find flat ground for the tents. He didn't even string the mules back together, handing their lead ropes to the best riders, giving Cody Jo one too. But her mule pulled back, and without a saddle horn she couldn't hold him. Fenton led him up the canyon himself.

It was a good place for a camp, backed up against aspen with grazing on the slides above. Fenton trimmed a deadfall so they could stack the saddles. Gus got lodgepoles for the A-frames and put Buck to work cutting them to size as he unpacked the canvas. Fenton belled two mares, saved out a third bell for Babe and pushed the stock out of camp. Then he got Gus and rode back with axes and the handsaw, tracking Tommy into the woods. It wasn't long before they heard Pinto nicker. They tied up there and went ahead on foot.

It got darker in the woods, the stream slowed, drifting across the floor of the canyon to form bogs, the stream and the bogs murky looking. The wetness pushed them closer to the canyon walls, where they found Tommy, high on some deadfall, looking discouraged.

"Rat's nest," he complained. "Logs all over. Bad shit."

It looked even worse to Fenton—the forest dark, the ground spongy, the stream spreading and uprooting trees, laying claim to the whole canyon. Tommy said the other side looked no better, the stream running close under the walls, a bog going almost to the cliffs. But it seemed to Fenton that's how he'd made it years before, never sure of a trail, just scrambling through, clinging to the hem of the canyon. It had been later in the year, drier. But he'd made it. He didn't want to give up now.

They worked their way across the canyon and found the bog, looking just as bottomless as Tommy predicted.

"I'm goddamned." Fenton looked at Tommy. "Got through once. Can't see how. You think it was that much drier?"

"Shit yes. Best is just before snow. That's when my people traveled. Down. Always down for winter."

"Yes, and in spring they came up," Fenton said. "They couldn't go down if they didn't come up. How the hell did they get up?"

"Same way everyone does. But them horse soldiers." Tommy enjoyed seeing Fenton swatting at mosquitoes. Mosquitoes didn't bother him. "Stayed high." He looked up at the cliffs. "What's up there?"

"Straight up, is what's up there."

"Not up top it ain't." Tommy was already starting. "There's other ways to get on top a cliff. Up there we maybe find a smart way." He swung himself up over the ledges, moving easily for such a big man.

"I'm thinkin' we're whipped." Gus knocked limbs off a deadfall to see what kind of ground was under it. "You must of come through before these trees plugged it up." His shirt was wet with sweat, spattered with mud.

Tommy's call was welcome. They wanted to get above the bugs. By the time they climbed up to find him, Tommy was convinced.

"See? Didn't move nothing. Used the country. My people."

They were on a shelf. For thirty feet to either side there was a clear way, like a good game trail. Across some shale Tommy found more. Then it was gone again. They combed back and forth, picking it up in bits—narrow, dropping or climbing to intersect other shelves, but there. They worked toward the South Fork, staying high until they found a clear trace that angled down to meet the broad alluvial fan. They marked it, followed it back, lost it entirely until it came to them that it switched back against itself, dropped into the canyon down a rough chute, cutting into the woods above the big bog. It crossed the canyon there, skirting a water-soaked meadow, and climbed the other side, found another shelf before dropping back, returning to the canyon floor just above their horses.

Fenton considered it as he rode up the darkening valley toward camp.

No trail, but there was a way. If he had to bring Tommy and Gus through with a few mules, he could make it. There would be steps to dig in the chutes, footing to hack into the shale, but it could be done. It was a different matter to bring a whole party through, most green as grass.

"No good for them people." Tommy spoke as if he heard Fenton's thinking. "Don't see the no good places." Tommy always worried about people from the city. They didn't seem to know what could happen to them in the mountains.

Fenton understood Tommy's objections, but they were so close. It might take three more days if they turned back, four if the weather changed. He was about to ask Gus what he thought when they heard bells high on the grassy slide. Babe whinnied, the bells pausing as if in answer.

They came into camp just after dark. Fenton belled Babe and pushed her out toward the others, knowing the feed would hold them.

He knew too that this was a good camp: the sleeping flies taut, water close by, lots of room around the fire, where everyone seemed to have gathered. He went to the creek to wash. When he came back they were huddled around Gus and Tommy, asking questions. Rosie gave him a bowl of thick stew and he moved away, letting the tiredness wash through him, hearing the talk without listening to it. There was so much to think about that he hardly realized they all had gone quiet, waiting for him.

He turned back to them, thinking things through. He told them about looking for the trail, the logs choking the canyon, only Tommy Yellowtail knowing they should look high. Cody Jo's eyes were on him as he talked, her face still.

"We've come this far," he heard himself saying. "We're awful close to White River. Guess it wouldn't hurt to give it a try." There was a murmur of approval. Subdued, not at all like the night before. They'd heard enough from Gus and Tommy to know this was a gamble.

Fenton squatted, drew a map in the dirt, feeling Cody Jo's eyes on him still. He told them how they could help, saying even if things went well it would take the morning to get the route ready. He hoped they could be on their way by early afternoon. That way, barring a wreck, they could be across the big river and camped on the White River benches by dinner.

Cody Jo and Rosie started putting things away as people drifted from the fire, talking among themselves. Fenton answered a few more questions, then slipped away. He had more thinking to do before he went to sleep. He'd been surprised by some of the things he'd said himself. He went past the saddles and looked at the stars as he took a long pee.

"You piss like a moose." A voice lifted from the darkness.

"Should of spoke up." Fenton knew Tommy slept by the saddles, watching the weather and keeping the porcupines away, but the disembodied voice gave him a start. "Might of pissed right on you."

"You done that already."

"Not 'cause I didn't know you were there, if that's what you mean."

"I mean you didn't have no idea what was gonna come out when you started sweet-talkin' them people. Me and Gus sure didn't. We just didn't count on you bullshittin' yourself."

"Truth is I *didn't* know. I was so occupied by how I got through there in the first place, I wasn't ready. Still don't see how I done it."

"Maybe you was so green you didn't know it couldn't be done. Most of us was that way once. It's best to disremember."

"Well, I made it. That's the thing."

"The wrong thing. And you went the wrong way. You was strong and dumb and lucky. Luck don't come that often. Don't pay to ask for it twice. Now you're gonna take these people through what you don't remember back when you didn't know no better than to try."

Fenton was startled to get such a long speech from Tommy. "Let's think how we will, not why we shouldn't. I might of chose wrong, but I chose. We just got to do it."

"Horse shit," Tommy grunted. "Even Spec would know better."

Special Hands, Tommy's son, was barely ten but already known for his skill as a hunter and skinner and woodsman. Fenton liked it when Tommy talked about Special Hands. He stood there waiting for more, looking up at the Big Dipper and listening to the creek. Tommy started to snore just as the cold came in. Fenton went back to his bedroll, moved around until he was comfortable and could concentrate on the day ahead. There was much truth in what Tommy had said. There were cliffs and bogs and snags all over the place. Something told him it was too big a bite to take, but something stronger told him to take it. He hadn't come all this way just to turn back.

They were up early. Rosie had a big breakfast ready at daybreak, pancakes and eggs and lots of bacon and coffee. Fenton sipped his coffee, watching Cody Jo turn pancakes and stack them on the corner of the stove while she did eggs to order in a big skillet. She moved easily about her work, a quality in her movements so graceful and sure he found it hard to start in on his day's work.

Buck and Gus were already at work, catching up the horses they needed, pushing the rest out for more feed, saddling fast. Despite his lingering, Fenton found himself heading down the canyon before the sun reached the valley floor. Behind him came everyone he thought he could use—and some he couldn't. There was so much talk in camp, he had little choice. Everyone wanted to help.

Fenton put Buck and Gus to work cutting away limbs and moving deadfall. He sent Tommy up on the cliffs with some of the teenagers, digging a path across the shale and cutting rough steps in the chutes. He dropped down to check where the route crossed the canyon, worried about how soft the ground might get after the first horses broke through.

Rosie organized things in camp, setting aside a lunch, taking the stove down, getting the kitchen tent ready for the packers. Cody Jo, still unsettled by the way Fenton had watched her, wasn't much help.

"Take this and go." Rosie handed her a sack of apples and a wedge of cheese. "Not much use to me, and you'll be a big hit with them."

Cody Jo brightened at the idea. She needed something to do. All the talk about cliffs and bogs worried her.

"Should I give tips on trailblazing?"

"Stick with the food. It digests," Rosie said.

They had the way open almost to the first chute when she found them. One log, still to be moved, had poles jammed under it. She stayed back as they tried to slide it, their bodies straining, faces red.

"Do better if you got her unstuck." Fenton's big voice came down off the chute. Then he was there with Gus, grabbing the longest pole, finding purchase for it under the log as Gus kicked a chunk of deadfall underneath for a fulcrum. Fenton levered down; the log came up. He braced it as they got other poles under it, slid it a few feet. They did it again, everyone falling in behind Fenton's strength and directions, moving the fulcrum, lifting and sliding the log until there was room for the mules.

"A short horse soon curried." Fenton tossed the pole aside. "What worries me is the damn bog. Might not have any bottom at all." Cody Jo watched him take his hat off and wipe his face, which seemed an even deeper brown against his white hair. Mud was splattered on him everywhere, drying and browning in the sun. There was a tear in his shirt. He looked big and strong and capable—yet somehow vulnerable too.

"Something to eat might help," she said, enjoying their surprise. They were happy she was there, telling her what they'd done, blaming and congratulating each other, pleased with themselves, the day, with Fenton—who made sure everyone had food before taking some himself.

"I believe you're our Florence Nightingale." He cut off a chunk of cheese and snapped his knife shut. "But I got this feeling she wasn't near so good to look at." The words came out of him so earnestly he was surprised himself, his throat tightening around them.

"I . . ." She felt her face warm. "Aren't there others ahead?"

"There are." Fenton cleared his throat. "Let's go find 'em."

Cody Jo was shocked by where he took her. She had to use her hands to get up the chute, cross the ledges and slides. They dropped and crossed the canyon to reach the others, the canyon magical to Cody Jo, sunlight filtering down to make the little meadow look rich, verdant. Tommy was on the other side, finishing up the chute they would have to climb.

"Ain't gonna do much better." Tommy popped a chunk of cheese into his mouth. "Test it with Babe. We'll patch where there's trouble."

Fenton put Cody Jo in front of him as they went back for Babe. He was embarrassed by how mud-spattered and dirty he was. They talked little, even when she hesitated crossing a chute.

"There's room," he said. "And the cliffs aren't what bother me."

"And the mules aren't what bother me." Cody Jo tipped a little. He reached out, gave her balance.

Gus and Buck had the horses ready for everyone to go back to pack up. They watched Fenton ride back again into the dark canyon, leading Tommy's pinto behind Babe.

"That Tommy, he can find a way through anything," Gus declared.

"And Fenton can clear the damn way." Buck was tired. "That man like to worked me into next week." He started up the trail. "Sure was determined. And by God he won."

Babe and Pinto handled the route with little trouble. Tommy met Fenton at the first chute and walked behind, shoring up the route, both worrying not so much about these horses as the others, especially the mules who might hit something and tip their loads off balance. Fenton grew more worried when Babe went up to her pasterns edging along the meadow.

On their way back the pinto went in still deeper, but there was nothing to be done. Jumbled deadfall forced them to skirt the meadow. All they could do was hope there was a bottom to it.

They were underway by early afternoon. Fenton noticed clouds but didn't make much of them. There could be buildups for days before a storm. He saw no sense in worrying about tomorrow with so much trouble ahead today, which came where he feared it would. Sugar, a little Tennessee mule Fenton favored, tried to climb above the mud, ramming her pack into a log that forced her back out into the meadow. She went down, tried to lunge up, went down again, rolling out over her packs, which kept her from sinking but now held her there, her struggles only miring her more deeply. She struggled a final time before giving up—her packs, off balance now, holding her fast.

Gus had already taken the guests through, each walking to lighten the horses. Tommy had followed, leading Babe, the mare the mules followed without fail. Fenton and Buck, alert for trouble, came last. Fenton was already pushing the other mules toward the stream when Sugar went down. He hurried the rest across, turning back just as Sugar lifted a mournful bray, which encouraged Fenton. If I can calm her, he thought, get her saddle off, she might fight free to catch up with the others.

When he got back to the meadow, he saw that Sugar's bray might have come from confusion as much as loneliness. Buck had worked some deadfall out onto the bog so he could stay on top of the mud. He was out there on the logs himself now. Fenton watched him reach across the mule and down into the mud, searching for the lash cinch.

Fenton saw Buck was off balance, but before he could call a warning Buck was catching himself on the pack, sinking Sugar still deeper. Buck's body lurched forward just as Sugar jerked her head up, hitting Buck's head like a maul on a wedge. He saw Buck go backward onto the muddy green, his face crooked, the blood coming so quickly he thought Buck's head had been split entirely.

He took off his boots, tied a lead-line to a tree, and started out through the mud. When he looked up, he saw that Buck was upright, blood streaming from his face as he balanced himself with one hand on a log, fishing around under the muck with the other.

"I see you come back for me. This mule has made my nose bleed. And I believe I've lost a boot in this murk."

"You ain't thinkin' straight." Fenton could barely see Buck's face through all the blood. "Let's get you unstuck. Worry about the damn boot later."

Fenton held the line as he went out but found the mud had a bottom after all. He used the rope anyway, hauling Buck out as Buck clutched at the boot he'd somehow found.

"Leggo that boot and I'll look at your nose." Fenton splashed muddy water on Buck's face. "It's moved some."

Buck felt Fenton's big hands on either side of his head and thought he felt something move, though he couldn't be sure.

"It's back near the middle." Fenton wiped his hands on his pants. "I'll cut them ropes now. Get the packs off our mule."

"If I knowed you was gonna cut rope, I wouldn't be in such a bad state." Buck scooped mud and water out of his boot, tilting his head and trying to clear his vision. "You told me never to cut rope."

"And I meant it. Unless you were gonna lose a whole mule. I was figurin' on you usin' some initiative when an entire mule come up."

"Initiative is what got me out there." Buck was struggling to pull his boot on. "I believe."

"Gotta study up on your brand," Fenton said, starting back toward Sugar.

☾⋅⟡

Cody Jo led her gelding until they crossed the last of the shale. Then she sent him on behind the others, turning and seeing Tommy leading Babe, Gus and the mules following. She saw no sign of Buck or Fenton.

She hurried back, sliding down the chute and crossing the stream on a log. She saw them then, watched Fenton peer down at Buck as though after something in his eye, saw Fenton's boots thrown aside. Only then did she see the blood covering Buck's shirt and running down onto his pants. And not until Fenton started back through the mud did she see Sugar, realize how ripped and broken the meadow was around her.

"He's gonna cut them ropes," Buck said to her. "He told me never to do that." He wiped his eyes. "He may get them packs, but I doubt he'll get Sugar. Pure sog out there."

Fenton waved a hand at Cody Jo. "Glad you showed up." He heaved a pack free and up onto the logs. "Buck got chunked." Somehow he got the pack saddle free as well, got all the gear to the edge of the meadow, stacking it there where it could dry.

"Wash his face up in the creek." He started back out toward the mule. "Just go easy around that nose. Pretty mushy."

Cody Jo saw Fenton pull Sugar's head this way and that. No matter which way he pulled, the little mule stayed put, her neck stretching out but the rest of her fixed deep in the mud of the disrupted meadow.

It grew darker, the mosquitoes thicker as they made their way to the ford. When they reached it Buck waded straight in, splashing water on his face before suddenly going down, his blood clouding the water. Cody Jo waded in after him, helped him back to the bank and cleaned his face with her kerchief. His nose was already purple across the bridge, a puffiness setting in around his eyes.

Fenton came and put Cody Jo in front, leading Buck across the stream and along the trail until they met Tommy. He was riding toward them on Pinto and leading Goose, the gentlest horse in Fenton's string.

"I wouldn't have hurried so if I'd knowed Buck was gonna wash up—in his clothes too," Tommy said, looking up at the dark sky. "Maybe this shower bath'll clean that blood off." Fenton was startled by how black the sky was getting.

"Buck here got banged up." Cody Jo was surprised by the urgency in Fenton's voice. "Slip him up on Pinto and get him back to the others. I'll take Goose back for them packs."

Tommy said not a word, boosting Buck onto Pinto and starting back before Cody Jo could collect herself.

"Go." Fenton pushed Cody Jo along behind Tommy. "When the lightning starts, them folks'll need some Cody Jo talk." Lightning ripped through the sky, thunder following so closely the pinto jumped.

"Maybe that'll scare our mule out of the sog." Buck was having a hard time staying in the saddle. "It sure got Pinto's attention."

"Maybe," Fenton called back. "And maybe there's gonna be so damn much water we'll lose her altogether."

9

Rain

Tommy put Cody Jo behind Buck to keep him in the saddle. They moved quickly after that, finding the others huddled under trees, eyes on the black sky, rain gear on. That morning Cody Jo, not wanting to tie her slicker on anyone's saddle, had stuffed hers into her duffle. Now Gus would either have to unpack the mules to find it or give her his, getting soaked for the kindness. Big drops were already starting to fall.

"I'll take Babe back." She climbed onto her gelding, not wanting anyone to see how miserable she looked. "We need Fenton."

Gus started to protest, but Tommy, ignoring a clap of thunder, handed her Babe's lead. "Gotta get him back before we cross." The rain was settling in now. "River could rise."

Cody Jo pushed them hard, sliding them off the trail once and clamboring back. The rain was steady, the trail soft. They slid down the chute into the canyon to find Fenton, all Sugar's gear tied onto Goose.

"Where's Sugar? We can't leave her."

"No choice. If this don't drive her out, nothin' will."

"But . . . " Suddenly Cody Jo found herself crying.

"Where's your slicker? You'll be soaked." Fenton pulled his own slicker from behind Babe's saddle and put it on her. She was shaking so hard her hands couldn't fasten the snaps. Fenton reached up and did it for her.

"Bet you gave yours to one of the kids," he shouted through the downpour. He reached into his saddlebag and pulled out a scrunched-up child's poncho. "Got this for an emergency." He put it on and mounted Babe, the poncho barely reaching his saddle. Cody Jo opened her mouth, but nothing came. Fenton pulled his hat down, water running off it like a waterfall. "Stick close behind old Goose," he shouted.

It seemed impossible, but the rain came harder. Fenton shouted something she couldn't hear and forced Babe up the chute, the shale blue-black and slick now, Babe struggling as she hauled Goose onto the thin trail above. The gelding, afraid of being left, scrambled behind, going onto his haunches once, Cody Jo clinging to his mane with eyes closed—leaving everything to her horse, to Fenton.

She couldn't believe how calm he was, how careful. She watched him ease past the slick places, riding slowly along ledges high above the canyon floor, the rain blowing so she thought the little poncho would be ripped from him—or he would be torn away himself. The shakes abated as she fought to stay in the saddle, but when they left the ledges and met the others, they came again, harder.

No one noticed, huddled as they were at the base of the ponderosas. Fenton was shouting directions before they knew he was there. In minutes he had them moving, checking cinches, mounting up. He tied his mules in strings of three, making sure a steady one was first.

Cody Jo did what she could to help, the shaking not as bad when she was in motion. Before she knew it they were following Fenton toward the river, riders with mules first. Even Buck led a string. Gus, leading Goose, rode behind him, the boy who'd been riding Goose clinging to his waist.

They wound through open timber, pushing against the rain until they heard the river and suddenly saw it: swift, brown with silt, the opposite bank lost behind sheets of rain. By the time Cody Jo got to the bank Fenton was half way across, water above his stirrups, Babe quartering upstream to take advantage of some hidden bar, the mules lurching under packs as they followed, crossing deeper water near the bank to reach the bar Fenton followed. He was turned in his saddle, watching not the mules he was leading but the ones behind, free now and floundering into the river as Gus set them loose to trail after him, the saddle horses waiting until the mules found the safest route.

Fenton hadn't had time to get anyone stationed in the river to steer them clear of the deep holes, keep them from turning back. All he could do was hope the storm would make them afraid to try anything on their own. It was a chance he had to take—the water rising, the downfall torrential.

Everything in him was concentrating on getting into camp, getting people dry—which is why he was startled to see Gus release Goose, shoo him into the river behind the mules. As faithful as Goose was, there was nothing to convince Fenton he would follow a string of mules through this river, not with every horse but Babe behind him, waiting on the bank—or still winding through the timber toward the river.

Goose reached the rocky bar and was pushing his way against the current when he saw no horses ahead. He looked back, turned toward the horses and slipped off into deeper water, the full force of the river rising to his packs, taking him deeper into the ominously smooth water that cut under the bank, exposing roots and boulders. His packs went under first, then he was gone, slipping beneath the water as if pulled. Fenton cursed himself for how tightly he'd tied on the packs as Babe turned toward the shore, made her way through the last wide rapids and up the steep banks toward the White River benches.

Tommy was checking the crossing for the others when he saw Goose slide under. He motioned the rest to cross, shouting through the downpour for Gus and Cody Jo to lead, hurrying others in behind, all of them too numb with wet and cold to fear the crossing as their horses stumbled, caught themselves, pushed their way through the swollen river.

Behind them Tommy saw what he'd wanted to see. Goose's nose came up first, the current pushing him against the shelf Fenton had used to reach the rocky bar. Tommy watched the force of the water lift Goose until his feet were under him, watched him scramble onto the shelf, staggering under the packs. Goose blew streams of water from his nostrils and stumbled as Tommy forced Pinto into him, Tommy cursing so fiercely it startled Goose upright. The other horses were fading through the rain, but Tommy was counting on them to pull Goose along. Goose lurched forward, water pouring from his packs as Tommy cursed him again, watched him go down only to fight his way upright, desperate to reach the others, the safety of the shore.

c-ɔ

Fenton rode through sheets of water into the big opening where White River slowed before sliding over a slab and dropping down into the South Fork. He tied Babe, his mules finding their own shelter under trees, then dropped the packs with the big canvas flies, rolled out the tarps as Gus found the lodgepoles they'd stashed there. Buck tried to help, but he was too confused and weakened. When Goose trotted into camp, Buck was so startled he backed away and fell.

"The drowned horse," he said. "He's come back."

Fenton paid no attention. "Get them candles and help Gus start a fire." He continued to roll out the tarp. "Tommy must of swum down and cut rope. "Damn, I hate cuttin' rope.""

Then Tommy was there himself, lashing the poles into two big A-frames. Together they heaved the tarp over a center beam, raised it and tightened lines to form a high, open shelter. Fenton got everyone under it as Gus and Tommy snapped twigs from the base of trees, hacked chunks of pitch from their trunks. They sheltered a candle until Tommy got a flame then covered it with the twigs and pitch, a fire finally lifting up against the rain.

Buck fed it until it had a life of its own as Gus caught up the mules, leading one after the other under a second high tarp where Tommy and Fenton unpacked. They worked fast, storing duffle and bedrolls, stacking saddles under manties.

When the rain slacked, people drifted out from under the tarps to warm themselves, clothes steaming from the sudden heat, saying little as they watched the men work, the camp growing out of nothing.

Before dark everything was established: stock belled and turned out, tents up, wet gear and clothing hung on lines around the fire and along the walls of the cook tent. People were eating by the fire or huddled in the cook tent with Rosie and Cody Jo.

Buck's face was swelling fast, the puffy skin turning purple. But he had worked hard, all of them had, not warming themselves at the fire, not asking for coffee, accepting only a swallow of the soup Rosie produced. Now they took spoonfuls of hot stew, eating as they worked—tightening lines, bringing in wood, covering saddles, digging drainages.

"Best I don't go in by that fire," Fenton said, thanking one of the men who showed concern. "Might warm too much from the outside. Then these hands wouldn't be worth a damn." He snapped a rope taut and tied it off. "Warming from the inside. A body tolerates that."

Cody Jo kept returning to the door of the cook tent to watch. Each time she looked, more had been done. Fenton never stopped: shaking out gear, stacking rope, giving directions. But the camp was subdued. And it went beyond losing Sugar. The bench they were on was not so high above the big river that they couldn't hear its steady rumble, boulders lifted from the river bottom and cracking into one another. The rain had diminished to a mist, but it had come with such power that Gus thought a foot had fallen. No one argued. Wherever they stepped there was water. They hardly needed the sound of the runaway waters to be reminded of what they had crossed—it seemed everywhere around them.

"You'd think I'd sleep tonight." Fenton took a plate from Cody Jo. "And I might, if this ground would drain and the river went down and Sugar'd come alive." He looked at her. "And Buck would heal."

"He turned to the man who'd wanted him to come in to the fire. "If you offered me some of that brandy, I just might accept."

The man was happy to dig out his brandy for the big packer. Cody Jo watched as Fenton poured some into his cup and passed the bottle on. It went around the fire, the teenagers getting approval to have some, the boy who'd ridden behind Gus tasting it and making a face, the others taking healthy portions, sipping, looking at the sky, pointing to a patch of blue opening to the west.

Tommy went into the woods and came back dragging part of a big stump. Fenton helped him lift it onto the fire, the pitch sending flames high into the air, startling everyone with its sudden heat. Cody Jo listened to the talk picking up, the laughter. She watched the patch of blue grow bigger, darker, the long day folding into night.

When she looked around, Fenton was gone, his plate clean, his brandy untouched. She found him with Rosie over near the saddles. They were putting out Buck's bedroll, covering it with a dried tarp. She took off Fenton's slicker and went over to them in the fading light.

Fenton held a bucket of water. Rosie was wetting a towel in it, holding it to Buck's face. "That'll help," Fenton said. "If we had snow, I'd use that. Can't be cold enough for what you need."

"How's a man supposed to sleep? Get up ever' hour and freeze my face. Don't warm before you ice me again."

"If we don't slow the swelling," Rosie said, "you won't find your bed anyway. Lose sleep now so you can see to find it later."

"Couldn't have found it now if Fenton hadn't rolled it out. I been trippin' all evenin' long."

"Gettin' dark," Fenton said. "I'll slip off and do things. Keep that cold on, Rosie. He's like a bronc mule. Gotta trick him into good sense."

Cody Jo held out his slicker, but he just smiled and waved it off.

"He is one crazy bastard," Buck said from under his cold towel. "I doubt he knows he's tired."

Cody Jo knelt down, wringing out another towel, handing it to Rosie. "Will his eyes swell closed?"

"Close to," Rosie said. "He's gonna look like a rainbow trout."

"A froze one," Buck complained as she spread the towel over his face. "Wish Angie was here to warm me."

A moon—just past full—lifted above trees and scattered clouds. Cody Jo went to her duffle for her jacket, pulling her slicker free as she did. She put on her jacket, took the water bucket and walked out to the big rock that slanted down into the currents of White River.

The water shimmered with moonlight as it slid over the rock. She filled the bucket, suddenly startled by Fenton's voice. He was high up on the rock, his hat off, his white hair combed.

"Tried for a bath before dark. Missed though. Not sure I'm made for this moonlight bathing."

Cody Jo walked up the slanting rock and sat. Fenton had on dry clothes, his wet ones wrapped in the torn poncho.

"I don't think anyone in the world could have done what you did today. And I had your slicker. You were soaking. I . . . mine was in my duffle."

"Don't things like that make you want to throw a fit?" Fenton smiled at her. "There was one time . . ." He watched her, his voice quieting. "But hell, that's another story . . . for another place."

"You got us here. Alive, except for poor Sugar. For a while I didn't think there was any way you could do that."

"Lot of guys could of done that. You see what's got to be done and you do it. There ain't a lot of choices."

"The choice was not to come down that canyon. Not to listen to us . . . Not to come into this country at all. It has so many ways to get you."

"People might get you," Fenton said. "But not these mountains. They don't want to get you or anybody else." They watched the water slide across the big rock, spilling down toward the rapids. "This high country, it's too big to care." He stood. "That's why I like it. You make do with what it offers. It took Sugar, but it let us cross the river. Make this camp. Things balance out."

Cody Jo was standing too. She took her hands out of her pockets and gave him a hug, a thanks for what he'd done, support for what was ahead. He found himself giving her a hug too. Then everything changed. He felt her breath on his neck, the curve of her stomach, the long warmth of her body, felt her words coming up through them.

". . . I could be good to you," she breathed into his ear, her body rocking just perceptively into his. "Do you . . ." She looked up at him. "Do you want me?"

Fenton's voice went thick. "What man wouldn't?" The words were scratchy, telling.

"Oh, dear." She pressed herself to him, her mouth wet and alive on his neck. Then she was backing away, looking up at him, her face torn. She left, almost running, scooping up the bucket and disappearing into the shadows toward camp.

Fenton was stopped there in the moonlight, which seemed more alive to him than the river moving beneath it. Finally the chill of the long day moved in and he shivered, made his way back to camp.

The root had burned low. Tommy was watching it, his world deep in the flames. Fenton found his brandy and sat.

"I have a need of this now. A bath out there gets brisk."

"I ain't dirty enough yet," Tommy said. "To freeze in that river or to drink that shit. Plays hell with my people."

"Pretty good to me when my day's work is done. Except for a mule Mother Nature buried for me," Fenton savored the brandy, "this day's is."

"Might surprise you." Tommy threw some pinecones on the fire, watched them flare. "Mules is tough."

"A duck couldn't swim out of there now. Likely sunk out of sight." Fenton warmed himself. "Just tell me," he sipped at his brandy, watching Tommy, "how in hell you got Goose off the bottom of that river."

Tommy watched the fire.

"Waited," he said finally. "Your people never understand. Wait. Good things can happen."

10

Sugar and the Bear

Fenton hated waiting, but the big river gave him no choice. He watched the water and paced and watched the water, the surging river going down much too slowly for his needs.

He'd gone to sleep thinking about Cody Jo, her lips wet on his neck, her slenderness arching into him. And with his confusion too—how much he wanted her, how troubled that made him. He'd tossed and turned with it until a deep sleep drove all thoughts away. Then in the night he'd heard it: the clear, lonely cry of a mule. He'd sat up, straining to hear more. But there was nothing—no bells, no movement in the night, no other hint of that mournful bray. The deep rush of the river was so constant he thought no cry could rise above it. But he'd heard what he'd heard. He slept little after that, thoughts of Cody Jo and the lone call tangled in his mind, pulling him back from rest whenever it crept closer.

He told Tommy Yellowtail about it as they tracked the horses, following them easily across sandy benches under water just hours before.

"A sign," Tommy said. "Sugar. Talkin' at you."

"Not a mule in the world could clear that bog after all this water," Fenton said. "Even if she did, we'd never hear her above the river."

"That's right. You wouldn't. A fuckin' sign."

They heard the bells on a side hill and climbed to get the horses, Fenton shifting the feed bag to his other shoulder.

"Probably just a dream. They can get pretty real."

"Fuckin' sign," Tommy said. "Telling you."

"What in hell is a mule going to tell me, dead or alive?" Fenton shook the feed bag to get Babe interested. "That we broke the rain record?"

"Fuck them records. Wait. Some signs ain't all bad."

Tommy had a way of knowing things. If Sugar had died some grotesque death, Fenton needed to know it for himself. He hated to give up on things, but he'd given up on the little mule. With all that water washing down the canyon, the bog would be underwater; most of her would be too, if a bear hadn't got that part already. He wondered if he should have shot her, given up at the outset. But that was wrong too. Who could predict such rain?

He took his gun belt out of his saddlebags and strapped it on. The trail would be gone. He'd have to walk. He wanted the Smith and Wesson with him, not Babe. Where there were dead mules, there were bears.

He spent the morning going down to watch the river then climbing back to watch Buck fumble around repairing the breeching on a pack saddle. Buck's face was mostly purple, with yellow around the edges. He had to hold his head at an angle to see.

"Leastways you didn't lose your teeth," Fenton said. "Those loose ones'll tighten. Takes time."

"I might could lose this thumb if I don't do better bangin' at these rivets. Ever' time you come back from that river I hit it. If you'd stay down or stay up, it might still be attached when I get done." Buck tilted his head to bring Fenton into view. "What *is* keepin' you so jumpy?"

"You're a sight," Fenton snorted. "Surprised you can see the damn saddle. . . . Cody Jo showed up yet?"

"Rosie and her took a walk. Let me rest up from the towels." He cocked his head to see better. "River's a noisy bastard, ain't it?"

"Must of poured up at the flats. River's hardly dropped at all."

"Slip on down for another look. I have better luck when you ain't leerin' at me." He craned his head back to see Fenton. But Fenton was gone again.

In the afternoon the river began to drop. Fenton saddled Babe and waited, resigned to getting wet as he crossed. But it went down fast, and by four it looked almost normal. He was mounted and ready to go when Cody Jo showed up, leading her gelding with Buck's saddle on it.

"I've decided to help," she said. "And I have my slicker tied on this saddle. Which is much too heavy for such a simple purpose."

"A slicker's sure useful on a sunny day. But it won't keep you dry in that river, or in that bog. You'd be lot more comfortable right here in camp."

"You men," she smiled. "Helpless when you don't get our help; confused when you do."

Fenton felt the blood lift into his face. This wasn't the same girl who'd come to him in the moonlight, left him sleepless and twisting with want. But then he didn't know who that girl was either.

"I may even rescue you a few times before we get back," she added.

"Let's go then." Fenton didn't know what else to say. "Try to get back before supper. That's when I Iike bein' rescued most."

C—⊃

The trail was slick but the crossing wasn't bad, the rapids running harder but the rocks firm, the horses negotiating them with little trouble. The currents had fashioned a giant eddy in the pool where Goose went under, the water dropping gravel and small rocks onto the shelf Fenton had used to get his mules into the river. They crossed it easily, the water barely up to their stirrups.

The timbered flat leading to the canyon was swept clean by the rain. It was quiet, churchlike, long aisles opening through the woods where the sun slanted down in shafts. Fenton hardly saw it, pushing ahead hard, moving Babe into a trot. When they hit the first slide he saw what he'd feared: The trace was all but gone. They tied up and walked, the route difficult, shale washed away from the gullies, exposing the bedrock. Fenton had to reach back to pull Cody Jo across the dangerous places.

The ford was not the one they had crossed either, if you could call it a ford. Deadfall had clogged the course of the stream, forming new channels everywhere. They crossed on logs and ridges of silt and twigs. In the fresh mud on the other side Fenton found the track he didn't want to see, claw marks extended, pressed deep into the new earth. He hurried Cody Jo past it, his voice growing louder in the still woods. Cody Jo, gloomier and gloomier as she thought about Sugar, was relieved when they reached a tall fir, the ground dry and solid around its roots.

"That meadow's just ahead," Fenton said. "Probably as underwater as Sugar. I'll take a look." He clicked something on the big Smith and Wesson and started to walk away, then stopped almost immediately, studying the ground ahead.

"What is it?"

"Mule track." Fenton looked off into the woods. Then he called, lifting his voice in a long "Come-on," the lingering call he used when he brought feed to his animals. It broke clear through the quiet woods. Then a deeper quiet. Not even a whisper of wind. Silence.

"Maybe he scared her out of that bog when we couldn't." His meaning was lost on Cody Jo. All she could think of was that the mule could be alive. He lifted his voice again, the call haunting in the hushed woods. Again he listened, as much now for something moving off as for a mule coming near.

"We'll track her," he said. "She'll be downright relieved to see us."

They followed the tracks for almost an hour, looping and back-tracking and angling under logs no mule should be able to get under, the tracks leading them closer and closer to the big river but never crossing the log-jammed drainage of Lost Bird Creek. Fenton was worried. The river was still more than a mile away, and darkness would be on them soon. He stopped, resting against a big deadfall, pleased that Cody Jo had kept up. He was about to say so when Sugar's bray lifted so close to them it made them jump. She was not twenty feet away, blending into the willows. They watched her lift her head again, offering an even more anguished cry.

Cody Jo began to laugh. Fenton had to as well, a pressure lifting from them both as they went to the mule, calmed her as she quivered and whimpered and paced in place, liking it as their searching hands moved over her, brushed at the mud, smoothed and cleaned her.

"You are a sneaky one," Fenton said. "Scared too." He got her free of the willows and let her nuzzle him. "And lucky." He pulled the belt of his trousers free, the heavy gun belt still in place. He threaded his belt through her halter and turned to lead her, weaving his way back toward the crossing.

They moved quickly. The long day was ending and Fenton knew he'd pushed Cody Jo hard, would have to push her still harder to clear the canyon by dark. He put her in front and when they came to the big fir she stopped, breathless, leaning against the tree and watching Fenton lead Sugar toward the crossing, which was dark and murky looking. It stopped Sugar as suddenly as she'd cried out minutes before. Her haunches dropped; she scrambled back, almost pulling the belt from Fenton's hand.

Fenton saw it right away. "Mud." He spoke as much to the erupted streambed as to Cody Jo. "Gotta get Babe."

"Hold her." He handed Cody Jo the makeshift lead and crossed the streambed in big, loping strides. Just as quickly he was back, looking down at her, taking her by the arm.

"Take it." He unholstered the big Smith and Wesson. "She's cocked, so leave that trigger alone. Unless you get downright serious. Then just shoot it in the air and hang onto Sugar. I'll be back before she drags you anywhere spooky." He was across the stream and gone.

"Why spooky?" she called after him. "We have Sugar."

"Never know," his voice called back. She heard rocks tumbling as he went up the washed-out chute. Then nothing.

Quiet came in again. Cody Jo put the heavy revolver on a log, rubbed her hand along Sugar's neck, talked to her, calmed her—pleased to have some time with the little mule. Sugar shivered, pulled away. Cody Jo stepped after her, across the heavy roots of the tree. They were well away from the mud, but still the mule shook. Cody Jo eased after her, soothing away the tension with gentle strokes along her neck, her flanks.

The shafts of light slanted in almost flat now, the greens of the forest deepened before Cody Jo saw it: the fresh scar on the fir—claw marks higher than Fenton could reach, gouges deep and even and repeated, sap oozing up like blood lifting from a fresh wound.

Cody Jo squatted, a sickness washing through her as it all came to her: Fenton's voice, big and constant. The pistol. Sugar's fear. The deep quiet. She gathered strength to lift herself, ease forward so she could get the revolver.

And there was the track. If she rocked forward, her knee would be in it. It was just as they'd said it would be but bigger, toed inward, the pad wide as it was long, claws reaching far beyond the thick toes. She watched water trickle into it, felt vomit come into her throat.

She swallowed it back, shivering, the fear in her mouth acrid. She stood up, leaned against the quivering mule, saw willow branches moving. She tried to fix on them, but the light was low. Her mind was wild. She'd even forgotten the revolver, only feet away.

Then there was Fenton's big voice urging Babe along. She heard the rumble of rocks dropping from the ledges. There was a crashing in the willows. "There he goes," Fenton called. "Scared by our big pistol, no doubt." And then he was with her, taking in her fear, talking to Sugar and Babe at once as he snapped a lead on Sugar, tied the stirrups across Babe's saddle, ran the lead through the stirrup strap to keep it up.

"Mr. Bear's on his way. And we are too," he said to Cody Jo. "I believe," he holstered the revolver, "we'll scramble out with no trouble. Babe's our leader. You follow. Sugar might need encouragement."

"I . . . I want to go with you."

"And you will." Fenton started across the streamed in the fading light. "Just two animals back." He let Babe pick her way. Sugar followed like a colt, trusting Babe to find firm ground, stepping where Babe stepped, anxious to be free of that place at last.

They wove their way across the stream in minutes, Cody Jo's legs shaking as she passed the willows. Sugar went up the chute, more goat than mule, charging into Babe's rump and leaving Cody Jo scrambling to keep up. When they came to the steep gullies, Fenton unsnapped the lead-line and let Sugar make her own way.

The steady pace drove Cody Jo's fear away. She pushed herself to keep up, Fenton's big voice soothing her as they moved into the timber. The gelding nickered as they grew close, rubbed his nose on Fenton as he tightened cinches.

"Them grizzlies! Won't take a grown elk or a horse or anything big unless he's hurt, out of commission some way." He looked at Cody Jo in the last light. "Or if one's dead and got ripe. They like that."

"Did you see him?" Cody Jo asked. "Was he there?"

"He was."

"Was he huge? On the tree . . . he clawed it . . ."

"Bigger'n average. Red-coated. Maybe young. Curious, I guess."

She looked at Fenton, his face in shadow but the shape of him, the size, and his ease with his horses and his own place in these woods offering safety, even comfort.

"Fenton Pardee," her voice was low as she turned to him, grasped his open Levi jacket, her face barely visible in the shadowy light. "We are going to make love. . . ." It was as though the words came with her breath. "I know. . . . You know."

She climbed up on the gelding, looked down at him, her voice level now, conclusive. "We will. . . ."

They rode back along the new routes made by the rain, Babe sure of her way. The moon, just clear of the horizon, leaving swatches of light dancing on the river.

Babe didn't hesitate, plunging directly in, Sugar and the gelding happy to follow. The crossing was deep but easy, the horses turning the water into new moonlight as they splashed through.

"Tole you some signs is good," Tommy said, looking solemnly and without surprise at Sugar. He took the lead-line and started away. Then he turned back. "All I know is you didn't hear *this* mule last night."

Rosie gave them food and they sat by the fire, answering questions, everyone astonished that Sugar had made it through the storm. They laughed, inventing stories about how Sugar had outsmarted the red-coated bear, extolling Fenton's skill as a tracker, making the bear bigger and redder—more dangerous. And they asked questions. It seemed to Fenton he was answering the same questions over and over again.

But they kept coming. After awhile Cody Jo took his plate away, smiling and whispering, "Afraid to tell them about us?"

She came back with a steaming cup of coffee, and Fenton watched as one of the men laced it with brandy. "Maybe," she whispered, passing it to Fenton, smiling and looking as though she were talking about the weather, "this will give you courage."

She watched the fire then turned back again, poured more brandy into his cup. Amused.

"I like courage," she said.

11

Fenton and Cody Jo

After that day of sun the clouds closed in and stayed. No more big rain, but each day it was there or threatening, misting or drizzling, starting and stopping. They seemed to live in their slickers. When they moved camp Fenton packed under the big fly, keeping water off the gear. But the dampness was everywhere. They were clammy when they rode, clammy in their tents, even clammy around the fire. Only the fishing got better, the wranglers eating so much trout that Gus went to Tommy to complain.

"Take them where the trout ain't. I'm about to grow fins."

"Keeps 'em happy," Tommy answered. "Don't mind the wet when they wade in it. When there's big cutthroats."

Gus saw it was no use, watching glumly as one of the men came into camp, his creel full of two-pounders. Gus figured he'd steer clear of the kitchen, let Tommy and Buck do the eating. They were harder to fill.

Fenton was busy keeping people as dry as he could, and as happy. And watching his horses. That's when he could think about Cody Jo—following clear tracks up some draw to find the horses quiet under a stand of timber, their bellies full, their tails to the weather as they waited out another rain.

One day he had to go far up the South Fork, picking up tracks early, following them through wet duff and across soaking meadows, thinking about Cody Jo: the way she touched him as she passed, brushed against him; the way she sat by him with her coffee, organizing the children for another day of dodging the rain, inventing games to play in the tents.

No matter the age, everyone looked to Cody Jo for diversion. She offered awards at the close of each day, got the children to put on skits, tricked Gus and Buck into telling their stories, even worked up a play that had everyone—even the actors—guessing who the villain was. And

as they clamored around her she would look at Fenton, her gaze
steady.

Her directness unsettled him. He was even more unsettled by how
full of her he was. He would watch her with the children, sometimes
his throat going so dry he dared not meet her eyes. He would turn
away then, move on to more chores, gathering wood, checking tents,
doctoring people—keeping his equipment covered, the bedrolls dry.

The weather broke two days before they would go out. Everyone
took baths and dried out clothes, became excited all over again by the
big country they'd traveled, climbing high on the canyon walls to look
back at it, studying the maps, talking about where they would go the
next time, and the next.

The last day they rode out under a cloudless sky, the Mission Range
rising up across Swan Valley like a postcard. Cody Jo pulled away from
the others and rode ahead of Fenton, Fenton leading his string, light-
loaded now and easy to manage. She was a graceful rider, and he
watched her movements with a concentration that made him ache.

He was scheduled to take another party in when this one got out.
He would pick up the guests, turn the stock around, and climb back
over the pass the next morning. But for the first time in his life he
began to doubt why he did it, wonder if he had anything left to give
these new people.

Cody Jo didn't have any doubt at all, chiding him about his devotion
to his mountains, her voice amused. Not until they were in the corrals
sorting through the piles of duffle did she talk to him as she had at
White River.

"You are going back into your mountains. Now I know why." She
looked up at him, her face smudged from helping Buck lift packs from
the mules, her voice halting—as though it were hard to find just the
right words. "Maybe I will be with you a little bit—in the night." Her
smile was crooked, uncertain. She reached out, straightening his collar,
touching him. "I know you, Fenton." She gave up on the smile, seemed
to surrender everything. "I need you . . . to know me."

Fenton got his kerchief from his pocket and wiped at the smudge on
her face, wanting to say something, too full of her to try.

Then they were calling her for their pictures. Fenton watched her
go, wondering if there were any Kodak made that could catch the
things he'd seen in her face.

⌒〰

It was a full summer for Fenton, and the fall just as busy, fishing and hunting parties overlapping seamlessly with his Forest Service packing. He seemed always in his saddle, or in his camps, or saying farewell to one party as he greeted the next. He didn't pull his hunting camp out until late October, the snow falling hard then and this time staying. Even the pack station was covered when he finally reached it, unsaddled in the half-light of a gray afternoon, spreading his canvas all over the barn so it could melt where it had frozen to itself.

He didn't get the shoes pulled and equipment oiled until December, when another storm came in and he turned to getting enough wood up on the porches to see him through it. A day into the storm Cody Jo came out of the woods, traveling all the way from Murphy's on snowshoes.

"No school for a week," she panted. "And I have gingerbread."

Fenton shook the ice and snow from her coat in the shed off the porch. He put her by the fire and brought her pack in, fueled the stove to get her something warm. "I'll make dinner," she said as she took off her boots and warmed, stretching toward the fire. "I know what you like. For dessert . . ." She smiled up at him. "Gingerbread."

"This storm might be getting worse," Fenton said.

"That's right." Again she smiled. "It is."

Fenton went out and started up the generator. He brought more wood in from the porch and poked up the fire. Cody Jo made him sit and tell her about each trip, who he liked, how Sugar did, and Buck and Tommy and the rest. She wanted to know if there were women. If they fell in love with him, talked him into going places he shouldn't, doing things he shouldn't.

It got dark, and she found Fenton's bourbon and watched him sip it as she made dinner. And after dinner she found music on the radio and they danced, her body moving so easily with Fenton's there seemed no separation at all between them and the music.

She put her head on his chest. "Later we'll dance naked." She looked up at him now. "Right here. With just the fire."

Fenton could find no words. He held her closer, the music filling him now, the music and the way Cody Jo moved to it.

"There's no hurry." The tempo changed and they changed with it, as though it were in them. "I'll be here for three days. At least."

They made love and Fenton found himself spilling out of himself so quickly he despaired. She calmed him and loved him. They ate gingerbread and then slept, and in the night he came to her once more. In the morning he wanted her again. But she made him wait while she brought coffee and biscuits on a tray. They talked and laughed until they wanted each other too much to wait any longer. They had time now, and it was nothing Fenton had ever imagined. She came to him again and again, and he loved her so it left him wanting her still, even after he ached from loving her so much.

"I was so a part of you." He kissed her shoulder, her neck, the hollows above her collarbones. "It made my old head hurt."

For four days they lived in one another so completely they thought of little else. They would rise, do the chores together, then return to make love, playing with one another, taking in one another, slipping back into sleep when they were through. After a late lunch she would watch him and talk to him as he worked on his tack, cutting leather, replacing the old, splicing and patching, happy to lose himself in the sound of her voice.

They would have a drink as they made dinner, sit by the fire afterward and listen to the station, dance to the music and talk about what it meant, tell stories, hold each other with their memories, their words. And they would go upstairs and make love again, by lantern now, the generator off, going farther and farther, testing and exploring and freeing themselves in one another.

One night Cody Jo sat above him, brought herself to climax. She leaned over him, letting her breasts swing against his chest, watching his face with her wide eyes as she reached behind him, easing her finger into him, moving it, watching him. "I want," her voice was low and steady and serious, "to be inside you, the way you are inside me."

On the fifth day she had to go back. Fenton caught up Babe and Goose and took her on horseback through the drifts to Murphy's. They had plowed that far and her little Ford was there, ready to take her on to her school.

Fenton led Goose back in a daze, letting Babe make her own way. He wondered how such good could come so quickly, not quite believing—even when he looked at the bed they had shared, the dishes washed and drying by the sink, the biscuits she had made—that it had really happened.

But it had, and it didn't end there. A week after she left him, he heard something against his window and looked out to find her there, packing more snow, throwing it, laughing in the moonlight, taunting him to let her in. He called out that he had never locked any door. And before he was down the stairs she was beside him, warming against the length of him, reaching shamelessly down for him, bringing him to her, into her, Fenton realizing he had never wanted anything so completely.

She stayed until Sunday, and when they rode back through the drifts, crusted now from the thawing and freezing, he brought feed for Goose, leaving him in Murphy's corral so Cody Jo would have something to ride back to him on—when she was ready.

And she would be. Never getting word to him, just being there, turning Goose out in the corral, letting herself through the unlocked door, arriving at one or two in the morning, once just at dawn, coming into his bed and taking him inside her, loving him, loving them together, even as he worried about how much he was coming to need her, how he would pace the nights away when she wasn't there. He would wake to some noise and rise, thinking it might be Cody Jo, then not sleeping but pacing and poking up the fire and wanting her, hoping she would come to him before the dawn.

It went on into the spring that way, the Murphys watching as Cody Jo caught up Goose, rode him into the dark of the woods. They said nothing—not to Cody Jo, not to Fenton, whom they saw seldom. Not to anyone. Cody Jo hid nothing, but she told them little. What she was doing they hardly acknowledged to each other. But Fenton's happiness, when they saw him, was clear. They just didn't see where it would go. How it would end.

When summer came Cody Jo left to see her father in Kansas, her aunt in Chicago. Fenton went back into his mountains, packing mostly for fire crews but also for the fishermen and hunters who came in from New York and Washington and San Francisco. Now and then Tommy Yellowtail or Buck would bring in a letter from Cody Jo and Fenton would go off alone to read it. But he talked little about her. They were surprised to see, when he brought a hunting party out in the early fall and found her standing there at the corrals as though she'd never been away, the relief on his face, the pleasure he took in just seeing her there.

He was back across the passes the next day, but knowing she was back made it different. There were no more long silences. He joshed the fire crews until he had them laughing, no matter how tired they were. He argued with Tommy Yellowtail about tracking and with Buck about his crazy ideas for campsites. Sometimes he wouldn't set up the canvas until the first raindrops fell, telling everyone it would clear if they'd just quit shaking their heads, swearing, telling each other how bad it could get.

It wasn't long after the snows drove them from the mountains that she came back to him. He was startled by the difference she made, the hungry way he took her in, began planning his days around her, his trips to Murphy's, to Missoula, even reasons to stop at the schoolhouse.

Happy as it made him, something about it worried him too. It wasn't that she was so young, but that she made everything seem so right, no matter the time of day or night or whether the Murphys, or anyone else for that matter, were there to watch them. She put her arm through his at the little Thanksgiving rodeo, touching him so lightly it seemed no weight at all, but the air rich with the sense of her. They were watching her students whip their big, slow horses around the barrels. She looked up at him, slowly started singing the same song they'd danced to the night before, dancing easily in front of his fire as she had unbuttoned his shirt, undone his belt, watched him watch her as she moved. She'd looked at him steadily as she danced, teasing him and wanting him just as hungrily as he wanted her. And now she sang to him with that same look on her face, watching him there in the cold by the long corral where the big horses labored, the children on them pounding at their sides and flapping at them with their reins as though it might actually make a difference. Listening, feeling the touch of her arm through his, Fenton felt dizzy with his need for her.

೧

And then just before Christmas she came to him, told him all of it.

"I love you, Fenton Pardee," she said. "And I'm mixing us all up. It's time you knew."

She told him about going off to the college in Massachusetts when she was seventeen, learning from the New York girls how to smoke, do the new dances, tempt the boys into driving up from New Haven or taking the train out from Boston. It was all new to her, and she liked it more than she should have. She'd paid little attention to her classes when her mother, sickish ever since she could remember, died. Her father brought her home then, kept her home after the funeral to help in his doctor's office there in the Virginia horse country of her mother's people.

But the young men from the hunt clubs wouldn't leave her alone any more than the boys from the colleges had. So he sent her to his own family in Michigan, sensible people who had sent their sons and their daughter off to the university. But they saw all that life in her, knew she should be back in the college where she'd started. So she went back, soon finding she could do her studies with hardly any effort. She thought maybe she was smarter than the others. She wasn't sure, though she knew she was wilder.

After her mother died, her father signed with the Medical Corps. They sent him to Fort Riley, and after the war ended he stayed on. When college was over she went to be with him, stopping to see her father's sister in Chicago, where she taught at the university, going on to St. Louis and then to Kansas City, where her father met her and drove her back to Junction City. Young men from the Virginia hunt crowd were still at Fort Riley, taking to the cavalry as naturally as they took to the hard riding and hard drinking of the regular officers. And soon they were bringing the regular officers to meet Cody Jo, to dance with her, drink with her—the men taken by this new breed of college girl who came so alive at the officers club and the horse breeders' parties outside Junction City.

And finally she told him about the captain, about going with him and the married couples to Kansas City to hear the great jazz players. How she went back with him again and then again—fell in love with him and found herself sneaking into the bachelor officers' quarters to see him. She told Fenton something must have been wrong with her mind, that she knew one wild thing would lead to another still wilder, but she saw too that nothing could hold her back, nothing would keep her from what she wanted.

It wasn't until after they shipped his regiment away that she learned the captain was engaged to a colonel's daughter in Washington. And she didn't learn that until after she learned she was carrying his child. She wrote him no letters. She didn't tell her father, going instead to her aunt back in Chicago, waiting with the students until it was her turn to go into the book-filled office to tell her everything.

The aunt was direct and capable. She said nothing as Cody Jo's story unfolded, just watched, listened, made her wait while she consulted with a friend at the university. In a few days the three of them went into Canada, where they met with a man who would end the pregnancy.

The aunt didn't like it, didn't like how it had happened, didn't like not telling her brother, didn't like any of it. Some things have to be done, she told Cody Jo, but you must learn from the doing. The aunt's friend was softer, taking the distraught girl into her arms, holding her through the long night, cleansing her.

Cody Jo looked steadily at Fenton, telling him all of it, looking away only when considering where to take him next, say it without excusing herself, putting the blame elsewhere. "I . . . I was desperate for him," she said. "I think I was crazy. It wasn't just him." She cupped Fenton's face in her hands, holding him. "It was me. He wasn't the first." She said it slowly so there would be no confusion. "There was this boy from New Haven. I think he did it on a dare, a bet with his friend. I . . . I'm not sure."

Fenton was so unsettled he couldn't speak. He thought anyone Cody Jo paid attention to would want to stay with her always. What worried her seemed backward to him, making him love her so much he took her in his arms, rocked her, wondered how he could be good enough for her.

"There may be all that in me still, Fenton." Her face was wet against his chest. "I sometimes think it's you that holds me together. Are you ready for that?"

"Yes." Fenton was so full of admiration for her that all his worries went sliding away. "I am." He kissed her hair, so moved by her candor that he was surprised to feel himself aroused—wanting her.

They lay in bed for a long time after they made love, quiet in one another's arms. After awhile Cody Jo sat up and looked at him, smoothing his hair, his shaggy eyebrows. "Something happened when they did that," she said. "There won't be any babies, ever, for me. You have to know that too."

Fenton reached up and brought her to him. "I wondered about that," he said. "If you want, we could go see one of those docs at that Minnesota clinic. Had one on a trip once."

"They can't help." She looked at him, and he saw that her eyes were wet again. "It's over. It's done."

Fenton was quiet for awhile. "Well," he touched her hair. "Saves me from shoppin' for a slow horse. Nothin' in my string that'll slow down enough to match those dobbins your kids rode in that Thanksgiving rodeo."

⌣⌁

And so the wedding was scheduled for the spring in Fenton's big barn on the edge of his pasture. Cody Jo's father came out and looked Fenton over for a long time before he made his toast. Cody Jo's aunt and her friend came out too. Fenton had a long visit with them, listening as they talked about having the vote, what the labor movement would do for women, how Cody Jo could be the best graduate student at the university.

He never doubted she was smart, he told them as they watched her making everyone at the wedding comfortable, pleased with her and with themselves and with the promise of this day.

"I just got this feeling," he turned back to them, "that she gets a lot more pleasure from the teaching than from the learning." They listened, sorting out what he meant, liking his directness, the size of him. And they watched the way he looked at Cody Jo. They liked him most of all for that.

Fenton liked them too, in his big easy way. He just came away with the idea that Cody Jo's aunt got a little walleyed when she was excited.

"Had a mule like that once," he would tell Cody Jo. "Rolled down a cut bank and hit her head on a rock. Worked fine after that. Just got walleyed in a tight."

No matter how many times Cody Jo tried to straighten Fenton out, he never got that out of his mind. "Don't you worry about your aunt," he'd say. "My mule would go walleyed too." He'd shake his head. "Damndest thing."

Ty (1937)

Spec could read the woods, and Ty wanted to know everything he read.

12

Lessons

Ty learned fast. He had no choice. He learned time on the trail was all Loco needed. He learned what made a good camp, what meadows held the horses, why to track them before the sun hit the ridges. He learned to take care of the stock first, then the cook, then the rest—himself, always, last. He learned an hour in the morning really is worth two at night. And he learned the hardest lesson of all: some things you couldn't predict.

"Never can tell the depth of a well," Fenton would say, "by the size of the handle on that pump."

He took to Loco and Cottontail, putting them in his string whenever he could. Loco had trotted into camp all by himself that first wet morning on White River, his packs askew but riding. The last thing Ty remembered, before drifting into sleep even as Jasper poured him coffee, was standing out in the rain with Spec, pulling off Loco's saddle, watching him break into a lope as he headed out after Cottontail.

Ty and Spec grew naturally into one another. Ty learned tracking from Spec, would get him to tell hunting stories as they walked down the herd on those cold Montana mornings. Spec could read the woods, and Ty listened to everything he read. Spec said he'd learned it from his father, Tommy Yellowtail, and his grandfather, Sings at Night. But Ty thought it was something Spec just had in him. Simple as that. His tribe called him Special Hands, but Ty could see it was more than his hands. Spec could skin out anything as neatly as you'd want, but what impressed Ty was that he could find what he was after, passing by this elk or that mountain goat to get what he wanted, sometimes getting it in his sights and not taking it at all. Stalking for the pleasure of it, easy in his woods, liking to watch just as much as shoot—maybe more.

And Spec liked to watch Ty with his stock, the boy moving quietly into the herd, getting the ones he needed with so little fuss the rest hardly noticed.

"Maybe packing's not so bad, leastways for you." Spec had just come into the high camp in Lost Bird Canyon. He liked where Ty had put it, the tents tucked into the last stunted stands of fir, the big U of the upper valley wide and treeless above them, its floor dotted with boulders and rocky outcroppings where it lifted into the cliffy bowl. "You ain't rolled nothin' yet, and you can get through the woods without knocking down half the saplings."

They were watching Buck ride toward them through the scattered firs. He had fresh supplies packed on three mules, and he waved as he hurried his string along, edging around one tree so tightly his second mule passed on the other side. They watched the tree bend as the lead-line hit it, the mule pulling away, eyes rolling as the sapling bent to the ground before the rope cleared it, the tree popping up and startling the last mule so he wrapped himself around still another.

"Take Buck." Spec watched the mules pull back, wild-eyed as trees bobbed, popped up, bobbed down again. "Got a different style. Might tear down the trees and lose a mule before it comes to him he's got a problem."

But Buck had noticed the commotion, letting loose such a string of language that the mules lined themselves out.

"Shit-fire." Buck looked at them. "They come along right smart until they seen you two jawing away in the middle of these woods."

"More like a pasture up here," Spec said. "You must have a system. If there was just one tree, I believe you could locate it."

"Shoot!" Buck watched as Ty and Spec caught up the mules and started unpacking. "I just take 'em to where Fenton says and hope it don't rain."

Jasper made a wonderful dinner, and Ty ate as though he hadn't had a good meal for a long time. The truth was he hadn't. He and Jasper had moved the camp alone, building a makeshift corral and getting things ready for the season's first hunting party. Buck and Spec had been gone for a week. Without any resupplies Jasper had been down to flapjack mix and peanut butter—and the cutthroats Ty caught when he dropped down the canyon to fish the big pools.

But he didn't do much of that after he began seeing grizzly tracks, picking them up the third morning on the other side of the stream. He saw them the next morning too, which made him worry about being away. Jasper's hearing wasn't good, and everyone knew he was mortally afraid of grizzlies—unless he was into his cooking sherry.

Fenton had ruled out hard liquor for Jasper, using the cooking sherry to keep him going. When Jasper got into more of it than he should, he wasn't afraid of anything, which posed a problem. Ty wasn't sure what Jasper would do if he'd had some sherry and found a grizzly nosing around, and he didn't want to find out. He hid the last two bottles of sherry under his pistol and left a rifle out. That's all he could think of to do, and it didn't seem to him like a long-range solution.

The temperature dropped below zero one night, and the next morning Ty couldn't find his horses anywhere. He talked it over with Jasper, who wasn't all that concerned.

"Don't believe Spec could track over this froze ground. They likely left them meadows to warm." Jasper made some peanut-butter sandwiches with leftover flapjacks. "Take that nose bag and go high." He handed Ty the sandwiches, enjoying how skinny the boy was despite all he ate. "To where the sun is. He waved Ty out. "Probably hidin' from big Fenton. Sneak up sideways. Might not see you're there."

It was almost noon before Ty was high enough to see back across the valley. He'd found nothing in the the chutes and slides horses might use: no scraped rock, no frost knocked from grass, no droppings. He climbed even higher than horses could go, wanting to see all the upper reaches of the canyon.

When he saw a chute angling up the cliffs, he went higher, climbing fast, reaching up for handholds. Now and then he would stop, but it was more to look for a way up than to see where he'd been. And then he was on top, looking across still another canyon, the head of it forming a rock-strewn bowl even bigger than the one he'd left.

He looked back, barely able to make out the white of the tents far down the valley, scanned back from there. Nothing. When he looked back at the way he'd come up, a chill lifted up his seam. It seemed impossibly steep; he couldn't tell how he'd done it.

He pulled the last sandwich from the nose bag, stashed there with ropes and halters and grain, ate it before reaching beneath the ropes for some grain. He ate that too. Chewing, he felt better. He was sure there was a way down; he just needed a place to start.

He looked at the country, high cliffs crowning the valleys, boulders spilling into flat greens where lakes once lived. Below them the forests grew a deeper green as they followed their streams. Somewhere under the purplish haze was the South Fork of the Flathead River, running north, different from other rivers. And better, he thought, protecting all the meadows and streams and game a person could want. He liked being where it all started, watching patches of snow drip into rivulets, feeding the high lakes drained by the streams that gave the woods their voice, bubbling their way down with life for the big river.

He turned and looked into the bowl behind him, liking the soft green of it, the way winter snows had scattered the big boulders. One of the smallest boulders seemed to move, inching toward another, making that one move too. It took a moment for him to realize he was looking at his horses.

He was so glad to see them that he was half way down into the bowl before he thought to be thankful this side wasn't as steep. Not until he was down did he realize how big the canyon was, how uneven the floor. Smoky nickered as he came over the last rise. He let her nose into the grain, rubbing her neck and talking to her. The others moved in, their bells ringing, comfortable after their easy morning in the sun. He made sure they each had a bite before catching up Smoky and Cottontail. Where they went, the others would follow.

He swung himself up and led Cottontail, the rest stringing out behind, bells ringing as they settled into a ragged line. When they came to the first timber, Smoky acted as though she wanted to go off into a jumble of deadfall, but Ty pulled her back, seeking the broad lanes along the stream. The others hesitated there too, finally following, their bells ringing as they wove down, the stream at last merging with the one draining from camp. Ty guessed they'd dropped a full three miles, with about that much to cover climbing back up to camp. There was no way to get back before dark now, and they took their time, Ty using the last light to look for the tracks they'd made coming down. He could find nothing. No sign at all.

They went through slides and in and out of timber, Smoky moving surely even when darkness fell, helped by a sliver of moon topping the trees. When they neared camp, Sugar worked her way ahead, breaking into a trot as they pulled up the last rise.

Ty was startled to see no light in camp—more than startled to hear, in the last dark patch of trees, a cough that came from something big. Sugar left the trail, scrambled up a bank, hit something and rolled back down, knocking Smoky to her knees before she struggled up—below the trail now—hurled herself back, hitting Loco, going down again. All the animals had turned before Smoky righted herself, spun around to follow them. Cottontail yanked the lead from Ty's hand as he grabbed Smoky's mane, the rest of them ahead of him now, going at such a breakneck speed he barely had time to realize he'd just confronted the grizzly.

That might explain the dark camp, but there was little time to think about it as Smoky veered so sharply he almost went off, crossed a long slab of rock and followed the others into the woods. They hardly slowed as they skirted rocks and jumped downed timber, going so surely he knew they'd traveled this route before. They were headed directly back to the canyon he'd left a full three hours earlier. But they were taking their own route, crossing a low shoulder he'd thought impassable.

Soon the choked route slowed them, Ty flattening on Smoky to get under limbs, leaning deadfall, trees twisted and bent almost parallel to the ground. They came into the canyon in the same jumble of deadfall he'd made Smoky leave earlier. Immediately they began grazing, still edgy but hungry now, blowing, nosing at one another, oblivious to Ty, who slid off to try out his legs. They were wet with Smoky's sweat, wet with a warmth that chilled so fast his legs began to shake. But it was more than the cold. He wasn't sure how he'd stayed with the herd, why he hadn't been left back with the bear. He walked in circles to settle his blood, try to think.

He unsnapped the lead from Cottontail and got back on Smoky, the sweat on her back cold and coarse now. He got everything in front of him this time, letting Smoky push them back along the cutoff, back toward the dark camp and Jasper.

It took longer going back, but Smoky warmed. His legs felt better as the mules calmed, and he let Smoky take up the lead again. He wondered how they'd found this route in the first place, the way twisting and turning back to join the trail to camp. Smoky slowed as they neared that last dark stand of timber, and Ty decided to sing, make noise to comfort the mules, to warn the bear too. He settled on "The Bear Went Over the Mountain." That seemed about right; no need to worry about the words.

As they entered the timber Smoky skittered, not liking something in the trail. He sang louder as a chill ran up his back and into his hair. Then moonlight again, the bells telling him the rest were following, trotting through the trees, made bolder by Smoky.

Still no light in camp. He saw no smoke coming from the cook tent and called out above the jingling bells as they forded the stream and moved into the corral. Only quiet. A deeper silence.

He took off the bells and put out feed. Called out again before walking toward the cook tent, looking for anything out of place—a tent torn, something knocked over. Everything was in place. The tent flaps were tied. He reached his hand in to untie them, pulled back the canvas, and was blinded by a beam of light.

"Jasper?" he called. "Jasper?"

The light wavered, outsized shadows playing on the tent walls as Ty's eyes adjusted to see Jasper slowly lowering the Smith and Wesson, which clattered onto the table. Ty saw the bottles of sherry as Jasper dropped the flashlight and hunched deeper into his coat.

"Lucky you ain't that red-headed bastard. For a minute I thought you was." Jasper poured more sherry into a jelly jar.

"You been gone so long I was commencin' to think you got et." He took a long swallow. "He sure as hell wasn't gonna get Jasper Finn. Not while I got this." Jasper shoved the pistol across the table. "And my rifle." He reached for it, knocking it down. "Let's have us a drink. If he gets interested, we'll fight the son of a bitch off right here. You ever find them rascals? Tell about your day."

Ty lit the lantern and got the stove going. He picked the rifle up, took the round out of the chamber and set the safety. He put it out of reach of Jasper and uncocked the pistol, rolling the cylinder over an empty chamber. Then he went back to the stove, warmed his hands, feeling the shakiness drain from his legs as his pants began to steam. He told Jasper what had happened, going through everything but the part about not knowing how he'd gotten himself up the cliff.

"I looked down there for tracks," Ty said. "Didn't think to look above that rock. Might not have shown there, though. Thing's frozen solid."

"You done good," Jasper approved. "Had you a learning day." He dug some cold flapjacks from his bread box, loaded them with peanut butter.

It was a theory of Fenton's packers that Jasper was a great cook for the first half of a sherry bottle but no good at all after that. Ty didn't mind. He was thankful for anything. He even liked the sherry, the way its sweetness warmed him. The peanut butter tasted good on top of it. And he liked Jasper's company.

"You shoulda told me about that bear, Ty." Jasper shook his head. "I'd of got him if I'd knowed he'd been around. Seein' him there is what startled me." Jasper told Ty about the bear, across the creek, downwind and up on his hind legs, his reddish head high, testing the air.

"Didn't have a fire going. Nothing around but those flapjacks. For you to eat, not that damn bear." Jasper took another swallow, liking the attention Ty was giving him.

"I was only partly scared, Ty." Jasper nodded as Ty stoked the stove. "You'd of been proud. Went to your duffle quiet as Spec. Found the gun, sherry bottles right there." He patted Ty's arm. "Good to have them handy." He took another sip. "Snuck back and seen that rifle and says to myself, Ty sure looks after Jasper." He smiled, poured more sherry into Ty's cup.

"I was afraid he'd chased you out of camp." Ty folded the last flapjack over and took a bite. "Or got you. Why didn't you answer when I called?"

"I did hear somethin' out there, Ty. But I don't hear too good in this coat." Jasper undid the snaps of his big coat. "And you can't never trust them bears. They snoop around mild as milk. Then all of a sudden they act like you pissed in their boot."

"All you had to do was answer. I could of got shot."

"Hell, you know I wouldn't shoot wild." Jasper poured a little sherry in Ty's cup and took more for himself. "Fenton'd raise hell if I put a hole in his tent."

13

Deep Woods

Ty was so glad to have Buck and Spec back in camp, he didn't protest when Buck poured him a little whiskey. Buck even poured some for Jasper, after he'd made sure Jasper had dinner ready.

The whiskey burned. Ty drank only a little, but he thought he'd never tasted anything as good as Jasper's dinner. He had thirds and then cleaned out the pot, pleasing Jasper, who sipped contentedly at his whiskey—then accepted the rest of Ty's. He sang to himself as he cleaned up, giving Ty a chance to tell Spec about finding the horses, about the bear, about coming into a dark camp and almost getting shot.

"Lucky to find them that way. Lucky to get them home." Spec looked at Ty, approving. "And you done it twice. But you took a chance comin' into that tent. Jasper's not all that careful when he's sober."

"I was just stayin' snug so I could shoot that hairy rascal." Jasper was drying the last plate. "Wasn't about to shoot no holes in things. Ty just come in too quiet. Startled me."

"Give a bear an empty camp and he's likely to explore it," Spec said. "But they ain't usually all that tidy. More likely to walk through a tent than fiddle with the flap."

"Never can tell what a bear might do." Jasper dried his hands on his apron. "I wasn't takin' no chances with that red-headed bastard." He shook his head and sat down, patting Ty's arm. "Was I, Ty?"

The next morning Ty took Spec to the pile of bear scat that had spooked Smoky. It was in the big stand of fir right across the creek.

"Surprised him during a pleasant moment." Spec nudged the pile with his boot. "Pine nuts. Gettin' ready for winter."

"He sure has been curious," Ty said. "Jasper's right about that."

"Why not? His canyon. The way he sees it, them's his pine nuts too. You'd be just as curious if someone come into your dining room."

Fenton brought the hunters in the next day. Big-bellied men from Cincinnati who hunted a little each morning, playing cards and drinking the rest of the day. But they wanted trophies, most of all a grizzly. Spec did what he could, getting them three elk before a snowfall made them stay in camp with their cards and Jasper's stories. Spec went out anyway, taking Ty with him and hiking down the canyon through timber and brush for two miles until he came to a hollow choked with fallen trees. Ty didn't realize the ground gave way until he came to the very edge of it.

"His den." Spec pointed at the jumbled deadfall. "Under there."

Ty looked around. It was darkish in the timber, snow falling slowly. He couldn't imagine how Spec had found this place.

"If you're out with Fenton and them and they get over this way, lead them past," Spec said. "Stay away from here."

"They want a bear. You got this big one right here." Ty looked into the dark woods. "Or near here."

"I might get one. Leave this one be. He done that for us."

They continued down through sloping woods. "I been thinkin' about him," Spec said. "What he needs to know." Ty wondered how Spec knew it was the bear that had been watching Jasper. Jasper had only said the bear was big, reddish. Ty didn't think Spec had even seen it. But Spec knew things that Ty didn't question. He wasn't even sure Spec knew he knew them, much less could explain. Ty listened and watched, answering when Spec asked him about the horses but mostly trying to see what Spec saw, walk where Spec walked.

They came into a glade, the snow not sticking as well now, the tracks of a smaller bear showing clearly. "Dressed out a elk over there on the first day," Spec said. "Figured it would draw something." He looked at a lodgepole, its lower branches broken away, bark almost polished. "Scratching himself." He looked at Ty. "I'll come back later. Maybe tomorrow."

It snowed hard the next morning, then cleared. But the men were into their cards, laughing and smoking and starting to drink well before it began to lift. Spec slipped away without anyone noticing but Ty, who left with him, needing to check his stock. They walked down the canyon for a mile before Ty picked up tracks and left Spec to seek his horses. He found them a long way from camp but comfortable, pleased to see him, happy to nuzzle into the nose bag and warm themselves with his feed.

He fed them what he had, talking to Smoky Girl and Sugar, rubbing Loco's neck, giving Cottontail a little extra. He left them to climb up to the timberline cliffs, where the sun broke through and eased the chill. He watched his horses warm in a meadow below him and looked across them at the drainages tilting down to the big river, looked beyond to other valleys lifting up to the China Wall. That was where the waters started their run to another ocean, where in a day's ride the country changed so much it supported a different kind of life—different trees and grasses, different animals. It made him think how much Spec was a part of this country, these woods, these animals. He thought about the bear too, probably liking this sun as much as Ty's mules, stretching in it, rubbing his back, gathering feed for winter. He hoped this would be one of those times Spec would see what he was after and decide to pass it by. He had little doubt Spec could kill the bear, which was why it held no excitement for him.

After awhile he dropped back down to camp. The men were out in the sun now, stretching their legs and talking with Fenton before they went back to their cards. He hadn't been back long when Spec showed up, something big and bulky lashed to his hunting pack. Spec motioned to Ty, and they walked through the trees to the corral, Spec opening the lashed manty to show Ty the pelt, asking him how to tell the men he'd taken the bear without them.

"We would of had to bring them on horses," Spec said. "Make a ruckus. I doubt they would have got a shot. This way I killed him clean."

Fenton came up and told Spec not to worry about the men. "They'd as leave shoot from a rockin' chair, if we set one up right." He draped the pelt over a log, smoothing it. "You done fine, Spec. They'll be tickled."

"You knew where to go," Ty said. "You were too smart for him."

"Don't have to be smart, with this." He gestured at his rifle. "My people had to be . . . in their times."

Fenton was right. The men couldn't have been more pleased, calling Spec Natty Bumpus and cutting cards to decide who would claim the bear. The man who won was so happy he made everyone drink with him, even Ty. He kept stroking the pelt, asking Spec questions. Later, when Spec rode out with him, the man paid him an extra fifty dollars, taking the hide in a special duffle back to Cincinnati to show his friends.

Three more hunting parties came in that year, the last strong young men from Missoula and Hell's Gate, friends of Horace and Etta Adams needing meat for the winter. They wanted to see the country too, get to know Fenton Pardee. But Fenton saw they knew what they were doing and left with Buck to pack out Forest Service people. "You'll be all right," he told Spec. "Point 'em to where there's elk. I'll be waitin' when you and Ty pull out the camp." So Spec stayed, hunting with the men, showing them the country, helping Ty learn the woods.

But when Buck came back to take the men out, Spec had to go too. Tommy Yellowtail had taken sick, and Spec wouldn't have it any other way than to be with his father. Jasper was already scheduled to go out, which left Ty alone to pack out the camp.

He didn't worry. He was mostly concerned with keeping track of the stock, which was easier now. Buck had packed in feed. It kept them close, the grass sparse, the snow beginning to stick. It was only a matter of time before it would cover what grass was left—then close the passes.

"Take you two days to knock down the tents and manty things up," Spec said. "You got plenty mules. If the passes close, go down. Follow the South Fork to Hungry Horse."

Fenton called it their "emergency exit," but both Spec and Ty were pretty sure it wouldn't be needed. The sky looked as blue as Wilma Ring's eyes that day they pulled her father out. And Spec knew Fenton's cutoff to the pass, told Ty about the big boulder that marked the route.

"Save you riding all that way down and climbing back up the drainage," Spec said. "Come in right at them meadows where Ring camps. Save half a day, maybe more."

That sounded good to Ty. With the days getting shorter, that was time he could use. It meant starting early, riding late. But with no camp to make it could be done in a day, which is what he wanted to do.

"Track us," Spec said, swinging onto his horse and taking the lead-line from Ty. It was such a clear day that Spec wasn't even complaining about packing. "We'll be at Fenton's by dark," he called out. "When you leave, get started earlier. You got more to bring."

Ty liked the picture they made, stocking caps pulled low, rifles in their scabbards, elk racks top-tied on the packs, breath steaming in the cold. He watched them cross the stream and waved as they dropped from sight.

He looked around at the camp, manties thrown over the saddles, tools stacked, tents snug and tight, the high country lifting above them. He'd learned a lot setting it up, meeting Jasper's needs for his cook tent, placing the corral, the guest tents. But there was so much more to learn—things he had no way to know were important that first day when he'd wound up biting down on Loco's ear. Spec had most of it in him already. He decided it was best to hang around Spec, hope some of it rubbed off. He tossed his coffee into the snow and started working.

It warmed, and he worked all that day gathering tools and equipment, lining out loads to be packed, knocking down everything but the big cook tent. He made a dinner of rice and eggs and elk steak. After dinner he went back to work, getting as much as he could balanced, ready.

The next day it was cloudy. He brought the horses in and gave them feed before going on about his packing. By noon it had begun to snow, big flakes coming gently at first and then thickening into a white curtain. He moved his work into the cook tent and considered waiting it out. There was plenty of food and he'd brought in lots of wood. But the snow was coming hard; it might keep coming for a week. If he waited too long, he might not even be able to get to the South Fork.

He decided to try for it the next morning. He'd ride to the cutoff, and if things weren't too bad, make a try for the pass. If the snow kept falling, he'd go on to Hungry Horse, an idea he didn't like at all. He didn't know where to camp, what meadows would hold his mules— didn't even know if the trail was marked. Traveling in snow wasn't all that easy when you *knew* where you were going; it was miserable when you didn't.

Whichever way he went, he'd have to leave early. He worked late getting everything ready, even eating a cold supper so he could pull the stove apart. When he'd done all he could, he put on Fenton's canvas coat and went out to feed, the cold hitting him so hard he felt lucky Fenton had left it. But cold meant clearing; there were only a few flakes falling now, stars showing off to the south.

Smoky Girl nickered as he neared the corral, came to him. The mules shouldered one another aside to get close. He buttoned the coat higher against the cold, watched them for a long time before going back. He knew there wouldn't be much sleep anyway.

He fired the lanterns before dawn, the sleepless night all energy now. The snow had stopped but much had fallen, blanketing everything, beaten down only where the mules had moved in the corral, pissing and dropping piles, huddling against the cold. He rigged a lantern and began to saddle, wanting everything ready for first light.

As dawn came, he was knocking down the cook tent, mantying it on the bare ground where it had stood—the work slow but his ropes tight, his knots sure. Snow was starting in again, big flakes drifting down and sticking on the ropes. He wished he had Spec or Buck, even Jasper, to hold the packs while he tied them off. It took over an hour to get everything right, but he made sure it was, that everything would ride. It was going to be a long day whichever way he went. He didn't want to spend half of it making right what he'd done wrong in the first place. He put the eight mules together quickly, Cottontail first, then Loco, each behind one he favored. He tied little Sugar in last, knowing she hated being left, would push the string along. He pulled Fenton's big canvas coat on over his Levi jacket. He could hardly get into Horace's anymore; if he could, he would have worn it too. The packing had kept him warm, but the sky was dark, the cold in to stay.

He lined the mules out, circling so each would know his place as he checked to see if something forgotten poked up through the snow. Then Smoky splashed across the creek, brushing past snow-heavy trees as she sought the trace leading from the canyon.

Snow was falling hard now, the woods changed. Drifts made the deadfall look cushiony, soft, the floor of the forest so smooth it seemed you could ride anywhere. The trail was gone, but Ty trusted Smoky to know where to go. His own eyes were on the woods, the pack string. He looked ahead for drifts but mostly looked back, turned in his saddle as though on a pivot, watching to make sure the packs balanced, no mule broke from the long line.

They moved through the snow for an hour, and Ty felt better. It wasn't so cold in the deep woods—no wind, the big flakes floating in so gently he could read their patterns on Smoky's mane. He thought about Fenton's cutoff, wondering if he'd even find it, wanting to mark it as he rode past on the way to Hungry Horse. That seemed the only way out—until next year.

He hunkered into the coats, watching. It was like riding into a new world, moving through this white. The trampled route behind them was the only thing that marred its surface, leaves and branches churned up as the mules felt their way along the forest floor. It was easy to see where they'd been. Where Smoky was taking them was the mystery, the woods so open and inviting any direction seemed possible. Ty liked riding through the white, watching it lift and resettle as Smoky made her way.

They went down so quickly he came off as though dismounting, his foot going boot-deep in snow before hitting something solid. He pushed off instinctively, found himself coming back into the saddle as Smoky struggled up, Cottontail already stumbling over the buried danger.

His hands were shaking as he slowed, easing the rest over the log, exposed now and manageable. He watched each mule step across, cursing himself for letting the snow lull him so, make him immune to all the trouble it could hide.

He took stock, worried that something bad had already happened. Steering Smoky wide of a drift, he leaned off the saddle to look back for blood on legs, blood on the snow; look ahead for something safe, some sure footing. But there was no way to tell, just the silent white, the easy fall of big flakes. He worried about how far they'd drifted from the trail, saw there was no way to know that either. He must have been in a trance when they left it. He couldn't remember crossing any drainages; wasn't even sure whether Smoky had been taking him up or down. He peered back through floating snowflakes, hoping for some landmark, then swept the woods before him. There was nothing to help him in either direction, just the silent white.

I could tie up, he thought, take Smoky back, find the route, then track back to the string, take them to it. But how far back? How much time lost? Where would that put us when night fell?

He focused on what was ahead, every other sense suspended—no sensation of the cold, the saddle under him, the lead-line in his hand. His mind spun: if he were going to turn back, it had to be soon. By night his tracks would be buried with everything else. Besides not knowing where to go, he wouldn't know where he'd been. Still he didn't stop, couldn't bring himself to pull up, tie his mules, go back.

His mouth went dry as he saw how little there was to work with. All he had was the ragged scar his mules left in the snow. He tried to calm his mind, make use of it. He looked back as far as he could and got direction from his own tracks, following them forward as a man might follow a pointer.

He looked ahead for something to fix on, found an uprooted tree, dirt showing through the twisted roots. He started for it, found a lightning-topped fir beyond the root, fixed on that. Then a leaning deadfall. He went from target to target, looking back to keep his course, ahead for some point to fix on—seeking always for something to tell him he was crossing the trail, paralleling it, some way to get it back so he would never lose it again.

His mouth went drier still when it came to him that the trail might be below them already, that he might ride until night with nothing showing up at all, that when his mind had drifted from him he might have missed not only the drainages but the buried creek too. The shifting snow had leveled the woods, changed everything he knew.

And still he went on, trying to hold his direction but bending and twisting his string of mules as the forest grew thicker. His heart sank as he eased them through places more and more difficult, knowing something might stop him at any moment. He was turning to check his course one more time when his eye caught something high in the timber. It was behind them—something out of place, wrong. He strained to make it out through the falling snow, finally turning back and riding toward it. He was almost under it before he realized it was a limbed lodgepole, almost fifteen feet long, high and braced on branches where nature could never put it.

He rode under it, dismounting into the knee-deep snow, feeling his legs shaking as he saw the woods opening in a lane, coming at the lodgepole at cross purposes and going off again down the canyon. He looked again, sure now that he'd found the trail but surprised that the lodgepole pointed off still another way. And where it pointed was Spec's big boulder, marking the way to the cutoff as surely as a signpost.

Spec had done it, he thought. Stopped with the hunters, found the lodgepole, lifted it into place. Shown him the way.

He took off his stocking cap, shook the snow from it, noticing the sky was getting lighter, the snow stopping. He felt blood rushing through him, his heart pushing at it. He realized he needed to pee but went to his mules first, checked their packs, their legs for cuts. Then he stepped away, emptying himself as he dug under his coats for his pocket watch. Soon he'd need to look for a camp. He was thankful he'd packed feed.

He looked at the watch, put it back, walked over to Smoky and rubbed her neck, thinking of what Fenton would do. He took out the watch again, put it to his ear, made sure. He looked at it still another time before he put it away. Then he tightened Smoky's cinch and climbed back on.

It was not yet noon.

14

Snow

"Let me tell you about snow." Fenton was carving a spoon for Jasper. It was August; they were camped up toward the China Wall, going still higher in the morning to pull out a fire crew. Ty couldn't figure what snow had to do with anything at that time of year.

"On that spring snow you can walk your mules over places you wouldn't dare, could you see them," Fenton said. "Don't need to know where you are so much as where to go—if the goin' ain't too steep and you start early." He compared the spoon with the one Jasper had broken rescuing the Dutch oven from the fire. "Use it right, old snow solves your problems. Gets you over places a goat couldn't navigate come summer."

He sipped at his coffee. "Fall snow is different. Might hide where it's bad, but it don't save you from it. Mostly air. Won't hold a pinecone." He looked at Ty. "To get out of these mountains in the fall, you got to know where the hell you're going." He looked back into the fire, whittling again.

"Most of them who lose their mules," he added, "don't."

Ty was well along the cutoff when Fenton's words came back to him. The truth was he'd made his decision without them, sitting there on Smoky for a long time thinking more about what Fenton would do than what he would say. It seemed to Ty that Fenton talked most of the time when he was doing something, but hardly ever about what he was doing. And it was hard to predict what he would do. He just did it, not a word about why.

Ty wasn't sure himself why he'd taken the cutoff. He'd just watched the snow and thought about Fenton and then found himself leading his string past the big boulder. He still wasn't sure it was the right choice. All he knew was how anxious he got when he considered riding all the way down the South Fork to Hungry Horse.

But he was feeling better. Remembering what Fenton said about snow helped. That the snow had stopped helped more, the sky still dark but nothing new coming down. And the way was surprisingly open. Now and then he could see where Spec had broken twigs off the trees or a dip in the surface of the snow where Spec's horses must have gone. He didn't know exactly what was under that snow, but at least he was on Spec's trail. And if everything went right, he'd soon be in a place he did know. The cutoff was supposed to come out in the meadows where Bob Ring's camp had been. Ty had scarcely known what he was doing that day, but everything about it was with him as though it were yesterday—pulling Ring's horse along the trail, watching the man fight his pain, hearing the girl cry, feeling every bump and switchback as though jarring something broken in himself.

He crossed the blanketed meadows by midafternoon, passing Ring's campsite and breaking ice to ford the stream. The weather had lifted. He could see the headwall now, some of the trail exposed before disappearing into wind-blown drifts. If I have to come back and camp, he thought, I'll have to turn everything around up there. He looked back at his string. There was a lot to turn around.

At the base of the switchbacks he stopped and dug under the manty where he'd stashed the feed bag. He went down the string, giving each some sweet-grain before letting Smoky and Cottontail finish it. He tucked the nosebag away, checked cinches and unsnapped all the lead-lines except Cottontail's. He snugged the shovel under her pack-ropes, mounted Smoky and started, his mules coming without hesitation, lining out as naturally as though still tied.

They went up the first switchbacks quickly, the mules following so closely he wondered why he hadn't thought to free them when they were in the woods. He remembered and it unsettled him: how lost he'd been, the blind luck that had led him to that lodgepole. He tried to put it behind him as he came to the drifts building across the switchbacks. Smoky pushed through the first ones easily, forcing herself through to make a way. The drifts grew as they climbed, Smoky backing off and pushing in again as Ty urged her ahead, her legs shaking from the effort.

The wind picked up, gusts of it blowing snow in flat sheets. The mules didn't like it, turning their heads away, pushing at one another to move faster. They came to a drift too high for Smoky, and Ty was off before she could move into it, the mules crowding forward, hating to stop in that wind. Ty pulled out the shovel and pushed into the drift himself. It was high but the snow light. He worked fast to make a rough trough, keep them centered in the trail. The wind swept the snow from his shovel as he worked, new snow blowing in where he'd shoveled, the wind shifting and rising and swirling snow so swiftly it was hard to gauge his progress. He kept his head down, tried to dig the trench faster than new snow could fill it. He felt sweat break out under his coats as snow exploded from his shovel, Smoky pushing at him as he dug, the two of them inching their way, the rest crowding behind on snow they packed themselves, shifting and stutter-stepping to move ahead.

And then they were free of it, the wind-swept trail almost bare again as Ty led Smoky around the switchback, leaning into blasts of wind and looking down as his mules came through the big drift, Sugar last— crowding the mule ahead of her. Ty pushed into the wind, his stocking cap pulled low against sheets of sleety snow, walking almost backward as he led Smoky, turning to break through more drifts, twice more having to shovel, but the drifts not as bad as the first, Smoky's legs no longer shaking. He grew hot and wet under his coats despite the wind and swirling snow.

The saddle of the pass had been under spring snow when he'd led Bob Ring and Wilma over it. Now he could see they'd crossed a moonscape of boulders and heavy sand that stung and tore at him until he had to walk sideways. They topped the crest into an icy wind that lifted everything before it. He walked backward into it, starting down now, making sure all the mules were following, seeing one hesitate, turn his tail into the blast until Sugar took over, pushed him toward home.

Suddenly they were back in snow, a field of it that settled into sweeping drifts where the winds quieted. Far across it, below him, he saw the trail snaking out, crossing more rock and sand before starting down the switchbacks. He kept moving into the snow, not worrying about how deep. Knowing he had to cross it. Knowing there was no way to turn back.

He was back on Smoky and half across the snowfield before he realized the wind had stopped, the quiet so sudden it seemed another noise. He could hear the creak of leather, the squeak of dry snow as the mules moved belly-deep through the white.

It was a quiet that made him uneasy, the light fading, blown snow sifting down, eerie as a moonless night. He made noise himself—took off his hat and beat ice from it, brushed sand and snow from Fenton's coat. A streak of pale sky appeared out across the Swan, the valley itself below them, buried in clouds that shifted and darkened with the storm. The streak widened, took on color—above him clouds, below him clouds, the blue strip growing and changing shape out where the Mission Range should be, the strip brightening with the colors of the setting sun. And then he saw the Missions themselves, looking high and close, white serrated ridges rising from the clouds, lifting up, declaring themselves.

The wind came again as they crossed the snowfield, sheets of snow whipping and swirling around the legs of the mules before settling back onto the drifts. Ty paid no attention, his eyes on the widening expanse of blue and purple and orange out across the Swan Valley, framing the high peaks of the Missions with colors impossible to catch, shifting and blending even as clouds rolled up from the Swan to swallow them, narrowing the scarlet line of color until it slipped back into the relentless dark.

The cold returned with the darkening sky. Ty shook himself. The sky had taken him so completely he'd paid little attention to what was ahead. He was startled to see they were following tracks, that the snow was broken out on the trail. He leaned off Smoky to look, using what light was left. Two horses, he thought, no mules. But why? Who? And on such a day? All he knew was to be thankful. He wasn't sure he could get off and shovel again.

He would be at the corrals by ten, he thought, knowing now there would be no way to get to Fenton's except by horseback. Not through this snow. He'd do what he could to help whoever was ahead of him, bound to be snowed in, then head for Fenton's barn. Maybe he'd make it by midnight. Knowing when didn't bother him now. He'd made it. He had his mules. His packs were balanced. And someone had broken the trail out. He'd made do. He just knew it had taken more than a little luck to do it.

That did bother him. He looked back through the fading light at his string, looked ahead at the tracks, letting Smoky set her own pace as she followed them. He knew nothing but dumb luck had saved them. And Fenton had taught him never to count on dumb luck.

The drifts opened for them as they dropped into the dark, and with the dark came more snow. Ty tried not to think about it—thought instead about the Missions hanging there across the Swan Valley, the shifting colors lighting the sky behind them. He doubted he'd ever see anything like that again, thinking maybe it was enough that he'd seen it at all. If he stuck with this life there would be other things to see, things most people had no way to imagine. Maybe those things would stay with him too, the way he knew the Missions would: the sky cracking open in a blizzard and framing them in purples and golds.

That was a kind of luck he didn't mind counting on. It was different from the other. It might even be that you could earn it—if you knew your mountains the way Fenton knew his.

Even before he got to the corrals he realized his feet were too cold. He got off and led Smoky, tried to wiggle his toes as he walked, the snow freezing in cakes around his pant legs and over his boots. But even with the drifts broken, it was hard going. After awhile he got back on. It was easy to see that Smoky was better at staying in the tracks.

He was surprised to find no life at the corrals. No animals, no lanterns or snowbound trailers. He rode on, so tired he didn't bother to tie his string back together. They were too tired and hungry to go anywhere anyway. And too close to home.

He was concentrating so hard on keeping his mind from drifting that he didn't notice he was still following the tracks until he was walking again, this time mostly to keep awake. His feet didn't feel cold anymore; they didn't feel much at all. He kept reminding himself to wiggle his toes, kept stomping his feet to get some feeling in them, so thankful for the tracks he'd given up wondering who made them.

He was back on Smoky when the trail forked to Fenton's corrals, the tracks so full of new snow he couldn't tell which way they went. He heard the generator's hum before he saw lights, a lantern in the barn. Maybe it was Buck. With a little help it wouldn't take long to unpack, feed his mules, turn them out. They deserved it. He hadn't made their day an easy one.

He circled to pull all the mules into the corral before dismounting, pleased his legs held but feeling nothing in his feet. He was stomping them when the barn doors opened and light spilled across him.

"Well, I'm goddamned." Fenton, unbelieving, stared at him through the falling snow. "Chose an invigorating day to crawl over that pass." Fenton got the lantern, held it high to look him over. "See you remembered to bring out my coat." He swept Ty's hat off his head and beat the snow from it. "From the looks of you, it's a good thing you did." He tossed the hat at Ty. "Let's unpack." He led Sugar into the barn. "We'll make short work of all that hair. Cody Jo might not rest until she takes some scissors to you."

Ty led Smoky in, liking it that she nickered when she saw Easter and Turkey nosing at grain in the feed trough.

They had the mules unpacked in half an hour, the saddles stacked, manties shaken and spread out to dry.

"Now let's look after you," Fenton said. "When all that ice melts off you, you might sting some. Your walking is already irregular."

"I walked a little coming out. I think it made my feet feel better."

"Good thing you could feel them at all. Blood don't get around much in a saddle all them hours."

Ty put feed out for the mules while Fenton held the lantern high to see what was left to do. "All that ice on them pant legs might of helped," Fenton said as they walked to the house. "Ice insulates. Sometimes."

Fenton was so unpredictable Ty thought he might be starting in to talk about snow again. But he was wrong. "Now that you been cold," Fenton said, "it's time you warmed. But not too fast." They went into the shed off the kitchen. "Cold is one of them things where too fast is bad."

Ty took off his coats, shaking the snow and ice from them, brushing off his pants.

"We got dry clothes you can use." Fenton was pushing open the kitchen door. Ty could hear Cody Jo's music on the record player. "First you best set in a tub of warm. You'll hurt, but it might get us by with no blisters." He pushed Ty into the kitchen. "Here he is, Cody. Raggedy." He looked at Ty. "But he's ours."

Cody Jo was suddenly there, her smile dying as she saw the way Ty looked. "Oh, dear." She stared at him. "You . . . you've grown all up." She hesitated, then took his arm. "Why, you're too tired to think."

Then she was all business: There was a big bathroom off the main room and she had him in it in a minute, getting warm water in the tub, getting towels, clothes. "I'll cut that hair tomorrow," she said. "We're putting food in you tonight." She looked at him, worried. "Feel that water with your hand. Make sure it's not too hot."

Fenton came in with a cup of thick soup. "Warms you from the inside." He tested the water with his hand. "That helps. Water will too. Let's make it luke. Them feet are gonna hurt."

"I'll be all right," Ty said. "I'm just glad I got here."

"And you should be." Fenton was turning to leave. "I just ain't sure how. Didn't seem to me anyone could cross them drifts."

Ty's feet hurt so much he had to lift them from the water. When he did, it came to him at last. It had been Fenton and Easter on the pass. Fenton leading Turkey to break out the trail. Fenton worrying about him, Fenton leading him home.

Got to thank him, he thought. Tell him about the colors behind the Missions.

He decided he wouldn't tell him about getting lost.

And then he was asleep.

15

Warming from the Inside

Ty's feet were red and sore, but no blisters. Later his big toenails turned black and he lost them. Fenton said he'd probably bruised them kicking at things to get the feeling back. Fenton had lots to say about Ty's ride out, especially that first night: waking him to drink more soup, keeping the water warm—talking all the time about warming from the inside.

"Them boys are always surprised, after they hold their hands half in the fire, that back in the cold they can't tight a rope. Something that says to work right a body needs to warm from the inside."

He left, coming back with more soup and a sandwich. "Food warms. He fussed around for something more to do. "Probably didn't eat a damn thing coming out over that pass."

He was right. Ty had some jerked elk in his saddlebags, but he'd eaten only one stick, chewing it until he decided to unhook the mules. But he didn't tell Fenton about that. He didn't tell him about getting lost either. That wouldn't leave him alone.

"Don't believe I could have made it if you hadn't broken that trail out," Ty said. "I was sure thankful."

"Watch mules on a cold mornin'." Fenton held out the sandwich. "Buck and fart, tear all over hell and gone. But I think what warms them most is that sweet-grain. Makes sense. Look what warms a bear."

Ty wasn't sure Fenton had heard him. He started in to thank him again but the words drifted off. Fenton put the sandwich back on the plate, put his hand in the water, checking the temperature.

⌒〜

"I think Fenton should have been a doctor," Cody Jo said the next morning. Ty was surprised that Fenton's pants almost fit him. He'd

rolled up the extra length and was shuffling around in an old pair of
Fenton's slippers. His feet were red and itchy, but otherwise he felt
wonderful. He loved the big breakfast Cody Jo had made.

"I don't even remember him bringing me the blankets," Ty said. "I
must of slept deep."

"I brought the blankets." Cody Jo put more flapjacks on his plate. "He
doctors, I comfort. He thinks the more it hurts the better it's getting."

"There's somethin' to that." Fenton brought in firewood. "Sounds
crazy but it ain't. Take Ty's feet. Itchy. Blood gettin' back in there." He
poured some coffee and sat. "Bound to feel some hurt when a body
corrects."

"I just wish you wouldn't take such pleasure in it."

Fenton turned to Ty. "In these mountains you got to remember to
set anything that's broke, sew up anything that needs sewin', right off
the bat. Nature's smart enough to make us plumb numb after we take
a whack. When you're numb is when to move things around. He
sipped his coffee. "Set old Buck's nose that way once."

"You did." Cody Jo grimaced. "Look at poor Buck's nose now."

"Didn't have much time." Fenton's arm went around her. "Least
not enough to be no Michelangelo."

"No." Cody Jo rubbed his hand. "But you could be a doctor. You've
got that way. Just promise never to do anything like that to Ty's nose."

Fenton headed out to the barn to put away the equipment. Ty got
up to go with him, but Fenton wouldn't have it, telling him to read
Cody Jo's books—there were things to be learned. "You'll be workin'
like a coolie in a few days. Repair first."

It snowed off and on for a week, so there was plenty of time for
helping. By the next day Ty was doing what he could, seeing what was
needed and doing it without a lot of questions. He liked being there,
liked the work, liked his little room off the barn, liked watching Fenton
and Cody Jo.

It was a happy time for him. Cody Jo had arranged for him to go to
school in Missoula, and Mary wrote that she and Will were pleased he'd
have the chance. Ty liked talking with Cody Jo about classes, the books
they'd be reading. In the mornings he'd oil and patch saddles, listening
to Fenton's stories, asking questions, learning even when the answer had
nothing to do with the question. In the afternoons he'd fire up the
woodstove and read in his room off the barn. At night Cody Jo would
play the piano and they'd sing, or they'd listen to her records. She even
started teaching Ty to dance, telling him it would be good for his feet,

that he'd be a hit at the schoolhouse dances. She thought he might have natural rhythm, but he needed to relax before she'd know for sure.

The fourth day it cleared. Fenton saddled Easter and took two mules, opening the trail to Murphy's so he could get supplies for Cody Jo. When he came back he brought Buck and Angie with him, and the Murphys too. They'd run out of things to do at the store and decided to come through the snow to stir up some excitement. They wanted to hear Cody Jo's new records, which they'd brought along with her mail-order things. They wanted to see Ty too, not sure whether to believe Fenton's story.

"There he is." Fenton unpacked the mules at the backdoor. "His feet are scratchy, but the rest is tuned up keen."

"Wait'll Spec hears." Buck passed the groceries across the snow. "He claimed you'd have to come out down Hungry Horse way."

"And he didn't say how much you growed." Angie watched Ty carry the groceries in. "You could break some hearts, Ty."

Ty took the horses to the barn and threw out feed. When he got back the women were talking about what food to have and Dan Murphy was already mixing and stirring his favorite concoction.

"I'll make a special for you." He looked at Ty. "Made me nervous just ridin' here from the store. Don't know how in hell you made it all the way from Ring's meadows."

"He was in a worse place than Ring's meadows." Fenton was watching all the mixing. "And it wasn't luck that got him out. If he'd counted on luck we'd still be looking for him."

"This is a Murphy special. Take a taste. People drive miles to partake." Murphy watched Fenton sip it. "Save some for our hero."

Fenton rolled it around, swallowed. "I like most everything that's got a bite. Try it, Ty. Your taster's not so contaminated."

"Here." Dan Murphy handed Ty a cup. "Then tell your secret. Fenton says he don't see how you made it." He watched Ty take a swallow.

"Oh . . ." Ty wiped at his eyes, sucked air to cool his mouth. "No secret, but maybe not knowing what's ahead when you saddle." He wiped his eyes again, hearing the music start up from Cody Jo's victrola. "This sure warms you."

"Slop me a little more, Daniel." Fenton held out his cup, amused by Ty. "Appears your special is right special."

Dan Murphy mixed a big batch of it in a bowl. Rosie put out some cheese and bread and they asked Ty lots of questions about his ride through the blizzard. He did his best to answer, thinking it probably wasn't as dangerous as they thought, though there was no way to describe the wind. It was hard to believe that himself. He said no part scared him more than any other, which was true. He hadn't had time to get scared, except for the getting lost part—which he didn't mention. When he finally said how grateful he was that Fenton had broken out the trail, Fenton hardly listened.

"'Bout the only luck he did have. Wind taking that snow ever' which way. I was damn sure no one could come up from the other side." Fenton got up and stirred the fire. "Good you got out when you did, Ty. Don't know what you'd be feeding them mules by now."

Ty took another sip, relieved it didn't burn so much this time. They played some of Cody Jo's new music and Rosie came over and got him to dance. Buck and Angie were already dancing, and Rosie was so energetic he forgot all about how awkward he must look. When they put on the next record, Angie said she wanted to dance with "Mr. Intrepid."

"Learn these steps, Ty." She started in to lead as soon as the record began. "No fun bein' a wallflower."

Cody Jo brought out a pot of chili, and they ate it with slices of elk steak and more of Rosie's bread. Ty found himself dancing to almost every record they played. Later in the evening they got Artie Shaw's swing band on the radio. When they played "Green Eyes," Ty found himself dancing with Cody Jo, and after a few steps the music seemed a part of him. He hardly felt her in his arms, though he knew the music wouldn't mean nearly so much if she weren't. The others stopped and watched. When the song ended Angie and Rosie clapped, Angie saying Ty won the prize as best dancer.

Cody Jo went to Fenton and took his arm. "Well," she said. "I believe he does have it. I wasn't so sure at first."

"What's he got?" Rosie was winding the phonograph, putting on another swing record. "Besides a big appetite?"

"Rhythm." Cody Jo watched Angie go over to Ty, swaying in place while she waited for the next record. "That's what he's got."

"Packers don't have a hell of a lot of time for dancin'." Fenton started in to dance with Cody Jo as the music began. "But when he's out of the woods, you girls can take over. Might need a dance or two by then."

Ty danced a bit longer, but nothing seemed as right as the dance with Cody Jo. After awhile he decided to go to bed and read. He took a lantern and went out through the snow, surprised by how hard it was to stay on the packed path.

The next morning he was thirsty and dry-mouthed and couldn't remember whether he'd read before he slept or not. He went into the barn to pee, went outside and got some snow to eat. He ate more as he got dressed, dressing fast in the cold. He ate still more as he walked up to the house, saw where he'd gone off the trail the night before.

Cody Jo was talking with Fenton in the kitchen. She smiled at Ty as she poured him a glass of juice. "You had a time last night. Told you those dancing lessons would pay off."

"Horace's old bunkhouse ain't too bad." Fenton put a mug of coffee in front of Ty. "Like your room in the barn. Better. Electrified."

Ty drank the juice and sipped at the coffee. He wasn't sure what Fenton was talking about. Then Fenton said something about the Adams's chores, and it came to him that they were talking about where he'd live while he went to school.

"It's a place to study, Ty." Cody Jo put a plate of scrambled eggs and toasted slices of Rosie's bread in front of him. "Etta will feed you. You'll need to eat." She smiled again. "Even when you feel a little funny."

c-ɔ

Two days later the roads opened. Spec showed up in Tommy Yellowtail's pickup and Ty got a ride into town with him. Tommy hadn't gotten better, and though he had faith in the medicine man, Spec wanted all the bases covered. He'd even filled out the forms for some government doctoring, much as he hated to do it.

"Papers and more papers." He spit out into the snow as they drove. "Then they act as though you're lucky to be allowed." He stopped at the bar in Seeley Lake and had a beer, buying one for Ty too, the bartender looking at Ty before deciding there was too much snow to worry about laws.

"Thought you quit this." Ty took a sip of beer, trying to keep Spec from fretting so much.

"I did. In the mountains." Spec bought more bottles for the trip. "It ain't worth it out here."

"Must of took the cutoff." Spec was sipping beer as he drove. "Stuck a log in a tree for you."

"That saved me. I was about to ride on past it."

"You would of found the way. Or that Smoky mare would of. You do good in the woods."

"Well," Ty looked out at the banks of snow. "I'm not so sure."

Spec dropped Ty off at the department store. Cody Jo had made him promise to buy something that didn't look so worn before he went to the Adams's. Spec wrote down the address of a bar where Ty could find him and went off to the government offices. An agent had promised to meet with him even though it was Saturday. Ty worried about that. The beer didn't seem to be calming Spec down.

The clerk tried to sell Ty some Levis Ty thought were too short. "Cowboys like 'em that way." The man eyed Ty's worn clothes. "So they don't drag in all that cow shit." Ty bought a pair one size up anyway, adding a shirt to that, and left, the man still telling him things he needed as he walked out the door.

He had time, so he walked along Main Street looking in store windows. When he came to an outfitter's supply store, he went in to look at the panniers. A man in an apron came from the back and stood there, smoking and looking at Ty.

"Snow drive you out of your mountains?" The man stubbed out his cigarette. "You boys always look a little lost come winter. Or drunk. It's a toss-up."

Ty asked some questions about the panniers, saying they didn't look as stout as the ones he used. The man smiled, lit another smoke.

"You work for that big bastard Pardee? He sings the same tune about them panniers."

"I do." Ty was pleased to be identified with Fenton. "Ours has a little more leather. They get worked awful hard."

"To tell the truth I do too, every time Pardee stops in and tells me to cinch this up or add leather there. It's a lot more pleasant to do business with that wife of his. She sure lights a place up."

Ty stayed on awhile, enjoying the man's stories about how frugal Fenton could be, how Cody Jo could get him to do what he'd just said he wouldn't. When he left he passed a bar where the nickelodeon was playing one of Cody Jo's favorites. He leaned against the building and listened, wishing he could see the mountains lifting on the outskirts of town. The clouds were in and he couldn't see them at all.

He walked on, thinking of different campsites, the miles he'd covered tracking horses, the way the sun broke through the clouds and gave such color to the Missions. And he thought about how Fenton and Cody Jo had taken care of him: Fenton coming for him through the snow, Cody Jo feeding him and cutting his hair and giving him books to read. He thought about dancing with her too. She'd shown him you don't even need to think when you dance with someone like Cody Jo. He thought maybe when things were right, you didn't have to think about them at all. But then he thought that could be another thing you never got to know for sure.

He checked the address Spec had given him, thinking he'd rather be headed for one of his camps in the mountains. Or for one of Cody Jo's dinners in the big log building Fenton had built for her up in the Swan.

Missoula (1937–1941)

Ty figured out that what he learned from Spec in the mountains was a lot more useful than what he learned from Spec in Missoula.

16

The Bar of Justice

It was dark when Ty finally got there. But he found nothing barlike, just a medium-sized brick building, the porch tilted where the ground had settled. Other plain-looking brick and clapboard buildings were scattered along the street, no stores in sight at all, and only one streetlight, its glow filtering across melting banks of dirty snow. There were a few cars in front of the building. Tommy's pickup wasn't one of them.

Again Ty checked the address, making sure before he crossed the trampled snow and rapped on the door. A voice called, and he opened the door to see a lone man playing solitaire. The man turned his cards twice more, putting down an ace before looking up at Ty.

"Spec's buddy?" He got the cigar going again. "Said you was green." He went back to his cards. "There." He jabbed over his shoulder. "Or upstairs."

Ty was so relieved the man knew Special Hands, he didn't think to ask any questions. He went past him into a larger room where there was a small bar against the back wall. Behind it was an open door leading to some stairs. A nickelodeon was against one wall, a few tables and chairs near it. Except for three bar stools, there was no other furniture. At one of the tables a man sat reading a paper and drinking coffee.

A woman was behind the bar, chewing gum and cleaning glasses. Ty went over to her and asked if she knew Spec.

"Know you too. Want a beer? A whiskey?" She looked him over. "How 'bout a quickie?"

She was younger than he'd thought, fleshy and pleasant faced. He wasn't sure he'd heard what she'd said.

"Well, I'll . . ."

"Whatever, hon. You name it. Spec said you wasn't to pay for nothing." She wiped the bar. "I'm Jeanie. Just say what you want."

"Would you have a Coke? It was a long walk."

"Might." She took a longer look at him. "Your buddy's havin' a good old time." She slid him a Coke. "Told us about you." She took her gum from her mouth as a man came in, sat at a table. "Didn't tell us you was cute."

She left to see what the man wanted, coming back to get a beer from the cooler. "I'll be waitin'. Just ask for Jeanie." She went back, put the beer in front of the man, and sat.

It was quiet as Ty sipped his Coke. He was thankful when the man got up and put some money in the nickelodeon. The music was twangy, not like Cody Jo's, but the noise made him feel more comfortable.

Two other men came in and a big, smiling woman came out from the back, calling them by name, laughing before pouring a jigger of whiskey and opening a bottle of beer for each. The men went off to one of the tables, and a wiry woman came in and sat down with them.

"You're Spec's friend." The big woman looked at Ty. "Got orders to take real good care of you." She opened a beer, came partway around the bar to give it to him. "This here one's on me. You just tell me what you want, hon. Beth's the one who'll find it." She winked at him and went back, putting some ice in a glass and pouring whiskey over it, stirring it with her finger. "Or I'll take you up myself." She lifted the glass at Ty and took a sip. "You boys never take much time."

It came to Ty then. He felt his face flushing. "Oh," he said. He got up from the bar stool and looked at the woman. Sat back down on the bar stool again. "I didn't know . . . Is this place called The Bar of Justice?" He looked behind him at the nickelodeon, at the tables. Jasper had told him about such a place one night in the mountains; he was sorry he'd only partly listened, thinking Jasper was into the cooking sherry again.

"Ain't no soda fountain," Beth smiled. "What'd you think?"

"There's no sign. Spec just give me this address." He still had the crumpled paper in his hand; Beth looked at it, threw it away.

"He's a caution." She didn't seem too happy about Ty's confusion.

She leaned across the bar. Ty could smell sweetish powder. "Sip on that beer there, honey. Tell me how old Fenton's doing. He ain't been around here since I was skinny."

"Well," Ty took a swallow of beer and tried to tell her about Fenton, about the mountains, watching her as he talked, not sure she understood. It was hard to keep straight what he was saying himself. The men would call out for drinks and she would be off to take care of them. She seemed to know them all, and Ty felt funny sitting there at the bar all alone with his beer, drinking it faster than he meant to.

More men were coming in. Ty saw that Jeanie was gone. But three or four other women were there now, some of them dancing with the men, their shiny dresses swinging out, showing bare legs.

He was almost through his second beer when Spec showed up, putting his arm around Beth, pulling her close. "There he is," he said, looking at Ty. "Only bastard I know can shoe a bronc mule, cross a snowed-out pass, and keep Fenton Pardee happy all at the same time."

"I sure didn't do them things at the same time." Ty looked at Beth. "Don't believe I've satisfied Fenton yet."

"She knows all about satisfying Fenton." Spec gave Beth a squeeze. "Hustle up some of them boilermakers. Ty's thirsty."

"I'll stick with these beers." Ty didn't know what a boilermaker was anyway. And he didn't like something in Spec's voice. He reached for his money but Spec grabbed his wrist.

"You ain't spending a goddamned penny." Spec's voice was hard. "This is my deal." Ty looked so surprised Spec had to smile. "Have a hell of a time, kid." He threw crumpled bills on the bar. "Got all this money from them government people. Have a drink on them bastards."

Beth's eyes hadn't left Spec. She seemed relieved when he let go of Ty's wrist. She put two jiggers of whiskey on the bar, a beer beside each.

Spec drank his jigger in a gulp, then took a long pull of beer. "Damn." He brought the bottle down hard on the bar.

"You don't have to drink that fast, honey," Beth said to Ty. "Spec's way ain't for everybody."

"He's been learning things from me in the mountains. No reason to stop here." Spec handed Ty the other jigger. "Is there, Ty?"

Ty sipped at the whiskey, felt his lips burn.

"You boys go sit." She put the drinks on a little tray, took them over to a table. "Take it easy, Spec. Ty ain't sure what hit him."

"He sure as hell will be," Spec said. "Take you another taste, Ty. That shit improves." Beth shook her head and got up to serve someone at the bar. Spec followed her and came back with another jigger of whiskey, lifting it at Ty.

Spec was right: Ty's whisky didn't burn as much the second time.

They talked, easing down their whiskey with beer, Spec relaxing as Ty told him about coming over the pass in the storm.

"Had you a hell of a year, Ty," Spec said. "You do good in the woods."

"Fenton wants me to keep at it." Ty wiped at some beer that had spilled on the table. "You be around next year? Show me some things?"

"Teach you to hunt. If I can get you free of them mules." He seemed to consider something. "Who the hell is Natty Bumpus? They never did say."

"Cody Jo says he's a hunter . . . in a book."

"In a book?"

"Never said the book."

"Well," Spec said. "Shit on that."

A girl with dark eyes that slanted off toward dark shiny hair sat down. Ty thought she couldn't be much older than he was. She was so pretty he couldn't keep from looking at her, watching as she took Spec's whiskey and drank it in one swallow.

"Thought we was going to have a party." The girl wiped her mouth, her lips scarcely moving when she spoke.

"This here is Ty," Spec said. "And this here is a party. Got my government money. Got my mountain buddy." He got up for some more whiskey. "Shit goddamn," he said, going to the bar.

"Ain't he a hell of a thing?" the girl said, drinking some of Ty's whiskey.

"Loretta enjoys a drink." Spec returned with more whiskey, Beth following him with beer.

"Don't you and Loretta drink too fast, Spec." Beth put down the beer and messed up Ty's hair. "Ty's just gettin' to know us."

"Loretta is why I was late. We had a hell of a time."

"I guess." Loretta looked at Ty. "Wanna dance?" She didn't look very interested, but when she stood up, Ty did too.

They shuffled around in front of the nickelodeon, Ty wondering why she'd wanted to dance in the first place. She didn't pay a bit of attention to the music, just held him close, tightening her legs on his thigh whenever she got the chance. When the song ended, Ty said he thought they better sit down. Loretta didn't object, sitting and drinking her whiskey before going off to another table.

"Hell, she'll be back," Spec said, pushing Ty's beer in front of him. "She don't take much time with them guys."

Ty watched her talking with a man over by the record player, the lights making different colors in her dark hair. Her expression didn't seem to change at all, but before he knew it, both of them were gone.

He began to think it wouldn't be right to go to Horace and Etta's after he'd been here. And it was getting late. Maybe he ought to ask

Spec about someplace else to sleep, but he didn't know if Spec planned to leave at all. He didn't even know where the truck was, which direction to start walking even if he could get his things out of it.

They drank more, and Spec got in an argument with a man at another table. Beth came over and quieted things down, and a big man who'd come in from the front went back out again. Ty wondered what had happened to the man playing solitaire. He wondered where Loretta had gone. And he didn't like what was happening to Spec, whose voice was getting hard as he found more and more things to argue about.

"Take that Loretta upstairs," Spec said. "It's a fuckin' government present. I'll sit here and think how to get more money out of them bastards." He looked at Ty. "What the fuck's the matter with Loretta?"

Before Ty could answer, Jeanie had plopped down next to him. "Anyone here gonna buy a girl a beer? I've worked me up a thirst."

Ty was surprised by how relieved he was to see her. He was at the bar asking Beth for the beer when Spec spun him around. "Told you this was my deal, goddamn it. You ain't buying no beer." He had turned Ty with such force they both went a little off balance.

"You boys are lucky." Beth acted like there was no commotion at all. "It's on the house." She pushed three bottles across the bar. "Here's some change too. Play somethin', Ty. Play "Minnie the Moocher.""

Spec took the beer back to Jeanie. Ty went over to the record player and pushed the buttons for the song. He pushed the buttons to play others too, songs that Angie and Rosie had played that night at Fenton's. He was looking for more when Beth came over.

"Don't be so low, hon. Spec was just happy to see you. Got so excited he wouldn't have it no way but his way." Beth pushed the buttons for "Pennies from Heaven." "You'll be like brothers come morning." Before he could say anything Jeanie was there and they were dancing. She was a lot more energetic than Loretta.

"You remind me of Angie," Ty said. "She sure likes this brand of music."

"Buck's wife? Bet she don't like my brand of lovin'." She pushed away and did some fancy steps. "That's the lindy." She slowed, dancing with him again. "You dance nice." She hummed the tune. "When we goin' upstairs? Spec give me my orders."

"Well," Ty said, looking at Spec and Beth sitting at the table, feeling a little dizzy and uncertain. "Well . . ."

They danced the next dance, then had a drink and danced again. And then Ty found himself in a tiny little room, hardly space enough for the bed. Jeanie was already out of her clothes, her heavy breasts swinging as she did something over a washbasin.

"Like these?" She cupped her breasts and held them up, the wide aureoles pale in the uncertain light. She looked at him. "Can't do much with them pants on." She dropped her breasts and undid his buckle. "Way you mess around, you'd think we had all night."

They rolled around on the bed and she wiped at him with a warm cloth. Then they rolled some more.

"Goodness, honey," she said after awhile. "You gonna poke that thing into the mattress or me?" She shifted her hips and took hold of him.

It was over so fast Ty wasn't sure he'd enjoyed it.

"Wasn't that good?" She pulled her dress back on and looked around for her shoes.

"I reckon." Ty still wasn't sure. He pulled his pants up, buckled his belt. "You know . . ." He sat back down on the bed. "I hardly know where I'm at."

She pulled him up and started him out the door. "You're cute." She gave him a little kiss on the cheek. "But scoot on in the potty there and clean up. It's Saturday; I got fish to fry."

When Ty got to the bathroom Loretta was coming out, holding onto the the door for balance. She was pale, her hair stringy with perspiration. Ty reached out to help her but she pushed his hand away. "Crapper's in there, kid," she said, going on toward the stairs, using the wall to balance.

Ty took a long pee and splashed cold water on his face. The room smelled of vomit, and he was glad to be out of it. He went down the stairs and found Spec sleeping at the table, his head on his arms, an open bottle of beer in front of him. Jeanie was talking to a man at another table. She gave Ty a wave and turned back to her conversation.

"You want the rest of this beer, hon?" Beth asked. She was going around with a tray picking up the empty glasses and bottles from the tables. "Spec sure don't." She held up the bottle for Ty, who shook his head. "Well, better get him on home. His truck's out back."

"I don't know where to take him," Ty said. "I don't know where to go."

"Well," she lifted one of Spec's arms, wiping the table under it, "I'll get Leonard. Maybe he knows."

Leonard turned out to be the man who'd been playing solitaire. He looked old, but that didn't seem to slow him. He got under Spec's arm and had him out of his chair so fast Ty had to hurry to get under the other. Spec woke a little too, which helped. But he looked bad, his head rolling and saliva running off his chin.

"I wouldn't expect him to drive," Leonard said as they took him out the backdoor. "Though I seen worse who did."

Spec didn't protest as they pushed him into the truck, picking his legs up so they could stuff them in and close the door.

"I don't know where to take him," Ty said. "Where to go."

Leonard spit a brown line into the dirty snow. "You know there ain't a goddamned thing you boys can't do up in them mountains. Why in hell is it just the opposite ever' time you get to town?"

He spit again. "You work for Pardee too?"

"I do." Ty wished Fenton were there to fix everything.

"Well, I'm damn glad it ain't him we had to carry. He's a big bastard." Leonard turned and started back in.

"Where would Fenton take him?" Ty called out. "If Fenton was here?"

"Beats me." Leonard had the door open, but he stopped, considered. "Jasper claims he's got some kin out Indian town way. Try that."

♡⌒つ

Ty had taken so many turns and bumped across so many rutted roads that he was sure they were lost, but Spec seemed to sense where to go. Each time the road forked he'd rouse himself, pointing before his head rolled back against the window or slumped down on his chest. Ty just hoped for the best, not even sure Spec would wake up when they got to wherever they were going. And now it looked as though they had, Spec reaching over for the wheel as though turning it sharply might stop them.

He pulled in with other cars and trucks, some with the doors off, the seats gone; others with no hood, wires hanging where the engines had been. The cars were scattered in front of a low building. An old corral, tilted and broken, leaned against one side of it. Spec got his door open and fell out into the muddy snow. A dog jumped out of one of the trucks, barking until he got close enough and then whining, going to Spec on his belly, his tail flapping in the ridges of mud and snow.

Ty helped Spec up, and the three of them crossed the lot to the plywood shelter that shielded the door. That and the tilted corral were all that broke the perfect rectangle of the building. As soon as they were under the shelter, the door to the house opened. There was no light, but Ty could make out a big presence in the doorway.

"Drunk or sick?" a woman's voice asked.

"A little drunk, I guess." She had an overcoat on against the cold.

"More than a little, looks like." She came out and shut the door behind her. "Pull them muddy boots off, and I'll put him on the couch." She pushed a wooden box over with her foot. "He can sleep it away."

Ty sat Spec on the box, leaning him against the plywood so he could pull off his boots. Spec peered up at the woman, saying nothing as Ty got him on his feet, shifted his weight over to her. The woman helped Spec inside and closed the door behind her.

Ty stood there, pulling up the collar of Fenton's coat and stomping his feet to stop the tingling starting up in his toes. He went back to the truck, the dog trotting along with him and watching as he got Horace's coat from the back and climbed into the cab. He thought of calling the dog in for what warmth it could provide but decided against it. He closed the door and stretched out on the seat, pulling Horace's coat over him.

He twisted and turned for awhile, trying to get comfortable, finally propping himself up on the driver's side and stretching his legs out across the cab. He slept that way—pulling up the coat, nodding off and waking and nodding off again, thinking about Spec. He decided what he learned from him in the mountains was probably more useful than what he learned from him in Missoula.

17

Town Learning

Spec was shaky when he came out of the house but clean, his hair combed. By then Ty had begun walking up and down the road, dodging the slush and jogging in place to get the feeling back in his feet. His pants were muddy and getting muddier from the jogging.

"Wondered where you went." Spec climbed into the truck and started the motor. Ty hopped in too, Horace's coat piled in his lap.

"Want a beer?" Spec bounced the truck over the ruts. "Couple of beers might make me horny again."

They went to the Elkhorn, Ty getting hungrier by the minute. A waitress gave them menus.

"You sleep in a leaky barn?" she asked Ty.

"How about two beers," Spec said. "We got a thirst."

"Age disqualifies your partner. And Sunday disqualifies you."

"Coffee, then," Spec said. "Which ain't what we need."

They ordered and Ty went to clean up. When he came back, Jasper was there, wearing a suit and a little fedora. He took the hat off when he saw Ty. Ty was so happy to see him he said nothing about the clothes.

"Told you to be careful where Spec took you." Jasper shook a finger at Ty. "Safer with bears. Lucky you steered clear of that big turd who works with Leonard. I give up on him. Leonard can bring his cards here to play."

"I'd like a beer," Spec said. "Would a beer suit you, Jasper?"

"I'd tolerate one. I been to church."

"You have?" Ty was surprised. "You never told me . . ."

"Beth keeps some cold." Jasper's thoughts were with the beer. "And that big shit don't work on Sundays."

"He might spend Sundays in church," Spec said. "Purify himself."

"Assholes don't purify. You and Buck should know that."

The waitress came with plates of eggs and potatoes and ham steaks. Ty was almost as glad to get the subject changed as he was to get the food. The last thing he needed was a beer—or The Bar of Justice.

He turned out to be the only one with money, which shamed Spec and Jasper into taking him directly to Horace Adams. Horace didn't seem all that pleased when they got there.

"Ty?" He took in Ty's clothes. "You're a day late. Your friends make you change their tire in a muddy place?"

"You remember Jasper and Special Hands," Ty said. "They drove me over . . ." He held out the coat. "I sure thank you for your coat."

Horace just looked at him, finally opening the door wide. "If you boys come in, this conversation might pick up."

Jasper and Spec were surprised. They'd never been in Horace's house. They hardly talked as they carried Ty's things through and out to the bunkhouse.

"You can clean up here." Horace opened a door to a tiny bathroom, a shower in one corner. "Then maybe you won't smell like a gin mill."

"We come in yesterday," Spec explained. "Ty's first time in town. After the mountains."

"Yes. And where you took him may stick with him longer than the damn mountains," Horace said. "Though he'll wish it didn't."

Etta came in with towels, excited about seeing Ty.

"Oh." She looked at him. "Are you hurt?"

"We brought his things in," Spec explained. "We come in yesterday. I needed to see the government people."

"And he seen them." Jasper held his fedora against his chest. "He still has one of them checks they give him."

"That ain't all of it." Spec couldn't help himself. "I'm gettin' more."

"Yes." Etta left the towels. "I'm sure."

It was quiet after she left, all of them looking at Ty.

"Well," Jasper said. "We best go, Ty. I thank you for the breakfast."

"You boys can see him when we clean him up," Horace said. "But not too often. There's school."

Jasper fitted his hat back on and left, but Spec hesitated, wanting to say something. Ty was relieved when he gave up on it, just held up a hand and followed Jasper out to the truck.

"You could stand a wash," Horace said. "Your friends may have set out to look after you, but they missed by some. Lucky you got any money left at all." He turned to go. "I'll show you the chores after."

He hadn't smiled at all.

╰╌╮

Ty was embarrassed by the fuss the school made about his late enrollment. At Crazy Pete School they understood ranch work might interfere, but they didn't seem to look at it that way in Missoula. He wasn't even sure they understood that if he'd had to ride all that way down the South Fork, he might still be wandering around in the snow.

Only the principal, Mr. Trout, who seemed to know Fenton, understood. He listened to Ty's story carefully, smiling each time Ty mentioned Fenton. Then he sent him off to Miss Wright, the English teacher, to get his schedule. Miss Wright was young and earnest and dedicated. Trout's guess was that she was so taken with the literature she taught, Ty would have no choice but to like it himself.

The other place he sent Ty was out to the football field. It was still midseason, but Trout had a feeling the strong young boy from Pardee's pack station would like it. And he was right. Ty was surprised himself by how quickly he took to the game, an attachment that became a mystery to Miss Wright—who was mostly interested in repairing his grammar.

But for the first week Ty was so busy he hardly had time to consider grammar, though Miss Wright tried to correct him each time they talked. She gave him books to read so he could catch up in English and history; she arranged to have him meet with his mathematics teacher each evening; and his afternoons were filled with football.

It turned out that Mr. Trout was always on the lookout for players. He'd liked the way Ty looked in his oversized Levis and guessed that running around on the rocky field at Crazy Pete School was worth something and throwing Fenton's heavy packs around was worth more. It didn't take the coaches long to see Trout was right. It was easy for Ty to wrestle down boys scooting this way and that with the football, flopping them down like calves ready for branding.

In the mornings he got up and fed the horses. Then it was off to school and Miss Wright. And after school, football, where an assistant coach stayed after practice to explain what an end had to do to keep a runner from going down the sidelines. It was from him Ty learned that Trout had been called Bull Trout when he played for the university, that after graduating he'd taught at the school and been the coach himself—before they made him principal.

Some days at their practices Ty would look over and find the big man watching, hands buried in his pockets, doing his principal's work right there on the field. The teachers seemed to have no choice but to go out on blustery afternoons and confer with him there. One day Ty even saw Miss Wright huddle with him, slender and out of place, holding her hair against the wind as Trout took his hand out of his pocket, pointing Ty out.

Football was one of the reasons the Adamses so quickly forgave Ty his bad start. The other was his steadiness. He did his chores on time, was always there for dinner, helped with the dishes—when Etta would let him.

But Horace's fascination with football helped more. He was a regular at the high-school games, the university's games too. He'd seen Bull Trout play in his first college game, been a fan ever since. He'd followed Trout's career as a coach and been even more unhappy than the sportswriters when Trout left coaching to become principal. That's why he was so pleased when they decided to move Ty up to the varsity for the big game with Butte.

"Bull knows," Horace said at supper. "He's forgot more than most coaches learn."

"He knows Fenton," Ty said. "I think most people do."

"Well, Fenton's hard to miss, Ty," Etta said. "He's so big. And he says whatever he wants—like family."

"They remember him at the university." Horace laughed.

"Do we have to hear that story?" Etta gave Horace a look, then took dishes into the kitchen. But Horace stayed and told Ty about Tommy Yellowtail and Fenton bringing Ty's grandfather's—Eban Hardin's—mules down the Bitterroot to ford the Clark Fork right there at the university.

"Water low that year. River wide and shallow. Bridge kinda dicey for those mules. Everything fine until some students started runnin' around with cameras, settin up tripods—every damned thing. All hell broke loose."

Horace described the chaos: mules tearing up the lawns, running up the stairs to buildings and being chased back by ranch kids bolting from their classes. Mule shit everywhere. "Took about three hours to calm things down and get those mules into the river. One of those deans and the police chief tryin' to give Fenton a ticket—or some damn thing. Bull Trout and all those football players down by the river watchin' the mules ford." Horace laughed. "Fenton just rode up to all them students. 'Sorry for the mess,' he says. 'But it'll repair. Could get more education cleanin' up my mule shit than from them books anyway.'"

"He said that?" Ty was stopped. "Did it cause trouble?"

"Not that bothered Fenton." Horace stood, knowing he had some making up to do with Etta. "Bull Trout still loves to tell that story."

The Butte team looked big in their black uniforms, confident. They hadn't lost a game. Ty watched the other Missoula players clench their jaws and double up their fists, making vows. He was surprised at how worked up they were. He wondered if Fenton and Cody Jo would be at the game. Etta had told them about it. She'd even sent a card to Will and Mary.

Ty listened to the coaches, thinking how different this was from the way he readied his mules for a tricky place in the woods or before he took them across some slick snow. He wanted them settled, comfortable about things. The coaches seemed to want the players more excited than they already were. By the time they explained their game plan, the players were so anxious Ty wasn't sure they understood any of it.

He listened but felt apart somehow. He hardly knew the other players, each night hurrying back to do his chores. And what he liked about football was the opposite of what made them so serious. He liked it that there was nothing to worry about, no bogs to skirt or deep river crossings or places you might roll your mules. He liked the freedom, took joy in knocking the others aside so he could get at the runner, swing him to the ground and bounce up for the next play. He hardly thought about how to do it, knowing it all instinctively, as if he were cutting off runaway horses.

When the game started, he understood what worried the coaches. John Lamedeer, the Butte runner, would sweep wide, going outside and turning upfield for ten or fifteen yards before they could force him out of bounds. He seemed to run without effort, just enough ahead to make the tacklers miss, sometimes even turning inside the Missoula end so quickly tacklers would trip over themselves trying to recover.

After Lamedeer scored his third touchdown, the coach called Ty over.

"Maybe you can stop that Indian from running around us," he said, his eyes on the field. "Or through us."

The boy Ty replaced was upset, kicking at the ground and throwing his helmet and swearing as he passed Ty. On the field the Butte players looked bigger, the grass stains on their uniforms darker. Ty saw some of them were looking at him.

Before he was sure he'd lined up right, they were coming at him, two players shoulder to shoulder, John Lamedeer behind them with a hand out, guiding them. Ty managed to slide between the blockers and Lamedeer turned upfield too soon, the others there to pull him down.

He had gained, but not so many yards as before. They were back at Ty again on the next play, Lamedeer planting a foot as though to turn up the field then sweeping past Ty like water around a boulder. Ty reversed himself just in time, cutting the runner off against the sideline. Lamedeer slowed to a trot as he went out of bounds, tossing the ball to the official as he came back, looking at Ty.

It went that way through the afternoon, Ty sometimes laughing as he forced Lamedeer to run inside or sprinted wide to pin him against the sideline. On one play the Indian almost got past Ty with speed so sudden Ty had to dive out to grab his jersey, Lamedeer's momentum whipping them out of bounds and scattering players as they rolled over one another and into the bench. Ty looked up and saw the boy he'd replaced standing over Lamedeer, swearing and gesturing before being yanked away.

It was Fenton who had done it, dropping the boy right in front of Bull Trout, who was coming over to take care of things himself. The player looked small between the two big men.

"Your boy is playing a fine game, Mr. Pardee." Trout looked at Fenton as though the boy weren't there at all. "A little short on technique, but he runs them down. I didn't know packers could run without a horse."

"You should see him wrangle mules," Fenton said. "Or run alongside a hay truck. This would be child's play if it weren't for that fast Indian."

The players had gathered around when Fenton pulled the boy away. They stepped back as Ty and Lamedeer made their way onto the field.

"Better let me run," Lamedeer said to Ty seriously. "We should be beating you bad by now."

"You're way ahead. I don't think we can catch up." They were on the field now, starting to jog. "It's fun, isn't it?"

"If I can't run it ain't," Lamedeer said, going back to his huddle.

"Them boys would of whipped you a lot worse had you not figured out that runner," Fenton said. They were having dinner in the Elkhorn, Ty so glad to see Cody Jo and Fenton he hadn't even thought to ask about his parents.

"Mary and Will wanted to come, Ty," Etta said, as though to remind him. "They said there was some business at the ranch."

"I see you improved on the company you keep." It was the waitress who'd fed them after their night in The Bar of Justice. "And you tidied up. Last time you didn't look so prosperous."

"Bet his pards didn't look much better." Fenton spoke up as though they were old friends. "I tell those boys they'd fare better stayin' in the damn mountains. Then winter comes and my advice goes to hell."

"He was a beautiful runner, Ty," Cody Jo said. "It was like watching some medieval contest. The two of you dueling it out with one another."

Ty liked hearing her talk, hearing all of them talk. He felt good. And he hadn't been so hungry since Jasper's dinner high in Lost Bird Canyon.

⌐⌐⌐

He didn't see Will and Mary until three days after the big Christmas snow, and he was lucky to get into the Bitterroot then. Horace got him a ride out with a drummer who had tire chains. It took them five hours to get to the Missouri Bar.

Dan was sweeping it out. Ty got a broom and helped, surprised to see he was bigger than his brother now.

"They tell me you played football for the Spartans," Dan said. "Dad worries you'll get hurt and he'll be out more money."

"He likes to worry. Tell him they got insurance."

"Ma don't worry. She enjoys having Jennifer around."

"Jennifer Malone?"

"No one told you?" Dan looked at him. "She's in the family way. Jimmy married her."

"He did? That the business that needed tending?"

"Ma don't like to talk about it. And Pa hardly talks about anything but how he had to sell our cows."

On the way home Dan told Ty how Will had sold almost everything to the big outfit that had the Hardin ranch. There was just the crazy milk cow left—and some saddle horses. But there was lots of work with the big outfit, which Will claimed was enough. He hadn't liked worrying about his own cows anyway.

Jimmy was plowing the road when they turned in. He waved from the big outfit's tractor as they went by. They parked by the barn, and Ty saw that all the mule rigging was gone. In the kitchen Mary gave him a hug and got a little tearful at how he'd changed. Jennifer was there, just a hint of the baby showing. To Ty she looked even sweeter than when she'd taught him his numbers at the Crazy Pete School. Ty could see that his mother was pleased about the baby, though she said nothing, not even when Jimmy came in and shook Ty's hand, talking about all his work with the big outfit.

In the morning Ty went out to feed. Jimmy had plowed a wide track for the tractor, and the big outfit's cattle knew to gather behind the clatter of the engine. It was easy to pull the hay wagon along behind, Jimmy setting the throttle and stepping back onto the wagon to help Ty with the hay, the tractor making its own way along the rough track. The cattle drifted in behind, bunching around chunks of hay. Ty saw some of Will's mother cows in with them. And a skinny yearling looked like the calf he'd saved when he broke his arm.

He only stayed three days. There was little for him to do. Dan was off at the store every day, and Jimmy had things to do for the big outfit. Jennifer and his mother were thick with their own concerns, and every time Ty sat down with his father, Will would go on about how bad things were. When Dan said a lumber truck was pulling out for Missoula, Ty hitched a ride.

He didn't see them again until May—the morning Mary died.

☙

Winter passed quickly, Ty settling into a routine to manage his chores and his schoolwork and repair the tack Fenton and Horace left with him. Fenton even brought in the Meana saddle, saying Horace wouldn't need it for another year and Ty should rig it to his liking. Ty oiled it, adding a flank cinch and new latigos and making scabbards for different tools. When the weather was good, he'd saddle one of Horace's horses and work him hard. It wasn't long before all the horses were in better shape than they'd ever been.

Horace liked Ty's quiet way with animals. He would look at the Meana saddle and smile, say he expected Ty would own it some day. "Just can't figure out whether Fenton's gonna give it to you or trick me into doin' it for him."

Ty liked being kidded by Horace, but he could never think of what to say. And he couldn't even imagine owning the Meana saddle.

He learned algebra and studied history, looking at the maps where Lewis and Clark had tried to cross the snow-choked Bitterroot. He was mystified about why they would try after the Nez Perce warnings but impressed that they didn't lose any horses. He read Twain and Crane for Miss Wright, talking with her about the stories before she sent him back to read more. And Cody Jo brought him books by Dreiser and

Dos Passos, taking him out for Cokes when she was in town, asking him why he thought they wrote the things they did.

When Jennifer's baby came, Mary called from the store at the Missouri Bar. A healthy boy, she said, with strong hands. Ty could tell she was anxious to get the baby home. But a few weeks later she was in the hospital herself, sounding so worn he didn't recognize her voice. They found out what was wrong, she said, only then saying anything was wrong at all.

"It's that fever." Her voice was weak. "They knew right off. They have medicine. It'll make everything right."

Horace closed up the feed store the next morning and drove Ty out to the hospital. But they were too late. The medicine didn't make everything right.

"It would have," Jennifer told him, the baby tiny under all the wrapping. "If they had known earlier."

"When?" Ty wanted to know. "When did it start?"

"A week." They stood outside the curtained room where Ty had seen Mary, the blotched skin, the hair still wet from fever, the body worn. "She took to drinking water. The way she does. She wouldn't complain."

"Couldn't he see? Tell how sick she was?"

"She wouldn't say anything, Ty. She said you weren't to blame him."

"She would. That doesn't make it right."

Will was already with the doctor, hands moving along the brim of his hat. The doctor was careful: spotted fever, he explained. The medicine not soon enough. The fever high. Blood pressure low. Lungs filling.

Will thought Ty should come home, that they should talk.

"It's okay," Ty said. "You got things to do. I'll go back to school. We can talk at the service."

But they didn't talk at the service. Will seemed to have forgotten, looking forlorn as the minister spoke. They lowered Mary into the grave and gave him some dirt to throw in. Then he left to finish up with the funeral people. Ty waited with the others under the weak spring sun.

"I'll go back to Missoula," Ty said to them. "He'll be all right. I've got that work in the mountains. I'll help if you need me."

"Oh, Ty." Jennifer was rocking her baby. "Ty . . ."

"It's all right. "I like it up there."

Will came back, still holding his hat in front of him, turning it.

"You coming, Ty? Jennifer will fix a supper."

"I got school. And that work in the mountains."

"Well," Will said, his mind someplace else. "Don't have no accidents."

In June Ty was back with Fenton, shoeing, bringing in hay—getting things right for the season ahead. He liked it, doing well from the first the work he would do for the rest of his life. He liked the mules and the horses; better still he liked the mountains, the way they provided food and comfort. The way watching his animals there taught him to make it a home.

☞

Bob Ring watched Ty ease his mules into the clearing, the lumber extending well beyond each but Ty moving the string so carefully there was no trouble, even on the switchbacks. It was Ring's job to build the lookout shelter. He'd packed in his own tools, but bringing lumber in was another matter. He was impressed to see Ty manage it alone.

Limping with a hitch he would have always, he went to help unload, surprised by how quickly it all happened. In no time the mules were belled and turned out, Ring hardly helping at all but admiring Ty's efficiency.

After dinner they climbed to the lookout site, sat on a ledge in the late sun. To the north, parallel to the broad valley of the South Fork, was the China Wall, where the waters started their long run east. The sun gave life to the ridges, deepened the greens of the forest below.

"Not much more than a year ago you pulled me out with my leg broke," Bob Ring said. "They had a time making the repairs."

"I won't forget. I was pretty scared."

"Fenton did what he could. Not many could do more."

The sun was almost gone, its light holding on the highest peaks.

"They tell me you came to be a fine player for those Spartans," Ring said. "Willie and I would like to see a game sometime."

"It's fun." Ty looked to make sure Ring wasn't kidding him. "It's just not serious." The sun had left a blush of color on the cliffs, as though within them they held some light of their own. "Like this."

18

Honeymoon

"Like a cow pissin' on a flat rock." Buck looked gloomily out at the summer downpour. It was Ty's fifth year of packing. They were camped with Miss Wright and her new husband at Danaher Meadows, which looked more like Danaher pond as the runoff filled it with pools, the trail now a stream.

"Bet the fishing's good." Ty came around from behind the cook tent with his shovel, his slicker dripping water. "Get that last tent ditched, I might turn Doc into a fisherman. Warm rain like this, they jump right in your creel."

"I'll ditch the damn tent. Angie's so keen on bakin' camp bread she don't even know I'm here." Buck put on his slicker and went out into the rain with Ty. "Come down like this once at White River. After I squashed my nose. Can't recollect if it was this steady."

"From what Fenton told me about that time, this is just a sprinkle."

Ty had placed them in a stand of timber well above the meadow. There was almost perfect drainage for the tents, but it was Ty's way to make sure. He felt even more responsible on this trip. Miss Wright had married the young doctor who'd seen Angie through the scarlet fever quarantine, and what she'd wanted more than anything else was a honeymoon in Ty's mountains—with Ty's friends. Her reasons mystified Ty, but he was more than willing. She'd come to mean a lot to him; he wanted to give her the best trip possible.

"Should we read a book each day?" he'd asked. "Study up for dinner?"

"None of that." She liked it that he could tease her. "No grammar." Her eyes grew earnest behind her lenses. "Just show me your mountains."

⌒⌒

By 1941 everyone knew Ty was Fenton's best packer, some said the best in all the Swan. And Alice Wright had grown more than fond of his quiet ways. He read every book she gave him, talked with her about them in his direct way. But she always sensed things withheld, unsaid. She'd even taken to going to his football games, surprised by the satisfaction he found in a sport so violent. It made her wonder about him, why he lost himself in some things so completely: being around his horses, working on his saddles, certain books. He had a way of disappearing into whatever he liked, making her think there was much to learn from that country that took him in so completely as soon as the snows melted.

She wanted her doctor to know Ty better too, hear how Ty put things, talked about his pack animals, his mountains. She wanted to see if Thomas found the same odd promise in this boy that she did.

"He likes Sherwood Anderson," she said on one of their walks. "Who would think some packer would like Sherwood Anderson?"

"Who is Sherwood Anderson?" Alice Wright had linked her arm through Thomas Haslam's, touching him so lightly yet completely it made him dizzy.

"He writes about people most of us hardly notice." She watched him watching her, needing her. "Pinched people. People with odd troubles."

She thought how both Ty and her doctor were drawn to people others overlooked. They just came at them from different directions. She wanted Ty to know Thomas too, understand all the good in him. She squeezed her doctor's arm, knowing that wasn't going to be easy, not with him as lost in her as he was. She turned to him now, taking pleasure in the way he looked at her, and told him about the people in Anderson's stories.

⌒⌒

Thomas Haslam was so smitten with Alice Wright his mind wouldn't leave her, despite how bewildered she made him. He still wasn't convinced she'd like a honeymoon of long hours in a saddle and cold nights in a tent. And he already knew the young packer—and liked him, had ever since the time Angie had knocked Buck through their bedroom window. He and Ty had sat on the steps long into that night considering what would have happened if Angie had cut Buck up with all those broken bottles.

"He'll bring Buck and Angie to help." Alice had seemed pleased just saying their names. "It will be so beautiful up there. Romantic. So . . . western."

"Western is right here in Missoula," Thomas told her. "And in Indian town, where we haven't money enough for inoculations. The people drunk half the time. . . . Eating the wrong things."

"The best of it may be up in those mountains." She took his hand. "Maybe not letting them stay in their mountains is where we went wrong."

"Maybe." The doctor felt himself surrendering. "It's just not the best place for what I have in mind."

"Oh, my." She put her hand to his face. "We'll have plenty of time for that." She touched his lips. "I'll make sure. We'll want lots of time for that."

He felt his need for her wash through him. "I just wish we didn't have to go into the mountains to find the time," he said.

Thomas Haslam had a hard time making sense of what Alice Wright did to him. She was a model of decorum at her school. Bull Trout was devoted to her, had her pour tea at school gatherings, serve cookies. At the faculty meetings she would pass bread warm from her oven, keep minutes in her perfect handwriting. Older teachers chose her for their special committees and studies. She volunteered for the most difficult tasks, deferring to her colleagues, offering her own ideas only when asked.

But all that propriety dropped away when she was alone with Thomas—on picnics, or in the car, or when she snuck into his room. Then she would touch him everywhere. Kiss him. Mock him. Swim naked with him in cold mountain streams.

"Wait until you can go inside me," she would say when they were back on their blanket, kissing and holding one another. "Just wait."

And she did make him wait, telling him she wanted to save only that one thing. He would feel sick with his need, wanting her so he would turn away, angry with himself, with her, with the wantonness that filled him.

He was a scientist to the bone. But he found nothing instructive about what she did to him, his obsession baffling him as much as the heartbreaking restraint that came over her just when they wanted one another more than life itself.

"We mustn't," she would say, her hair wild, her breathing heavy, pushing him away, reaching for her glasses. "We can't. Not yet."

He would hold his temples, wait for the throbbing to subside, so consumed understanding seemed impossible.

The night after the wedding they made love in the big guest bedroom at Cody Jo and Fenton's, coming together in such a rush it did little to settle him—a passion remaining that was hardly compatible with seven hours in a saddle, numbing baths in mountain water, freezing nights in a tent. He was thankful Cody Jo had sent a puffy double bedroll, thankful that Ty would set their tent a little apart each night. But his yearning was constant.

When the warm rain started in and the women went to making camp bread, he saw his chance. He got his books and took Alice's arm even as he heard what he dreaded.

"Do you need me to help with the baking?" Alice gave him a look, gently pulled her arm away. "I'm ready to help."

Angie waved a floury hand. "Take your cow-eyed man and go. He's bordering on desperate."

Horace Adams, in his rain gear, ready to fish the swollen river, enjoyed it. "Want to watch me put a fly where they can't resist?" Horace studied his flies. "Mostly pure science. You would take to it right off."

"No." Thomas's mouth was dry. "We'll be all right. Ty said he'd show me later." He held up his books. "Got reading."

"Well," Horace looked at the books before stepping into the rain. "Don't you two steam up them pages. Might be handy if we got to start the fire."

Thomas and Alice sat naked in the middle of their rumpled bedroll, books thrown aside. Alice held Thomas's flooded penis as his hand traced the soft line of her breast. There was no way in the world, he was sure, that a man could be happier. He was leaning to kiss her when they heard the sucking sound of a shovel, as though someone were digging under the tent. Alice pulled away, reached for her glasses.

"Ty?" she called out. "Is that you?"

"Should be." Even with the clatter of rain, Buck's voice made them jump. "Much as he loves ditchin'. But it ain't. He's already dug trenches from here to Texas." The shovel hit the tent wall and rattled the canvas.

"Now he ain't gonna be satisfied until I dig a canal around the two of you."

Alice smiled at Thomas, began to laugh. She looked so beautiful in her nakedness, her smile wide, her glasses misting, Thomas thought his heart might break.

"I'll come out there and help," he called out, resigned. "You shouldn't have to worry about our tent."

"You keep right on studyin' your books." Buck's voice was so clear Thomas thought he might be about to come in. "If you can read above this racket. Shovelin' is more along my line anyway. Read up for when my kids get sick again." Suddenly his voice came from the other side of the tent. "Or when Angie decides to whack me." Then there was only the steady rattle of rain.

Thomas began putting on his pants, picturing Buck out there in the downpour, leaning on his shovel, thinking.

"She does things so sudden, Angie does," Buck's voice finally continued. "When I was courtin' her, she wouldn't have anything to do with me until Sugar jerked his head and flatted my nose. Don't believe I looked good at all when I come out of the woods. But then it seemed she couldn't do enough for me. Worried over me and washed me up, and when I asked her to marry she couldn't of been sweeter.

"'Of course I will, Buck,' she says. 'You poor thing, you,' she says. I got busy and come up with the papers before she changed her mind. And that's when we got married. Maybe mashin' up my nose wasn't such a bad thing after all."

"You think it was the nose that won her over?" Thomas was in his rain gear standing there with Buck now, the rain finally letting up.

"Can't think of what else," Buck said, studying the doctor's face. "Surprised me as much as when she hit me with the bag of bottles." He started to shovel again, still thinking.

"There's been other times she surprised me," Buck added. "She ain't all that predictable."

19

Angie and Buck

Angie *wasn't* all that predictable. But she was a good mother and a good wife and she knew a man like Buck needed excitement. She just didn't like him to have it when she couldn't have some fun herself, which is why she made him sleep on the cot in the woodshed while she and the children were quarantined with scarlet fever.

Buck didn't like it. But there wasn't much he could do. When he got back with Fenton's new mules, Angie was already incarcerated.

"Sleep on that bed in the shed," she'd said from the window. "Doc Haslam says that'll do fine. I'll just knock on that wall each night so you'll miss me. . . . You can knock back so I'll know you're not hellin' around."

Buck was so disappointed he couldn't crawl into his own bed with his own Angie that the reality of the arrangement didn't come to him for two or three days. Each night she'd knock, and he'd knock back. "Good night, Angie," he'd say, and then he'd toss and turn through the night thinking of her—sometimes even thinking of Jeanie down at The Bar of Justice. After a few more nights he found himself thinking of Jeanie more than Angie, which is why he got Ty to come over and spend the night.

"When you hear her knockin'," he said. "Knock right back. Say good night right back too. Can't tell who's who through that wall anyhow."

Ty was too tired to argue. It was football season, and the minute he came out of the mountains they'd put him in the games. Mr. Trout had figured that if Ty started school that late each fall, they deserved to have him for a final semester, and this was it. By now the schoolwork was easy, at least compared to all those practices they put him through. His only worry was that he wouldn't wake up when he heard Angie knocking on the wall.

"Don't get in any fights, Buck," he said as Buck headed out. "Angie always seems to know."

But this time she didn't seem to know anything. When the knocking came, Ty woke up and knocked right back. And when she called out, Ty said his good night right back. A little before dawn, Buck was back himself, smelling of beer and tobacco and crawling into his sleeping bag.

"Jeanie says hello." Buck passed gas so sharply he sounded like one of Ty's mules going up a hill. "A fartin' horse'll never tire," he said. "A fartin' man's the one to hire." He rolled over and sighed. "Jeanie sure is a good old girl." He was asleep before Ty could tell him he thought so too.

Ty lay there and thought of Jeanie. He'd been back to The Bar of Justice a few times since that night with Spec. He'd danced with Jeanie, with Loretta too, when she wasn't too drunk. But he had not gone upstairs. Not that he had anything against it. He just didn't remember it being very satisfying. And most of the time when he was at The Bar of Justice he seemed to be getting Buck or Spec—or even Jasper—out of some scrape.

And one of the cheerleaders, now gone on to the university, had surprised him by how good she was to him. She was older and had a way of making things so natural and uncomplicated he got to looking forward to seeing her more and more. When they did see one another it was mostly her idea, Ty sometimes wondering if she weren't a little embarrassed that he was a packer. But she was so nice to him that he didn't let that trouble him. She even came down from the university and took him for drives into the country or to one of the diners out toward Bonner before kissing him and loving him in the big backseat of her father's car.

All of it gave Ty a good understanding of what Jeanie meant to Buck. He even slept in the woodshed twice more before the Butte game, which they played just before Angie's quarantine ended. John Lamedeer had graduated and the Spartans finally beat the Bulldogs, Ty catching a pass and running like a jumped deer to score the final touchdown.

Buck was there, so excited about Ty's run he almost knocked Horace over pounding him on the back. He went with Ty to the locker room, waited until Ty dressed and went back to Horace's with him to help with the chores.

"Bet you're wore out," he said finally. "All that runnin' and tacklin'."

Ty saw what was coming. He wanted to see how Buck would say it.

"After dinner you could slip down and rest up in the woodshed." Buck acted as though the idea had just struck him. "Course after the quarantine there won't be any need," he added. Ty closed the feed bin and waited.

"Hell, Ty," Buck said finally. "Truth is I won some money on that damn game. Thought I'd use it to try out some dance steps with Jeanie."

Buck was sitting on the bed drinking beer and listening to the radio when Ty got there, figuring he'd read himself to sleep. "Want one?" Buck reached into a laundry bag he'd filled with ice and beer and pulled one out for Ty. "Sure puts a song in your heart."

Ty could tell Buck was feeling his oats. He sipped at his beer and watched Buck slick his hair before putting on his hat. "I'm so tired I doubt I can finish this beer." Ty leaned back on the pillow. "Don't get too wild now. In a few days Angie'll want to show you some dance steps of her own."

Buck was two blocks away, the sack of beer slung over his shoulder, when what Ty said came back to him. He stopped and considered, a yearning for Angie coming over him so completely that before he knew it he was headed back for the house. The night was mild, and he felt so good about things he thought he might drink a beer as he walked, deciding instead to drink one with Angie while they talked through the window.

It wasn't until he'd rapped on the window that he realized Angie might ask some questions about his being in his best shirt with a sack of beer over his shoulder. He was frozen by that thought when the window opened and there was Angie, shushing him and smiling and looking pretty as a picture in her nightshirt. Before she could say anything to change his mood, he'd tossed the sack in and tumbled after it, rolling across the floor a few times.

"I got to missing you so much, Angie," he said, sitting up. "That I thought I'd bring you this beer."

"You dummy. I'm still in quarantine. What in the world are we gonna say to Doc Haslam?"

Buck opened a beer and gave it to her. "Tell him you put a song in my heart." Then they were tumbling on the bed, Angie shushing him to keep him from waking the kids, loving him and scolding him and loving him more.

"Better we don't tell him what the song is," Angie said.

When they were through Buck drank the beer and got more. They lay on the bed talking, Buck telling her about Ty's game and how Missoula had finally beaten the big kids from the mines. "Don't know why they call themselves bulldogs. More like oxes. Least when Ty ran right past the lot of them." He laughed, content with himself.

He didn't tell her that he'd won any money on the game, a fact that had almost slipped his mind, along with any thoughts of Jeanie or the girls at The Bar of Justice. He was comfortable where he was, and pleased—balancing a bottle of beer on his stomach as he talked.

"Angie," he said, smiling contentedly. "Just knock on that wall once."

"Why in the world would I knock on that wall?" Angie asked. "With you right here in my arms?"

"Give a knock." Buck took another sip of beer. "Won't do no harm."

"You are a silly one, Buck Conner." Angie gave the wall a few raps. "That satisfy you?" She was looking at him when three knocks came back. Buck grinned at her.

"Give a 'night night'," he said. "See what happens."

Angie looked confused. "Good night," she called out.

"Night, Angie," a muffled voice came back. It gave Buck such a laugh, he sprayed beer across the bed.

"Ain't that a stitch?" He was laughing so hard he had to hold the beer with both hands to keep it balanced on his stomach. Angie cracked him so hard she knocked it loose anyway. Buck looked at her, startled.

"Son of a bitch!" She jumped up from the bed and tripped over the bag of ice and bottles. "Bastard!" She picked up the sack and swung it.

Buck saw something had gone wrong. He grabbed his clothes, ducked the bag and reached the window just as she brought it around again, some of the bottles breaking as she knocked him through. He rolled away, clutching his clothes and realizing she was coming out after him.

Ty heard swearing and glass breaking and was running toward the corner of the house when Buck passed him going the other way, running crooked in his bare feet. "She's got the beer," he said, running past. Ty didn't have a chance to slow down before he turned the corner and hit Angie. She seemed to fly a little before coming down and rolling over the bottles. She began to cry and reached into the sack to throw a bottle off where Buck had disappeared.

"Should of known that reading light wasn't for him," she said as Ty helped her up. "Can't hardly get him through the Sunday comics."

Ty quieted her and put her back through the window to calm the children and call the doctor. After awhile she came out on the porch with some blankets and they sat drinking beer, keeping warm with the blankets, waiting for the doctor.

"Wish he could be more like you, Ty." Angie didn't seem to blame Ty at all. "Not so knot-headed." She cried a little, sipping her beer and lighting a cigarette. "You think I drove him right back to that Bar of Justice? Where those girls will patch him? Make over where he's hurt?"

"I didn't see any blood." Ty wanted to make her feel better, but it was hard. He saw things in such a straight line he was embarrassed even being around people who lied. But he looked at Angie and knew this was one those times it would help if he could think one up.

"It isn't what you think, Angie." Ty sipped his beer. "Buck is so good natured. He goes mostly for the companionship." He wished the doctor would show up.

"Companionship? Seems to me it's more like fornication."

"Not always. Lots of guys down there just like to kid each other around. You know how Buck takes to that." Ty looked for the doctor's headlights. "You know, Angie, I've never even seen him go upstairs."

Which was technically true, but skirted the many times Buck and Spec, egged on by Jasper, had talked about that very thing, the three of them trying to get a rise out of Ty, who tried not to think about their stories now.

"He misses you, Angie." He patted her shoulder. And that much was true. Everyone knew how much Buck missed Angie, though no one could predict what form the missing would take.

"Oh, Ty!" Angie hugged him, gave him a little kiss on the cheek. "You've always been a good man." She sighed, put her head on his shoulder. "Even when you was a boy." Ty saw tears running down her cheeks.

He had put his arm around her and was trying to think of something else to say when he saw the doctor's car pull up. He was so relieved he went across the yard to meet him, explaining that Buck and Angie had broken the quarantine. And now it looked like he had too.

Thomas Haslam listened, asking a question here and there but not nearly as upset as Ty thought he would be. "The communicable period is almost over, Mrs. Conner," he said. "I don't think drinking a little beer with Mr. Conner will be a problem. Unless you drank from the same bottle."

"I don't recall we did."

"You didn't use the same utensils, did you?"

"Well," Angie began to cry again. "You could say he used his and I used mine." She turned and went in the house, wiping at her eyes.

Thomas Haslam watched. Ty knew there was more he had to tell him. He fished around in the wet sack for a beer, offering one to the doctor.

"This'll take some explaining," he said.

They sat there for over an hour, talking and drinking the beer, the doctor asking questions about Buck and Angie, finding himself as interested in Ty as he was in them.

"Well," the doctor said finally, getting up to leave. "They are vigorous people. If I don't see them about the scarlet fever, I will about something else. I doubt any of it will do them in."

Ty watched him drive away, liking the direct way the doctor looked at things. He hoped he hadn't given him the wrong idea about Angie and Buck. The way Ty saw it, they were pretty much like the others up in the Swan.

Just more so.

20

The West

Ty stood in his slicker, watching Buck and the doctor as they talked, the rain letting up. Ty liked it that two people so different got on so well up here. And Buck and Thomas Haslam certainly were different. He remembered the look on the doctor's face when Buck told him why he'd broken the quarantine, the doctor questioning Buck as he looked him over for scarlet fever symptoms.

"Well, Doc," Buck had explained, "it's plain to see I'd take Angie over Jeanie, could I have her. Trouble was, I couldn't. Until I did. Hell, the reason I had her knock on that wall was to show how much I loved her."

Whatever other questions Thomas Haslam had seemed to drift away as he stood there, looking at Buck, considering.

But Ty could tell the doctor was drawn to Buck, see he was interested in Horace and Etta too, saw it when the doctor looked them over to make sure Ty hadn't passed any germs along. His enjoying them so was part of the reason Ty got them all to come along on the honeymoon trip. The other part was that Ty thought Miss Wright would have a lot more fun with Angie and Buck and Etta and Horace than she would with anyone else, especially those schoolteacher friends of hers.

Anyone else, that is, except Fenton and Cody Jo. He was sure Miss Wright would like them more than anybody. But they had other things to do: Cody Jo going back to Chicago for her Red Cross training, saying that if we weren't going to help those people in Europe now, we would certainly have to later; Fenton packing for the Forest Service, which counted on him more and more.

With Spec locked up in Deerlodge, that left Ty to run the pack station. He was managing, but there was a lot to manage. He had Buck to wrangle, and Gus Wilson ready to help if there were a need. He had Angie and Jasper taking turns at the cooking, even ready to work together. And he'd convinced the Murphys to handle the booking arrangements, knowing he'd have to spend most of his time until the snow fell in the saddle—even after they let Spec out.

He'd come out of the mountains for the wedding, and to make sure everything was ready. Miss Wright considered the trip his wedding gift, but to Ty it was much more. It was his way of thanking her for her books, her patience; for getting him into the right classes, making sure he had the right help, coming to his games, and being so nice to his friends. It was his thanks for her befriending Buck and Angie—even Jasper, who would stand straight as a lodgepole when she appeared, stammering and fussing until he could slip away and drink, Jasper being at a loss around schoolteachers. Cody Jo was the only one he could tolerate. And even Cody Jo left him edgy.

☞

To Ty it was a wonderful trip. Each time Etta and Angie chased Alice Wright out of the cook tent, it was a chance to show her his country. It was as though he could share his own literature with her, things no book of hers could explain. He hadn't ever wanted anyone to like the mountains the way he wanted her to like them. And when he saw her appreciation was tied to the doctor's, he felt the same way about him.

That was why he took them out each night after dinner, showed them where his horses were grazing or how the moonlight danced on the rapids; why he took them on detours from the trail to get special views; why he got them up at dawn each morning and put fly rods in their hands. It was hard for Ty to think of anyone who wouldn't get excited about fishing when cutthroats were rising as they were on that trip.

Except, Ty had to admit, the doctor. He soon saw that the doctor's appreciation of the country turned mostly on their camping. "How many miles will we travel?" he would ask each morning. "When will we be in camp? Good places for the tents? The kitchen? Our tent?"

At the end of each day Ty would watch Thomas Haslam wash the dust away, seek out Miss Wright and slip off to their tent. In the years to come he would wonder why he hadn't understood the doctor's need for Miss Wright right away, how important it was to Miss Wright that he had that need. He guessed that to him Thomas Haslam had still been too much their doctor, Miss Wright still too much his teacher.

But in its way it worked. Certainly Thomas Haslam and Alice came to love the high country as few others did: Alice taken by its beauty;

Thomas learning from it, liking the order lifting above the chaos of deadfalls and avalanches and huge troughs carved by glaciers. And they both learned from watching Ty, seeing how at one he was with it—a natural part of a landscape more imposing than any god mankind could invent. In his own way Ty showed them where the waters begin.

꒰⸝⸝◜◝⸝⸝꒱

None of this was in any of their heads that rainy day in Danaher Meadows as Ty shucked his slicker and handed the fly rod to the doctor, pleased the rain had finally stopped.

"Go on, Doc." Buck was all encouragement. "They'll be plump as ticks."

"Ever occur to Buck that trout may not be all a man's soul requires?" the doctor asked, following Ty to the river.

"That might throw him off." Ty pointed to a slick behind a rock. "With the trout rising this way."

It took three tries, but the first time the fly touched the slick a big cutthroat lifted, twisting in the air before slapping back and running. The doctor moved down the bank, playing him, his mind now only on the river, the fish, the rod, the movement of water.

He caught fish for half an hour before they quit rising, the sun out now and Ty relaxing on the bank, pleased with the concentration Thomas Haslam gave his fishing.

"Let's slip out and check the stock," Ty said. They'll be out from under the timber now."

"I'll hang around camp—try to hide from Buck."

"He's persistent. But he's interesting. Give him that."

"All of you are." Thomas Haslam looked at the high ridges. "You have this country. It makes a difference." His eyes came back to Ty. "What will you do when this war comes, Ty? How will you leave this?"

"I'll go." Ty handed him the creel, full of fish. "I've been talking with Cody Jo. She keeps up on what they've done." He was moving again, picking up a nose bag, sticking a lead-line in it, heading out to check his mules.

"I'll go."

The last day the sky was blue as china, the country spread out below them in mottled greens—forest and meadow darkened by shadows from the peaks. Ty had them on the pass before noon, at the corrals by three, Fenton there to greet them. Soon they were saying their good-byes, picking through the gear for their duffle, telling Fenton about the trip, thanking Ty, who still had much to do. He and Fenton were taking Forest Service people in the next day, and then Ty had a last fishing party before hunting season—when Spec would be back.

"Well, we've seen it," Alice said to her doctor. "The West—no fences or stop signs or roads. Hardly any trails."

"This was here before anyone thought to call it 'The West.'" Thomas Haslam put his arm around her, loving the touch of her. "Before anyone. I think your 'West' is these people."

He watched Fenton and Ty as they grained the mules, checked them for sores, Ty talking to them, keeping the nose bag away from Loco until he was sure Cottontail got her share.

"What makes them may be this country." He held her closer. "But it's these people. I think it's something inside them—that's 'The West.'"

War (1941–1945)

Fenton had fixed Bob Ring's leg, Ty thought, and now Cody Jo had fixed his—helped him dance so he would know he could walk.

21

Army Mules

They let Spec out for hunting season. Fenton knew the judge, who worked it out so that Fenton and Tommy Yellowtail were the parole officers. The stipulations were that Spec keep working for Fenton—and stay away from The Bar of Justice. The judge couldn't say that; The Bar of Justice wasn't supposed to be. But everyone understood. Tommy Yellowtail brought Spec directly to the pack station, not even stopping at the Seeley Lake Bar. Fenton gave him a horse and a pack mule. Two days later Spec was in Lost Bird Canyon with Ty and Jasper, setting up the hunting camp, listening to Jasper's stories, finding out what Ty had come to know about the woods.

Ty saw he was quieter, but he saw too how much pleasure Spec took in the mountains. He would be gone before dawn, checking the meadows, the game trails—reading the country. Then he would be back, helping Ty set up wall tents or lashing the lodgepoles into a corral, liking it that Ty didn't want to use nails anymore, if he could help it. Ty had decided to be like mules crossing frozen ground: he'd leave no tracks. Spec liked that—Ty wanting the country to stay the way he found it.

And Spec liked the camp, the same one his father and Fenton had found years ago when they'd forced their way through the canyon below. That was the one time his father had considered leaving Fenton, afraid Fenton was so smitten with Cody Jo he'd lost his judgment. It wasn't that Tommy didn't understand. The young braves were always doing hare-brained things when they were moonstruck. He just didn't like the prospect of getting out of all the trouble a moonstruck Fenton could cause.

Spec didn't dwell on those old stories, but Ty saw he took to the camp as much as his father had. He would slip away each evening after

Jasper fed them, sometimes not coming back until dark and then staying late by the fire, letting the flames tell their story. Only once did he say anything about the government man he'd almost killed—or the big bouncer he'd waited for outside. And what he said, he said only to Ty.

"Wish I'd hit him harder." Spec's voice startled him. Ty was graining his mules in the hidden glade above camp. He didn't think anyone else knew it was there, yet here Spec was, coming to them so silently the animals didn't stir—until his voice broke the stillness.

"Which one?" Ty went back to his feeding. "I heard you came close to doing them both in, though they say that bouncer came out worse."

Spec rubbed Loco's neck, pleased the mule had begun to trust him.

"Both . . . I guess."

Ty was surprised. There was no anger at all. Just matter of fact. He moved the nose bag to Loco, feeding him while Spec rubbed.

"See any sign? Fenton says a big grizzly hangs out below."

"Watched him. Red-coated. He watched me too. . . . There's others above. We'll hunt there, leave that roan bear be."

They left the mules and worked their way down to the camp together, Spec talking about getting someone to take care of his father after he enlisted. It seemed to Ty that Tommy Yellowtail was the only thing outside the mountains Spec cared about when he was in the mountains.

It was different when he was out of them.

They moved the camp three times before hunting season was over, Ty cleaning everything up before moving on, storing his trimmed lodgepoles where even Spec would have a hard time finding them. Spec and Jasper looked to Ty now for what to do, when to do it, the two of them staying in the back-country the whole of hunting season, not leaving the woods at all until Ty pulled everything out. But each time Ty went out to get a party or to move a fire crew or to resupply, they were anxious to hear the news.

"Cody Jo and Fenton don't think we can stay out of it," he told them. "They about flattened London. And they've sunk another ship."

"Them army people will likely object to an Indian with a record." Spec poked at the fire. "But that judge said he'd fix it. If I wanted. Maybe we'll be settin' up one of them military tents next year."

"Quit that talk." Jasper, sipping his cooking sherry, didn't want to hear it. "You sure as hell don't want to be in no war."

But to Spec and Ty they were as good as in it already. They didn't so much talk about what they would do as about what was happening—reading the magazines Fenton and Cody Jo sent in, looking at the pictures in *Life*. And Cody Jo made it all too real: families pushed from their homes, ships sunk and sailors drowned, tanks rolling through the cities.

It was a late fall, and with no football to worry about Ty didn't move them out of the mountains until November. He went right to work, pulling shoes, patching, oiling leather. Spec made sure his cousins would look after Tommy then headed for town to join.

"Think I'll become one of them marines," he said, stopping to see Ty on his way. "That judge says they go at things more direct."

"You'll be good in whatever you join. They'll see what you can do when they give you a rifle."

"Maybe. Hope there's not too much paradin' around."

Ty felt blue as he watched Spec drive away. He wasn't as sure of things as Spec was. And he'd heard the marines took a lot of chances. Spec didn't need to be encouraged in that department.

Two weeks later Ty signed up, with the army. Fenton tried to convince him to take over the Forest Service packing, saying it would make him draft-exempt, that he could go to the university and play football just like Bull Trout wanted him to. But he could see that Ty was going to join. And there was a part of him that thought he should.

Not all of him, though. He knew it would be a different Ty who came back. If he came back at all. And he liked this one, liked his strength and judgment and gentle way with animals—with everyone, except on the football field. He liked the way Ty took to the mountains, moved through the roughest country with no fuss, making decisions each step of the way but never fretting, just doing it—finding feed for his animals and shelter for his people, letting them ease into the country he'd come to love.

∽

Ty signed up on a Wednesday and was scheduled to leave the next Monday. A band was at the Elkhorn, and Fenton decided they'd have a farewell dinner. Cody Jo got Etta and Horace to come along, and at the last minute Angie and Buck showed up.

It was a good time. They danced and ate and drank and danced some more. After awhile it seemed to Ty everyone he knew was there.

He saw the cheerleader dancing with the man she'd been dating at the university. And Bernard Strait was at a table with Bob Ring and Wilma. Bernard was high enough up in the Forest Service to be draft-exempt. He danced all the slow numbers with Wilma, Wilma waving to Ty and Fenton from the dance floor and not looking at all like a young girl anymore.

Ty felt light-headed from all the beer, but the music was so good and he was dancing so much that he just kept on drinking. He danced to "Sing Sing Sing" with Angie, who bounced around until they were both out of breath. He danced to "Blueberry Hill" with Etta, who got embarrassed, saying that music was for Cody Jo, not for her.

He finished it with Cody Jo, and they stayed on the floor to dance to "Sunrise Serenade." Ty thought he might be dancing with air, even though Cody Jo was right there in his arms. After awhile he quit thinking about the dancing, just let the music move them.

When they got back to the table Bob Ring was there, and Wilma, stopping to say hello before they left.

"Ty's joined," Fenton said. "Better give him a good-bye dance, Willie."

"You've been drinking," she said, as they started to dance.

"I have . . . I just may do some more."

Then they were dancing to "Indian Summer," and instead of saying what she was about to say, Wilma put her head on Ty's shoulder and gave in to the music. For a minute Ty thought he was dancing with Cody Jo, but Wilma was even slimmer, and for the first few steps she seemed a little tentative. Cody Jo was never tentative.

"You don't look like you did when you were leading Apple over that snow," he said.

She leaned back, looking at him, her eyes pools of blue in the smoky light. "No." Her face came back against his shoulder. "I guess I don't."

They danced again, and then again, Ty seeing that Bernard was watching, and then that Bernard had gone over to join Buck and the others.

When they came back to the table, Fenton had a woman with a camera there. She wore a shiny dress, her hair piled up on her head.

"Let's get a picture," Fenton said. "Be awhile before we're together like this again."

⌒⌒

The next day the Japanese bombed Pearl Harbor. Everyone gathered at Etta and Horace's to hear the radio reports, listening through the day and into the night. Ty finally gave up and went to bed, but no sleep came. Everything he'd imagined about joining had suddenly changed. He supposed he'd changed too.

He still felt that way as they called out his name at the loading dock. Cody Jo, not looking so certain about things now, gave Ty a long hug. She swallowed back tears as Fenton gave Ty a razor that came apart and fit perfectly into a small leather case. Miss Wright showed up too, gave him a gift-wrapped package. He put it in his grandfather's kit bag with the razor and some sandwiches Etta had made.

Fenton stayed with him on the train even as it began to move. "Don't let them make you do something foolish." He looked at Ty and for the briefest moment hugged him. "Don't go gettin' yourself killed."

It was awkward—Ty was almost as tall as Fenton now. But Fenton was gone before Ty had time to realize he was embarrassed. He watched Fenton swing off the train, jogging with it a few steps before dropping back. He leaned out to wave good-bye, but Fenton had already turned back toward Cody Jo, looking tired to Ty. But then he'd looked more and more tired each time Spec and Ty had talked about enlisting.

Ty ate one of the sandwiches and opened the package Miss Wright had given him. It was a leather box, not much bigger than a pocket bible, with a little drawer. "T.H." was stamped in the leather, and when he opened the drawer a music box played a few bars of "Red River Valley." On a card in the drawer, in her perfect hand, she had written "For important things." Ty dug around in his kit bag and found Fenton's razor. He put it in the drawer, listening to the music box one more time before he put it away.

They changed trains in Denver, then stopped and started through the night, reaching the training camp at dawn. A big sergeant lined them up and said things about turning chicken shit into chicken salad. "Play ball with me," he barked, "I play ball with you. Don't play ball with me, I stick it up your ass and break it off."

It was like that all the way through basic. When Cody Jo sent the picture, Ty had to go into the bathroom after taps to look at it. It was a good picture, but it seemed to Ty it had been taken in another life. He was smiling at the camera, looking silly, he thought. On one side of him was Cody Jo, laugh wrinkles showing even though she was hardly smiling at all. On the other side was Wilma, serious and pretty and a little sad. Horace was next to her. On the other side, next to Cody Jo, were Bob Ring and Bernard, who was looking at Wilma. In back were Fenton and Etta and Angie and Buck, Angie mugging for the camera, Buck's arm across her shoulders. Fenton was next to Etta, looking even taller than usual, more sober than the rest.

He was looking at Ty.

They kept them so busy through basic training Ty was surprised he learned anything. But he did, winding up in charge of one of the squads. After basic they made him a corporal, and after he filled out a questionnaire they shipped him to Colorado to work with the mules of a mountain-combat division.

Everyone was surprised the army had sent them a man who knew about mules, but they put him to work right away. He tried to teach the men to be quiet around the animals, not to yell and swear and frighten them. But it wasn't easy. Most of the men were from cities. They wanted to drive the mules like cars. And to Ty the army manuals for packing had the loads too high, sometimes with the heaviest piece of equipment highest. Ty wanted to lay it all out and pack again, his way. But the lieutenants said to·follow the manuals. So Ty did, but it seemed to him like rolling a rock uphill.

The mules were good though, big and leggy. After walking them around on level ground for a few weeks, the soldiers led them up a railroad bed to Pikes Peak, two men for each mule—one leading, another behind, Ty ranging up and down the line trying to keep everything balanced.

A colonel waited at the summit. "Think we can do that in combat, soldier? Get ammunition through the mountains like that?"

"Maybe. If you got a railroad bed to walk up and time to rebalance these packs," Ty said. "Wouldn't make any bets along a mountain trail."

The colonel was surprised. "What the hell did you do before this war?"

"Packed mules," Ty said.

Ty learned that the colonel was the cavalryman, Jeb Walker. His mule regiment was being called the last chance for the horse cavalry. The rest of the cavalry was still at Fort Riley, using tanks and half-tracks and little jeeps instead of horses.

Ty didn't know any of that that morning on Pikes Peak, though it wouldn't have changed a thing. It was easy to see they were using too many men to pack too few mules. And packing them wrong.

But the army wasn't ready to give up on their mountain-combat experiment yet. Ty's battalion boarded trains and headed for the Hunter Liggett maneuvers in California. Jeb Walker had convinced them to test his mules against the new vehicles they claimed could climb anything a mule could.

As soon as they had their tents lined up and the encampment established, he called Ty in. "Look." He showed Ty a picture of a Cossack firing at a German tank across his fallen horse, snow everywhere. "Horses and that miserable Russian winter turned the Germans back."

"Take a lot of trucks to bring feed enough to get us through a winter like that." Ty didn't like the picture. The horse was frozen.

"Listen, Hardin." Suddenly Walker was all business. "Three nights from now we'll get an objective. Those motorized troops will have the same one. Do whatever you want with your mules. Pack how you want. Just get there first." He looked out at the coastal range lifting behind the rows of tents. "I believe mules can do what those vehicles can't."

That night Ty let the mules off the picket lines to graze. The young officers didn't like it, but the word was out. Jeb Walker had made up his mind. This man Hardin could do it his way.

Rain came in that night. By morning it wasn't draining away from the tents anymore. Ty found other places for them, higher, where the runoff was good. No more neat lines of tents, but no water in them either. The men began looking to Ty for direction, and he got them to help him set up a big fly where he could rebalance the pack loads. He worked all that day and into the night, balancing, explaining, rearranging.

The rain didn't stop until the morning before the march. Ty caught up the mules and put them on the picket lines. He had them brushed and saddled by the time Walker came with his maps.

"It's twenty-two miles to that ridge, a three-thousand-foot climb," Walker said. "Can we do it?"

"Hooves have more purchase than tires. And mules don't break down," Ty said. "But it's awful wet. I wish we had a bell mare."

The colonel walked out ahead with his staff, all in combat gear. Ty put the mules in short strings, a few men assigned to stay with each. But the entire troop had to get to the ridge and deploy their equipment. The other men fell in behind, all knowing it was going to be a long night, only a few thinking they'd make the ridge by dawn, if at all.

The rain had stopped but the footing was bad, the men struggling through mud churned up by the mules. After two miles most had dropped out of sight, and Ty's mules had overtaken the colonel's staff. He stopped, gave his mules a breather as he untied the short strings, setting each mule free, telling the men still with him not to worry if they couldn't keep up.

There was moonlight, but it didn't help—the trail was like grease. Soon they slid into a dark swale and ran into Jeb Walker. "Can't get my men up the other side of this," Walker said. "Too slick."

"Mules might make it." Ty's mules were sliding down into each other. "But they'll be stopped soon. We need to get off this trail to where no one's been." He looked at the map under Walker's flashlight. "Maybe we can travel up the ridges. Stay out of these runoffs."

On the map they located a shoulder angling out above them, steep in places but showing a route all the way up to the ridge.

"If we can get onto it through this brush," Ty was already turning, pulling his lead mule back out of the draw, "we might follow it to the top. Bound to be better than this."

⌒⌒

There was a hint of light in the east as Jeb Walker came out onto the fire break that ran along the ridge's spine. His uniform was torn. He was caked with mud. But he was there. He watched Ty rig a picket line and start unpacking, taken by the soldier's steadiness, surprised to see him produce a feed bag and grain each mule.

"Didn't have to repack a one." He looked at Ty, satisfied.

"We were lucky. Had good mules."

"Damned if that one didn't pull me up here. If you hadn't told me to grab his tail, I'd be down there with the rest." Walker looked at the picketed mules. "Why the hell didn't he kick me back down the mountain?"

"Had other things to think about," Ty said. "Like not gettin' in a bind himself. Mules know. They pull a lot of folks out of a tight."

"You like these mules, don't you?" The colonel enjoyed the tall soldier. "They made it. It's my troops that can't get up the damn mountain."

"These are fine mules," Ty said. "And those are good men. But in this country four legs do better than two."

"You're here, aren't you?"

"Someone had to bring the mules."

They looked out over the steep country, the ravines dark with wet.

"Sure isn't the way I thought I'd be fighting this war." Ty turned to the colonel. "Pulling mules up a ridge they got no reason to climb."

"You'll have your war. Maybe even with these mules."

Then they heard the whine of motors lifting and falling, then lifting again.

"They got here." Walker looked at Ty. "How the hell did they do that?"

They saw the lights coming along the ridge, stopping down the firebreak, the men climbing out, looking at the mules. The captain in the lead jeep double-timed up to Jeb Walker and saluted, as surprised to see the mules standing there as Walker was to see the trucks.

"You got here, sir." The captain looked at the colonel's torn uniform. "Looks as though you fought your way."

"We did. This soldier brought these mules where my men couldn't go." He looked tired to Ty, still in charge but no longer so determined. "Damned if I know how he did it."

They learned that the trucks had been driven through the night, going two hundred miles around the designated ridge to find a graveled road that approached from the back. They had fixed flats and made repairs as they went and still arrived at dawn, their men fresh, their equipment dry.

c⌐੭

On the train back the colonel sought Ty out. "You beat them, Hardin. But those bastards won. They've decided there isn't anything over there we can't get to with those trucks and jeeps—and those damn tanks."

"We might work mules to death to keep up that pace," Ty said. "I'd rather risk the vehicles."

"Maybe you're right." The colonel sounded resigned. "Maybe we're all finished with horses and mules. Except for show. For little girls and rich men. If we can feed and equip our troops better with those goddamned vehicles, that's what we'll use."

The train was winding its way back through a deep gorge in the Rockies. Ty looked at the canyon dropping below them, cliffs climbing up to high peaks on the other side.

"I don't believe we're through with them." Ty looked back at Walker. "Give them enough time and they can get you into a different kind of country . . . up where you can see."

Walker was gone before he finished. Ty watched him move down the car, talking to his sergeants, encouraging his men, giving his troops what he knew he had to give them. Ty figured if they had to fight a war, it wasn't a bad thing to have a man like Jeb Walker in charge—a man willing to try something new, if something new was best for his men.

22

Wounds

They made Ty a sergeant before the division went overseas. He had his own squad now, and he'd watched Jeb Walker enough to know how important it was to keep his men cheerful. That wasn't easy on the troopship. He hated to go below to do his inspections, the men sleeping on canvas racks, duffel-bags jammed around them or thrown in the aisles. Each night he checked on them before making his way up to the partial shelter of an anti-aircraft station. It was cold and miserable, but there was air. He would wrap himself in his blanket and sit, wondering if the passes were open, if Fenton had the mules shod, if Cody Jo was listening to the same music they heard on the ship's radio. He got little sleep, nodding off only now and then but at least free of the crowding, the complaining. He got sick only once, throwing up all night before forcing himself below for morning inspection.

He tried not to think about the mountains, but he craved openness so much it was hard not to. The men, edgy as bears, grumbled and snapped at one another. The smells of bodies and Cosmoline and tobacco, the creaking of the ship, the clamminess of the hold and the constant wet of the winds made it a kind of hell. He wondered if the other men, taken up by their poker games and pinups and stories of weekend passes, had the same yearning for quiet that he had.

The men came to him for things, liking his quiet ways. They would choose him for different contests with the ship's crew, tests his years of packing helped him win without much fuss. He knew knots, could tie them quickly; he understood balance and was able to hold the course longer with his surprising strength. One day the big Greek bosun's mate was testing the soldiers, standing face to face with one after the other, a broom handle held high above his head. They would twist at it, straining for only a moment before the big man would turn it on them, laughing, his height and great strength too much for them. They came for Ty, bragging away their boredom, placing bets, dismissing his reluctance.

Ty took the handle and was startled by the power of the smiling Greek, the man's bulk massive against Ty's leanness—the two equal in height but that, and hands hardened by ropes, the only things the same. Ty stopped the twist before the bosun could start his turn. Now it was the sailor who was surprised, Ty's spare frame carrying no suggestion of such strength.

The mess call came and went. Still the two held one another off, the men leaving and returning to watch and, high on the bridge, Jeb Walker watching too. Ty thought he could hold on no longer when the bosun, suddenly weary, gave way, the handle turning at last and Ty locked to it so completely he found it hard to loosen his hold.

"You're a skinny bastard." The big sailor wiped sweat from his face. "We'll try it when I'm fresh."

He was a peacetime stevedore from the Jersey docks, his strength a part of the ship's lore. Word went out, and with more days still at sea Ty took to avoiding him, staying clear of them all. It wasn't so much that he feared reprisal, he just didn't want any more of it, even if his hands were working again—and they were bad, the calluses torn from the flesh.

But his men wanted more, liking the betting; the sailors wanted more too, wanted their money back. It gave them things to talk about. Ty liked that even less. It seemed the wrong way to keep the men from getting blue.

To Jeb Walker it was another matter. "See you surprised that big sailor." He stopped to talk with Ty as Ty waited in the long mess line that wound up and down the ship's ladders.

"He was already tired, Colonel. I was lucky."

"Lucky? Maybe. Maybe not. You won. Good for the troops."

But Ty understood how lucky he'd been. The man's strength had come as a shock. He doubted Fenton ever had such power. He needed a week for his hands to heal. He figured the bosun's mate just needed a few hours' rest.

Only later did it come to him that Jeb Walker knew more about it than any of them. At least he knew what to do. He filled their last days with so many inspections and drills there was little time for anything except getting ready. The work kept Ty from feeling so lonely, and it ruled out a rematch. For that Ty was thankful.

⌒⌒

They arrived to find Le Havre reduced to rubble, beaten down by the Allies coming in, the Germans falling back. The people looked as worn as their city, as though something deep within them was gone. But there was no time to linger over that; Walker moved them too quickly out into the pock-marked countryside. What they saw wasn't good: farmhouses shelled, dead horses bloating, tank routes churned deep through abandoned fields.

Their days filled with moving and bivouacking and moving again, the big guns firing over them. Walker pushed them hard toward the oily smoke that rose always from somewhere out of sight. They moved in behind the pounding, rarely seeing Germans until suddenly they were their prisoners, their youth showing through dirt, deep weariness, fear. To Ty they looked more like scared boys than the fighting men in the training films. He was troubled to see anyone in such a state. His men were surprised by his patience, which broke only once, with German officers making demands, insistent and haughty in their fear. He turned away, let his men prod them in with the rest, curse them more than the rest.

He had three squads now, the responsibility heavy. Day after day they would move on, sometimes deployed to move down lanes and across torn fields. But mostly they moved by truck, even by rail, until they reached another front and moved into position, the men counting on Ty for their safety, for finding them cover, shelter. They went north of Paris and then dropped south again. Always working east, always toward the Rhine.

The shelling from their big guns was constant, and when the return fire came in, they took their own casualties, Ty's squads staying intact but having to bring others out, patching the torn bodies themselves until the corpsmen arrived. They began to take more prisoners—boys, frightened and wary even when Ty's men gave them food from their own rations.

In December the German tanks came at them hard. They pulled back and dug in, holding on until their own tanks came up to give them relief, Walker coming in behind them, pleased with Ty's men, where Ty had placed them, that he'd had no wounded.

"Think about taking on more men, Hardin." He pulled Ty aside. "We keep losing these damn ninety-day wonders."

They were having coffee in their bulky canteen cups, the colonel's driver keeping it warm with lines from his jeep's radiator.

"It's enough keeping mine alive." Ty shook his head.

"Don't cave in on me, Hardin." Walker looked at him. "We need you."

Ty watched the colonel move off to the next entrenchment, thinking how much the man gave of himself. He supposed he should be thankful, but most of all he just yearned for an end to it. He wanted to see the late sun on a Montana peak, wanted his men back in their homes. He even wished it would end for the colonel, though he had a hard time thinking what he would be like without these men to worry about—without this war to fight.

By January the Germans began pulling back again, but seemed to begrudge every foot. Walker's troops kept pressing, moving through the winter and into early spring to cross the Rhine at last. They were joined there by a battalion of black tankers, men trained to move fast and glad to have the colonel's troops riding on their big tanks. The men camped together in the barns and taverns and little stores that were still standing, then moved on again, the big guns preparing the way as they pushed on, weary beyond considering but buoyed up by the farmers and timid children and townspeople who dared to welcome them.

They turned farther south, getting rest in a village hardly marked by the war, glad to settle in and get clean as they waited for the mess tents and supply trucks that would give them hot food and fresh clothing. Mail. News. They wanted to know what was happening at home, in Washington, in the Pacific—even where they were. They'd long ago learned that news from the rear was more accurate than anything they could learn right there in the middle of it.

Ty got two letters from Cody Jo and one from Wilma. Cody Jo included one Special Hands had sent, asking her to forward it. It was from out in the Pacific, but it was too cut up by censors to know where. "We've been gone for ____ days," it said. "It looks like it'll be ____ before we get to ____." And then there were some things about hot weather and how he missed The Bar of Justice. That was all. Short as it was, it was a long letter for Spec.

Cody Jo wrote that there was too much to do at the pack station for her to go with the Red Cross, though she was still training the others. She told him about Buck and Angie and Smoky Girl. She wrote about everything she could think of—telling a funny story about the Adamses, even filling him in on the squabbles the Wilson brothers were having. She said some things about politics too, but the censor had cut most of that out.

Fenton had added a P.S. to her letter. "Don't get your ass in a sling," he wrote. "Miserable to pack with your ass in a sling."

Wilma wrote about the university, the courses she was taking, how the football team had done badly since most of the players enlisted. She wrote about the "Hit Parade" and the songs they were playing. She liked "Do Nothin' Till You Hear from Me" and "I'll Be Seeing You," but her favorite was "I'll Get By." She said she was sending a box of brownies and they all missed him and she hoped he'd write. The censor had hardly touched her letter. Ty guessed she'd written it so there wouldn't be much to worry about.

He read all the letters a second time. And then he read them again, thinking about all the things Spec had taught him about the woods, how pretty Wilma had looked that night in Missoula. Each time he read them he felt more blue. It wasn't so much because he missed them as because the letters reminded him of what it was like to be free of noise and commotion and fear—the worry that one of your men might stick his neck out where he shouldn't.

He wanted to know what the weather was like in the high country, whether Fenton had put shoes on the mules, how soon it would be before they could get over the passes. He missed going over the passes, going into a country so untouched it had its own way of keeping you alive.

"I've 'liberated' us some kegs of beer," one of the sergeants announced, saying no one was to drink too much. The tankers and Walker's men were enjoying it on the playing field of the village school. A football turned up and a game started, the players tackling each other happily before taking themselves out for more drink. Ty's men were trying to get something going against the tankers, who were fast and flamboyant, pleased with the beer and the smell of food cooking.

Ty drank some beer as he watched the game. He saw no one was bothering to keep score and soon found himself in it, enjoying it just the way he had back in Missoula. He scored one touchdown, catching a pass thrown across the field and surprising them with his speed. They got the ball again, Ty running with a short pass when he ran into something so solid he thought he'd hit a boulder in the South Fork.

A tanker helped him up. "That was Otis Johnson." The man watched Ty try to clear his head. "He's regular army. Shouldn't fuck with that man."

Otis Johnson brought two canteen cups of beer over to where Ty was sitting. He gave one to Ty and they drank together. Ty was afraid all his men were a little drunk. He thought he might be too. But he knew he felt safe here, safer than he'd felt since Le Havre—and more relaxed.

Otis Johnson didn't seem drunk at all.

"Hit you a little hard." He looked at Ty somberly. "Didn't want my men lettin' you run around so quick. I make it a point for them to be quicker."

"Gave me a thunk." Ty was enjoying his drink. "Haven't been hit like that since the hay bales landed on me." He took a long swallow of beer. "It was fun playing again." He laughed a little. "You reminded me you don't always get to run where you want."

Otis Johnson broke into a smile. "I try to teach my son that." He shook his head. "But I don't think he learns so good."

Jeb Walker's jeep pulled up and the colonel got out, looking around at the soldiers gathered in groups as they drank the beer, the football game diminished now to a few men throwing the ball around.

The sergeant who had found the kegs stepped up, saluting smartly.

"We uncovered rations in the town brewery," he said, his arm snapping back to his side. Ty enjoyed how serious they were when reporting to the colonel. "It was provide some here or risk getting it requisitioned, sir."

Jeb Walker returned the salute. "See you solved that problem." He looked at the men, who were smoking, laughing as they drank and waited for the big dinner. He looked back at the sergeant, his face showing nothing.

"Just take it slow," he said finally. "Don't want them too sentimental."

He turned and saw Otis Johnson, who had left Ty and was saluting the colonel himself.

"Is there anything the colonel needs?" Otis Johnson's voice was so soft Ty could barely hear him.

"Otis Johnson!" Ty had never seen the colonel so pleased. "Sergeant Otis Johnson." He was shaking Johnson's hand now, smiling, Otis Johnson smiling too.

"Hardin," the colonel said. "This man is the best horse soldier in the United States Cavalry." He turned back, looking at Otis Johnson. "Hardin knows horses. Mules too. Might know more about mules than you."

"It's tanks now, Colonel," Otis Johnson said. "Tanks at Riley."

"Yes. And it's infantry for Hardin. But what you two know best is shod and has four feet. Never forget that."

Four days later Ty saw Johnson again. He was giving his rations to the half-dead skeletons reaching out to him at Gunskirchen Lager. Ty's men had moved in on the camp fast, trying to feed and clothe what was left of the stick-figures who clutched at them. But Johnson's tank was there first, Johnson speaking to them, telling them things were all right now, his voice gentle, his eyes unbelieving. The smell of the camp was everywhere—human waste and rot and death lifting from the ground, the buildings. Ty covered his nose and mouth with a hand and watched Johnson surrender himself to the clutching forms—his face tortured, baffled.

Two days later there was Johnson again. Ty's men—the smell of Gunskirchen Lager still with them—were calling in their own artillery to disable a lone German tank fleeing the Russians and panicked into firing as Ty's men blocked its retreat. But it was to the Americans the Germans wanted to surrender. Ty knew it, understood it. He was moving to call off the strike even as the round came in. He saw the German's head poke up from the hatch, arms raised, saw him disappear in the blast as Johnson's tanks rumbled in to capture what was left. Only then did Ty realize he was no longer standing, no longer could stand, the wet soaking his pants and running into his boot was his own blood—realize that he was not hurt so much as sick, sweating, and cold all at once.

And then Johnson was there, tightening a tourniquet across his thigh, swearing in a singsong, soothing voice as he pulled Ty free from the rubble around him. Johnson twisted the tourniquet still tighter, pressing on the ooze below it, pulling something away. Ty felt nothing, just the suck and the release of something coming free.

"Ours." Johnson had it in his hand, the soft swearing stopping as he studied it, wiped away the blood. "I thought so."

They took Ty to the field hospital, where they probed for more and sewed him up, the stitches neat and even. They gave him morphine and told him to sleep. That he would be all right.

When he woke a Red Cross volunteer was there. They'd brought his pack in and she'd found Alice Wright's music box. He'd carried it all the way across Europe, keeping Fenton's razor in it, using it when he had a chance.

"Shall I give a shave?" The woman held the box, her face kindly. She looked solid and permanent in the blocky British uniform. "You're a lucky one, y'know. You'll be on your way home now."

She opened the drawer for the razor. The tinkle of "Red River Valley" lifted and Ty found himself crying. He looked away, tried to stop it.

"There, there. You'll soon be home." Her voice seemed to bring more tears. She lathered and shaved him while he fought for control, talking to him cheerfully as he wept.

Ty couldn't even thank her. He wasn't sure what had started it. But he knew talking might start it all over again.

That afternoon Otis Johnson came in.

"Didn't mean to treat you so rough when you got hit." He stood at the foot of Ty's cot. "Best to do things quick when you get a hurt like that."

"That's what Fenton claimed." Ty was disoriented from the morphine. They'd given him a big shot after the Red Cross woman left.

Otis Johnson looked puzzled.

"Fenton Pardee." Ty tried to clear things up, saw Johnson was confused but didn't know how to explain.

"What did you say your son's name was?" Ty wanted to get back to something simple, to talk about anything but the wound.

"I didn't. But it's Walker. Walker Johnson. We named him after the colonel."

23

Healing

There was no way Ty could foresee the bond the war would would fashion for the three of them, though there was a hint of it in the letter Walker had waiting for him at the Fort Collins hospital. It was written in Walker's careful hand, attached to the commendations his staff had submitted for the medals.

> We should offer you something more tangible than medals, Hardin. But they will have to do. The truth is that men like you and Johnson are the ones who won this war. It was a war we had to win.
>
> I am sorry about the wound, but I am thankful it was Johnson who brought you in. He knows how to care for men as well as horses. He is the best soldier I know. You are one of the best too, even though you hated doing what you had to do.
>
> It was necessary. Never forget that the wound you'll live with was suffered for the right cause. You were there because the world needed you. It gives thanks.

The colonel went on to say that if the urge to sleep on the ground ever came upon him again, he intended to have Ty take him into his mountains. "I want to see if you handle mules in high country as well as you handled them in California mud," he wrote.

He signed the letter "With admiration." Ty slid it into the music box under the razor case, thinking he should write back. For a few days he even considered what to say. Though he never wrote that letter, it was weeks before he was free of what the colonel had written him. There was plenty of time to consider it as they put him through his rehabilitation, the nurses making him walk morning and afternoon, massaging his wound until the feeling began to come back, lifting his leg until he could lift it himself, easing him into the shiny whirlpool baths, the jets coming in above the wound, below it, the water hotter and hotter.

The cause may have been right, he would think, but wars end badly for anyone touched by them. He thought of the wounded he had patched, the dead he had waited with until the corpsmen came. He thought of the German tanker too, blown apart as he surrendered. And most often he thought of the starving wretches at Gunskirchen Lager.

He couldn't get them out of his mind, even when the throbbing and itching would call back his own wound, making him worry about dragging a game leg behind him as he went out for his horses. He thought about the pack station every day—and about the mountains. When he couldn't sleep he would let his imagination take him along a trail he knew, consider each camp: where to stack the saddles, put the kitchen tent, find wood and water, feed for his horses and places to sleep for his people.

And after awhile sleep would come, dulling the ache of his wound, sinking him beneath his pain. His dreams were mostly of the mountains, his biggest fears not finding his horses or being stopped by deadfall on the trail or by snow on a pass. But those things didn't seem much of a worry now, not after what he'd just left. He didn't like his dreams about that: Confusion and smoke. The rumble of the big guns. Explosions ripping open the night. Bone-thin arms reaching out to him.

He was in the hospital for almost three months. Cody Jo came to see him halfway through his stay, driving almost nonstop all the way from Missoula. He was walking by then, needing a cane but putting more and more weight on the leg each day.

"You're so thin," she said, as he limped into the sunroom. She hugged him, held him for a long time, looked at him again. "And you're older." She touched his face. "It's in your eyes."

"You look the same." Ty saw she was thinner too, her hair shorter, the laugh-lines around her eyes deeper. But she was the same Cody Jo, laughing, asking him questions and half-answering them herself, making him feel important and entertaining all at once.

She arranged with the nurses to take him out for dinner, and they went to a roadhouse outside of town. It was there that she told him Spec had been wounded too, hit by a sniper's bullet on Okinawa.

"We think he'll be all right," she said. "One of those marine officers called Tommy from Washington. Told him Spec had done something very brave. That Tommy should know what a good marine Spec was." She made a face. "As though Tommy needed to know Spec would do something 'brave.' That was his problem every time he got to town."

She got up and put some money in the jukebox.

"I hope that wasn't your problem, Ty," she said, sitting down again. "I hope you didn't try to do something brave."

"I didn't. Truth is I hardly remember what I did do."

"Supposin'" was playing. Cody Jo drummed her fingers on the table with the music, as though she were dancing as she sat there.

"I can't wait until you get well enough to dance." She put her hand in her lap. "These songs bring back so many things."

Their food came and they talked and she told Ty about Fenton, that he didn't seem to have the energy he used to have, that he'd had to get Buck and Bump to come over and do the shoeing that spring.

"He'll raise hell if those shoes come off." Ty couldn't imagine Fenton as anything but the big unpredictable presence he'd always been.

They laughed about that, and then they heard "Daybreak" playing. Cody Jo got him on his feet and coaxed him into moving along with the music. They stayed pretty much where they were as they danced, the other couples giving them room. After awhile Ty leaned his cane against the table and kept moving to the music, using his wounded leg for balance.

It came back to him what a marvelous dancer Cody Jo was the moment he put down the cane. They hardly had to move their feet, but the music was in both of them. They swayed and hesitated and swayed again as though the music came from some hidden place only they shared.

"You haven't lost it," she said when they finished. "That rhythm." She watched him, then smiled. "That's why those nurses told me to get you well. I bet they want to take you dancing!"

The next night she drove him to the big hotel in Colorado Springs to hear the dance band. They were playing on a terrace, tables arranged around a dance floor. The musicians were wonderful. It was easy to tell how much they liked the swing tunes they played. It wasn't long before Cody Jo was making friends with them, asking them to play her favorites, his favorites too: "Green Eyes" and "Frenesi," "Have Mercy" and "Perfidia."

They played all the songs that had kept Ty's men going too. Every time they'd found a radio they'd gathered to listen, memorizing every word, each intonation. It was hard to believe that he was hearing those songs now, played by a live band while they ate elegant food, used napkins and had wine. Knew they were safe in the soft summer night.

Cody Jo coaxed him into dancing to each slow number they played. Before long he was moving much more easily than he had the night before. They even stayed on the dance floor for some of the faster songs, Ty shuffling in place as Cody Jo moved around him, came into his arms and swung out again—as though they'd danced that way forever.

They stayed on the terrace long into the night, dancing, drinking more after their dinner. Some of the musicians joined them between sets, talking about how much they liked watching Cody Jo dance, even asking if Ty wanted to sit in at their drums. Ty refused, embarrassed to realize they were serious and drinking more than he should. He was surprised when they played "The Sunny Side of the Street," saying it was their last number. It seemed the wrong song to end with, but he loved dancing to it, the musicians smiling, Cody Jo and he the only dancers left on the broad terrace. The song was almost over before he realized his leg hardly bothered him at all.

Cody Jo gave him the car keys. "I might take a nap," she said, tipping a little. "I don't think I danced that last brandy away."

Ty was pleased he was able to work the clutch and startled by how quickly Fenton's Buick picked up speed. He hadn't driven a real car in a long time, and he slowed to make sure he had control. . . . He hadn't danced away his last brandy either.

He wished they were headed back for the pack station now. Dancing with Cody Jo had brought so much back to him that he felt a little dizzy. She tilted against him and he shifted around to make her comfortable. They drove that way back to the hospital, Ty thinking about when he'd met Cody Jo and Fenton, recalling his first day: Fenton setting Bob Ring's leg, Ty leading Ring out across snow while Ring drank and sang hymns, going back that same day to ride all the way to the South Fork, the coyotes calling, the moon giving only a hint of the country he would call home.

Fenton had fixed Ring's leg, he thought, and Cody Jo had fixed his—made him dance so he'd know he could walk. He understood why she'd made them stay late. It didn't bother him. He wished she'd worry that much about him after his leg got better. Besides being in the mountains, he couldn't think of anything he'd rather do than dance with Cody Jo.

The nurses had cleared their late return and the M.P.s waved them through with no questions. Cody Jo didn't wake up until he slowed the car, stopping in front of his ward.

"Home again, home again." She lifted her head. "Jiggedy jog."

"I don't call it home. But it's sure improved since you arrived."

"You've been drinking." She smiled at him. "I like that."

"Can you drive?" He lifted his leg with his hands to clear the door. "The nurses could find you a bed here."

"I can now." She slid under the wheel. "After resting up from the dancing." She ran a hand through her short hair. "You improved. Bet it didn't hurt your old leg at all."

"Your dancing fixed it." He looked at her through the window.

"You fixed it." She kissed her fingers and held them to his cheek. "People who dance like you just self-repair."

She looked at him with only the hint of a smile. Then she was gone, the car not even swerving as she headed for the gate.

Ty didn't see her again for six weeks, not until Horace drove him out to the pack station in his pickup, though he got two letters from her. The first thanking him for their night of dancing.

The second telling him Spec was dead.

24

Indian Signs

"Like one of them Indian signs of Tommy's. Finds its own way to come true." Horace was driving carefully, worried about how thin Ty looked. "Special Hands was all patched and on that hospital ship home when the plane mashed itself right into them. Killed Spec and three others." He turned to Ty, unbelieving. "Barely hurt that ship."

Ty hardly saw the country they were driving through.

"How did Tommy take it?" He'd gone to see him in Indian Town. But he didn't think Tommy recognized him.

"He roused himself when they shipped Spec back. He took that flag all folded up. Watched them lower the coffin. But he never thought Spec was in there. Not for a minute. Just started in to drinking again."

"Might not have been in there." Ty looked out the window again. "Not much left when a man gets hit right on." They were getting close to Seeley Lake. Ty was remembering when Spec had driven him in the other direction, celebrating Ty's first year in the mountains. He'd been so honored to have a hunter like Special Hands take him to town he probably would have gone to The Bar of Justice even if he'd known what it was.

"I guess those kamikazes think it's an honor." Ty saw Horace needed an explanation. "They're different from us."

"You must of seen some bad things." Horace looked over at Ty. "Etta and me are sure glad you come out of it all right."

They went by the bar at Seeley Lake and Ty remembered when Spec had bought him beer there, wouldn't let him pay, the bartender seeing Ty was too young but serving him anyway—because Spec told him to.

"I'm not sure any of us came out of it all right," Ty said. He saw two men drinking on the porch where he'd first seen Gus Wilson, chairs tilted back. He also saw the worry on Horace's face and thought he'd better change the subject.

"We've all changed over those years. You and Etta too."

"Does slowin' to a crawl qualify as change?" Horace asked, still concerned about Ty.

He began asking Ty questions: what Ty's medals stood for, how the Germans acted when they surrendered. He asked questions all the way out to the pack station, offering his own answers when Ty grew quiet.

"Mostly it was confusing," Ty said. "Everyone going different directions. Roads out. Waiting. Then rushing for somewhere else."

He didn't talk about the frightened boys they took as prisoners. He didn't talk about his wound, or about the smells of Gunskirchen Lager—the starved people reaching out, needing someone to touch.

Cody Jo came out when she heard the truck. She'd been baking and had flour on her jeans. She looked so natural and happy Ty had to swallow away his feelings. She hugged him and made him walk for her, told him that Dan and Rosie were coming for dinner. Buck and Angie too. That Fenton was putting in a hunting camp and wanted Ty with him right away.

"Hold on," Ty said, as they went into the house. Music was playing. Music always seemed to be playing when Cody Jo was cooking. "I'm not even sure I can ride."

"You can dance, Ty. If you can dance, you can ride."

Ty saw the big house was finished at last: the floors polished, railings in on the stairs. Over the mantle was a painting of an Indian packer. A long, shiny table was where the makeshift one had been.

Cody Jo told him to take the guest room, but he took his things out to his old room off the barn. Someone had put a bed where the cot had been. And there was electricity, a lamp to read by.

The army had shipped a sleeping bag back with him. He spread it on the bed and went through the corrals to see what horses Fenton had left, pleased to see Smoky Girl sunning herself out in the pasture. Cottontail and Loco were there too. He got a nose bag and went to them, worried that his limp might make them wary. But they came to him right away, Loco peering around Cotttontail to make sure before nosing in for feed, trying to get it all.

He saved the last for Smoky, then led her back to the corrals, knowing the sooner he found out if he could ride the better. He began brushing her, wondering how Fenton was and why no one talked about that. It was hard to imagine anything wrong, though. Fenton seemed too permanent.

He looked up at the high ridges of the Swan. The sun was warm on his face and he felt at home at last—or at least near enough to see where home was, up where the air was thin and the nights cold.

He'd saddle Smoky after lunch, see if he could ride without too much pain. But even as he walked into the kitchen for lunch, he knew there would be no waiting, that no matter the pain, he'd be headed for the pass in the morning. He wanted to see Fenton, needed to see the country. He just wished Spec were there to see it too.

⌒⌒

"You're older, Ty." Rosie put a bag of homegrown tomatoes on the table. "You're getting some of that sad look Will used to have."

"Just makes him more handsome," Angie said. "Mysterious like."

"You been breaking any hearts, Ty?" Rosie was going through Cody Jo's records. "Hear those nurses were trippin' over themselves to get you on your feet."

"They sure tried to get me rid of this limp." Ty felt awkward with all the attention. "The doctor says it'll go away—in time. Says to do whatever I can. Just not too fast."

"That's what Fenton said after you were half-frozen." Cody Jo passed out the drinks Dan had made. "I thought we'd never get your blood moving again. 'Take it slow,' he said. And for once he was right."

"He's right about a lot of things, Cody Jo. You tease him too much."

"I don't think I tease him as often now, Ty." She looked at him. "And we miss it. It was one of the ways we made love."

Then she was busy, making a cheese sauce, frying elk sausage. They drank, dipping their bread in the sauce and listening to the songs she'd collected during the war years.

"Those songs meant a lot to us," Ty said. "Made us happy and sad all at once."

"Well let's be happy listenin' to them now." Buck got another round for everyone. "It's best to be glad about who's here, not sad about who ain't."

Things picked up a little after that. They listened to Benny Goodman and Glenn Miller and Artie Shaw. Ty thought they might start dancing, but nobody did. They just listened and drank, eating the sausages with the tomatoes from Rosie's garden.

It was all right with Ty that nobody wanted to dance. It hadn't been easy getting on Smoky in the first place, and it wasn't much better after he did. Not until he'd worn her down a little and loosened himself up. Ty guessed she hadn't been ridden at all since he left, a suspicion Horace verified that afternoon before he drove back to town.

"At first we didn't get on her because of you bein' away," Horace said. "And then we didn't cause she wouldn't let us. By the time Fenton got her, she wasn't fit for anyone but him. And he was busy with Easter. 'Wait till it's over,' he says. Which most of us were doin' anyway."

Horace got in his truck. "And we did. We all waited. A lot stopped while you boys was gone. Didn't change, just stopped. Hope you can start things up again."

Ty watched him drive away before going back to Smoky. It took three hours. But when he finished, they were reacquainted. And he knew he could ride. At least that much was started up again.

They had a lot to drink that night, but not even Buck got boisterous. Mostly they listened to the music and tried not to worry about Ty's limp.

"I can haul them supplies in for Fenton," Buck said. "No reason for you to be on the trails until that leg heals."

"And let you knock over all those saplings?"

"Been workin' on conservation since you left." Buck sounded hurt. "Cottontail and me."

Ty saw being funny was no good. "Truth is, Buck, I want to go. Want to see Fenton. Find out if my leg is good enough so I can help."

Buck got more drinks and Angie and Rosie cleared the table, all of them making nice to Ty, saying they were sure his leg would hold up, saying how much help he would be. . . . What they weren't saying was what bothered him.

"I want Fenton to see you," Cody Jo said. "He'll be so glad to see you."

Billie Holiday was singing "In my solitude . . . you haunt me . . . " Cody Jo took it off and played "Daybreak," saying it was the last record because daybreak was when Ty had to get going. She got Ty up to dance with her, but it wasn't at all like that night they'd danced on the terrace at the hotel. The song seemed sad.

He went out to his room and pulled his sleeping bag over him. He lay there thinking of his favorite camps, wondering what fords had washed out, thinking about all the things that could have changed . . . and thinking about Spec. It wouldn't be the same in the woods without Spec.

⌒〜

"Spec may be gone," Fenton said. "But he'll stick with you the rest of your goddamned life. You'll see." He was sitting by the fire with Jasper, drinking the whiskey Ty had brought in. Gus Wilson was there too, and Ty could see why Gus was needed. He'd pulled Cottontail and Loco into camp in the late afternoon, Fenton there to meet them and looking so much thinner and smaller Ty hardly recognized him. If Fenton's voice hadn't held up, steady and insistent, Ty was afraid he would have been staring at him still, making sure it really was Fenton.

"Them you learn from are always with you," Fenton said. "Telling you things. Helpin' you see." He shifted to get more comfortable. "That's all the immortality a man gets, far as I can tell." He sipped his whiskey. "When you think about it, it ain't a bad kind to have."

"Let's talk about somethin' cheerful," Jasper said, enjoying the whiskey Ty had produced. "Like havin' Ty back. I feel safer already." He patted Ty's arm. "You always looked out for me when them chips was down."

"He might have to do more of that if I don't shake this goddamned ache." Fenton started to get up for another drink, but Gus brought the bottle over, watching as Fenton settled himself back down.

"Been off my feed, Ty. Off my industry too. With you here maybe we can catch up to where I let Gus down."

"If you'd see the doc you might not worry about who you let down," Gus said. "Or fret over what you shouldn't be doing in the first place."

"I know what I *should* be doing. What pisses me off is I can't. With Ty here I just may go see Doc Haslam. Not that he'll tell me anything new."

"Don't let 'em poke you with their knives," Jasper said. "Costs all that money and not a nickel worth of repair."

"Poke me wherever they want if they get rid of this ache. It's hardly tolerable without whiskey."

"They sometimes cut the ache out," Gus said. "But you got to see them first. Ty can finish up here, take care of them hunters comin' in."

"I'll take you up to the pass tomorrow," Ty said, poking the fire. "You can instruct me on what to do. You've probably missed that opportunity."

"I have. But it's hard to crack the whip. This ache keeps me preoccupied."

Jasper shook his head, knowing that if Fenton didn't protest about doctors poking him with knives, things were bad. He took another sip, thinking it was one of Tommy's Indian signs.

A bad one.

Death and Life (1945–1947)

In the meadows the snow looked windblown and rippled, holding for a time behind raised clumps of grass before lifting away and settling—like winter's dust.

25

Home

Ty threw himself into his work until his hands blistered. He got gloves from Jasper and kept on, Gus surprised by how determined he was not to bruise the country. They built the three-bar catch corral in the lodgepole grove, used deadfall for rails lashing them to standing trees. They dug a fire pit rather than use rocks for a ring. They set up a small wall tent for their gear and two bigger ones with stoves for the hunters, putting them where the ground drained to avoid ditching. And at the end of each day Ty would explore the country on Smoky, thinking where Spec would send hunters, how he would handle it if they asked him to do their hunting.

He wasn't looking forward to the hunting, but he liked getting ready: looking high for game, listening to elk bugle at sunset, the coyotes' wild calls—spotting bears as they foraged.

Jasper took pleasure in feeding Ty, watching his appetite return. Gus watched Ty too, saw he didn't like to talk about the war, about Fenton. Gus figured, in his country-wise way, that hard work was good medicine. Sleep would heal. The harder the work the deeper the sleep for Ty.

He was right. Ty made his bed under the makeshift saddle rack. The manties thrown across them offered all the shelter he needed—and a place to look out at the stars, listen for the night noises. He would lie there with his leg throbbing, the throb slowing to an ache as sleep washed through him. He barely stirred one night when a deer rummaged around looking for salt, only half-woke when the belled horses drifted close. The safety of his woods was so comforting, his weariness so absolute, Gus wondered if even a grizzly roaring through camp would unsettle him.

Fenton was his worry—one he tempered by knowing Fenton was seeing Thomas Haslam. Gus had decided to talk less about Fenton's well-being and more about the work he'd left them to do, but he'd seen the look on Ty's face when he came down from the pass, Ty's eyes on something else as he unsaddled and turned Smoky out. He thought Fenton must have said something, though there was no way to guess what. Fenton was too unpredictable. And they'd run into Bernard Strait up there. Gus thought Bernard had grown even more touchy during the war years. It was hard to tell what he might have said, seeing Fenton in that condition, Ty looking not so much older as different—as though he'd traveled an uncommon amount of country during the war, none of it pretty.

⌣⌒

And Bernard *had* behaved strangely up on the pass, at least Ty thought he had. He was putting in a benchmark, dressed in his olive ranger pants and his brown ranger shirt, the brim of his hat straight across his brow.

"Well, you're back." He looked more ready to talk than Ty expected. "This is the Bob Marshall Wilderness now. I got charge of the South Fork District. I believe you're startin' down those switchbacks a little early."

"Can't get started too early in the mountains," Fenton said.

"That's true, Bernard," Ty said, knowing Fenton was hurting. "Fenton always said an hour in the morning's worth two at night. Missed hearing it these last years."

"Hell, this was the Bob Marshall before Ty signed up." Fenton looked around. "Doesn't hurt the country, I guess. But I think the man was crazy."

Bernard looked at Fenton as though Fenton might be crazy himself. "He was a famous conservationist. What's the matter with you?"

"Only thing he wanted to conserve was some country to test himself in." Fenton shifted to find comfort. "I seen him come into camp and see he hadn't made his fifty miles and go right back out to make it up. Wind up so sick he couldn't watch the sun set or hear elk bugle."

"Maybe that's why they dedicated this country to him." Bernard couldn't believe what he was hearing.

"Count yourself lucky he dropped dead back east. Never would of heard the end of it if he'd died in one of them blizzards he always got caught in." Fenton started Easter down toward the switchbacks.

"Got to wait an hour before you go down." Bernard was cleaning his glasses. "Stock might be coming up."

"Would you tell me what in hell you're talking about, Bernard? If someone's coming up, I'll get out of the way. Or they will."

"It's the regulation now." Bernard put his glasses back on. "Stock goes up in the morning. Down in the afternoon."

"You think we would of got your Bob Ring and his broke leg out if we listened to them paper pushers?" Fenton sounded so weary Ty was sure Bernard would see he was sick. But Bernard stepped in front of Easter, looking determined.

"It's an official government regulation. That's all I know."

Fenton's face was gray, but what he said was clear. "And you are an official government asshole." He moved Easter forward until Bernard had to step back to let him pass. Ty followed, watching Bernard's face go tight.

The pass was broad before dropping into steepening switchbacks. Ty rode up to be with Fenton. "Loosen him up, Ty," Fenton said. "Maybe he'll see even old Bob Marshall couldn't regulate where a horse shits or what a bear eats or when a man finds himself sick on a god-damned pass."

"Guess Bob Marshall wasn't so good at regulating himself."

"He wasn't. But he wanted to regulate us. I think the man was from another world, one where you don't have to learn from the country. You just use it for your excitement. Tommy thought so too. Thought too many of us were like him. And Tommy has a point." He leaned from the saddle and spit. "Before you're through they'll be makin' heroes out of folks *because* they get themselves killed. Used to be the opposite. If you got killed you were dumb; got caught with your britches down."

"I been dumb a few times." Ty remembered the big snow.

"Not dumb enough to cash in." Fenton wiped his mouth. "Somethin' tells me this may be my time. Thought it'd be different."

"See Doc Haslam." Ty didn't like hearing it. "He'll know what to do."

"Hell, he'll just tell me official what I know unofficial already . . . But I promised Cody Jo. I'll go."

Ty reined in, watched as Easter took Fenton down the switchbacks.

Bernard was having his lunch when Ty got back. He got out some jerked elk and they sat, warming in the high sun.

"I could give him a ticket for that," Bernard said. "I might yet."

"Ticket?" Ty was surprised to hear such a word. "They're for parking. Or speeding. Not for up here."

"We write them up when people don't follow the regulations. It doesn't work out to have everyone do what they want."

Ty looked at him. "Seems to me this country tells you what you can and can't do all by itself. You could see Fenton needed to go out."

"He did look tired. But that don't mean he can ignore regulations."

Ty saw Bernard's mind was set. He let it go. The sun was warm, the air pleasant, and he could see far out across the country.

"Working for Fenton regular now?" Bernard asked.

"If I can keep up."

"Heard you got some medals in the war."

"They give some out if you get hurt."

"Maybe I'll bring Wilma in to your camp when she comes up. She was asking around about your wound."

Ty got up and tightened Smoky's cinch. "Tell Willie Cody Jo says I can still manage a dance or two." He mounted. The thought of Cody Jo dancing made him smile.

"Wilma dances mostly with me these days." Bernard spoke so earnestly Ty was amused.

"That makes you a lucky man. Do I get a ticket if I cut in?"

Bernard saw no humor in that, so Ty said his good-bye and headed for camp.

⌒⌒

In four days they had the camp more than ready. Ty and Gus rode out to pick up the first hunting party, Ty taking his mules out for supplies, Gus deadheading saddle horses out for the hunters to use. Ty was anxious to see Fenton, find out how he was and tell him about the camp. He liked talking about the country with Fenton. And he was still learning packing tricks from him—tail-tying, tucking a manty just so, different ways to top-pack. He even learned when Fenton drifted far from the subject. "That's why you can't beat a tight rope," Fenton would conclude, which might have nothing to do with what he was saying but everything to do with what he meant.

They'd been so efficient at getting out of camp they were on the pass early—Ty's need to see Fenton so strong he hardly slowed as they crossed and started down the switchbacks on the other side. A half-mile above the waterfall ford he saw horses below them, and from the way the first rider sat his horse, he was pretty sure it was Bernard. He'd forded and pulled well off the trail by the time they met, Bernard leading a pack horse, another rider behind him.

"You came out over that pass awful early, Ty," Bernard said. "We might have had a wreck."

"You're safe as water in a bar," Ty said. "Saw you coming and made sure."

"Ty Hardin!" Wilma Ring turned out to be the second rider. She pushed by Bernard and rode up to Ty, leaning off her horse to give him a kiss. "You could have said hello before you disappeared into your mountains." She straightened her hat, smiling. How blue her eyes were came back to Ty in a rush. "After I sent you all those brownies."

"They must of been censored too," Ty said. "Never did reach me."

"You're getting worry lines, Ty. Around your eyes."

"We were going in to check out your camp," Bernard said, still not sure whether or not to be official. "Thought you were coming out tomorrow."

"You check it out, Bernard. If you can find it. And offer a drink to Jasper. He'd enjoy some social life."

"You just dodged a ticket," Bernard said. "Wilma's here and we got a long ride ahead."

"Hope that's not the last time you rescue me, Willie." Ty tipped his hat. "I sure enjoy it."

Gus was headed back to his sawmill to check on his brothers, their fighting a constant worry. He helped unsaddle first.

"Reminds me of Cody Jo," he told Ty.

"Willie does?"

"When Cody Jo come here we all tripped over ourselves to get close."

"They seem different to me," Ty said.

"Watch." Gus stacked the last saddle, his scar looking pale against his sunburned face. "You'll see."

Ty was puzzling over that when he saw Fenton's Buick coming, a cloud of dust behind it. It was almost to the corrals before he saw it was Thomas Haslam driving.

"I told Fenton I'd come pick you up," the doctor said. "We need to run more tests."

"What tests?"

"Routine. Though there's nothing routine about your friend Fenton."

"What'll they show?"

"We aren't sure. Things don't look that good."

"What things?"

Thomas Haslam looked at Ty. "Let's go see Cody Jo. You two should hear it together."

26

A Last Trip

Ty was back on the trails before he could digest it. Nothing Haslam had said made him optimistic. There was a cancer. They weren't sure where, but that hardly mattered. It was into the lymph nodes. They would try to arrest it while they searched, cut it out when they found it—if they did.

"Are there cancers where you can't operate?" Cody Jo had asked, her voice steady. "Places you can't reach?"

"Yes," Thomas Haslam said. "The pancreas. The small intestine. But there are places we can. There's a clinic in San Francisco. We'll use whatever they have."

It had come at Ty too fast: lymphoma, metastasize, sarcoma. He'd felt lost. But he'd seen Cody Jo would find out in her way as much as the doctor would in his. "If it is bad," she'd asked, "how long do we have?"

"Not a year. Maybe a year, for Fenton. No more."

Cody Jo had looked out at the willows, turning golden as winter came in. "Better get started for the clinic," she'd said.

Ty took the news back in to Jasper, with some cooking sherry. Jasper didn't touch it until after dinner, then he talked late about Fenton.

"If Fenton goes," Jasper said, "he'll take a lot of what opened up this country with him."

"Only wants it open so far." Ty watched the fire. "Likes it this way."

The hunters he'd brought in were experienced. Ty told them where to hunt, and when they got something he'd get it with Cottontail and Loco, working quickly, gutting and quartering and bringing the meat back for Jasper to hang.

When he took that party out there was another, more social, winning Jasper over with toasts and special dinners. They would gather each night to tell their stories—deferring to Ty as he came and went—quiet, competent, showing them the meadows and waterfalls, not telling them about the country so much as helping them see it.

It grew colder, the elk moving lower for feed. There was time before the last party came in, and Ty moved the camp to Fenton's old spot in Lost Bird Canyon, just above where the canyon narrowed, flattened—where the big bog began.

"They can hunt for goats on the cliffs, go below for elk on the South Fork flats," he told Jasper, using the lodgepole rails he'd hidden with Spec, setting up the camp as though returning home.

In the morning he left Jasper to make a food run for the trail crew. He was gone for four days. When he returned with Buck, Jasper was wild with worry about a bear—although he'd seen none.

"One hasn't been around, Jasper," Ty reported. "No tracks at all."

"May not have left any sign." Jasper was testing the sherry Ty had brought in. "But he's out there. Fenton told me one hangs around here. Spies on us." He sipped his sherry. "Scary bastard."

"Might be that red one that chased Sugar out of the bog," Buck said. "That was after I squashed my nose." He drank, thinking about it. "Only reason Angie married me." He laughed. "That bear's all right. I never would of thought to break my nose."

"Spec told me some live to thirty years," Ty said. "Maybe more."

"This one's considered me his main course for so long I'll bet he's got longevity." Jasper looked at Ty. "It was bad for you to leave me here, Ty. You know my hearin's thin."

"Buck'll stay when I go out next time. You'll be fine. Hasn't been a bear around here anyway. That I can tell."

Ty worried about that as he rode out for the last party, his string rustling through aspen leaves and climbing through bear grass toward timberline. Maybe a bear hadn't been hanging around camp, but that morning he'd realized one wasn't far away.

He'd tracked his horses up a slide just after dawn, moving slowly on his game leg, finding them sunning high above camp. He'd found a big pile of bear scat too, only two or three days old. He couldn't tell what drew the bear so high: no berry patches, no pine nuts. He'd rested, looking down on the camp and thinking of his last time in Lost Bird

Canyon, just after they'd let Spec out of Deerlodge. Spec had shown him tracks near the bog, not a day old—big and toed in, the tracks a big bear leaves when it has a full belly and time to spare. Later they'd picked up tracks of a sow and her cubs.

"He won't be with her. That ain't a bear's style." Spec had remounted and looked at Ty. "But she'll have an affection for them cubs that'll make her more unpleasant. Ain't that the way? Those gals down at The Bar of Justice change when they foal too. Nature passed us by on that one, Ty."

"On what?"

"Carryin' our own," Spec had said seriously. "Bringin' in a life."

Ty pulled up to rest his mules, thinking Spec had always been that way in the mountains, finding value in things the rest hardly considered. He'd just had few ways to say it. When he was in Missoula it was different. Whatever made him see so much up here seemed to disappear down there. He wondered what Spec would make of Jasper's fear of the bear. He doubted he would dismiss it. And he knew Tommy wouldn't, not after seeing that big pile of scat.

He looked back down the long drainage of Lost Bird Canyon, their camp lost somewhere in the hazy gold of fall aspens. Beyond them he could make out the thick stand of timber that sheltered the bog, the stream drifting there in lazy bends that turned back almost into themselves as they flooded the canyon floor.

Bog today, meadow tomorrow, he thought. Smaller timber moving in, making soil for bigger trees, the forest taking over until some heat deep in the earth heaves everything up, tilts it to make new streams and lakes, the spring melts washing down to start it all again. The country lifting and falling, changing, a place where humans can make do sometimes, sometimes not—but a home always for animals. He could see why the bears took such comfort in it, as much a part of it as the streams and the seasons, the great jumble of it their home.

He wondered if the big bear was watching the camp now, studying all the commotion. Tommy Yellowtail would look for some sign in that. But Spec would probably find some balance. "Hell, it ain't breeding time," he might say. "No reason for him to tear around. By now he's likely eatin' more for fun than need. Got time to puzzle over us—tents, corrals, smoke. Wonder why we ain't as efficient as he is."

Ty made a trail camp that night, watching the fire as he chewed jerky and thought about Jasper and Buck. He doubted they were considering the bear at all now, sneaking down another bottle of sherry and taking comfort in one another as people did. His animals did it too, Loco and Cottontail looking to Smoky Girl for comfort, all of them sticking together. Bears were different, breeding early and going their solitary ways. The sows accepting the boars for their need, but having their cubs alone, getting them going even if it took a few years, then leaving them too, going their lonely way, readying themselves for the long winters.

It takes something more to get humans through the winters, he thought; they need to do some caring, be cared for. He fed wood to the fire and thought of Horace and Etta, Angie and Buck—even the girls at The Bar of Justice. Jasper too. Jasper needed people as much as the rest, maybe more. And it was hard to imagine Fenton without Cody Jo, or at least Fenton not thinking about Cody Jo. Hard to imagine it the other way around too, Cody Jo without Fenton to fill some hollow place in her life.

He looked out from his little ring of light, heard a bell across the meadow, a coyote far down the canyon. He thought bears must have something too. Know how to find a snug place in the high country, a place to watch the seasons, be a part of where it all begins.

He caught up his horses before dawn. When he got out he found Cody Jo waiting at the corrals, Thomas Haslam with her. The hunting party had canceled, she told him, which Fenton saw as an opportunity: the camp set up; supplies ready; Ty bringing out the mules. Fenton wanted to go in, wanted them all in Lost Bird Canyon again.

"It's all right, Ty." Thomas Haslam spoke quietly. "We can treat him when we get back. He wants to be in his mountains—one more time."

☞

"Ty's got most all his strength back." Fenton watched Ty walk a log closer for him. He sat, hunching toward the flames, elbows on his knees.

"If he hasn't, he soon will." Cody Jo poured whiskey into Fenton's cup. "All that work to get us here."

"He knows to tight a rope." Fenton looked at Ty. "Haven't packed a mule since we started. You done it all."

"Wish I'd top-packed a folding chair. You could use some comfort."

"No goddamned chairs," Fenton said. "Just clutter things up. Stove and tent is luxury enough. Half the time I resent them."

"I'll admit I'm partial to Jasper's stove," Ty said. He looked around to see what else he could do. He wanted Fenton free of the pain. Whiskey helped, but morphine helped more. And Thomas Haslam was fishing.

"We camped here," Fenton said. "Bog down below like to do little Sugar in. That's where she rearranged Buck's nose."

"My first trip." Cody Jo looked at him. "Brown as an Indian, you were. I think you got us into all that trouble just to prove you could get us out of it."

"Truth is," Fenton said to Ty, "I was so muddle-headed over her I didn't know up from down. It was wrong to try it. Tommy, he knew it."

"You won my heart," Cody Jo said. "You always do."

She went into the kitchen to help Alice and Angie get dinner, all of them wanting Buck to bring Thomas back so he could give Fenton the morphine. They chased Jasper out, which was fine with him. It gave him a chance to sip Fenton's whiskey.

"Think that red-headed one still camps in here, Fenton?" Jasper swirled his whiskey and took a taste. "Spec said them rascals live a long life. Buck seen one down in there. Seen a big track too."

"Buck might of seen a black bear." Ty didn't want Jasper to talk himself into a worry. "He's not that reliable at distinguishing."

"Might be that roan bear." Fenton looked into the fire, thinking. "Might not. Could be his reputation is what's got the longevity."

"This one's a slippery bastard." Jasper warmed to the idea. "Been interested in me and Ty since before the war."

Ty poured more whiskey for Fenton. "I think Jasper jumbles his stories together just to keep our interest up."

"That happens too," Fenton said suddenly. "The damn stories grow. But bears do come back. That's a truth." He began to sound like the old Fenton, coming at things from a direction no one expected. "There was that bear up around the forks. Raised hell with every Indian party that camped in there. Indians claimed it was medicine. Said it was a tough Gros Ventre warrior come back to play hell with the Flathead and the Blackfoot." Fenton looked at Jasper. "Told that story down through generations, longer than any damn bear could live. I thought it was foolishness, but Tommy claimed near every time they camped up in there, they got hit by a grizzly."

"Hear that story enough," Ty said, "imagination provides the bear."

"That's what I told Tommy. Tommy wanted to know what kind of imagination it is that kills dogs and horses and rips the shit out of tepees."

"That's different. Maybe coincidence. Different bears. It happens one year in five and imagination fills in the rest."

Jasper listened. As far as he was concerned the bear watching him had nothing to do with his imagination.

"It's more than that, Ty," Fenton said. "There's things you can't explain. The night after that big rain, when I'd plumb give up on Sugar, I heard a mule." Fenton leaned forward, cradled his whiskey in his big hands. "Even if Sugar had called, we'd of never heard her. River loud as a train."

"Could have come from Loco, one you'd turned out."

"But it didn't." Fenton finished his whiskey, his voice quiet, no argument in it at all. "It didn't come from our mules," he said again, as though speaking to himself.

Jasper didn't like being in the camp alone. "My hearin' is so irregular," he told Haslam, "a belled mare could sneak up and steal my lunch."

They all saw how much the bear worried him. He was sure something was out there. And though Ty made light of things, he'd seen what he'd seen. He couldn't ignore Jasper's worries.

That's why he left Buck in camp with a rifle when he took Fenton and Cody Jo down the canyon. They wanted to see where Sugar had bogged down so many years ago. Thomas Haslam came with them, just in case, which was fine with Ty. He needed to ask him some questions.

"The cancer's holding off. For now," the doctor answered. "And he knew where you were camped. I doubt we could have kept him out."

"How long will it hold off?"

"Never know. We're lucky to have the time we do."

"Can't that treatment fix it?"

"May arrest it. There's no cure . . . except some miracle."

"What does Fenton think?"

"Fenton? He accepts it. . . . A lot better than you do."

They ate lunch at the ford: cheese and jerky and apples. The air crisp.

"In those willows is where I saw that roan bear." Fenton settled on a root of the big fir. "Had darker hair down along his backbone."

"This place still gives me a chill." Cody Jo looked around. "He'd been watching me. I . . . I thought I was going to get sick."

"Just curious. And not scared." Fenton looked at Cody Jo. "The way I was that night you tricked me into going to your school recital."

"You wanted to go." She smiled, almost shy as she looked at Fenton. "You were hungry for some culture. For my cookies."

"The cookies weren't what hungered me."

"Buck said he found that track near here," Ty said suddenly. "Bet it's just a black bear."

He left, hiding what was in his face. He hadn't gone a hundred yards up the stream before he saw it, in some mud the stream had left as it dropped. Buck was right; it was a grizzly, the claws extended far beyond the pad. He'd been right about the size too. Ty saw that no matter how he put his boot down in the pad, there would be plenty of track left over.

He squatted, knowing it looked bigger because of the mud but also knowing it was the biggest track he would ever see. It was clear this bear was more than just big: he was seasoned and smart, comfortable in his solitude. Ty counted back to that first trip of Cody Jo's. Not so many years had gone by that this couldn't be the same bear, in the same country, with the same habits. And there was Jasper too—Jasper sensing this presence, knowing something was out there no matter Ty's denial. He worked his way back, wondering what Fenton would say.

But he didn't have a chance to ask. Fenton's pain had come back. Haslam was giving him morphine as Cody Jo held him.

The next day he took Fenton and Cody Jo all the way to White River. Haslam came with them, his doctor's things in his saddlebags. Fenton almost seemed his old self as he told them how Tommy and Gus had carved their way through the canyon, how Sugar had smashed Buck's nose, how they had given up on Sugar and almost lost Goose in the South Fork.

The river was low. Fenton led them across easily, Easter knowing this crossing as well as any horse in the mountains. They pulled up the steep pitches to the old camp. Grass was growing in the fire pit, showing a softer green where the tents had stood. But where everything had been was clear, looked inviting in the October sun.

They had lunch, Fenton comfortable enough to turn down Haslam's offer of morphine. Afterward he took Cody Jo to the long rock that slanted down into the White River. He wanted to hear the waters spill down into the South Fork. When Ty came to join them, Cody Jo was on her way back for morphine.

"Good to watch the water from here," Fenton said, seeing the way Ty was looking at him. "Cody Jo and I watched it together one night. Long time ago . . . moonlight on it."

"Let's get you out of these mountains." Ty reached out to pull Fenton to his feet. "It's time for that treatment."

Fenton waived him off. "Hell, Ty, that treatment has less chance than a fart in a storm."

Ty found no way to respond.

"It's no big deal, Ty." Fenton tried to cheer him up. "Next year you'll be in these mountains. I won't."

He watched the waters for awhile.

"Important thing is what'll stay. The South Fork. White River." He held out his hand, let Ty pull him to his feet.

"Remember this country," he said. "It ain't goin' nowhere."

27

Fenton and the Bear

The last evening Ty took the rifles off to the big rock that held the sun and broke them down, putting the parts in order on a manty, cleaning them the way Spec always had.

"You still do them things Spec taught you." Jasper stopped by with the canvas water buckets. "While you forsake your loyal cook."

"I'll get your water soon as I'm through." Ty checked the action of the Winchester as Jasper ignored him, walked past to get the water himself.

"Offered to get his water for him." Fenton sat down and hunched forward. "Believe he thought it was too much for me." He shook his head. "Sorry damn state of affairs."

"Spec used to do this." Ty looked down the bore one more time. "While he told me what a miserable life a packer has."

"Packin's somethin' you took to. Spec saw things different. Took no pleasure in a well-packed string . . ." Fenton's voice stopped as he saw movement in the willows below them. Then the bear lifted up into the sunlight, rising higher and higher, the hair reddish in the late sun, the head nosing upward, testing. Ty eased back the action of the Winchester, slid a shell into the chamber.

There was stillness, their eyes moving from the bear to Jasper, dipping his buckets into the aspen-lined creek, then back again to the bear. The only other movement was the bear's, its huge head high, questing, reading the air.

Ty snugged the rifle into his shoulder, the stock cold on his cheek. Jasper struggled up from the creek, water slopping from the heavy buckets. He was abreast of the bear before he saw him. The buckets dropped, the canvas collapsing, water pooling out as Jasper staggered back into an aspen and fainted, sliding down its trunk.

The bear came down onto his forelegs and moved toward him—big as a car.

Ty's finger tightened on the trigger even as he considered the risk. He knew this bear wouldn't go down with one shot—with many shots. He knew too that the bear would charge. He just wanted the charge at him, not Jasper. He was farther away. He was uphill. He had the Winchester.

Then he heard Fenton's voice—the voice conversational, Fenton's attention on Ty, not the bear, not even on the crumpled body. "Jasper has passed out." It was as though he'd seen a landmark. "Or maybe his heart's give way." His voice got louder. "I believe we're more interesting to our bear than a passed-out Jasper. Take your finger off that trigger. Let's see."

Ty let up on the trigger, holding the bear in his sights as the bear looked up, searched to find that voice. His head turned back to Jasper, still motionless at the base of the aspen. Then they heard his deep cough, a kind of grunted dismissal. Ty felt a weakness wash through him as the great body turned and melted back into the brush, the rustling of willows all that was left.

"Hand me that Springfield." Fenton's voice grew urgent. "I'm steady enough to shoot. Keep your eye on them willows. I'll watch Jasper."

Ty kept watch as he passed the Springfield to Fenton.

"If he don't charge back," Fenton pumped a round into the chamber, "better try to revive Jasper. He'll want a drink."

"Saw that bear's track." Ty still watched the willows. "Should have told you."

"No matter." Fenton looked beyond Jasper's still body. "It's your hand now. Play it. Keep things calm. I'm bettin' calm is all our bear wants."

"Should of told you." Ty was trying to see into the deepening shadows. "You know things I don't."

"Your problem now, Ty. I'm done with it . . . or it's done with me. It don't pay to second guess."

"You'll soon be runnin' things like always. "

"Don't pay to lie to yourself either." Fenton motioned to him. "Ease down there for Jasper. I'd like to get this over."

Angie and Alice cooked dinner as Jasper recovered with Fenton's whiskey. Fenton was sure he was the same bear that had chased Sugar from the bog, just twice as big now. He had the same reddish pelt, the same stripe along his backbone. Ty had seen that clearly, along with the scars—his record of a long life in these woods.

Fenton had other theories too, figuring the bear saw few people in this canyon, probably none but those with Fenton or Ty. Few other packers even knew about it, and all of them were wary of Fenton's routes.

His guess was that the bear was mostly curious, didn't want to face them any more than they wanted to face him. "Hell, bears take an interest too. Want to see what's what even if it don't make much sense."

They talked about it, figuring the bear's age, listening to Fenton, to Ty, asking questions, all of them getting comfortable with what had happened—except Jasper. Jasper was still shaky. "Never can tell what that devil might do. One time he near got Ty shot." Jasper held his whiskey with both hands to keep it from spilling. "Ain't that true, Ty?"

"It wasn't the bear squeezing that trigger."

"No, it wasn't. But it was that damn bear that got my interest up." Jasper accepted more whiskey, somehow sounding pleased and belligerent at once. "Don't you deny it."

⌒⁀つ

It took them two days to get out. Two days after that Fenton started his treatment. Ty pulled shoes and put away the gear, and when the snows came he moved into town himself, setting up his saddle shop in Horace's barn, making sure Fenton got his treatments on time.

Bull Trout came in to see him there, talking about college and football and watching Ty move around his workshop. "That leg has mostly healed. And Jasper's put some pounds on you."

"I don't limp anymore." Ty saw where the conversation was going. "But even if I could run again, it wouldn't be fast."

"You're tougher than you think, Hardin. Get that meat back on your bones and you could play again. If you've lost speed, play linebacker. Not many got by you."

"There's packing. That's what I like."

Trout looked at him, watching how sure he was with his tools, how straight he cut the line of leather.

"You're not packing now," he said after awhile. "You can't pack in the winter. And they have this new bill. You don't have to play football, you know."

A few days later Cody Jo said the same thing. It made enough sense that Ty went in and registered, signing up for a course in history and one in geology. That gave him something to think about between the times he was off helping Fenton, which he did each day after his classes.

They could all see he took the treatments as seriously as Fenton did. Maybe more. He was at the hospital regularly, making sure Fenton was on time, talking with the doctors, more troubled than Cody Jo when Thomas Haslam accepted the teaching job in San Francisco.

"We won't move until June, Ty. And no matter when we go, the treatment will go on. I'm not the one giving Fenton the medicine anyway. What I seem to be doing mostly is calming you."

He looked at Ty, considering. "You know Fenton and Cody Jo may be more concerned about you than they are about themselves." He spoke slowly now, making sure to say it right. "Fenton is dying, fighting mostly just to keep Cody Jo's spirits up. What makes you think he can keep yours up too?"

"I'm not asking . . ." Ty's throat closed on his words.

"Think about it, Ty. Every time you see him you look more like your father. If Fenton taught you anything, it's not to walk around like you've been dealt a bad hand. You haven't. You have brains, health. Use them."

He put a hand on Ty's shoulder. "Offer him life. Not despair. That's the legacy Fenton's left you . . . life."

That night Ty drank beer with Buck and Angie and Jasper, trying to cheer up, wanting to talk about what Haslam had said but afraid it would make him low again. They didn't seem blue at all, talking about Fenton and the bear and the mountains as though they would all last forever.

The next night he went to The Bar of Justice. When he told Beth about Fenton, she began to cry. "He was so full of piss, Ty. Always out-tricking the others." She wiped at her eyes. "The best ones always go. Or don't come back." She poured a drink, fixed one for Ty. "You hardly been here since you got back. And then just to drink. I ain't sure you're havin' any fun at all."

"I've been in the mountains," Ty said. "With Fenton."

"Watchin' him die?" She mopped at the bar. "Fenton would tell you to go on upstairs and have a good time. Spec would too."

Loretta came into the room and started talking with a man over by the jukebox. Ty saw again how beautiful she could look.

"Loretta's quit drinkin'," Beth said. "Got religion too, which may not be an improvement."

Loretta came over. "So you got wounded by the Germans. That's God's way, you know. He can take and He can give back."

"I'm not even sure it was the Germans," Ty said. "And tell me why He took Spec?" He thought about how much Spec enjoyed this girl.

"Spec never paid enough attention to Him," Loretta said. "You might pay more yourself."

A man came over and asked her to dance.

"Be careful," she said over the man's shoulder. "Don't get like Spec."

"Truth is," Ty turned back to Beth, "I'd like to be more like Spec. In the woods at least."

Beth filled his glass, not sure what he meant. "Just drink slower, hon. He made life awful hard."

Ty had another, drinking more than he meant too. It made him stop thinking about Fenton—or about anything else. He didn't even protest when Loretta helped him upstairs. But he didn't enjoy it either.

"I'd say you didn't get your money's worth," Loretta said. "Which is your own business. It's mine how much of that poison you pour down."

"You sure have changed." Ty struggled to pull his boot back on. "Why is what I drink a worry to you?"

"It is now I've joined," Loretta said. She was dressed, impatient to get back downstairs. "There's a meeting tomorrow. Want to come?"

"Joined?" Ty got the boot on and leaned back. "Some church?"

"That AA club. I had too much one night, and this guy knew it. After we was done, he said, 'Honey, you're in trouble. Better let go and let God.' Took me to a meeting the next day. And I did. I let go and let God." She looked in the mirror and patted her hair. "He's a regular now. And I'm sober."

"Havin' any fun? They say that's what I got to have."

"I'm makin' more money. Which I got to start doin' right now."

Ty followed her downstairs and drank some more. "Is Loretta serious about all this religion?" he asked Beth. "About that AA?"

"You bet." Beth's bosom jiggled as she stirred drinks. "The good news is she don't pass out when she's workin'."

"Is there bad news?" Ty found he wasn't so much drunk as sleepy.

"The bad is she's a pain in the ass." Beth laughed. "You get on home, honey, before you are too. She might talk you into one of them meetings. That'll be depressing."

Ty's head hurt the next morning. But he got to the geology class, giving up on taking notes when he realized the professor was saying in complicated words what Fenton had told him in simple ones. He went from there to the hospital and had coffee with Cody Jo while Fenton had his treatment. Wilma, doing her volunteer work, sat down with them. But she soon had to get up to console a logger whose wife had miscarried.

"Don't you go see her looking like that," she told the logger, her eyes so blue, her uniform so tidy that Ty was sure just her presence made the man's world better. "Help her laugh. Tell her you love her."

Willie smiled, encouraging and understanding at once. The logger left with his back straighter, his head up. Ty was taken by the way she'd cheered him up.

"Hope my pep talk did some good." Willie sighed, sitting back down.

"They're lucky to have you," Cody Jo said. "We all are. You make it make sense. The births . . . the deaths too."

"I just wish these visitors wouldn't look so low," Willie said. "Some patients look worse after they see their friends."

Ty blew on his coffee. Willie was watching him as she talked, reading his face, the set of his shoulders.

"It's true." She put her hand on Ty's. "Fenton hasn't much longer. What counts is what he does have. Help him. Show him his mountains in you." She hugged Cody Jo, who had begun to cry, and went off about her work. Ty sipped at his coffee, afraid to say anything.

"Sorry." Cody Jo brushed back her hair. "I'm not even sure I'm crying about Fenton. I think it's Willie, being so sensible—saying things I know but can't do." Her voice was husky, searching for something. "Am I just selfish, Ty? Is it that I can't bear seeing him this way? He's the strongest part of me. What keeps me whole." She looked at Ty as though afraid to let go of something she'd just found.

"Do that for some girl, Ty." Her voice came to him as if they were alone in the world. "There is nothing better you can do in your life." She let the tears fall, her face not changing at all.

Then Fenton was in the hospital for good. Ty would visit, talk about the trips he was planning, ask advice about where to go, which fords washed out and which didn't. Fenton listened, sometimes answering, sometimes not.

"They looked right shocked at my condition," he said one morning after the doctors had left. "They're right, too. I couldn't get water from the creek." He stared at Ty, his mouth dry, his eyes yellow. "Better not count on me, Ty." He forced himself to swallow. "I ain't got the energy." He looked out at the winter skies.

"That country's been good to me," he said finally. "Taught me." He looked at Ty. "It'll do better for you. No Cody Jo to turn your head." He wet his lips. "Sure wouldn't trade for the interruption, though."

He closed his eyes. Ty thought he was sleeping and started to go.

"Need to slip over soon." Fenton's eyes were still closed, but his voice was clear. "It's time." Fenton opened his eyes and looked at Ty.

"Rode across once. Slick rock a goat couldn't cross. Led a mule too. Back from the dead."

"Sugar," Ty said. "Sugar was the mule."

"And Cody Jo. She come along." Fenton looked out toward the Missoula hills, lost under the gray clouds.

"Never liked to be packed." He turned back to Ty.

"Who?"

"Cody Jo. Never would follow." Fenton's eyes seemed to come alive in the ravaged face. "Tight your ropes, Ty," he said. "Never can beat a tight rope."

The next day he was gone. They told Ty as soon as he got to the hospital. Cody Jo was there with Thomas Haslam.

"It's finished," Haslam was saying to Cody Jo. "He's free of it. It's what he'd want . . . It's over."

"That part is," Cody Jo said. There were no tears left in her now. "But not Fenton." She took Ty's arm, looked at Thomas Haslam. "I don't think Fenton knows how to be over."

28

Good-bye

With Fenton gone things went flat, as though they were in the eye of a storm: the wind settling, everything cold enough to freeze spit.

Fenton had wanted it simple—cremation, his ashes in Lost Bird Canyon. Cody Jo explained it as Ty drove her out to the pack station. She wanted Fenton's ashes as far away from the undertaker as possible, and she left the urn there on the big mantle, huddling in her coat and telling Ty she wanted him to spread them in the canyon as soon as the passes opened. There would be a good-bye in the school-house before he took them in, but right now she was going to Chicago. She needed to be away from all things that were Fenton until they settled in her mind.

They left the ashes on the mantle and drove back through the cold. It hadn't snowed in weeks, but old snow was banked in dry drifts along the road or had settled, windblown and rippled, out in the meadows. It was moving still, holding behind clumps of grass before lifting and settling again—like winter's dust. Cody Jo watched it and moved closer to Ty, taking his hand, holding it as she looked at the snow lifting and falling out across the meadows.

"We drove this a time or two," she said finally. "I think he could do it with his eyes closed."

"He could the trails. Most any of them."

"He had Easter for those. Or Babe. They made it easy."

"And he had you for these. You made that easy."

She squeezed his hand again, watched the snow moving in gray sheets.

"I don't think those ashes are Fenton, Ty. He's somewhere, but he's not in that awful urn."

"I know." He watched her looking out at the snow. "I know."

They rode that way, her hand in his, all the way back to Missoula.

The winter slid away. Ty gave up on his courses and moved his saddle shop out to the pack station, living in the big house, patching the sheds, helping the neighboring ranchers, organizing gear for the coming season.

Once a week he made the drive to Missoula, stopping at the library to get new books from Willie, staying sometimes to hear a lecture or to have a drink at The Bar of Justice, staying once because Willie had asked him to take her to the big dance.

It was the spring dance, and the students wanted their pretty librarian as one of the chaperones. It didn't take Ty long to see they were interested in her as more than a chaperone. As soon as she picked up her card they gathered, writing their names for this dance or that. It was all new to Ty. He had on a tie and one of Fenton's good coats, but he still felt out of place.

"Don't you sneak off, Ty." Willie seemed a little flustered by all the attention. "I'm saving the best ones for you."

She introduced Ty to student after student, many of them veterans too, though none much like Ty. They were all surprised their librarian had invited a packer to the big spring dance.

There was a swing band from Denver, and it was easy to see why it was popular. The band opened with "Big Noise from Winnetka," the floor of the gym instantly filling with dancing couples. It took Ty a moment to shake off his surprise, to realize he was dancing along with the rest of them—with Willie.

"Don't know why you didn't corral Bernard for this," he said as they settled in with the music. "He'd be more presentable."

They broke apart, Willie spinning, her dress whirling, her blue eyes on him as she moved back and broke away again.

"I wanted to teach you some new steps."

She came back with such perfect timing he saw no reason to answer.

"Didn't have such good bands here before the war," Ty said as they waited for her next partner. "Or such big dances."

"They had something, or you wouldn't be able to dance this way."

"Cody Jo. She taught me." The band started in again, a slow number this time. "She dances the way you do."

"Compliments from my packer?" Willie moved to the music as she stood there. "What girl wouldn't want to be like Cody Jo?"

"I think your partner got lost." Ty moved to her and they danced, the vocalist singing "I'll Be Seeing You," Willie easy in his arms. "Let's keep dancing. This band knows the right songs."

"They do." Willie's cheek was on his shoulder. "I wouldn't mind if we danced this way all night."

They were deep into the music when someone tapped him on the shoulder. "This one's mine," a voice said. "Now that I've found my partner."

Ty got some punch and went outside. John Lamedeer was pouring whiskey into his punch glass. He poured some into Ty's as well.

"You got invited too. This'll help us through it." Lamedeer tucked the bottle into his pocket. "Think they lost their standards during the war?"

"They lost some good people," Ty said.

Lamedeer looked at him. He'd been in the army too, but they'd found out about his football early, and he'd spent his time playing for service teams. Ty had already seen him play for the university. It seemed to Ty he was faster than ever.

"Sure you can't play with that leg?" Lamedeer asked. "We could use you."

"Can't run much anymore," Ty said. "And I'm a packer."

"So? I'm a Flathead. They let me play—go to their dances." He poured more whiskey. "They don't give a shit what we are."

"That's not what I mean."

Lamedeer was quiet. "Hear Special Hands didn't make it."

"He didn't. They sent back what was left."

They stood, talking about high-school games, the coaches at the university, drinking more before they went back in.

"This ain't my kinda dancing." Lamedeer stopped at the door. "I'll watch. See if you move good enough to play again."

Then Willie was taking Ty's arm. "Our dance," she said. "I need more dancing with you."

"Were you and that man Lamedeer drinking?" They were walking back to Bob Ring's house just below the campus.

"Yes. And it sure helped when I danced with those others."

"It certainly didn't help when *I* danced with those others," Willie laughed. "There were plenty of tipsy veterans in there."

"The way you look in that dress, they'll be checking out a lot of books now." Ty felt her take his arm, hold it close.

The night was warm and they walked past the house, going around the block three times before they stopped. Ty refused Willie's offer of coffee. He didn't want to be sitting there with Bob Ring after having such a good time with Ring's daughter. He thought it might show.

"Thanks," Ty said. "I thought this might be an ordeal. It wasn't—not at all."

He leaned down to kiss her cheek. But she caught his face in her hands, held him away, looking at him.

"You are so much more than a packer, Ty." Her voice was serious, almost stern. "Don't you see that?"

Holding him that way, she pulled his face to hers, her lips wet, almost wanton. Then she was up the steps and onto the porch.

"Chaperoning with you gets exciting," she said. "Should we try it again?"

But when it was time for the graduation dance, Ty couldn't go. He had to salt the trail to the pass. He wanted it open so he could get the lookout crews to their fire stations. And there were Fenton's ashes to take care of.

Willie took Bernard instead.

᠆᠊ᢏ

Ty had finished supplying the crews by the end of June. The country looked wonderful as he rode out: grass high, streams full, snow melting from the ridges—game everywhere. He was glad to have all his strength back and glad it was time to take care of the Fenton business once and for all. Willie had organized everything, even getting Thomas Haslam and Alice to come from San Francisco, the doctor to speak at the schoolhouse, both of them to be with Ty when he spread the ashes.

He left his horses at the Crippled Elk corrals and drove the pickup to the big house. Cody Jo had already been there a week, Angie and Buck moving into their old cabin so she could have the house to herself. She came out to meet him in the warm sun, hugging him and stepping back to look at him and not having it any other way but that he move his things in, take the guest room where he'd wintered.

That night Angie and Buck came with a big dinner. It wasn't long before the others began to show up: Horace and Etta with the Murphys. Thomas Haslam and Alice in from San Francisco. Even Jasper and Gus. All of them having dinner together, Cody Jo making everyone at home.

She was still Cody Jo, talking about the labor movement, the dangers of the bomb, the United Nations, but none of it overshadowed how much she cared about them, how she'd opened the house to them just as she and Fenton had always done. They all felt it and opened themselves to her, the stories about Fenton becoming so alive it felt like he was there, sharing some special amusement with each of them.

It turned out not to be as easy to talk about Fenton at the school-house. By the time Cody Jo and Ty got there it was almost full, some already settling for places outside, under the windows or along the porch where they could hear. All the Conners were there, and the Wilsons. The Jamisons were there too, with Sue, no longer a little girl now but married to Bump, her own little Conners lined up in a row. Tommy Yellowtail was gone, but his family came, the men big and dignified in their beaded vests, fresh feathers in their hatbands; the children settling in with them, quiet as wood.

Everyone who worked for the Forest Service seemed to be there, some inside on benches, some under the open windows. Every trail-crew member who could wrangle a day off was there too. Bull Trout had driven out from Missoula. There were cowboys from Big Fork and Creston, packers from Ovando and Augusta—two who'd ridden across the mountains from Kiowa.

The Elkhorn piano player was just winding up "Lonesome Road" when Beth came in, ample in her black dress and sitting down quickly when two loggers jumped up to give her their places.

Wilma had convinced one of the Sisters of Providence to oversee things. She welcomed them with a prayer, her voice clear and lovely, her face perfectly framed by her habit. Rosie Murphy read a poem, her voice sounding harsh after the sister's.

Gus Wilson followed. "I have something to say," he started out. But he couldn't say it very well, because what he wanted was for Tommy Yellowtail or Spec to say it—say how Fenton was most at home in his mountains. He got that much out, that he wanted Tommy and Spec there, but that was all.

Buck couldn't say anything at all, though he opened and closed his mouth a few times trying. Ty, sitting with Cody Jo, sympathized. That's why he'd backed off when Willie asked him to talk. He knew he couldn't.

Bob Ring was next. He told the story about Fenton's bringing him out of the mountains with a broken leg, saving the leg and saving Bob Ring too, as far as Bob Ring was concerned. "I don't think I could have lived without that leg," Bob Ring said simply. "I suppose there's a lot of us here think we can't live without Fenton. But I guess we got to learn." He looked around, swallowing. "Won't be easy," he said finally.

Then it was Thomas Haslam's turn. At first he didn't speak so much about Fenton as about the kind of person Fenton was. But soon he focused right in. "The thing is," he said, "I don't think Fenton Pardee knew how to complain. Except when he thought you wanted too much money for a horse or a saddle. And that complaining was mostly for fun. As far as I could tell, he saw life mostly as interesting, a chance to figure things out.

"With Cody Jo," Thomas Haslam looked at her, the room still as a pond, "he figured he got more luck than a man deserves. Maybe that's why he accepted dying so readily—the last chapter of a book he loved."

His voice was low but clear through the deep quiet. "I don't believe in this business of people being better in the 'hereafter.' It makes no sense. What does make sense is how Fenton made us better—here. How knowing him helped us . . . here."

Cody Jo squeezed Ty's hand so tightly he dropped the program they'd given him. As he picked it up, he heard someone begin to clap. He saw it was Buck, that Beth was behind him crying and clapping too. Lumberjacks near her stood, all of them clapping. Then everyone was standing and clapping, many crying too. Cody Jo held on to Ty as the Sister of Providence quieted them, got them all singing "My foot's in the stirrup, my pony won't stand, goodbye old paint, I'm leaving Cheyenne." Willie had chosen it, picked the right verses, printed them on the program so they could sing them together.

After the last verse, she'd typed:

Fenton Pardee
1871–1946

Cody Jo was crying when they finished. Ty gave her his kerchief, felt the room quiet as they waited for her. He walked out with her, her whole body shaking as they went across the porch and down the steps. There were tables there, and food. Dan Murphy had made sure there was plenty to eat. He'd even put out a keg of beer from his bar.

Cody Jo smiled at Ty in a hurt, crooked kind of way. "I should be stronger. It was what Thomas said. And that clapping." She handed him his kerchief. "You hold me together, Ty."

And then she was saying encouraging things to the first people coming out of the schoolhouse, helping them through their awkwardness, the things they didn't know how to say. The rest lined up, needing her to see they were there before they began visiting, sorting out what it all meant.

It wasn't long before Beth came out. She turned away when she saw Cody Jo, but Cody Jo went to her. "You knew Fenton." She took Beth's hand. "He would be so pleased that you came. Drove all this way. Remembered him like this."

Bernard Strait had come out of the schoolhouse behind Beth. He was shocked to see Cody Jo and Beth together and veered away, not wanting to hear anything Beth might say. But he needn't have bothered. Beth didn't say anything at all, flushing and crying a little and holding Cody Jo's hand with both of hers. Cody Jo gave her a hug before she went back to the others, saying things to the children she'd taught, to their parents, to the cowboys and packers—paying just as much attention to the last people in the line as she had to the first.

Ty watched Bernard. It was hard to predict what he might do, and Ty figured Cody Jo had enough to handle on this day. She was talking with Buck now, Buck saying right out how much he wished Fenton could have been there: "He could of told Gus how to say what he had such a hard time with. Maybe got me so I could talk too. Hell, he might of even added some things to what the doc said."

Buck hung his head, afraid he'd said too much. "He most always knew what to say." His voice broke a little. "I never could get the knack."

"Oh, Buck." Cody Jo put her hand on his arm. "You have the knack. You do. It's just . . . a different knack."

Ty thought Buck might start to cry, but he swallowed it away and walked over to Bernard Strait.

"Something pissin' you off, Bernard?" Buck wiped his sleeve across his eyes. "Somethin's wrong, I'll sure as hell make it right."

Someone handed Buck a cup of beer, and he took a big swallow. "Bet your fuckin' ranger hat I will." He took another pull before surrendering it to Ty, who took a sip and offered some to Bernard.

"I invited Beth," Ty said. The sun reflected off Bernard's glasses as he digested it. "Drink some beer. Let's talk about old times."

Bernard moved away, and Ty caught up with Beth as she was leaving. He walked with her to the car. Leonard was waiting there to drive her back.

"She's nice, Ty." Beth got into the car, a little teary. "Real nice. I can see why he didn't come back. . . . It sure hurts to have him gone."

She wound down the window. "Not much meat on her. But she must of had somethin' Fenton wanted."

"You did too," Ty said. "I know you did."

Dan Murphy collared him as soon as he got back.

"Them Indians is into the beer," he said. "That's a worry." But Ty looked and saw that the men were just as serious out in the lot as they had been in the schoolhouse, giving their children a little food, a few sips of beer. They stayed for awhile and were gone, slipping away as quietly as they'd come, some to Indian Town, others around the Missions to the reservation.

It was one of the packers and two cowboys that Dan should have worried about—and Buck. Gus and Ty cut the cowboy-packer problem off before it got started, Gus getting them more beer while Ty started them talking about the back-country rather than where the cattle should graze, what land the packers could cross getting to their mountains.

Jasper was a little drunk by the time Ty took Cody Jo home. He was telling Fenton stories to Buck, the two of them laughing and getting maudlin and enjoying each other. Gus told Ty he'd look after them. Dan said the same, that he'd clean everything up. Ty wasn't sure of any of it, but he still thought he'd better leave. Cody Jo had had a long day.

⌒⌒

He didn't learn about Buck and Bernard until he came out of the woods, and he wasn't sure Cody Jo ever found out. She'd already left the valley, and by then the fight was mostly just a matter of amusement.

From what he learned, Buck had been drinking happily with Jasper when something got under his skin. He'd walked over to Bernard and hit him, breaking his glasses and sending him backward through the dust.

Bernard had got right back up and knocked Buck down, though Jasper later made light of that, saying Buck was partway falling down from beer already. Jasper claimed Buck was lucky his first punch caught Bernard anywhere at all, much less right between the eyes.

As surprised as Buck had been to find himself on his back, he wasn't so drunk he couldn't get up and swing at Bernard again, missing entirely and winding up with Bernard in a headlock. The force of it had sent them both back down, where they rolled and punched at one another in the dust, ignoring everyone who tried to separate them until the Sister of Providence began hitting them with a broom handle.

"Get up," she'd said, her voice still lovely as she poked at them. "Quit rolling around in all that dirt."

Buck, whose parents had been Catholics, got up quickly, as did Bernard. They apologized, which surprised the sister as much as their stopping. They went off then, each in his separate direction as though their argument had settled with the dust.

Most of the people in the Swan thought it had too, that beer was what caused the fighting—beer and something that didn't like to bend in Bernard. They laughed about it and consulted Jasper about the details, but to them it was over and done with.

It was only Ty who didn't think so, who thought the anger would remain—in both of them. Ty and maybe Willie, who wouldn't admit what she felt about it even to herself.

It would be almost three years before they would learn they were right.

29

Ashes

Jasper and Buck were impressed by how alert Ty was at night in the mountains. "He always keeps an ear on the lookout," Jasper would brag. "Even after a big feed."

It was a different matter when he was between clean sheets and in a bed, no worries about drifting horses or marauding bears. He didn't realize Cody Jo was there until she was beside him, the warmth of her changing his sleep, changing his life, her hand sliding down his body.

"I need to be here." Her voice was a breath in his ear. "Hold me. Let me touch you. Let me," she breathed. "I need this."

He felt himself lifting, felt her hand along the flat of his stomach, tracing the hairline and then taking him, flooded now, into her hand, stroking him, bending to kiss him there, her breath a long sigh. She moved onto him, held his hands away as she moved, not taking him inside her but rubbing her wet along his hardness, moving and moving until he heard her gasp.

She let him hold her now, bent to kiss him, moved her hips until he was inside her—wet and open with a warmth that sucked away his breath. She began moving again, moving and moving until she moaned, arched, her hips coming forward to take all of him, her eyes on him as she saw he could take no more. Coupled, they turned until she was under him, her fingers rimming his lips, her tongue moving into his mouth, her hips rising to his. "Yes," she said. "Yes, oh yes" as he spent himself, as she was saying yes and yes and her hand was going across his mouth, quieting him.

They lay there, her hand still on his mouth, his want for her even greater than moments before when everything in him needed to fill her. He didn't know how long they were there. He only knew how much more of her he wanted—her neck, her lips, the nipples that grew and lifted under his lips.

Everything seemed right about it. Nothing wrong. The only thing that seemed strange—he came to see later—was that it was so right. Even when she breathed into him, saying, "You see now. There are two loves of my life. You are the other."

They waited to make love again. And did. Cody Jo moaning as she came to him. Cried out again, her face wild and fixed on his as she caught her breath again, then again. Once more he spent himself in her, wanting to put every part of him into her wetness—his heart, his senses, the tongue she seemed to drink from him. He wanted to turn himself inside out within her.

They slept then, though he knew he didn't want to sleep, wanted to be awake with her forever, touching her forever, inside her forever.

And just before dawn they were dancing, naked, there in the still room. They swayed to her humming, feet hardly moving, their bodies one. He felt no awkwardness, nothing but the sweetness of being one with her, moving easily, sensually, as she hummed "I Got It Bad," "Have Mercy," "Moonglow."

They made love still again. Old lovers now, savoring one another, Ty pacing himself for her, exhausting her until the end when he would lose everything in her. She saw it, wanted it too, wanted it for him, wanted it so she seemed to pull everything from him, milk him until he cried out, her breath matching his, her moans a muffled sob against his skin.

He must have slept then. He knew only that she was gone. There was the smell of coffee, bacon. A thin line of dawn was lifting above the Swan.

"Could we marry?" he asked. "I never knew . . . ," he sat there, lost for a way to say it, ". . . this could be."

"I know. You are my love, Ty. You are." She seemed sad and happy at once. She had never looked so beautiful, her hair loose, the color lifting in her face, her eyes on him—as though there were not enough of him.

And then the Haslams were there. She was feeding them too.

"Will you come to the corrals?" Ty asked. "See us off?"

"I will. With lunch. Cookies for the trail."

"I'll be saddled and packed before the sun hits the meadow." Ty put his hat on and stood in the door, looking back at her. "Maybe sooner." His eyes took her in. "I'm already hungry for that lunch."

He was waiting for them. The horses saddled, the packs balanced, hitches tight.

"A special lunch for Ty." Cody buckled sandwiches into his saddlebags.

"What about us?" Thomas was tying Alice's slicker behind her cantle. "For us it's scary, an adventure. For Ty it's all in a day's work."

"He might be tired," Cody Jo said. "Packers get tired too." She looked at Ty, her eyes alive, her cheeks flushed. "Saving lives."

"You've made mine," Ty whispered to her before he swung up on Smoky. "I never . . ."

"Yes," she said. "I know."

"One week. I'll be out in one week. . . ."

"Yes." She smiled up at him, her eyes wet. "One week."

⌒⌒

Fenton's ashes weren't on Ty's mind now. Cody Jo was. No matter how much thinking he did, nothing made it as simple as it had seemed that night, her needs pushing everything else aside. Now she was everywhere with him, in the streams and meadows, on the passes and along the lifting canyon walls. He even thought of her when he went below the big rock, saw the fresh tracks, knew the bear had come back, knew that Fenton's ashes would soon be drifting across them. It was a thing he couldn't tell Cody Jo, who had wanted no part of these ashes, but it wouldn't leave him, didn't leave him even as he and Thomas Haslam spread them, listened as Alice read the poem she'd chosen.

"Sunset and evening star," she read, standing on the rock, ash dust hanging in the slanting sun.

And one clear call for me!
And may there be no moaning of the bar,
When I put out to sea.

In that late sun Ty found himself thinking not so much about Fenton's being gone as Fenton's being there—how much Fenton had given the bear, these woods, him. The words in the poem caught none of it. Nor could he. He wondered if anything could.

Alice closed her book and they stood in quiet, Ty watching a last dusting of ash settle across the bear's track. They walked back to the camp together, shadows growing long, cool coming in, a fire needed.

"Didn't she say why? Where she was going?"

"Said she was headed for Chicago. Left you a letter with Angie." Gus was deliberate, careful, sensing something he didn't want to know. "She gave me a hug at the station, but she looked forlorn—or scared." The mill's big belts were busy behind him. "You look that way now."

"I just need to see her, that's all." Ty got back in the pickup.

Gus leaned in the window. "People think I got this scar from a bear." It was so unexpected that Ty stopped, his hand on the key. "I didn't. I got it because I was crazy over a woman. Which can hurt a lot more than a damned bear."

"C'mon, Gus." Ty started the motor. "A bear can kill a man."

"So can bein' moonstuck." The scar looked pale as Gus backed from the window. "Difference is you get to see a bear comin'."

Ty puzzled over it as he drove to Murphy's store. There was no way Gus could know what was eating at him. No way anyone could. Who could know how Cody Jo was that night? He could hardly believe it himself.

Angie, looking worried, gave him the letter. "You look discombobulated, Ty. Can't you give a smile?"

She hugged him and he left her there in the doorway, driving only a little way before pulling over and reading the letter and feeling his legs go weak, his stomach queasy. He drove to the house and sat down to read it again, his hands shaking.

> I love you, Ty. You'll be with me forever. In my waking and my sleeping.
>
> I told you there were two loves in my life. And a part of me knows your love is closer, even stronger than Fenton's— so fresh in me it hurts.
>
> But I know that it can't survive. It tears me apart to say it. My legs are jelly. I can barely hold this pen.
>
> It's not our ages. The same years separated me from Fenton. But Fenton and I could fill each other's days. I can't do that for you. You have some hollow place I can't reach. It would kill me to watch you, day after day, needing what I can't give.
>
> You are whole in your mountains. In time you will find a woman who doesn't pull you from them. She will give you

the children I can't. I will be jealous. But I'll know that is the woman you should have.

Fenton would understand. He would want me to love you, but he wouldn't want me to hurt you. I won't. I can't. I love you too much.

I'm falling apart inside, Ty. Your love, our love, is all that holds me together.

Cody Jo

Ty saw that her hand had been shaking when she signed it. He went into the guest room where they'd made love, went into her room, put a pair of boots she'd left into the empty closet. He went out into the sun and stood by the corral, tried to read the letter again, but found he couldn't.

After awhile he drove back to his horses, put out feed and went through his duffle to find the music box. He put the letter in and got things ready for the next trip, working steadily but without much plan, surprised when he turned to do something to see he'd done it already.

He slept at the corrals that night, used the lake to wash away the dust. But sleep didn't come, his mind playing over where Cody Jo might be, how he could get an address, where he could set out looking for her when the season was over. He thought about their night together too, the things she'd said, the songs she'd hummed, what she'd told him with her body. He tossed and turned with it, watching the cool stars.

⌒⌒

The guests were from Atlanta, the men clean shaven and boyish, the women pretty. They teased Angie and Buck with their soft accents as Buck balanced out their duffles. They'd spent the night at the big house, Angie and Buck telling them stories about Ty and Fenton and the back-country. They grew quiet around Ty as he chose their horses, sent them off toward the pass with Angie so he could finish packing with Buck.

Buck worked quietly for awhile, then said it: "Quit actin' like somebody pissed in your boot. It ain't that bad. She just wants you to run things. She set it all up with that banker."

"Then he must know where to reach her."

"Well, he knows where that aunt is." Buck tightened a rope.

"Then he must know where she is." Ty pulled the rope still tighter, a part of him wanting to start for her right now, another part saying wait—let things settle in Cody Jo. Get his own legs under him. When they pulled the string away from the corrals, he was calmer, quiet and steady—concentrating on his mules.

Except for his quietness it was a wonderful trip, the fishing better than good, the days long and sunny. The guests were drawn to the tall packer, liking it when he would stop to talk with them, point out things along the trail. But none of their schemes could draw him out. The men would smile, watch their wives use their southern ways to engage him. But not even the drinking worked, Buck and Angie getting entertaining and garrulous while Ty grew more private, pensive.

The rest of the season went the same way, Ty never busier, never more efficient, concentrating on his packing in a way that mystified Buck—and drove Angie to distraction.

"Can't you see? He's pinin' away. It breaks my heart."

"Hell, I try to keep up with him," Buck would say. "But he's on the go all the damn time, sometimes packin' for two parties at once, and takin' care of the fire crews too. I'm commencin' to think he likes it alone."

"He does, you dummy. And it's wreckin' him."

"Might perk him up if I got him into town."

"Stay the hell out of that place." Angie whacked him. "You got enough to handle right here."

When hunting season came Jasper took over the cooking, his fretting about bears lifting Ty's spirits a little.

"I wouldn't go sleepin' under that saddle rack," he'd say to Ty. "Somethin' might carry you off." Ty would smile as he muttered about bears. But the amusement wouldn't last long. Even Jasper worried about how often he'd come across Ty looking off across the country as though he didn't know what he'd lost.

When they pulled the hunting camps out and the snows closed the passes, Ty went in to see the banker, a man as mystified by packers as he was by Indians. He did all he could to help Ty, explaining that Cody Jo was in Europe on a walking trip with her aunt, the university in Chicago handling their mail. He explained how the bank was taking care of the accounts too, but Ty didn't hear that part. All he wanted to do was reach Cody Jo.

He went back out to the Swan and took care of the gear, finally writing a letter, asking the university to forward it. That winter a letter showed up, Cody Jo writing from Spain about the places they'd been, the things they'd done. At the end she wrote, "I think about you at night, Ty. I think about you always when we are in the mountains, wondering about you in yours—if you think of me, if you are dancing with someone new, if your life is good. I hope so. I love you so deeply." Ty read the words again and again, relieved to have them, lost about what to do with them.

He spent his days working in his saddle shop or helping out the lumberjacks and the ranchers. He got organized for the next year's packing too, signing Forest Service contracts, scheduling trips. He wanted the packing to go well. That was something he could do for Cody Jo.

And night after night he sat on the big couch, reading a little but mostly just looking into the fire.

Willie (1947–1949)

If at first he hadn't loved her the way he had loved Cody Jo, he found himself loving her more as their winter days opened into spring.

30

The Librarian

It was a relief to Willie when Ty would walk into her library. He was always working with colts or green mules, and she was afraid one might plunge off the trail, dragging the rest behind him. But she knew Ty was good at his work, gentle with his animals—as she was sure most packers were not. And she liked it that the life didn't harden him, not the inside of him. She made sure of that, giving him books that offered some balance.

Bernard Strait came in to see her too, but not for books. More and more of his work was with the Missoula office, and he would come with big Forest Service reports under his arm, studying them in the reading room and looking up to smile at her, making no bones about being there to enjoy Wilma Ring. He would take her to movies, to lectures and basketball games. The pretty librarian was well known on the campus, and Bernard was happy to be with her, enjoying her popularity, proud of her and pleased to see to whatever needs she had.

With Ty it was different. He was always polite, but he hardly knew what her needs were. He would grow quiet with her friends, stand a little apart, meeting them willingly enough but reticent—as though not sure it was right to intrude on her world. She liked it best when he took her dancing. She liked the way he relaxed to music, knew almost all the songs, humming them, sometimes speaking the words, his voice just a whisper. She didn't even mind the drinking. It didn't seem to change him much, just make him relaxed. She liked it most when Angie and Buck would join them, Buck laughing and dancing with her in his big, open way; Angie making over Ty, her energy contagious. Sometimes Buck would order shots of whiskey with their beer. Willie would sip hers, her eyes watering, but liking its warmth, liking the way Ty watched her as she drank.

"I'm not sayin' Bernard's the pick of the litter," her father told her one morning after she'd come home from Mass to cook him a big Sunday breakfast. "Just that he's a better bet than Ty. Not likely to leave you for half a year to moon around the mountains lookin' at sunsets."

"I like them both." Willie was surprised to hear her father being critical of Ty. The trail crews swore by him, called him the most reliable packer from Missoula all the way into Canada. She got out eggs, thinking about the night before at the Elkhorn—the music, the people. "Ty's just more fun to dance with." She broke the eggs into a skillet, stirred them.

"Probably fun to do more than dance with." Bob Ring still couldn't get used to how pretty his daughter had become. "It just might be fun that leaves you blue as night . . . after he's had his."

"Ty's not interested in me." She was flustered by the way her father looked at her. "He lost interest in a lot of things after Cody Jo went away."

"Healthy man like that doesn't lose interest in *some* things. You better be thankful that's not what he's after."

"Why be thankful?" She put eggs and bacon and toast in front of him and messed up his hair. "Librarians need excitement too."

"Watch your damn step." He pointed his fork at her. "Ty's not one of those altar boys down at that church of yours."

"Maybe that's why I like him." She laughed as she watched her father's face redden. "That old library gets pretty quiet."

"Ty does too," her father said. "Which might be when he's most interesting . . . and dangerous. Stay in your library. It's quiet *and* safe."

"Fathers! I think you'd like to lock us all up in a tower."

"With reason," Bob Ring said, getting it all out and starting to eat. "With damn good reason."

None of it was lost on Willie. She knew Ty didn't always stay with Horace and Etta in Missoula. And it was clear that the people he'd say hello to in the street weren't the kind you'd find at Mass—or anywhere near a library. The truth is she was glad he knew them, glad to see he had a life outside his mountains.

It troubled her that that was where he was most at home. She tried to accept it, tell herself it was just a young man's affliction. But it nagged at her. There was a firmness in the way he looked at things, a finality that made her wonder if he could ever be comfortable outside them, where to his way of thinking people were caught up only in what they could own.

It made their times together unpredictable, not so much because of Ty but because of something in her. There were times when she was startled by her own response to something he would say or do, or the way he would look at her. Sometimes she'd feel a flutter in her stomach and want to put her arms around him, other times she'd feel something close to fear, a rush of blood that frightened her.

Everything, *everything*, about Bernard was different. He was as predictable as coffee, polite, careful to seem thoughtful but still as stubborn as a mule, which hardly bothered her. She had so many ways to get around his intransigence that it almost seemed endearing. She would see it coming, watch him put his tongue in his cheek, considering before shaking his head as though answering some higher logic. And she would back away, come at whatever it was from a different direction a day later, enjoying his acquiescence, smiling as her idea became his invention.

She knew Bernard wanted her for more than his partner at university gatherings. But it wasn't difficult to hold him at bay. And there certainly was no shortage of interested men. There were all the veterans stopping by her desk for help. There were the young professors, shy and awkward in their pretensions, asking her for coffee or to go to some special lecture in their field.

And she was in no hurry. She liked her courses in the English Department, enjoyed moving from one class to the next, coming to grips with the literature—the authors and the different approaches her professors would take to them.

And of course there was Ty. More interesting than any man she knew. And despite his rough profession, perhaps the most tender. She would watch him watching her, see that look on his face as though he knew getting close to her might be both the best and the most painful thing he could possibly do. It perplexed her. And it drew her to him.

⌒

In the summer Ty got another letter from Cody Jo, this one from Italy. Then some cards. Then another letter, describing where she'd been, the hikes she'd taken. And always there was something that sent his blood rushing, made it hard for him to swallow.

"I watched a sunset with you last night," she wrote in a card. "You were inside me." In another: "Morning coffee. My moment with you. I taste you. Feel your warmth in the early sun. You surround me."

One of the letters was from Switzerland. "We are hiking in these wonderful mountains," she wrote. "You are everywhere, in the peaks and flowers. But civilization has climbed too high here. What we have is higher than civilization can go." She crossed something out. "Is that possible? Am I too filled with you to make sense?"

But he had no way to answer. All he could do was read her words. It was easy to see his letters weren't reaching her. She answered none of his questions.

He got a manila envelope for the letters and carried it in the bottom of his duffle, reading them over on some sunny rock after an icy bath. Or reading them before dinner, taking a drink and walking away from the others, reading them in the late sun and wondering where Cody Jo might be at that moment, what people she would be making happier, more alive.

His life fell into a pattern. He'd read a lot over the winter, pacing his trips to Missoula with the books he needed. Willie had helped him more than he deserved: suggesting books, cooking dinners, getting him to go dancing at the Elkhorn or at the big dances at the university. He liked the dancing, Willie always a little reticent at first then relaxing, dancing more and more like Cody Jo. One night after Buck got her to drink a jigger of whiskey, he closed his eyes as they danced and it seemed she *was* Cody Jo.

There was no more kissing. He was too immersed in his sadness. He even thought Willie might be happier without the kissing. She seemed to be content—watching him as though waiting for something.

"You keep looking at me," Ty said to her one night between pack trips. There was a good band at the Elkhorn and Ty was glad to be in town for a night so they could go dancing. "It's enough to make a man jumpy." The band was playing a novelty number, a polka. They were watching Angie and Buck try to dance to it, Ty not ready for a polka.

"You can be pretty amusing," Willie said, "with some drink and good music."

"You like to laugh at me, don't you?"

"I like it when you laugh." She was part playful, part serious. "When you have a good time."

"Maybe dancing with you is what makes for a good time."

And then Bernard Strait was there, wanting to polka with Willie. They went out on the floor, and Ty could see right away that Bernard was good, fast—his leg coming up and banging down with each step. Ty watched them, Willie catching the rhythms perfectly but willowy and giving as she moved to Bernard's energy. He saw that Buck was watching them too, Buck's face red from all he was putting into it. Ty thought Buck was going to dance over and give Bernard a good bump, but Angie cut it off, heading them in another direction.

Ty was glad she did. He knew how much Bernard liked Willie, and though Bernard didn't seem the right man for all her generosity and liveliness, Ty knew he had no business saying so. He felt lucky Willie was so good to him, uncomplaining when he would sweep down out of his mountains and rush into town for supplies, new books, conversation.

Once that spring she'd even offered to break a movie date with Bernard so she could go down to the Elkhorn with Ty.

But Ty wouldn't have it. Something about Bernard was troubling him more and more. He didn't want to make it worse. He'd stopped in at The Bar of Justice that night instead, not wanting to go upstairs so much as to have someone to talk with before he drove back to the pack station.

"You're looking a little better," Beth told him. "It ain't been pleasant watchin' you walk around sober as an owl."

"Got all my gear ready for the season," Ty answered. "Got to pack lumber to those Forest Service cabins tomorrow. Too busy to be sad."

"But you are." Beth patted his arm. "It ain't hard to see. Go on and take Loretta upstairs. She's slowin' down on the AA. That ought to perk somethin' up." She poured him a drink, pleased by that one.

Loretta came over. She'd been drinking and there was a lot of color in her face. She looked as pretty as she had that first time he'd seen her.

"I give up on that AA turd. I might marry a cowboy."

"Can one afford you?" Ty asked. "They aren't high income."

"Try them Forest Service boys," Beth suggested. "Uncle Sam pays regular." She laughed, mopped at the bar. "Those boys is still talkin' about when it took all of them to throw Spec out."

Ty hadn't gone upstairs with Loretta that night, which was probably a good thing. But watching Bernard and Willie polka, he couldn't help thinking of some of the things he *had* done that winter. They didn't make him like himself very much. He'd gone upstairs with Loretta while she was still "letting go and letting God" and dealt with her as silently and roughly as though she might have given him his wound.

He'd even gotten drunk one day and gone by the cheerleader's house. She'd made over him, given him coffee and been sweet to him. But he'd just said bad things to her. He couldn't remember exactly what, just that he'd made her cry, that it hadn't bothered him when she did, that he'd left not even remembering why he'd come.

And when old man Conner's cattle got trapped by a big snow he'd pushed Smoky so hard she'd almost foundered. Her legs shaking, icicles hanging from her bit, steam rising from her as he swore at the Conner boys, pushed her so hard there was no way the others could keep up. They'd led their horses back only to see Ty bring the cattle in at dawn, save them and almost lose the best mare in the valley. Ty saw it too, but said nothing, just looked at them in their silence, spitting and rubbing Smoky down in the shelter of their barn, his hands shaking because of what he'd put her through—the madness that had driven him in the night.

☾⁀

The dancers had been so enthusiastic the band played a second polka. Ty watched Bernard and Willie swing back into the music, watched them dance only a little before Willie turned and came back to the table.

"Bernard has worn me out," she said. Bernard stood there, still breathing hard from the polka, unhappy the dancing was over.

Ty saw it, asked him to sit, offered him a beer. Bernard did, talking politely even after Buck returned to the table, Buck looking a little sour because Bernard was there. But it wasn't long before Willie and Angie had Buck laughing, their talk so animated it even made Bernard smile.

Things stayed a little edgy until Bernard left, and Ty knew it wasn't all Buck's fault. Bernard always had trouble when the Forest Service listened to the packers; he had even more when Ty was the packer. And it wasn't lost on him how much trouble Bernard had when he saw Ty having fun with Willie. He just didn't like to think about it. It was too complicated.

By the time Bernard left the evening was almost over. The band played a last set: "Satin Doll" and "S'posin'" and "That Old Black Magic." Willie had had some sips of Buck's whiskey while she and Angie were fooling around, and as far as Ty could tell it made her dancing better than ever. The band finished with "Stars Fell on Alabama," and it was as though he *were* dancing with Cody Jo. Only this time he knew it was Willie in his arms.

When they got back to Willie's, he got out of his truck and walked her to the porch. "I'm sorry about this past winter," he said. "I haven't been much of a friend."

She watched, her eyes deep in the faint light from the porch.

"Things pass," she said. "If you give them time."

"You've helped with that. You and the music."

"Your mountains helped with that." She lifted her hand, touched his cheek. "Your mountains and their music."

Ty didn't get out to the pack station until almost two in the morning, and he had to get up at five to start saddling. He drank a glass of milk and went to bed in the big guest room. Angie had fixed up Cody Jo and Fenton's room so it could take guests. This one was pretty much his by now.

He got in bed, but sleep wouldn't come. He turned on the bedside light and got out the manila envelope, starting in to read Cody Jo's letters again.

It wasn't long before he was asleep, the light still on, the letters scattered across his chest.

31

1948

Looking back, Ty would find a certain symmetry about the year: marriages at the beginning and the end—no way to see either one coming. It was as though he'd stumbled onto some trail he had to follow because there was no other way. And no way to turn back.

Two letters from Cody Jo should have warned him. "We have been joined by my aunt's colleagues," she wrote. "One of them is Bliss Holliwell. He has written four books. Very distinguished." She went on to say that her aunt's friends didn't know about packers but that she was trying to explain, and learning much about the Victorians while she tried.

The next letter was from England. "They call this the Lake Country," she wrote. "There are mountains, but not like yours. They are open and safe, even when it rains." She told him she was learning about people who had time and incomes and snug houses, people who wrote about each other—what they were thinking, doing for society, how they spent their days. "It's a life packers might not understand. You are such men of action."

It clouded Ty's days to see the distance between them grow. Cody Jo still put time aside just for him. He knew he was with her, somehow. But he wasn't sure how. He *was* sure how she was with him: along every trail he rode, in the fires he watched and the music he loved. But he knew too that it was changing—as sunrises do when winter comes.

It confused him that she'd once needed him so much and now was so sure they should be apart—though he did his best to make sense of it. Cody Jo cared more about people than anyone he'd ever known. She was always sure of what to do, could explain it in that compelling way she had—direct, knowing just what needed to be said.

She was certainly direct when she told him of her marriage. "I have married Bliss Holliwell," she wrote. "But my love for you is so strong you were somehow there, wanting what's right for me. For us." She went on to say that she knew Bliss Holliwell was not the best man in her life, but he was the right man for her now—and in a way for Ty too. "He knows about you, Ty. He understands us. He is gentle, kind—a safe harbor for what will always be ours."

She ended saying, "You and Fenton remain the men of my life. But Fenton is gone. You are the dangerous one. My love for you is dangerous. With my declaration to Bliss we will be safe. It makes sense of us."

Sense was not what it made to Ty. It was as though she had torn away his insides. He got drunk the first day. And the second, the fire blazing, too lost and empty to find his bed. Then a storm came in and he had to fight it to feed the stock. That sobered him. He took to working on his saddles, making repairs in the barn—doing anything he could to keep from thinking, facing a world that seemed upside down.

It was Willie who put him back together. It wasn't that she said anything; she just accepted it, took it in as though it were a book read and put aside until it was absorbed. You could go back to it, read the words again, but the story was told. You lived with that.

⌇⌐

"Cody Jo has gotten married," he'd said to her, standing at her desk in the library with some books she'd given him. It was early February, two weeks after he'd read Cody Jo's letter. He looked a little surprised himself, still bundled against the cold in one of Fenton's ragged old coats. He hadn't meant to say anything at all. It just came out of him.

"Stay for dinner. I'm making a roast."

"No time. Things to do."

The thought of sitting over a meal and talking to Bob Ring and Willie was too much for him. He'd talked to no one since he'd read the letter, which was why the news burst out of him so unexpectedly. A bottle so full can't stay corked forever.

"Librarians need coffee breaks too." Willie checked to make sure no one needed her. "Especially when a well-dressed cowboy makes an offer."

Ty didn't remember saying anything at all about coffee, but it was nice to walk through the cold with her to the student cafeteria.

"Why is it such a surprise?" Willie watched him over her coffee. "She loves literature. Suddenly there's this great teacher. A worthy man to care for. She's wonderful at that. She loved taking care of Fenton."

"There's others she could look after." Ty never did know if Willie understood how he felt about Cody Jo. That day was the only time she even hinted at knowing.

"Some men don't want to be taken care of." She sipped her coffee. "You don't. You like to take care of others. Up there. In your mountains."

"I might tolerate being cared for. If she's so good at it."

"Maybe she tried, in her way." Willie's blue eyes were on him. "Maybe you wouldn't let her. Couldn't let her."

Ty took the books she offered him and headed back. There was no wind, but it was deep cold. He drove with the heater on high, but the chill leaked in everywhere. When he got home, he fired up the stove and drank some milk. Then he got out a pad and a pencil and sat down at the kitchen table to write Cody Jo.

Years later Cody Jo would tell him that was the best letter he'd ever written. It didn't seem that way to Ty, not that night. He just wrote what he had to write, wishing her his best, which he did; wanting the best for her, which he always had. He told her that he would take care of the pack station just as she wanted him to, but that he didn't see how he could take it over from the bank. He was holding his own with them. That was enough. And then he told her that he wanted very much to see her, that he loved her still. That was the hardest part, saying it so it wasn't wrong, didn't ask anything of her.

The next day he drove through the snow to Murphy's to meet the mail run. There was nothing more he could think of to say.

$\backsim$

The rest of the winter was a blur. He replaced all the worn rigging on the pack saddles, oiled and repaired the riding saddles, putting longer tie strings on each. He took on as much leather work as he could. And when the Conner boys got sick, he took over their feeding chores, quieting the half-broken team as he did. Old man Conner had a hard time believing it.

"Them boys should stay sick longer," he said, watching Ty work the team through high drifts to put out the feed. "You got things goin' so slick I forget to complain about this shitty weather."

Ty even filled in for Gus's brothers at the sawmill. They'd gotten into trouble in Great Falls and the judge kept them to work it off. Ty didn't like the sawmill, but he stuck it out. He'd had a soft spot for Gus since the first day he met him.

He didn't go to Missoula much, but when he did he'd stop and have coffee with Willie. She even got him dancing again, Ty surprised to realize he was the one who had to get relaxed—not Willie. But they had fun, Willie kidding him because he was no longer finishing the books she gave him. And when he told her Cody Jo wanted him to take over the pack station she got out a pen and asked him lots of questions, writing down the answers as though she were a bookkeeper.

"We'll see what we shall see." She put away her pen and stood. "But now," she led him onto the floor, "there's music."

The band was playing "How High the Moon," and with Willie so alive in his arms, it hardly seemed a chore to get relaxed.

The melt came fast that spring. Ty was in the back-country by June, supplying all the ranger stations and trail crews up and down the South Fork. Then an early fishing party came in and then another. And there were trail crews to move and Forest Service training sessions to supply and still more fishing parties. It went on like that, Ty sometimes having two or three parties in the woods at the same time—shuttling between them with his mules, moving camps, resupplying, tacking shoes back on, doctoring, keeping people comfortable.

There was so much work Ty had to keep Buck and Jasper busy all summer. Angie too. The work seemed endless, Buck getting Bump to help sometimes, Ty prying Gus loose from his sawmill when he had to.

But it was good work, and there were surprises that made it better. It was a surprise to have so much business from the Forest Service. It was a surprise to have Buck and Angie become such a part of everything, Angie organizing matters in the front country even better than Ty could in the back. The biggest surprise was when she showed up with two extra guests for the Haslams' trip.

"That man looks pretty damned official to me," Horace said. "Says he knows you." Angie had brought the Haslams and the Adamses to the Crippled Elk corrals. It was Horace and Etta's last trip, one they wouldn't be taking at all if the Haslams hadn't been so persuasive. They'd made their decision to go at Christmas and hadn't stopped planning since. Or worrying.

"The doc knows him. Met him at the Presidio back there." Horace was looking at the saddle Ty had put on Turkey, who—despite his willfulness—was the mildest horse Ty had in his string. "You gonna make me sit in this saddle for two days and nights the way Fenton done?"

"You sound like Jasper," Ty said. "You rode all *one* day and into the night. Not through it."

"Seemed longer." Horace stepped back, looked at Turkey. "This ain't no bronc, is it?"

"Hardly," Ty said, watching Turkey doze in the sun. "When are Doc's friends getting here?"

"They'll be along," Horace said. "Might be more your friend than the doc's. . . . Think we'll get rain?"

"Who?" Ty wasn't sure Horace knew what he was talking about.

"That man there." Horace shook out his rain gear and pointed at a military sedan pulling up. Jeb Walker got out, smiling at Ty.

"Hardin . . . guess I'll finally get to see you pack something besides machine guns and ammunition."

"Colonel Walker?" Ty was having a hard time believing Jeb Walker could be in anything but a uniform.

"General now," a voice Ty would never forget said. "It's General Walker." Otis Johnson was standing there, his smile as wide as the South Fork. "Thought you might reenlist."

The Haslams introduced them all around, explaining they'd met Jeb Walker in San Francisco, talked to him there about Ty. The surprise was their idea. Otis Johnson was Jeb Walker's.

"Two of my best soldiers." Jeb Walker was shaking hands with Horace. "Though Hardin didn't want to be."

Ty had trouble swallowing. There they all were—no uniforms or orders or big guns firing overhead. All of them safe in the morning sun at the Crippled Elk corrals. He turned away, picked out horses, collected himself.

When he was sure he could talk again, he got them mounted and sent them ahead, seeing right away how naturally Jeb Walker and Otis Johnson sat their horses. He was thankful he'd set time aside for this trip. And it didn't take him long to realize how thankful he was Angie had decided to come, Alice and Angie calming Etta, keeping Jasper in line, doing things with the food that made dinners the highlight of each day.

It was one of the best trips Ty would know in a lifetime of packing—and with some of the best people he would know in that lifetime. He took them to waterfalls, the best pools, led them high above the China Wall to see the breathtaking drop east, look back across the South Fork.

"You were right, Hardin," Jeb Walker said one evening at sunset. "It was our dream. But it was your reality. You'd left all this."

Ty wasn't sure what he'd been right about. He didn't remember talking with Walker at all about the country, just about mules. But he didn't pursue it. Jeb Walker might act less military in the mountains, but he was still Jeb Walker. His voice still made Ty stand straighter, move a little faster. But Ty saw he was different, saw that he spent a lot of time alone by the river, sometimes fishing, sometimes just standing in it, watching.

Otis Johnson took to it too, liking the little things: the way the bear grass took over, the rapids picked up, the wildflowers flourished. He liked Ty's way with animals best, learning about packing, going out with him to bring in the horses, squatting with him to look at tracks— elk, deer, bear.

Angie and Alice managed to improve Jasper's food so much Thomas Haslam claimed they'd topped "The Top of the Mark." Etta would sip a drink with them, laughing, forgetting how worried she could get about bears and weather and the language Horace used in the mountains.

"It's never been so civilized up here." She watched Angie put napkins and silverware out on a big log she'd fashioned into a buffet table.

"That's 'cause we always had Buck along." Angie tidied the silverware. "When Buck rides in, the whole camp starts downhill."

"Be fair," Alice said. "Buck has his charm."

"The trick," Angie said, "is to keep him from usin' it."

Jasper enjoyed hearing them talk, enjoyed even more the way they took over his cooking, giving him plenty of time to socialize. He just wished the general would offer him some of the bourbon he'd brought along. Angie had cut off the cooking sherry, which made no sense to him. He'd snuck in three extra bottles. No recipe required that much, not even these fancy ones. But the third night Jeb Walker spoke up and won Jasper's heart once and for all. He was impressed by the general already, but being impressed hadn't meant being comfortable around him.

"All right to offer your men a drink up here, Hardin?" Jeb Walker asked. "A cup or two might agree with this cook of yours." Thomas Haslam and Horace had joined Walker, Ty and Otis staying with their coffee.

"Jasper enjoys a drink." Ty's face revealed nothing. "And he's got time. They've all but fenced off his kitchen."

Jasper wasn't shy about accepting. After that he and the general shared a few drinks each evening. "Treats me like a guest," Jasper would tell Ty, sipping the bourbon and enjoying the fire. And he would tell his bear tales, tell stories about Ty and Fenton that Ty couldn't remember himself.

It rained only one day, a day they spent gathered in the kitchen tent around Jeb Walker's bourbon, Jasper embellishing on his adventures with the red bear—who loomed ever larger in his imagination.

One story led to another, and after awhile Haslam started talking about the Sierra Nevada, describing waterfalls dropping from high granite rims and packers claiming it never rains there at night. Walker knew those mountains too. When he was a lieutenant they'd asked him to ride across them on a rerun of a Pony Express route.

"Spectacular range," he told them. "Forgiving from the west; hard as the devil's teeth on the east." He looked at Ty. "Tough country for horses. Rock and more rock. You could pack it. Most shouldn't try. We lost a good remount not respecting it enough."

Ty listened for awhile, then he got his slicker and went to see which direction his horses had headed. Otis Johnson went with him, liking his talks with Ty. "My boy has taken to playing football," he said, as they picked up tracks. "I believe up here would do him better."

"You played football. I sure remember that. I did too, in school. Played end."

"He don't play like you and me," Otis said. "He's like smoke. Hard to catch hold of."

"Wish I'd been that way. You knocked me silly."

"Be good if he got knocked some too. Football's no game to float around in." Otis looked at Ty. "Life ain't either."

Ty was amused to hear Otis fret about how his boy would bend and twist, go out of bounds before they could bring him down. But he took it as Otis's humor. On the last day, when Otis asked again if Ty might have work for the boy, he realized it wasn't. It wasn't a hard question to answer, not if the boy was anything like Otis. Ty said yes. And that seemed to satisfy Otis.

A letter from Willie was waiting for Ty at the corrals. Buck had brought it out and left it on the dashboard of Walker's car.

"If it's from that librarian we met," Jeb Walker said, passing it on to Ty, "I'd answer 'yes'—no matter what the question."

Ty was more surprised by Jeb Walker's easy warmth than with the letter.

"Yes, sir," he said. "I always paid attention to your advice."

"Forget 'Sir.' That's over," Walker said seriously. "You've given me a trip I'll never forget." No "general" in his voice at all now. "I'll come back, Ty. Where you pack, I'll go."

"And don't you forget my boy," Otis said, smiling at him. "He might could learn from you even after I finish with him." He cuffed Ty with his hand, knocking him off balance.

Ty waved good-bye, rubbing his arm and wondering if affection like Otis's wasn't what taught the boy to be elusive.

Willie's letter was brief, but attached were pages of neat columns.

"It looks like you can do it," she wrote. "I've gone over Angie's records twice and have a firm promise from the bank. If business stays healthy, you can make the pack station yours."

Ty shuffled through the papers, shaking his head at Willie's efficiency. He knew the figures would be accurate and he knew he might be able to do all the things she asked.

But he also knew he wasn't likely to do them. Willie didn't understand that owning a pack station wasn't why he was a packer.

ᴄ-⊃

And then that fall it happened. Not in the mountains, where you can drop off a cliff or run into a grizzly at any moment, but in Missoula, where there aren't those dangers. Ty never was sure he had the story straight, but he never talked about it as anything but an accident. That much he could do for Willie.

He'd heard from Beth what happened down at The Bar of Justice. It was so out of keeping with anything she would make up that he knew it had to be true, or close to true—as true as Beth could see it.

There had been a lot to put away after the passes closed, the season so busy Ty had to buy what was left after a packer out of Ovando rolled his string and cashed in. That got them through the season, but it all needed rerigging, which kept Buck busy until Angie left to tend to her mother in the Whitefish hospital. That's when Buck moved into town to be with the kids, doing some work for Horace but mostly rattling around as lonely as an old bear.

"And just about as touchy," Beth told Ty after the fight. "At least that's the way he got when he saw Bernard. The man had never come in here once, but he come in like he owned the place, drunk as his Forest Service buddies and mean enough to start a war."

Ty pieced it together. Bob Ring's retirement was a big one. Forty years in the Forest Service meant a lot to all of them; Bob Ring did too. They liked to have him limp into one of their stations and cheer everyone up. He knew the packers, and he knew the rules, and he had a way of bringing them together so no one got rubbed the wrong way. Except Bernard now and then. Bernard was probably the hardest working ranger in the Forest Service, and the least bendable too.

Bob Ring had tried to put a little more bend in him at the going-away party the men gave him, saying that he was likely to be the last of an old school of rangers and Bernard was likely to be the first of a new one, that if he could leave a little of the old around it might make life a lot easier for the new.

The rest of them picked up on that, toasting Bob Ring and Bernard with such good humor they became as drunk on what was said as on what they drank. And they drank plenty, Bob Ring thinking he could sleep his off on the train to San Francisco, Bernard hardly thinking, just happy to be appreciated. Happy at first, that is, before he felt the numbness come over him. But the toasts went on, Bernard's numbness disappearing into a haze of fellowship and wild promises as they sent Ring on his way, waving at the train before going off to the Elkhorn for more.

It was there, Ty figured, that they hit on the idea of taking Bernard to The Bar of Justice, thinking the drinking had done him so much good they might as well take him the whole way and do him even better.

They didn't know that Buck would be there, lonely and sober. They didn't know what went on deep in Bernard either—things Bernard couldn't see himself. They just knew that it was fun, that they were laughing, that they had Bernard swearing and vowing crazy things and that for once he wasn't looking disgusted when they mentioned The Bar of Justice.

Buck was having a beer and talking with Beth when they came in, rowdy and swearing and full of liquor. Beth didn't like it from the outset, which made Buck try to calm things down.

"You boys better settle," he said, "or Leonard'll read you the riot act." A Sun River ranger wasn't too drunk to understand the warning.

"If you'll hold your horses," he told them, "I'll buy a round." That quieted everyone but Bernard.

"I see you're down here where you belong," Bernard said to Buck. And the way he said it wasn't so much drunk as mean.

"You come down here more often, you might improve too." Buck seemed to enjoy how angry Bernard was getting.

"I got no need to come down here," Bernard said. And then it just popped out of him, as though it had been waiting there to be challenged.

"I'm marryin' Wilma Ring."

Hearing something like that about Bob Ring's pretty daughter quieted them all. Buck's voice broke through, nothing amused in it now.

"You asshole. You couldn't fuck Willie with Ty's cock."

Bernard came at Buck so fiercely his own momentum did most of the damage. But the moment Buck landed the blow, he knew he couldn't have done better.

"Shit." The Sun River ranger looked at Bernard, sprawled across a collapsed table, blood flowing from his nose. "No need. He would have fallen if you'd stepped aside."

"I wanted to," Buck said. "It done me good."

Leonard came in, his big assistant looking ugly while Leonard shooed them out the backdoor, helping the last two pick Bernard up and giving them a rag to sop up the blood. "And good riddance." He looked at Buck. "You too. You're trouble drunk or sober. Oughta make you and the ranger boy pay for the fuckin' table too. It ain't fixable."

"No need to hit him like that, Buck." Beth was mopping at the bar. "Drunk as he was." She threw the rag at him. "Quit smilin' and get the hell out. If they come lookin', they ain't gonna find you here."

Ty had heard the first speeches at Ring's party before he went up to the university to join Willie for the lecture about Lewis and Clark. He was always impressed by how much they'd done, knowing so little about what was ahead. His guess was that in the early days few could see very far ahead, and even when they got to where they could, they were probably so far along the road that got them there it was too late to turn back.

He talked with Willie about that, eating ice cream after the talk, saying he guessed everyone's life was like that—a little.

"Only some people start out on rockier roads than others," Willie said. "Like one of those trails you use that no one else can find."

"I just steer clear of your ranger friends. They're gettin' so they want to do all your seein' ahead for you."

"I think you want to steer clear of everyone," Willie said. "Angie told me you've got little trails in there a goat couldn't find."

"I just go where the mountains let me," Ty said. He enjoyed the way she mocked him, pointing her spoon at him. "Let them do the choosing."

Ty was getting into his pickup to start the long drive back when a sheriff's car pulled alongside.

"Your buddy got himself into a scrape tonight," the officer said.

"Buck? Where?" Ty knew how restless Buck had been and what trouble he could get into if he put his mind to it.

"Down there," the officer said. "I'm not supposed to know."

That's when Ty went to see Beth, learning all he could before going off to look for Buck. But Buck wasn't in any of his usual places, and hadn't been—though most everyone knew something had happened.

Ty finally found him asleep at home, not nearly as worried as everyone else seemed to be. He got up and had a beer with Ty.

"Caught him right, Ty. Don't think you—or Fenton—could of done better." He took a long pull at his beer. "Sure made me feel good."

"No need to hit a drunk. Doesn't prove a thing."

"He *was* right drunk," Buck said. "Nice to have two good things happen to Bernard on the same night."

Ty slept there that night. In the morning he walked over to see Willie, buying her a paper on the way and hoping he could talk her into one of her Sunday breakfasts before he headed back for the pack station.

It was all over when he got there. And not long ago from what he could tell. She didn't answer his knock. He went in to find her collapsed on the floor in her own vomit. When she saw him she retched again, nothing left to come up now—just the retching, the fighting for air.

He lifted her onto a kitchen chair, wiped the vomit from her face, her blouse, found a towel and mopped at the floor. She tried to speak but couldn't. He brought her water, wiped at her face again. Waited.

It came slowly. But he got it. Bernard had been there, his face bruised and swollen, wanting her to marry him. She'd laughed, kidded him. Told him not to be silly. It was a beautiful day. He should enjoy it.

Then he'd left. And she'd heard it. Gone out. Seen it. She reached out to hold Ty, her face tortured.

Ty cleaned her. Took off the soaked blouse and put her in one of Bob Ring's old ones. Mopped the floor and wiped the cabinets. Then he went out.

Bernard's truck was backed into the drive. He could see it before he got there—hair and bone, the orange-red of drying blood smeared across the rear window. Bernard's body was over the steering wheel. His hand was under the collapsed torso, the Colt still in it.

Ty went back in.

"It wasn't that," he said. "He was cleaning it. It was an accident."

He went to the phone and called. "There's been an accident," he told them. "You'd better come."

Then he took a bucket of water and more towels and went out.

He'd cleaned most of it when they arrived. One of them the same one who'd told him about Buck the night before. They made him stop, told him he shouldn't have started. They asked Willie questions, but it was no good. They had to turn back to him.

"He told her he was going to clean it," Ty said. "I got here just after." Again they told him he shouldn't have touched anything, made him sit while they checked, talked with Buck, went to the corner store where he'd bought the paper.

More of them came, some from the Forest Service. A doctor from the Catholic hospital gave something to Willie. Ty covered her, let her sleep as they turned to him again, asked more, verifying things all over again.

"Checks out," the sheriff finally told him. "No thanks to you. And you aren't foolin' anyone." Bernard's body was under a sheet now. "The Forest Service boys want it that way too. No skin off my ass. You're the ones got to live with it."

⌒⋅⌒

"Don't leave," Willie said, waking. "Stay with me."

"I will," Ty said. "I will."

He made her bacon and eggs, everything on end now. Ty cooking. A breakfast ending their day, not starting it.

She wouldn't go to bed, so he sat with her on the couch, held her through the night. Two days later he drove her out to the pack station, not wanting to leave her and having a horse to doctor. He gave her Fenton and Cody Jo's room, but in the night she came to him.

"Hold me, Ty," she said. "I . . . it keeps coming back." She got in with him and he held her, thinking how different it had been with Cody Jo.

"Will you take care of me?" She sat up, looking at him. "Keep me from thinking this way?"

"Yes. You know I will."

She didn't feel safe to leave him until Bob Ring came back from San Francisco. But by then everything was pretty much decided. Bob Ring took the news calmly enough, more surprised that Ty would go off to listen to a priest than he was that Ty was getting married. He was sure any man would be lucky to marry his Wilma. He still felt that way, fragile as she was after what Bernard did.

Ty left everything up to the priest—and Willie, acting on his own only to get Buck to stand up for him, Jasper and Gus to help people get settled in the little Catholic chapel on the last day of the year. The ceremony was somber, but everyone was taken by how lovely and serious the bride was, how acceptable the lean packer, wearing a suit Cody Jo had bought for Fenton years before.

There was a reception, that somber too until the gin Dan Murphy and Buck had put in the vestry punch began to take hold.

After he'd had some of it, Bob Ring took Ty aside.

"She's as good a person as there is, Ty." Bob Ring watched him. "And she was always the happiest. This thing will pass." He looked across the room at Wilma as she said what she had to say to each guest, looking lovely and pale.

"I know." Ty was not sure he knew at all, not sure of anything since that long day with the police. "It will."

"Well," Bob Ring held up his glass to Ty, "here's to the two of you. I hope you're married to her—not to those goddamned mountains."

32

Marriage

If loving Ty and keeping busy could have driven away her demons, Willie would have shaken them in a few weeks. But they hung on. Ty would watch a cloud cross her face and know she needed touching, holding. Not that that was all she wanted. He was surprised by how naturally she took to lovemaking—from the start. Her church certainly hadn't driven that from her.

They drove to Helena for their honeymoon, if four days in a blizzard can be called a honeymoon. Willie didn't complain. She made the big room their own, discovering room service, exploring Ty's long body— her fingers tracing his roped muscles, the deep wound high on his thigh.

On the third day he found her looking out at the swirling snow, hugging herself into her robe as that lost look came over her. He eased her away, out through the storm to visit the capitol building, look at the Russell mural, explore the cavernous rooms. Later, with coffee, she was Willie again, teasing him, her eyes smoky.

"Shall we go upstairs?" she asked. "There's this bed." He felt her foot along his leg. "I could warm it for you. Warm you, for me."

"Was I worth waiting for?" She smiled as Ty tried to recover himself. "My father told me I would be." She moved a finger across his chest, studied his face. "Is this what he had in mind?"

"No." Ty held her more closely. "Fathers don't think that way."

But in his heart Ty suspected he had Bob Ring to thank for Willie. That her father had somehow freed her for him, made her unafraid of the rough edges Ty couldn't hide. Maybe it came from how comfortable Ring was with himself. Maybe it came from his giving her a world balanced and safe. And maybe it came from her having no mother to shade that world with darkness, the unknown. That had to count too. Willie hardly ever mentioned her mother, taken from her so long ago—the woman who might have warned her that someone like Bernard could turn her world on end.

But that mother might also have kept Willie from being so complete right here in his arms. And he was taken by how complete this Willie was. If at first he hadn't loved her the way he'd loved Cody Jo, he found himself loving her even more as their winter days opened into spring. He loved her candor and optimism, the way she could bring light into the darkest corners. Which is why he would pale when he saw her thinking of Bernard: what she could have done to hold that off, what she might have done to bring it on.

That first year Bob Ring had a lot of traveling to do. Willie and Ty alternated between his house in town and the big house at the pack station. It gave Willie a chance to do what she did more easily than anyone Ty had ever known: provide order and clarity and a generous pace to life. She rehung pictures and moved furniture and organized drawers. She scoured the kitchens, checking things off one list as she added to the next. She straightened out Ty's affairs too, paying the feed stores and suppliers and reviewing the packing accounts. A few more good seasons, she told him, and he would be sitting at a desk sending others out to pack. He enjoyed watching her so much it hardly troubled him. He couldn't imagine owning the pack station anyway.

At least he couldn't until Willie took him to the banker and he learned Cody Jo had already deeded half of it to him.

"You have equity now," the banker said. He was not much older than Ty, but so careful and proper the two seemed from different worlds. "You could borrow against it or just discharge the debt." He shuffled the papers. "I believe that's what Mrs. Holliwell would prefer."

That name jarred Ty back to life. "I . . . I'd just like to make sure I help Cody Jo's income."

"Mrs. Holliwell understands that. Getting it free of debt is her priority too. Then we'll discuss the distribution of profits."

"She wants you to have it, Ty," Willie said. "It makes sense. It could mean more money for her. In the long run."

"If you have more years like this, it won't be a very long wait. Twenty percent of the debt paid off." The banker looked at Ty approvingly, his face so smooth he looked as if he'd shaved minutes before their meeting.

"Is it true that you are the best packer from here to Canada?" he asked suddenly, unsettling Ty.

"Oh, much farther than that," Willie said, smiling. "I'd say on up into Alaska." She seemed so delighted the banker had a hard time looking back at Ty.

"Could you take some of us into those mountains? I've heard stories about pack trips. We all ride. We wouldn't be much trouble."

"Well." Ty tried to ignore the smile Willie was giving him. "That's something to think about."

"We'll keep working on the debt." Willie turned her warmth back on the banker. "We do want to pay it all off."

"Yes." The banker was a little undone by the awkward packer, how pleased the pretty wife seemed. "That's the smart thing."

It was a happy time for them. Ty surrendered to how well Willie did things: supper each night at dusk, town each Sunday for her church and a dinner with her father. She even scheduled a few minutes each morning, right after breakfast, for kissing.

"Just kissing," she would tell him. "Practicing up for the night." And if it went too far, if they wound up on the couch or back in bed or someplace that surprised them both, she would say "Oh, dear! We'll have to abstain tonight." But by night it would be different. "It won't hurt," she would say. "This once. We've been so good. Let's have a little reward."

Buck was around a lot that winter, Angie helping out at Murphy's store or in town with the children, the last of them almost through high school now. Once Willie got blue so suddenly she went out to the saddle shop where Buck and Ty were working. Ty saw the look on her face and took her in his arms right there, talked to her until it went away and she began to smile, kidding Buck about staring at them.

"You can just turn your back. Perfectly normal for newlyweds." She kissed Ty again and gave Buck a little hug. "Bet you were even worse with Angie." She headed out the door but poked her head back in, wagging a finger at Buck. "Probably had no restraint at all."

"Hell." Buck sighed, watching the door close behind her. "Ever tell you about Pa givin' me that sack of jelly beans when I married?"

"For the sugar?" Ty examined the leather he was about to cut.

"Nope. Just told me for that first year ever' time we made some love I was to take one out and put it in a jar."

"Did Angie know?"

"Nope. But I damn near emptied that sack."

"Then what?" Ty saw Buck wanted to make a point.

"After a year I was to take a bean *out* of that jar after each time."

"Cause now you needed the sugar?"

"Not to eat. Just to take out. And I'm beginnin' to think Pa's right."

"About what?"

"About I might never empty that jar." Ty saw how blue Buck was getting just thinking about it. He went to get two beers from the snowbank and gave one to Buck.

"How long you and Angie been married now?"

"Goin' on twenty-three years." Buck took a pull at his beer. "Lotta beans still in that jar."

"Maybe you miscounted. You count that time during the quarantine?"

"Yes. And other times you might not know so damned much about." Buck didn't like how sweet Angie had been on Ty after that night.

"You know for a fact I been workin' at it, Ty. It's just that seein' you and Willie made me think I ought to pick up the pace."

He took another pull on his beer, thinking about it.

"We sure had some good times, me and Angie." Buck watched as Ty turned back to his work.

"Hard not to have a good time with Angie." Ty checked to make sure his cut was true. "She's got so much life in her."

Buck decided once again not to try to apologize for what happened to Bernard. Ty would only say it was an accident, that Bernard had just been cleaning his Colt. Buck guessed it was pretty important for Willie to think that. And he didn't figure it was his business to make anyone think different. But he *was* sorry for his part. He had been from the minute he heard what happened. He was sorry even after Ty married and seemed happier than he'd ever been. Buck saw it as a sorrow he'd live with always.

And Ty *was* happy. He didn't think he'd ever been so happy—happy with Willie's schedules, happy with her planning, happy with the laughs she would have with Buck and Angie and Jasper, even happy with her ideas for how to pay off the debt.

But he was happiest of all with their times alone—at least when she wasn't blue. Only now and then did he think of what they'd do if she found herself pregnant. And each time he mentioned it she shushed him. "I know exactly what I'm doing," she would say, sometimes kissing him, sometimes putting a finger to his lips. "Don't you worry your packer head."

Ty wasn't so sure she knew what she was doing. And he was sure her church didn't, worrying that it might require things of her she wasn't ready for. But he kept his mouth shut. Willie was so certain about how to go at things he felt awkward when he questioned her.

That's why he wasn't so surprised when she told him she was going to have the baby. And he wasn't surprised at all that that's when her moments of sadness began disappearing.

She was taken with the whole thing from the first day, cheerful even when she found herself queasy. She got books from the library about pregnancy and child care; she looked up names for boys and for girls; her dinners became more and more elaborate.

"We must build our strength now," she would say, lighting candles and feigning a deep seriousness. "You'll need to be the hero—very soon."

There was no slacking off in the kissing schedule. If anything she found ways for Ty to break the "just kissing" rule more often than ever.

Happy as she'd been before Bernard, Ty could see she was happier still planning for this baby. And he saw from the start that she'd known better than Ty or Bob Ring or anyone else that shaking the blues was her business—no one else's.

He just hoped that having the baby was the right way to do it.

~

In December of 1949 in the delivery room of the Catholic hospital in Missoula, Wilma Hardin's daughter drowned in her mother's blood. The doctors could neither save the child nor halt the flow from the ruptured uterus, the mother dying moments after her child's lungs filled. One life extinguishing the other as though fulfilling the terms of a larger plan.

At an age when most men use what they have learned to fashion their future, Ty Hardin found himself seeing no future at all. Everything became a blur. The mountains that had given him life no longer seemed the ones that had taught him about life, filling with people they didn't need at the same time the people he needed left him.

It was a paradox impossible for him to digest.

Book Two: The Sierra (1950–1984)

The Sierra Nevada is five hundred miles of rock put right. Granite freed by glaciers and lifted through clouds where water, frozen and free, has scraped and washed it into a high country so brilliant it brings light into night. It lured Indians into its valleys even as it struck terror into the heart of a new world crowding west. It was higher than civilization could go.

Westering men found ways around it, skirted it north and south until they surrounded it. Only then did they creep back to see what had stopped them so completely. Some, probing higher, saw that what healed the glacier-torn range might heal their own wounds as well. A few found ways to be a part of it, to live with it, learn from it.

Ty Hardin became one of those men. Though he went to the Sierra to forget, the Sierra made him remember. It showed him once more that all is in motion, everything is flowing—animals and waters and rocks. That the ground we sleep on and the stars above us all are moving, never ending.

It made him see again that day follows night.

33

Cold Canyon

It was five years before Ty could tally it up. He was in the Sierra by then, the South Fork and Willie far behind. And it wasn't until Thomas Haslam's questions that he could say it aloud.

They were camped in Cold Canyon, a day out of Tuolumne Meadows, the trees edging the high meadow and the late afternoon warm, the wind soft, the Haslam children creeping out to the winding stream, looking for trout, exploring their world—alive with that fragile life that is the High Sierra.

Thomas Haslam had his bourbon out. He and Ty were testing it, Ty thinking back to how seldom Thomas Haslam had thought of a drink when Ty first met him, how comforting he found one now, liking to savor it, watch his children through its richness, think of the times he'd had; the times still ahead—for work, for Alice and their children. Even for the life Ty was leading.

"Do you like this country, Ty?" he asked. "You look as much at home in it as in your own."

"Higher. Sunnier." Ty looked at the clouds that had been gathering each morning, the puffs growing day by day, searching one another out until the white would deepen into gray, rain burst from them at last, spilling in sheets to clear again by night, the sky washed, the stars brisk and alive above the moon-splashed granite.

"Don't have to set up tents every time you turn around." Ty sipped his bourbon. "It's a predictable country. At least this time of year."

"And you don't have to worry about grizzlies," Haslam added.

"I never worried about them." Ty looked at him. "I believe it's their worryin' about us that made everyone so nervous."

But the death of the red bear should have warned him, a happening so sudden and violent he was numbed. The loss of Willie and the child was less numbing than final, bringing a heaviness that settled in like silt.

Thomas and Alice had read about it. It was in the papers all over the country. Two experienced hunters, exploring the little-known canyon. The huge red bear rising from the aspen grove, rising unbelievably high, watching them, scenting them until they fired on him together, firing again and then again until he was upon them, his charge breaking the arm of the one who lived—the one he flung away as he mauled and shook the other like some toy whose parts must never work again.

They'd read about the man with the dangling arm, blood dripping from his wounds, running and running until he'd come to the one packer who used the canyon, who on a whim had decided to take the season's last party through the wild canyon he knew as no one else did. The wounded man collapsing there, unable to go back with the packer—unable and afraid beyond reason. The packer had left him to be nursed by an ancient cook and two bankers and their wives, couples on their first trip into a country they would never want to see again.

They'd read about the packer finding the broken man still alive but knowing he shouldn't be, couldn't be for long. The packer watching the bear circle before charging back, the packer shooting and shooting and shooting until the huge beast dropped, almost upon them—the life gone from him at last.

And later Ty told them himself, told them what he'd told the Forest Service and the reporters and biologists and naturalists who had called and written and come to him, come to hear him and to examine the vast tawny pelt. The pelt that would soon hang behind the desk of the Forest Service supervisor so the young men of the Forest Service could see it, know what they were protecting. Know what they had to fear.

But telling it as he had had never meant thinking about it the way he did that afternoon in Cold Canyon. He told Thomas Haslam about hesitating over the hunter's torn body, watching as the wounded bear circled, wanting him to leave, nurse his great hulk deep in some hidden glade—live to reclaim his canyon, his solitude. About the bear's finally charging after all, as though to go out with these men who had betrayed him, injured him so deeply, go out with them or fix them so they could never injure anything again.

And so Ty had had to shoot, his bullet going to its mark but the bear withstanding even that, and another shot still. Only the final one, fired into the huge bear's anguished mouth, had finally put it all to rest.

And he told him about turning to the dying hunter, the blood bubbling from the torn face, an ear and the scalp gone, an arm all but ripped away, a leg broken and akimbo, the man speaking through the orangy froth of his battered lungs, Ty bending to hear him say, "Kill me." The voice pushing blood from the torn mouth. "Kill me."

But Ty not able to do it. Knowing he should but turning away, stumbling back—leaving some part of him behind with the huge bear and the dying man and the torn earth. He returned with the others to find the broken life still there. No talk from the ravaged body now, just the bubbling flecks of blood telling them how stubborn, against reason, life can be.

They stopped in Fenton's old camp, brought in what was left of the man on a crude litter, made a place for him to die as Ty dressed the wounds of the other, fashioned a splint for the arm just as Fenton had fashioned one for Bob Ring's leg in what seemed to Ty another life, another place.

The hunter died in the deep darkness of the overcast night. Ty mantied him up in the morning and packed the broken body out on Cottontail, as steady a mule as he had for a task more somber than any he'd ever known.

Word came out ahead of them. The Forest Service was there, waiting. Two of Spec's cousins, skinners, were already going back in to weigh and measure and dress out the great bear. The officers did their duty: sent the broken hunter on to the hospital, took the mantie from the torn body of the other, examined it, sat down with Ty to write their reports, to answer the hard questions reporters were asking. The reporters astonished as they looked from the body to the mountains and back to the haggard packer, wanting more but making do with the spare facts he offered.

"Hard to know what ate at me so," Ty told Thomas Haslam. "Must have been that the bear could live with us so long—with Fenton and Spec and the rest. Like we lied to him. To ourselves."

"About what?" Haslam asked. He was moved hearing Ty speak this way. "You had to pull that trigger."

"Not about that. By then one of us had to go." Ty looked out across the meadow, watched his horses moving higher, seeking the sun. "I mean about thinking we could have it forever."

Thomas Haslam thought of all those deaths pouring in on Ty at once, everything he'd counted on gone.

"I'm sorry about Willie," he said simply, looking at Ty. "The child."

"Maybe it was in the cards," Ty said. "Maybe she saw something coming."

ᓚ᠆ᓄ

If Willie did see anything coming, Ty never knew it. She was Willie until the moment they wheeled her into the delivery room. But she'd known shooting the bear had changed him, seen that look on his face when he came down from the mountains. It was the same he'd had after Fenton died. After Cody Jo left. The same look he'd had after Bernard.

Ty hadn't wanted to seem gloomy. He'd taken Willie dancing, big as she was. But she'd known something was missing. Something about the promise, always there in the way he danced, was gone. He couldn't lose himself in the music, surrender to its rhythms.

When the Sister of Providence came to him, the same who'd counseled Willie in school, saying her prayer in that clear, beautiful voice, Ty knew. He hardly heard the doctor's explanation. "Tried to hold the blood, save the child, the rupture unexpected." He'd turned away as though there was no need to hear at all, walked the night away through a town suddenly strange to him, across a campus finished for him, past houses closed to him.

And so they talked, Thomas Haslam and Ty, the doctor knowing most of it but not how it had come to Ty, not until that afternoon in Cold Canyon when Haslam found he had to swallow his own feelings away. Glad as he was that Ty could finally talk it out, he found it hard to hear it out, to watch Ty's face—the acceptance in it, the finality.

ᓚ᠆ᓄ

The Haslams had been in the South Fork with Ty earlier that very season, bringing with them Opie Kittle, a packer whose sons wanted nothing to do with the Sierra pack station the Kittle family had run for almost a century. They'd told Kittle about Ty, and it hadn't taken the old packer a day of watching Ty work before he offered him a job. By the end of the trip he'd offered him half-interest in his whole operation, which had only made Ty smile. Opie Kittle saw why when they came out of the woods and Willie was there, her belly a watermelon and her voice clear as mountain water.

"She'd make any man stay to home," he said to Ty. "But things change. Write when you're ready. Ain't seen a packer like you in a lifetime." He squinted up at Ty, liking everything about him. "High country's just right for you. And where I pack is the highest we got." He watched Ty settle Cottontail's breeching between the sawbucks, swing the breast collar onto that, the cinches up across all of it, lifting the saddle and pads together, switching them so the pads would dry where he stacked them. "It's where you ought to be."

Thomas Haslam reminded Ty of that when he came from San Francisco for Willie's funeral. All of them were there, Cody Jo and Bliss Holliwell too, even Beth and Loretta, trying not to be noticed but tearing up when they saw Ty.

He was with Bob Ring, looking at them all, speaking to them all. But it was as if he didn't see them at all, as if he were a wooden man being told where to turn and what to say.

They buried Willie and the child in the Catholic cemetery next to Willie's mother. Bob Ring limped along behind the coffin with Ty, his face creased—everything about him looking older with each crooked step he took. Ty seemed to be looking beyond the coffin, beyond everyone, looking at something else, someplace else.

Cody Jo began crying, holding Buck's arm as though it might save her from something, burying her face in his shoulder.

"Oh, Buck. He'll never have it now. I thought someone like Willie . . ." Buck held her, his eyes wet as he looked across her buried head at Bliss Holliwell, whose face was just as anguished as Buck's.

"I was so wrong." She looked from one to the other through her tears. "How could I have been so wrong?"

Ty didn't seem to hear it when Thomas Haslam reminded him of Opie Kittle. He didn't seem to hear it when the banker called him in and told him they would continue with the mortgage on the house but couldn't be responsible for the back-country, wanted him to convert the packing business into day rides, start a guest ranch, do what was safe.

But he heard something when Opie Kittle called and told him he still wanted Ty to come and run things, that the half-interest offer held. He didn't even seem to consider it, just said he would come.

Two weeks later Cody Jo heard about it. She wrote telling the banker to sell, to settle the cash on Ty, that she'd take care of the details.

When it was done, there was enough for Ty to buy a decent truck and a four-horse trailer and have some left over.

When spring came, he loaded Smoky and Cottontail and Loco, deciding to take little Apple too. She wasn't young anymore, but she was Willie's.

"They won't miss her," he told Buck, who helped him load. "Won't be much use to them anyhow."

But Buck knew better. Buck knew Ty wanted to take some of Willie with him when he left.

34

Coming into the Country

Opie Kittle—Mr. Kittle to almost everyone in Big Pine and up and down Owens Valley—had never seen anything like Ty Hardin.

"Pulled in here one night with two horses and two mules. Next morning had shoes on all four. Started on my mules next. Hardly said a word." He shook his head to punctuate it. "Ain't that the goddamndest?"

"Maybe you've got your man." Harvey Kittle, Opie's youngest son, watched as Ty caught up another. "Now you can move to Bishop like you had good sense."

Harvey was a dentist. He'd crippled a leg when he was a boy, doing things with Opie Kittle's mules he didn't like doing in the first place, which had set him against mules once and for all. But with one brother gone in the war and the other dealing faro in Reno, he knew Opie was his responsibility. It just wasn't easy, given his father's devotion to his mules.

"Glad he found you." Harvey Kittle watched Ty quiet a leggy mule who didn't like the rasp on his hoof. Ty let the hoof down, rubbed the mule's hock before turning to look at Harvey, who had the same scrunched-up features as his father. But his bow tie was so perfectly knotted and his shirt so perfectly white, he didn't look like he belonged anywhere near Opie's barn.

"Drove down from Bishop," Harvey said. "See if I can keep him from throwin' saddles on these mules and startin' up a trail a sane man wouldn't even salt. Not yet, leastways."

It was all right with Ty that there was no introduction. They knew about one another already, and they both had a soft spot for Opie Kittle.

"So far he spends most of his time bringing me Cokes from the cooler."

"That is restrained, for him. But it won't last. He was best for so long he still believes he is."

"Quit crabbin'." Opie Kittle appeared. "Ty's got everything under control."

"Then let's hop in the car and go. Got a root canal in the morning. Watchin' you and these mules makes my hands shaky."

"A beer won't hurt your hands. Got things to show Ty."

"Show him over the phone."

"Never learned to point over the phone."

Ty opened the cooler and got out the beer, handing them each one and cracking one himself. He was smiling. And he hadn't smiled for a long time.

ᘉ

It was the work that made things better, he thought, that and listening to Opie Kittle talk about the Sierra. Looking up at the great range didn't tell him a lot, but looking at the photographs spread around the little ranch house, hearing Kittle describe what was going on in them, did.

And he liked listening to Harvey and Opie talk, the dentist scrubbed and tidy but still his father's son, still comfortable with his father's language and eccentricities. People came to Harvey Kittle from up and down the valley, getting him to take care of their good teeth and pull their bad. And all of them asked about his father as soon as Harvey got his hands out of their mouth—what trips the old packer was taking, how many mules he was packing, what kind of help he was having trouble finding.

Opie Kittle was always having trouble finding help, the kind that did things the way he wanted. That's why both Harvey and Opie were so happy to watch Ty move through a day's work. In no time they were as comfortable with him as with each other. And when he talked, they didn't just warm up their own arguments. They listened. Partly because it was a surprise to hear him talk at all but mostly because he said things about packing that even Opie had forgotten, if Opie had known them in the first place.

What worried them now was how to introduce Ty to the Sierra. They could take him up to their corrals at Goat Creek, but what then? How was he to know what was beyond the passes? Opie wanted against reason to be the one to show him, but with all his ailments that was out, which didn't keep them from chewing at the idea anyway, arguing and swearing at each other and rooting around for a solution. It came the minute Sugar Zumaldi showed up and said he'd be happy to work a few trips—if Opie would haul his burros up to Goat Creek come August. That's when Sugar planned to take his whole family and vanish into the Sierra, the mountain range he loved almost as he loved the family he took into it.

"Lucked out," Opie Kittle told Ty. "Ain't a man knows the country better. He's took me places that surprised his goddamn burros."

In two months' time Ty would find out how true that was, be astonished at the little hanging valleys Sugar would slip into, where the feed was plentiful and the water good. Sugar seemed to find the same comfort in mountains that Spec found. He made Ty at home in them too—the mountains as much in Sugar's blood as Ty's mules were in his.

And there was reason. Sugar Zumaldi's father was among the last of the Basques to run sheep in the Sierra, his father's father one of the first. The sturdy drover shipped into a strange country to do what other men would not, knowing little of English but everything of animals and weather and mountains and learning the Sierra by seeking out every nook and cranny where there was grass. And each pass that led to more.

"Hoofed locusts," John Muir had called them, "leaving nothing." But the sheep of the Zumaldis always seemed to leave plenty, the Zumaldis more interested in what was on the other side of canyon walls, on the next bench, out of sight around the next reach of rock than in exhausting the feed where they stood. It was their legacy to Sugar, who found it in him as a hawk finds flight. Ty sensed it when they met, Sugar doing what needed to be done but his dark eyes on the great range—or on Apple, the little mare he took to as no other. Ty watched him favor her, brush her, give her treats, walk out to bring her in as quietly as Spec moving through woods—a Spec who liked horses and mules and packing in a way the real Spec did not.

Opie Kittle had moved up to Bishop by then, giving Ty the ranch house, Sugar sleeping in the bunk room where Ty had started out. But Opie was back with them more often than not, enjoying watching Ty and Sugar as he enjoyed nothing else—except his mules.

"Why call him Sugar?" Ty watched as the Basque brushed Apple. "Had a mule named Sugar once. Good one too."

Opie looked to see if Ty was serious. "Don't know about your mule. But watch Sugar with his burros and you'll know. He'll call and them rascals come runnin' and fartin' just to get close. He don't pack feed, just sugar lumps."

Ty watched Sugar Zumaldi go on with his brushing.

"Well, you can get some farther with sugar than with vinegar."

"With a colt too?" Opie Kittle liked knowing what was going on in his new packer's head. "A mustang?"

"With most everything," Ty said, "that you got to live with."

c·⌐

Two weeks later they herded all their stock up the twisting road to Goat Creek. The road dusty and hot until they reached the cool of the timber, climbing still higher to corrals perched by the tumbling stream, shaded from the late sun by the looming Sierra crest.

"We're higher than the peaks in the Swan." Ty saw the trail threading its way still higher along the canyon wall. "And we still got three thousand feet before the pass."

"That's why it's Goat Pass," Sugar said. "Grandfather claimed goats is the only ones not to get dizzy when they cross."

"I crossed once without gettin' dizzy." Opie Kittle had trucked up a load of hay, inching along so slowly he'd only then caught up with them.

"I believe I was drunk." He hunched into his coat, the cold coming in now. "Or hung over. I forget which."

"One's more fun," Ty said. "But harder to remember. You sure Sugar's girl can handle the cooking? We'll have our hands full with all this stock."

"Sugar's kids can do anything. And Nina's his best. It's when they leave that's got me worried. Once he gathers his family with them burros, he just disappears."

"Nina's a fine cook." Sugar tied Apple to the hitch rack and unsaddled. He'd led her most of the way, liking to walk more than ride. He looked so fresh to Ty he seemed ready to go another ten miles.

"The Basques eat good, so they work good." Sugar stacked Apple's saddle on the hitch rack. "Know how to live in the mountains."

"That's the trouble, you damn bandit. You ain't stayin' long enough to teach Ty. How's he gonna eat well *and* work good when he's alone?"

Ty looked at the trail climbing away above them, crossing raw cliffs to wind high above the plunging stream.

"I got an idea." He looked at Opie Kittle. "If Sugar'll show me that country, maybe I know who can take care of the rest."

"Better be a smart idea. Don't want that desert trash again . . . or them drunk boys from Olancha."

"It'll seem a smart idea on some days," Ty said. "Not so smart on others. But it'll sure keep things lively."

That night, after they'd set up the wall tent and Opie had gone back to Bishop, Ty lit the lantern and sat down to write Angie and Buck.

35

Over Goat Pass

They loose-herded the stock over the pass to cross the Sierra and pick up the first party. Sugar and the girl pushed the mules behind Ty as he let Smoky feel her way up the headwall. A chill went up his spine when they crested. He pivoted and pulled his hat tight, watching the mules gather themselves in the hard wind, noses to the impossibly narrow trail. Behind he saw the purplish gray of Owens Valley, ahead cliffs spilling their talus into blue lakes. Beyond the lakes the green of meadows, darkening pods of forests dropping into canyons. It swept him up like a leaf. He couldn't believe what they'd crossed to get here, what they found when they were here.

"I seen that look before." Sugar rode Apple up beside him as they skirted the first lake. "It ain't always this good."

"It's this country. It opens up so . . . it opens me up."

"It can close you down too. I wanted a good day. For you. But not this good. Ain't so pretty when it's lightning. Snow."

"But you come back. You can't stay away."

"Hard to stay away from a beautiful woman too. It might mean trouble, but it don't matter. Moth and a flame. You keep coming back." Sugar dropped back again. "You'll see. This country ain't so different."

They camped in the first timber, wind-battered trees edging their way up into a tilting meadow. Ty saw they had crossed the crest even above a great bank of snow that melted to start the first rivulets on their run west, becoming the stream they camped on before cascading down to join the Kings. Across the meadow his horses moved higher with the sun. He marked the place as darkness fell, wanting tracks in the morning.

The girl was busy before light. Ty and Sugar crossed the frost to follow the tracks high, then higher still to the horses—quiet as rocks, waiting for the sun. Ty was warm from the climb, winded. But he was ready for the morning, pleased with the slanting light of the new day.

He led Smoky in, the rest following, bells clanging as Sugar clucked and whistled them in behind. Ty picked his way down shallow cliffs, seeing now why Sugar so often chose to walk. The country seemed to come up through his legs as he skirted granite slabs, chose sandy fissures widened by winters into grassy steps. Sky pilot and rock fringe hugged boulders, purple-blue heads opening to the sun. It was as though a gardener had readied it: rocks perfectly placed, flowers lifting, a scrim of dew from the frost melt, the stream rippling past.

They were moving by seven, Ty so busy looking over the country he could hardly keep track of the trace. They merged with a main route, and he gave Smoky her head. He couldn't get over the way they threaded through it. The mules lined out behind Cottontail as they climbed north, up past lakes and tarns into raw rock, a line of quartz halving it as they closed on another divide, this one dropping them into the north fork of the Kings.

The mules crossed over with no hesitation, the trail carved through talus that left nowhere to go but forward. Wind blowing hard until they reached the quiet of switchbacks, a snowfield, the crunch of hooves the only sound—and Smoky blowing as she nosed across.

Ty was even more taken by this country: the canyons seemed deeper, the peaks higher, the cliffs more sheer. Down and down Smoky took him, the slender trail threading across cliffs golden in the late light, down into a canyon where Sugar moved ahead, looking for something, finally turning back to say:

"Been watching that Smoky mare. The old sayin' don't hold for her."

"What saying?"

"This trail jackassable; for horses impassable." Sugar smiled at Ty's confusion. "I think your mare *can* go where my burros go."

Without another word he was off Apple, leading her through willows and onto a slanting game trail climbing the timbered canyon wall. Ty was thankful his mules were separated, the trail steep enough to scare a deer. He heard Sugar laugh as he dismounted onto ground higher than Smoky. He led her then, the packless mules scrambling, Smoky sometimes lunging but willing, going where Ty took her.

And then they were up, crossing the lip of a tidy U-shaped valley, the middle of it a sparkling meadow. Sugar made his way across, fording a

stream and disappearing. Ty followed him into the timber only to find
him on a perfect flat, too hidden for anyone to come on by chance.

"I'll show you all over these mountains, Hardin." Sugar tied Apple
to a tree and began catching up mules. "They like you."

"More the other way around." Ty pulled the saddle from Smoky,
checked to see if she'd cut her legs on the rocks.

"That too." Sugar stacked saddles on a barkless deadfall. "Nina and
me seen it when you come over Goat Pass." He spread a manty over
the saddles, tucked it against the wind.

"What is it you saw?" Ty was already freeing the animals.

"That you was smitten." Sugar shooed the mules out of camp,
watched them nosing the sand for a warm roll. "Seen it happen before."
Sugar spoke matter-of-factly. "Mostly to Basque."

They sat with coffee, looking east over the deep canyon they'd left,
shadows creeping up the soaring peaks.

"The Palisades." Sugar watched the sun linger on them. "Used to
take our sheep into the basins below. Now it's just climbers."

"Have you gone back? With your burros?"

"Too rocky. Not like this." Sugar looked around, taking in the girl,
composed across the fire, the kitchen put away, beds laid out,
everything in its place. The only sounds were the busy stream, the bells
of the mares out in the meadow.

"It's beautiful," Ty said finally.

"Men die climbing into it. Too many."

"Have you climbed over there?"

"Some."

"He's climbed most of them," Nina said, hugging her knees against
the cold. "With that man Clyde. Grandfather thought they were crazy.
'Is there grass up there?' he would ask. 'Water? What is up there that
you need?'"

"He was right." Sugar held Ty with his dark eyes. "I thought I'd be
able to see more. Saw farther. Not more."

He stood, threw away the last of his coffee. "You'll see what I mean.
Norman Clyde, he's still smote. Like you. But you'll learn. See everything you need from a place like this."

"That's what grandfather always said." The girl stood too. "You've
made it your saying now."

"Yes. And if we do right it'll be Ty's too."

Ty stayed by the fire, wishing Spec were there to listen to Sugar Zumaldi.

A coyote called. Another answered, clear and haunting. Ty knew they were calling from those rocky basins Sugar used before his climbs into the Palisades.

$\backsim\!\sim$

After that Sugar rode in front with Ty, or walked—leading Apple as he told Ty about the country. It was clear Opie Kittle was right: No one else could know as much—where there was water and grass, where cliffs would stop you, how to get around them when they did.

Sugar was like a cat, burying everything he did, sometimes even walking the rocks beside the trail to leave no sign. He would use no fire rings, scooping out a place and taking the ashes away in the morning, kicking away droppings, sweeping away tracks.

They rode north, leaving the Kings drainage to cross a pass wild and high. They rode for miles along treeless lakes and meadows before dropping through broken rock to reclaim the forest in a canyon rich with the names of philosophers and wise men: Huxley and Darwin and Lamarck. Sugar seemed even wiser, pointing out this hidden route and that. Each night he would pull out a map, point to a hidden place where some prospector had made a scratchy start, mark the map to show Ty places no one thought stock could reach, pools you could dive into from warm granite: hidden places where water and feed and wood were as plentiful as the glade was secret.

They rode down the canyon of the philosophers, camping in lush meadows before dropping from its lip to meet another stream, follow it west toward its source to camp high, the grass sweet enough to hold the horses while Sugar told Ty more, helped him bring the country into his bones.

The next morning Sugar took them up the canyon wall along a trace sometimes invisible, climbing along shelf after shelf of grassy ledges, some narrowing to granite as they worked their way up and up the steepening canyon wall until Smoky seemed to be going straight up, just a chute ahead of them, rocky and forbidding—a danger Ty didn't like.

"Hell for sure on the animals." Ty stopped to give Smoky a breather before pushing her up it.

"That's what they call it." Sugar had led Apple up.

"Call what?" Ty looked back to see if his mules were rested.

"This pass," Sugar said. "It's hell for the stock and hell for the people. But it don't seem like 'Hell for Sure' to me. Seems like God fixed it. Made all them shelves to help us climb."

"You must have a different God. Mine's not that generous."

Sugar shook his head. It bothered him that Ty smiled that tight smile whenever Sugar talked of God.

Smoky went up the chute like a goat, the mules pitching and scrambling behind. Just across the pass stood a lone tree, its bark torn away by fierce winters, leaving a strip that spiraled up and brought life to a second trunk flourishing high above them.

"Foxtail," Sugar said. "Toughest tree we got. You had a strip of bark like that, you might survive the winters up here yourself."

"Must be thousands of years old." Ty was stopped by so much health emerging from such a narrow band of life.

"Been through some times." Sugar started down, this side not so steep.

"Might be older than that God of yours," Ty said.

But Sugar didn't answer. He was too busy negotiating his way down from Hell for Sure Pass.

A day later they met their party, businessmen from Fresno. They were pleased to be above the heat, pleased with the packers and the horses; pleased with the pretty girl who fed them and spoke about becoming a lawyer, a doctor, saying there were new opportunities for Basque women, ones she intended to know.

They brought a letter from Opie Kittle saying Opie would meet them at Tuolumne Meadows, that they had to haul the stock south to take the next party into the Whitney country. "Lucky it's the Haslams," Opie wrote. "They won't mind when you're lost. Better learn all you can from Sugar about where to go. The man dogtrots up cliffs that would lame a goat. Keep up. Ask questions. You'll need answers."

At the end he said Buck had called saying he was coming. Then he'd added a P.S.: "Hope your friends work out. Don't want to be up shit creek again this year."

Ty smiled, tucking the letter away and thinking that was exactly where Buck would think he was when he went over his first Sierra pass.

They took a main trail north, the guests riding ahead with Nina as Sugar told Ty about the country. Each day they would pass one or two hikers, but they saw only one packer, a huge man with a high-crowned hat and a gaudy kerchief, his pants tucked into high boots. He looked too big for his horse to Ty.

"You Kittle's new man?" He spit, wiped his mouth with the bright kerchief. "You must like that ass-packer as much as Old Man Kittle."

"Sugar sure knows the country." Ty moved his mules off the trail so the man could pass. "I learn from him."

"That girl's about ready." The man watched Nina as she rode on. "The ass-man done good."

Ty pulled his string back on the trail, knowing that Sugar didn't like the remark any more than he had. Nina registered nothing, but Ty thought she'd heard. He liked that even less.

"Call him Knots Malloy," Sugar said. "Tightened his knots so absolute once they had to cut rope." He looked at Ty. "Too strong to get things right, if you ask me."

"I did ask you. Anything that big I need to know about."

They were bathing in a tarn just above Thousand Island Lake. Ty was lying out on a slab of granite, drying in the sun.

"Something about that man," Sugar dried himself with his shirt, "runs against the grain."

Ty knew Knots Malloy troubled Sugar. Knew Sugar didn't want to give Knots any importance by admitting it. That was all right with Ty, but he knew it was hard to ignore people like Knots. He'd seen men try in the army—seen bad things happen when they failed.

A day later they crossed Donohue Pass and saw the big glacier filling the north cirque of Mount Lyell. Below them the Lyell Fork of the Tuolumne wound through broad meadows, stands of timber spotted in them as though placed by the gods.

"That Josiah Whitney said the glaciers had nothin' to do with all this," Sugar said. "I doubt he looked."

"Fenton would have seen it right off." Ty seemed to be talking to the country itself. "He'd enjoy this. How it opens up. No rain at night."

Sugar laughed, his spirits back. "Don't you count on that, Ty Hardin. We been lucky. You wait. It can be like God pissed."

That night they made do with a camp that had been used often. A fat bear came sniffing along as Nina got dinner ready. He rose, sniffed the air, came down and began pacing, working his way closer. Sugar banged some pots and shouted, but the bear paid no attention, pacing still closer, his fur loose over his big body like clothes that didn't fit. Sugar hit him with a rock. The bear hardly noticed, pacing still closer.

Ty had never seen a bear so bold. He had his Colt in his saddlebag, but he knew you weren't supposed to shoot these bears. And there was something comical about Sugar and Nina shouting and the bear paying no attention. He went to the fire and got a burning log, waved it. The bear ignored him, moving so close to the kitchen Ty had to throw the log, the flaming end hitting the bear in the side. He grunted, rose up and turned toward Ty, who was ready with still another log. They considered each other for a long minute before the bear came down and trotted away, stopping once to lick where the log had hit him.

"Persistent bastard." Sugar turned to Ty. "But you knew. Looks like you've had trouble with bears before."

"A different kind." Ty retrieved the log, put it back on the fire. "Wouldn't have bothered us like that." He sat on a rock by the fire. "Wouldn't have left us like that either."

"You mean grizzlies? Ain't they a whole different matter?"

"Yes, but I believe we're the ones cause them the trouble."

"We've ruined these. Find a road and they want a handout."

"Handouts aren't what interests my bears."

"What does? What do they want?"

"What you want, I guess." Ty felt awkward saying it. "A place to be alone." He got the buckets and started for the stream. "What we all want."

Sugar watched him go, thinking a place to be alone *wasn't* what everyone wanted. But it was what Ty wanted, wanted more than any man he knew. Even Nina saw it. . . . It was a worry to them both.

A day later they met Opie Kittle at the Tuolumne Meadows corrals. He had his two big ten-horse trailers, Ty's trailer too. Standing by it were Angie and Buck. Jasper Finn was with them.

"Jasper?" Ty could hardly believe Jasper was right there in the Sierra, looking a little worried but chipper nevertheless. "Jasper Finn."

"Got some years left," Jasper said. "If you want mountain grub."

"Yours I do." Ty thought of the persistent bear. "And you'll sure like these bears. They'll take to you too."

Ty laughed at how nervous that made Jasper. He was surprised more than anything else: surprised by how glad he was to see them. He was almost shy as he introduced them around, worried that Angie might get too affectionate. It turned out Sugar and Nina were the ones who seemed affectionate.

"Glad you have these people, Ty." Sugar shook Buck's hand. "Me and Nina want for you to have your own people." Nina looked up at Ty from where she was showing the kitchen to Angie and Jasper. Angie could tell by her look how lonely Ty had been.

"Wouldn't hurt to stop for a beer," Buck said when they turned the trucks south for Owens Valley. "I get thirsty just watchin' you drive this thing."

"Kittle's the boss. I just follow along." Ty thought of the hot drive ahead. "But Jasper's with him. They might hatch up a plan."

Opie considered things as he led them south, only part of him listening to Jasper's theories about bears. Before dark they had to meet Jeb Walker, the punctual general who would be with the Haslams at the corrals south of Lone Pine. But he knew Ty and the others needed something to eat. He settled on the Deerlodge as the best bet. Maria Zumaldi was planning to meet Sugar there. And he could talk with Ty about the Whitney country. He knew Sugar had shown him things on the maps, but he had more faith in himself than in maps. They might show where the trails were, but not the grass—which was what mattered.

"Bout time." Buck perked up the minute they pulled off the road. "It's gettin' so I got to prime up to spit."

"Lars'll fix that," Ty said. "Never met a thirst he didn't wet."

Lars Swenson was in his thirties and still wedded to old country ways and old country sayings, and he was honored whenever Opie Kittle stopped in. And Lars had liked Ty from the first. He'd heard about him from Opie, and he knew Ty must be a good packer just by the looks of him, his height and his quiet ways. When they walked in there wasn't enough he could do for them.

"I got sandwiches," he said. "It's a hot drive. You need beer."

"Two for me," Buck said. "For starters. And I'll buy Mr. Kittle's. Had he not stopped I'd of shriveled." He turned to Sugar. "Does everybody in California shrivel? I near become a raisin in that truck."

"Up there you won't." Sugar gestured toward the mountains. "Up there it's good. Cept for storms. Winter." He was wondering where Maria was, but the beer tasted so good he relaxed. He liked how much Ty enjoyed his friends.

Jasper went off to help Lars make sandwiches, and Angie went over to the jukebox and played "Tuxedo Junction" and "String of Pearls." She even got Ty to dance a little, Nina and Sugar pleased to watch them.

Sugar got his maps and spread them out on the table, showing Opie the places he'd pointed out to Ty. Opie was astonished.

"The hell you say. You never showed me them places."

"You couldn't get into them," Sugar said. "Ty can."

Ty smiled, enjoying them. Nina went to the jukebox and played a song by the Texas Playboys. She came over to Ty, shy but determined, asking if he would teach her to dance the way Angie did.

While they were dancing, Ty trying to get her to relax with the music, he saw Jasper and Lars were sipping whiskey while they worked, Lars fascinated by whatever Jasper was saying. When they brought over the food and Lars started asking Ty questions, it was clear Jasper had been into his stories about bears. It was also clear that getting to the corrals early was less and less important to Opie Kittle. It wasn't even that important to Ty anymore. The beer was good, and there was music. He'd watered and fed the horses before they loaded, and both Angie and Nina wanted to dance again.

When they finished their sandwiches, Lars—still trying to get Ty to talk about bears—decided the Deerlodge should buy a round of beer.

"Jasper here has sure been good for you, Lars," Opie said approvingly. "We'll bring him around more often."

"For Mr. Kittle, I buy two." Lars put a second bottle in front of Opie. He even made a toast, everyone enjoying his roundabout delivery.

They'd hardly put their bottles down when Maria Zumaldi came in, serene and gracious and as lovely a woman as Ty could imagine. Sugar put her in a seat next to Jasper and pulled over another for himself, Jasper so warmed by Maria's smile that he decided to buy the next round himself.

It took a few minutes for Ty to realize Maria spoke no English, that Sugar and Nina were filling in what she was saying: that a flat tire had delayed her, changed by her sons, who had talked all the while about going into the mountains with their father. They hardly noticed when Jasper's beer appeared, hardly noticed when Knots Malloy came in either, big as he was. When Ty looked up and saw him, the man looked even bigger than he'd looked in the mountains—as though the room couldn't quite contain him.

"I see your boys has left the horses in the sun while they butter you up with beer," Knots said to Opie, as though Ty and Sugar weren't there. "Ain't the way the famous Mr. Kittle usually handles his stock."

"I'm the one left them out there, my friend." Opie was as calm as could be. "Watered and fed; not a sore on a damn one."

Knots grunted and joined some cowboys at the bar who were enjoying Jasper's stories as they watched him sip whiskey.

The Texas Playboys were on again. Angie and Buck started dancing. Sugar and Maria decided to dance too, and Ty asked Nina if she wanted to try again. It was a fast number, and with the others out on the floor Nina relaxed to the music, let Ty move her around in his easy way. When it was over they were all a little out of breath, wanting to dance again but knowing they had to get going. Even Jasper could tell that Opie was getting responsible again.

Knots Malloy had put on a Gene Autry record and was ready to do a little dancing himself.

"Mind if I dance with this here little lady?" he said to no one in particular, taking Nina's hand.

"Oh," Nina said. "I'm sorry. I'm just learning."

"She has to make tracks," Ty said. "Got a foot out the door."

"How 'bout that pretty mother of hers? She looked awful good dancin' with the ass-packer."

Maria, not understanding a word Knots said, smiled and kept walking. Knots reached for her but Ty stepped in the way.

"She's about to trot along too."

Knots was surprised. "Who named you the rescue party?"

"I did." Ty realized again how big the man was. "I guess."

Malloy looked at him then looked over at Sugar. "You know," Knots said, "I hear the only thing dumber than a sheep is a sheepherder."

They were all at the door now. Lars Swenson was about to say good-bye when the quiet came. Lars and the others looked from Knots to Ty then back again at Knots. Ty was quiet too.

"I heard different," Ty said finally, his voice level. "Heard it's a guy who can't untie his knots."

Everyone knew where Knots had got his name, but nobody had ever said a word about it to Knots. Hearing Ty say it took them by surprise, the cowboys at the bar turning to watch. Knots, not sure he'd heard what he'd heard, was as quiet as the rest, his mouth a little open.

Opie didn't waste a minute. He herded everyone out and waved Sugar on his way to Goat Creek. Deciding a drunk young driver was better than a drunk old one, he pushed Buck behind the wheel of one rig, crammed Jasper in behind him. He told Angie to drive the pickup and hopped into the other rig with Ty.

As they left they saw Knots still in the door of the Deerlodge, his mouth still a little open.

"You did tell that big turd what's what." Opie looked at Ty. "He'll start lookin' for a way to tell you the same."

"Maybe." Ty was sorting out what he had to do. He figured they had three hours of light left. He had to water and feed again. Getting in before dark would help. "Didn't take to the way he treated Sugar."

"Me neither. But I'm too old to straighten them things out anymore."

They were quiet then, neither wanting to talk about it. Opie was looking out at the sagey floor of the Owens Valley.

"This country was all green once," he said. "Then they took our water and run it down to that Los Angeles."

"I guess a lot of what was in the mountains has gone off to the cities," Ty said. "Or the other way around."

The distinction hardly bothered Opie. He was asleep, leaving Ty alone with his thoughts. Ty looked forward to this trip with the Haslams, with Jeb Walker too. It would be good to have Buck and Angie and Jasper with them. He was anxious to see Mount Whitney too, and the Kern, the camps Sugar had told him about.

He tried not to think about Knots Malloy, though he was pretty sure Opie was right. It was one of those things he'd need to settle.

Knots would be a hard man to ignore.

36

Norman Clyde

They camped the first night under tall lodgepoles, grazing the mules in a big meadow above them. The climb had been hot and dusty, long switchbacks through a sagey, sandy country so steep the trail barely held. The sage gave way to timber as soon as they entered the basin, which was cool and inviting—trees spaced and stately, meadows lush, icy water spilling from cirques carved under the Sierra crest. From the camp they could see it: high, imposing, snow glinting from the crevices, cliffs dark and sheer—all of it seeming to lean toward them, as foreboding as it was seductive.

Just after coming into the timber they had overtaken a shaggy white-haired man with a huge pack, the man moving slowly but his pace steady. He didn't step aside until Ty was almost upon him.

"Nice lookin' mules." He took off a sweat-stained campaign hat and swabbed at his forehead. "Packed tidy."

"Helps when there's a climb like that one." Ty was surprised a man so old could carry anything so big, move so steadily. "This country sure tests you." He moved on, wanting to make camp so everyone could wash off the dust. Behind him Thomas Haslam pulled up and began talking with the man, taking off his hat as he said hello.

"Know who that was?" Haslam helped Buck and Ty unsaddle. "Norman Clyde. They call him 'The Mountain That Moves.' He's climbed more of these peaks than anybody."

"Goes alone," Sugar had told Ty. "Climbs anything, as though he's just warmin' up to climb somethin' else." Sugar told him how Norman Clyde had left his wife in her grave—his studies unfinished—retreated into the Sierra. He'd told him about Clyde's solitary ways too. Ty hadn't liked the way Sugar watched him as he described Clyde.

Just then the man himself trudged by, his pace the same.

"Ask him for dinner," Alice said. "We have plenty."

"We do." Jasper warmed to the idea. "With Angie stayin' back to help Mr. Kittle, we got extra." He liked this new country. Better still he liked having Jeb Walker along, a major general now, with an aide doing whatever Jeb Walker wanted and the aide's pretty wife as anxious to help Jasper as the aide was to help the general. And they were headed for Army Pass. The general enjoyed talking about that. Jasper looked forward to good evenings talking about Army Pass, sipping the general's bourbon.

"Let's," Jasper said to Ty. "He'll perk the general's interest."

They caught Clyde not far up the trail, his pace not a jot faster, as though wherever he found himself at sunset would do for camp.

"We've come to invite you." Jasper still held the knife he'd been using. "I've cut some nice steaks."

"He's right," Ty said. "We'd be pleased if you'd join us."

Norman Clyde watched to make sure they meant it.

"I could use a bite." He looked around. "Good camping here. Flat ground. Water."

He sat on a boulder and shucked his arms from the pack. Ty lifted it free, startled by its weight.

"Got enough for a mule here," he said.

Norman Clyde was impressed that such a slender man could handle all that weight so easily. "Why the hell use a mule?" he said. "When I can carry as much. Go higher too." He began pulling things out: a tool kit, extra boots, cans of food, moccasins. He found a pair of pants wadded down under things, shook them out.

"Ought to spruce up for the dinner," he said.

"Well." Jasper saw he was serious. "We'll make it nice. I'll just slip on back, get things ready."

He hurried off, leaving Ty to watch. Ty was astonished by the things that came out of the pack, how quickly they were arranged: two fishing rods, a ball of wire, nails, a skillet, a pistol, two cameras, an axe, climbing rope, a bedroll, books in different languages, a tarp. Finally Clyde pulled out a shirt, just as balled up as the pants had been. He shook it out and changed into it too. To Ty he looked the same as he'd looked coming up the trail, only more wrinkled.

Ty explained his plans for camps, describing some of Sugar's out-of-the-way places.

Norman Clyde listened, offering a suggestion here and there, but mostly he listened. Finally he settled himself on a rock and looked at Ty.

"You been talking to a man named Sugar Zumaldi?"

"I have." To Ty the question was a relief. He'd wanted to bring up Sugar's name but felt awkward about it. "He told me about this country. Said I should go up the Old Army Pass. . . . He even told me about you." Ty picked up one of the books. "Said you know as much about the Greeks as you do about these mountains."

Ty surprised himself, being so forthright. Something about the way the man watched him seemed to draw it out. "He's planning to meet me in a few weeks. In a place called Milestone."

"I know more about up here than about those Greeks." Norman Clyde kept looking at Ty. "The interesting history's here. And Sugar might be the best guide to it, if you can find his camps."

He studied Ty as he took a cup from his belt, poured water into it, dabbing himself here and there to clean off the dust. He rehooked the cup on his belt and settled his campaign hat.

"Must have faith in you if he said go up Old Army. His burros go up. None of these others even try. Mostly it's slid back to nature. You can try. Just send your friends up the new one. It's designed for people. Bad to take people where they can't go."

It was a happy evening. Alice helped Jasper lay things out in her special way, and Jasper's steaks had never been better. Jeb Walker got out his bourbon and found out Clyde enjoyed it as much as Jasper and Buck. They laughed and told stories as though they'd known each other for years. Alice and the pretty aide's wife—looking as crisp after their baths as Norman Clyde looked rumpled after his—a perfect audience. Doc Haslam watched Ty, who was pleased himself by all the life in his camp. That pleased Thomas Haslam.

Jeb Walker knew all about Army Pass, at least the old one. "Otis Johnson told me about it," he said. "Built by black troopers, from Georgia, back at the turn of the century. Good men. Inexhaustible. No one thought they could do it."

"They could do most anything—if you paid them a wage." Clyde's blue eyes stilled them. "Trouble is they had to build where it let them. Where the snow holds. Some years it never melts free. When it came time to reroute, they had the new tools. Could cut right through the rock, find the sun. . . . But that old one, that's the Sierra."

"Sugar Zumaldi," Norman Clyde said as Ty walked him back to his little camp, "knows another way across this crest. His people took sheep up it."

"He didn't tell me about that."

"Didn't tell you what a climber he was either. We went up the Palisades together. Tough climbs. The man gifted." He stopped and looked at Ty in the moonlight, his face craggy and strong.

"Then he just quit. Didn't like to rope up. 'A man can climb anything with all those ropes and hooks,' he told me. 'I don't need to get there that bad.'" Clyde walked on, shaking his head.

"Maybe that was right, for Sugar. Not for me. I just kept climbing. Not sure Sugar understands it."

They heard bells in the meadow, clear and reassuring in the cold air.

"More than one reason to bring them up here." Clyde cocked his head and looked at Ty. "Right pleasant company."

"Mules and mountains. Seems to me they go together."

"Mules are what those explorers Brewer and King used." Clyde looked toward the crest, inky blue in the night. "Rode them places Zumaldi opened up. Climbed some peaks. Put them on their maps. But I doubt they were first. Sheepmen probably been up before, getting high to look for meadows."

"Think they were up there?" Ty looked at the highest peak on the escarpment, massive in the moonlight.

"Likely. They used to call it Sheep Peak. Now it's Langley. That Clarence King climbed it. By mistake. Almost killed himself too. Found the hardest way. Thought it was Whitney. For a while everybody said 'Hurrah. You've done it. You're the best.'" He laughed.

"Wasn't he?" Ty knew Clarence King had discovered Whitney. Norman Clyde seemed to know something different.

"Hell, no. The best wouldn't miss a whole goddamned mountain." Clyde hunched deeper into his jacket. "The best is probably some Zumaldi we've never heard of. Those people had the mountains in them. Never hurried. Opened this country along deer trails, cracks in the rocks that started before we got upright."

"Did they find out he missed Whitney? The Basque?"

"If they did, they wouldn't have cared. A fisherman did. Rode his mule up from the other side." He smiled. "That fisherman cared. 'No wonder Clarence King had so much trouble,' he said. 'Found the wrong way up the wrong mountain and wouldn't admit it.'"

Norman Clyde looked at Ty, his voice serious.

"That can break your heart, you know."

"What can?"

"Making your wrongs look right." Clyde pulled his collar up against the cold. "To yourself. Rips your heart right out." He turned into the shadows to find his bed, his voice disembodied. "This country helps with that. Helps you tolerate yourself."

Ty tried to make sense of Norman Clyde as he walked back through the moonlight: his solitary ways, the odd focus he had on things. He was wondering what wrong the man was trying to make right when he decided he'd pick up Clyde's pack in the morning and top-pack it right up Old Army Pass. That way he'd learn the way and maybe learn more about Clyde. Why he kept climbing these peaks. Alone.

He realized how cold it had gotten and hurried back to camp, pleased to find Buck and Jasper still by the fire. "Your job," he told Buck, going to the water bucket and breaking a skim of ice to get a drink, "is to take everyone up that new trail. I'll take the mules up the old." He warmed at the fire. "We'll meet on top. If that pass lets me up it."

☞

But in the morning Norman Clyde was gone, the only sign the pressed earth where he'd slept. Ty rode with the others until they turned south to the new pass on the sunny side of the huge shoulder that shaded the old one. Then he rode toward Old Army, the route barely visible as he moved through meadows and along lakes, looking for Norman Clyde.

When he saw the pass at last, he took out the binoculars Alice Haslam had sent him that Christmas. "To see the good things ahead," she'd written. There was nothing good about what he saw now. The headwall looked impossible. And the old mountaineer was nowhere to be found. Ty scanned the huge bowl that steepened into cliffs, the apron of snow spilling from the high saddle. Nothing.

And there was no trail either. Not that Ty could see. He turned the glasses to the north, to the impossible-looking cliffs that led up to the still higher shoulder where the Zumaldis had taken their sheep. They must have crossed the crest along the top of those cliffs, coming from the north along a way only they knew, crossing a thousand feet above Ty's pass. He scanned the boulder-strewn chute below the cliffs and saw something was wrong, different. He focused on it and saw it inch higher—realized then that he was watching Norman Clyde's pack, the man seeking his own way to that high shoulder so few had known.

Ty turned back to what was before him, remembering what Clyde had told him the night before: "It'll surprise you," he'd said. "Can't tell where you're going till you're there. Sugar knows. Sugar should be with you."

"Or Norman Clyde," Ty thought, deciding there was nothing for it but to see for himself. He set his mules free and gave Smoky her head, moving along the lake below the headwall. To his surprise a trace appeared at its upper end. They were on it, then it was gone, then they were on it again, the route twisting and turning and taking them up between boulders and above cliffs and through chutes, the mules spread in a ragged line, but all of them on the course, all with their packs low and balanced, handling their impossible task as though it were not impossible at all, their noses to the faint trace as if knowing it would lead them to water and grass, a country good to be in.

He was so impressed with what they were doing that he scarcely looked at where Smoky was taking him, trusting her as she scrambled up and up, angling away from the high saddle, away from the big snowfield as she climbed high on the side of the bowl, almost as high as that snowfield, when suddenly she turned back, going along a natural ledge that had looked impossible from below. It proved to be a long traverse leading directly into the saddle. He rode along it, the ledge sandy, tilting down into the cliffs that fashioned the bowl, snow hugging their ledges. Sometimes there was snow above him too. But his route was clear, clear even as he came to the big snowfield where the sun-warmed rocks had slid the snow away to offer him a cool corridor above the vast white. They emerged into a wind so strong he had to grab for his hat, Smoky bracing herself as she crossed the final steepness to the broad pass.

It was wider and wilder than Ty could have imagined. Beyond the pass the country was serrated and vast, mountains opening to more mountains, a forested country dropping away in between, distant ridges rising into the sky like the teeth of some crazy saw.

He rode onto the pass, trying to place things in his mind as Sugar had placed them on his maps, as Clyde had described them. It was a moonscape where they were, so windswept that what little life there was had to hug the ground to survive, edging the rocks in pale greens and blues, as fragile as it was exquisite.

Ty was surprised by how quickly he'd come up the impossible-looking bowl, immediately finding the main trail where Buck would join him.

What was ahead—dropping into the Kern—seemed easy compared to what he'd done.

He dismounted, caught up his mules and tied them into their places, vowing never again to try something like that without exploring it first. He even walked back into the wind, peered down into the bowl to recapture his route. But it was too wild to tell where he'd been, everything fell off so. It was as though they'd been lifted on a cloud.

To the north he could see the high summit of Langley, even see the passable route King had missed in his haste. But he could see the cliffs on Langley's face too, understand how King might think it was Whitney.

And on those cliffs was that speck of dark again, moving ever-so-slowly upward. He used Alice's binoculars, and there it was—a pack with legs, a pack that could swing itself out and around boulders, inch its way up cliffs, find a purpose in going higher, always higher.

He looked back to the south and saw Buck appearing, the others strung out behind. Buck's eyes wide as he huddled in his coat, fighting off the wind.

"What crazy bastard put California way up here?" he shouted, shaking his head at the thought of it.

Ty was so pleased he had to laugh. He lined his string out, looking forward to the lush meadows far below.

37

Big Trees

That wasn't the last Ty would see of Norman Clyde, the two crossing paths with one another for the next twenty years. Mostly in the mountains, best in the mountains, Ty learning more about Norman Clyde each time he saw him—but never everything. It was different for Norman Clyde. He seemed to know everything he needed to know about Ty.

They came to know things about one another's life in the valley too, where things weren't always as good: Norman Clyde writing to describe his climbs—and getting so impatient with pestering teenagers he'd frighten them off with pistol shots. Ty drinking too much at the Deerlodge—finding himself in the morning with some dancer who knew the songs but not what they meant. But what they came to know about one another outside their mountains never interfered with what drew them together in them: Ty liking to learn from Norman Clyde; Norman Clyde liking to teach Ty the things he thought he'd left forever at the university.

Only a few days after Old Army Pass, Ty saw the mountaineer again. They were behind Mount Whitney now, camped in a hidden meadow below Crabtree Lakes. Ty was watching Thomas Haslam and Jeb Walker fish the upper lake when he saw that pack moving again, working its way along the boulder-riddled crest that met the trail to Whitney's summit. He used his glasses to make sure. There was Norman Clyde, headed for the highest peak of all. Not on the trail that made it possible and safe and predictable but getting there his own way—in his own time, for his own reasons.

A day later he was in their camp. "When I hit the trail, I left my pack and went on up without it." Clyde accepted another helping from Alice. "Didn't stay long. Too many people up there."

"How many?" Jeb Walker asked.

"Three. All talkers too. Came back and slept where I'd left my pack." He watched Jasper stirring something. "Then came looking for you folks. . . . My cooking's just not up to Jasper's."

He was pleased he'd found them, and it was as pleasant as he'd remembered. More pleasant, he thought, accepting an after-dinner drink from the general. And it had been very pleasant the first time.

He took his drink out onto the rock where Ty was watching his horses far across the lower meadow.

"Think I know why you're so interested in those two."

"King and Cotter?" Ty pulled himself away from his view.

"What else you been askin' about?" The mountaineer's blue eyes were on Ty. "It's because they came along so recently. Began opening up a country we're still opening ourselves."

"Eighty years ago?" Ty looked at him. "That's not yesterday."

"Hell it isn't." Norman Clyde snapped his fingers. "Like that." He cocked his head. "That's not even right. That's about how long we've been upright. The history those boys started is about as long ago as a snap inside that snap." He snapped his fingers again, liking the comparison.

"Not very long," Ty said, watching the gray creep up Whitney, the sun dropping.

"Fact is human history's so new up here we're part of it." Clyde liked it that Ty gave him plenty of time to make his points. "That's why everyone wants to know how the hell I climb these peaks."

⌒

In the morning Clyde was gone. Ty half-expected it, picturing him off along some high route known only to him. But it was no matter. When he met Norman Clyde again, they'd pick up where they'd left off. He felt lucky to have learned what he had, looked forward to seeing the country Clyde had described: the deep Kern trough, the power of the river; the Kaweahs and that shelf Sugar talked about; the Chagoopa Plateau; the Big Arroyo crashing down to join the Kern.

They rode north along a high meadow, deer watching them and twitching muley ears. Above them, across the deep fault of the Kern, the Kaweahs jutted out from the Western Divide: higher, closer, more impossible than the divide itself. The snow-choked bowls beneath them fanned out into an airy shelf of timber and grassland and lakes tilting down into cliffs dropping to the Kern. That was the Kaweah shelf. And Sugar was right—it was as alluring to look at as it was impossible to reach.

"Dropped into it once with Norman Clyde," Sugar had told him. "But we didn't stay. Climbers don't. They climb down the Kaweahs to get in, turn around and climb up them to get out. No reason to stay. Nothin' to climb."

Ty saw right away why Sugar was so taken with it—the meadows green, the lakes sparkling. He watched it as their route started them down into the Kern, the trail following a fast flowing creek, down and down toward the big river. The Kaweahs hung above them across the canyon, the Kaweah shelf going out of sight as they dropped—just as tempting to Ty at the end of the day as it was at its beginning.

Above Junction Meadows, where waters spilling from the Kaweahs join the Kern, the river spread into a ford. They crossed, camped by the faint trace leading up the Kern-Kaweah, a route that skirted the high cliffs guarding the Kaweah shelf to climb the other side of the canyon, crossing the divide and dropping into the Kings River country.

From their camp Ty could see the Kern arcing through a wooded meadow, the water deep enough to look peaceful. He freed his horses and went to watch the river gather its power to send its waters thundering across big boulders into slicks that rose in bubbling pools of white and green. He could see why they needed bridges below, the river funneling, straight as a plumb for ten miles, before widening into shoals that might provide a rocky crossing—in late summer, the water low.

In the morning they recrossed, took the trail down the river's east side to reach the hot springs, where a log bridge crossed the river once again. Sugar had told him to go downriver from the bridge, close to the springs but away from the trail. They camped there under ponderosas, the women returning crisp and clean after their baths to chase Buck and Jasper away. The two were happy to go, the hot springs all theirs.

"Smart of you to grab that sherry." Buck, clean and scrubbed, sunned himself. "It's hardly tolerable in the valley. Improves considerable up here."

"It is tasty with this warm." Jasper passed the bottle to Buck and lay flat in the hot water, studying the towering canyon walls. "Haven't felt this clean since Ty married Willie."

The thought of Willie quieted them. They passed the sherry back and forth.

"Ty's gettin' more spirited," Jasper observed. "He sure likes that man with the pack."

"Hope he doesn't take up backpackin'. He's too good with mules."

A voice broke in on them so suddenly Buck almost dropped the bottle. "You sure as hell won't do! I was lookin' for them pretty women you're supposed to be packin' around with Kittle's mules."

They saw that Knots Malloy, big as the big horse he was riding, had led his mules off the trail to look them over.

"Count yourself lucky you got a peek," Buck said. "We took first in several beauty contests last winter."

Knots was moving before Buck finished. They couldn't make out his answer, just heard something about jackasses.

"Hope Ty's up to beatin' the shit out of that man when the time comes." Buck relaxed again, passed the bottle to Jasper.

"Why?" Jasper settled back into the hot water. "Ain't we still workin' on gettin' Ty happy?"

"Someone's got to do it. I'm not up to anything that big."

"Maybe I'll take him on." Jasper lifted a skinny arm from the water and took a long pull. "This makes me right perky."

Buck reached for the bottle and took some himself.

"You'll need more perk than what's in here," he said.

Ty's camp was so hidden that Knots Malloy saw not a sign of it as he crossed the log bridge and headed down the river. He was thinking of the swinging bridge still ahead. He knew they'd pulled the cables as tight as they could, but the bridge still rattled and swayed. Once he'd had to beat a mule so hard to get her across he'd pulled something in his shoulder. The mule always fought him after that, and his shoulder still wasn't right. He had bad memories of that time. In fact he couldn't think of any good memories involving that bridge. He was working so hard on not thinking about it he didn't even notice Ty's tracks leaving the trail.

Jasper was glad Knots had missed them. The general was so polite he might have offered him a drink, a waste of the bourbon Jasper was enjoying as Alice got them singing. She and the aide's wife knew all kinds of songs. They got everyone singing around the fire each night— no one but Ty worrying about the horses or the bears or anything else.

The next day they crossed the bridge and rode under Chagoopa Falls, the water a mare's tail as it spilled from the canyon wall. Then they climbed the wall itself, their trail following another plunging creek, switching and turning so steeply across cliffs Jasper was afraid to look back, the canyon floor fifteen hundred feet below. He felt better when they climbed into the big timber of the Chagoopa Plateau. But that didn't last long either.

Ty trusted Sugar's directions completely now, which was a worry to Jasper. They crossed the plateau, skirted a huge meadow and left the trail to go through untracked woods to the opposite rim of the plateau. Ty rode along it, looking down into the Big Arroyo until he found his route. He set his mules free and took an angle down the bluffs, sliding and slipping over little short switchbacks until there was no way to switchback at all, Smoky leading the mules straight down the timberless arroyo wall. Jasper, too frightened to dismount, rode it out, eyes closed, his body leaning so far back his head touched his horse's rump. Then, miraculously, they were down—safe on the floor of the Big Arroyo itself.

"There's a ride that would give the cavalry pause." Jeb Walker looked up at the impossible descent they'd made, exhilarated. He watched his aide, who'd abandoned his horse, cling to shrubs and roots as he made his way down.

"Haven't had so much fun since my aunt had her accident," Buck said, watching the aide.

"What accident?" Walker asked.

"Time she caught her tit in that wringer," Buck said, his laugh breaking out so richly the general had to laugh too.

They camped right there on the river, Buck telling more stories, liking the camp, liking it that there was no trail at all here, liking how much all of them were coming to like each other.

He told about the winter Fenton packed the frozen Chinese from the mine, sawing the bodies in half to balance the packs and enraging the families when he couldn't match the halves up.

He told about the buffalo calves his grandfather trained to plow, only to learn they'd only plow north in the spring, south in the fall.

"So he decided to plant narrow," Buck said. "But it got so it took two days to trot in for lunch. That's when he broke them to milk."

"That's the only time his granddaddy didn't get done what he said he would." Jasper had hardly known Old Man Conner, but Buck had told him so many stories he felt like family. "When he died his wake was so good they postponed the funeral."

The Haslams listened happily. And Jeb Walker had a way of getting one story to lead into another. Everyone enjoyed them so much the storytelling caught on with the rest of them, the stories and singing making each night better than the last. They even told stories about Ty, waiting until he left to check on his horses and talking quietly, seriously—about how Fenton and Cody Jo took him in, the time he rode through the blizzard, killed the red bear because he had no choice. Only when Willie's name came up was there quiet, all of them looking into the fire.

They eased their way up the Big Arroyo, fishing the river and taking side trips to the lakes above. Then in a swooping day they turned west, crossed the divide at Kaweah Gap to enter the Kaweah drainage, the headwaters a bottomless lake, cliffs plummeting into it.

After the lake the country seemed to stand on end, snowmelt feeding shelves of green, bursts of paintbrush and shooting star and lupine. A lake below seemed unreachable until the trail took them into the cliff itself, tunneled through a buttress to wind its way through talus and juniper, meeting the lake at last. Then more than two miles along a cliff, the trail following ledges, barely going up or down as it clung to the sheer wall, Ty's mules loose behind him, moving easily. But nothing about it easy for Jasper—his eyes closed, knuckles white on his saddle horn, dizzy with the thought of the chasm dropping to the Kaweah River far below.

"Like a stairway to heaven," he told Buck, still shaking.

"Cliffy and steep?" Buck unsaddled. "Hard on the stock?"

"No, goddamn it," Jasper said. "Impossible."

They were nearing Wolverton, the other side of the Sierra where the road from the Central Valley wound its way up into the big trees. At Wolverton Jeb Walker's people would leave them; the Haslams would stay, other friends joining them for the trip back across the Sierra. Ty was looking forward to it, to recrossing the Western Divide, this time at Colby Pass, completing a full circle around the Kaweahs to ride back under that Kaweah shelf and rejoin the Kern. They would camp again at the Kern ford, then follow the big river north to its source, turning off at its headwaters to meet Sugar in Milestone Basin.

Ty was anxious to see Sugar, talk about the places he'd been, where he'd camped, his meeting with Norman Clyde. He hadn't thought there could be anything in the world like this country. He knew Sugar had seen it coming.

༒

The last night Alice put on a skit about a packer who fell in love
with his mule, convincing Buck to play the lead with Cottontail as the
love interest. After that they sang songs, Ty watching and thinking of
Fenton's theory about warming from the inside. It seemed to him these
people knew all about that, letting the fire take care of the outside,
counting on each other for things that ran deeper. He considered trying
to tell them about Fenton's theory but decided against it, not sure he
could make it make sense.

The next day he sent the rest out early so they could ride through
the sequoias in Giant Forest. He would take the cutoff and meet them
at Wolverton, where their trails converged. Ty hadn't expected to see
any big trees himself and was startled when his trail dropped into a
sequoia grove, the trees huge, some with their cores burned away by
ancient fires but still healthy. His string went silently through the deep
duff. All he could hear were birds, the blowing of his mules, the creak
of leather. The rest was still, sunlight filtering through, ferns barely
moving in the soft air.

"Some of those trees were there," Norman Clyde had told him,
trying hard to make Ty understand, "when Homer wrote about that
siege." He'd held up one of his books, as though offering proof.

"What siege?" Ty didn't understand. "You mean before Jesus?"

"Jesus came later." Norman Clyde had looked as cranky as a crossed
professor. "Maybe a thousand years. Those trees were there before we
started our damn history." He'd thrown his book aside. "And think
how long these mountains came before the trees."

He'd given a kind of snort, sipping Jeb Walker's whiskey as he did.

Ty thought about all that as he pulled Smoky up for a breather, his
long string diminutive beneath the great trees. He dismounted and
walked to one of them, went inside the charred hulk to look up and see
light, the tree topped two hundred feet above him by some winter
storm. He went back and looked up at limbs big as trees flourishing a
hundred feet up the trunk, craning his head, taking in all that life
reaching out from the giant husk. He let Smoky nuzzle at his hand,
rubbed her ears. "Some things got tougher hides than others," he said,
his voice seeming to violate the deep silence. Then they were moving
again, Ty thinking of all the things these trees had been through, how
serene they were despite it.

When he got to Wolverton, everything changed. The military car was waiting and Jeb Walker was once again the general, his aide moving fast to keep up. The door of Walker's car slammed, the driver raced the engine and they were gone—back to the general's world of troop movements and motor pools and helicopter landings.

"And so ends their trip." Alice looked at Ty. "Not with a whimper but a bang. I'll miss them. Will you miss him?"

"I will. Him and Otis Johnson are the only good things that came out of that war."

"He and Otis," Alice said.

Ty smiled. "I still got you to teach me to say it right. And the doc." He began unsaddling. "And your kids. And I got those binoculars. I'm on the lookout for the good things ahead."

38

Milestones

Ty liked heading back for the Western Divide. The Haslams' friends could hardly be nicer, but he let them ride with Jasper and Buck so he could watch the country—imagining how it was fashioned, the benches so orderly, the meadows so green.

On the fourth day they climbed to a long lake, the trail clinging to granite swept by ancient ice. Above it the sparse timber gave way to a snowmelt meadow fed by a snowfield. They crossed it, the sun cups deep but the pitch shallow, and scrambled into talus, the scratchy trail winding up steeper and ever tighter switchbacks, on and off snow until onto the pass at last. Ty watched the others come onto the divide, the Kings River behind them, the Kern ahead, Jasper clutching his saddle horn, his eyes closed against the heart-stopping drop back to that field of snow, tiny now, a thousand feet below them.

They looked east, looking across the giant trough of the Kern from the other side now, Whitney there beyond it—massive and regal. The jagged peaks of the Kaweahs leaned over the Kern, declaring themselves, and there was the Kaweah shelf again, even more inviting now. The cliffs fell away in sheer granite to isolate it from the north as abruptly as from the Kern, the soaring Kaweahs patrolling the rest of it—guardians assigned by some god.

"Your Elysian field, isn't it?" Thomas Haslam watched Ty, knowing well what held him there. "Bet it's just as elusive too."

"Looks pretty, that country," Ty said. "Everything you want."

"Things seem that way. Until a man gets them." Haslam was looking at the shelf himself now, his voice gentle. "I guess the cure is to have our dreams come true. Get appointed to some job and find yourself stopped by the ones who did the appointing." He smiled. "Find yourself loved by a woman and learn she loves what you will be—not who you are."

Ty liked thinking of Willie and Cody Jo up here—or out there on that shelf. But he knew Thomas Haslam had a point. They might not like it at all.

"I'm not much good at figuring what women want," Ty said.

"But you yearn for something. What is it?"

"Not much." Ty felt awkward saying it. "A safe place. It looks peaceful over there. Feed and water. Wood. The Kaweahs above. The Kern below. Whitney to catch the late sun. You could watch the colors at sunset."

"Probably just rock over there. Or swamp. Might be no flat for a camp—or bogs everywhere. No place to sleep. You can have illusions, you know." Thomas Haslam looked out at the dazzling expanse of peaks and canyons, the waterfalls dropping into the valley they would follow to the Kern. "Even in country like this."

Ty was surprised. It sounded a little like Spec's reservations about packing. Only Spec would have sworn a lot. Thomas Haslam just seemed resigned.

They dropped into the treeless U of a high valley, following the course of an old glacier that made room for lupine and gentian—wild onion edging the stream. To the north Ty could see the profile of Milestone, looking like a tombstone. It jutted from the knife-edge ridge as though chiseled, closing this side off from the basin beyond— cutting anyone off but some Norman Clyde, some lonely climber who had it in him to challenge places like that.

In an hour they were down into timber, the trees hard-bitten and scruffy as their trace dropped steeply down a moraine. At the bottom another glacier had intersected theirs, the bigger U of that valley open and inviting, lifting back toward the high pyramid of Triple Divide, the peak that separated all the places Ty had been: the Kern, the Kings, the Kaweah.

It came to him then that they'd been circling this mountain, not the Kaweahs he'd watched so closely. Camping on waters separated by this mountain—even though it was the Kaweahs he'd used as his compass.

Fenton would enjoy that, he thought. Thomas Haslam too. Even Spec. His going all that way with his eye on the wrong thing. Sugar Zumaldi would see it differently. He'd claim the Kaweahs had seduced him, promised him the things the way a beautiful woman might.

Thinking of Sugar, he led his string away from the faint trail toward another of Sugar's camps, riding toward Triple Divide Peak until the timber grew sparse. He forded the stream and rode back down the other side to camp under big lodgepoles. It was everything Sugar had promised: the timber open, wildflowers edging the rocks, the stream alive with pools and shallows before dropping into the canyon below. Ty wouldn't have to worry about his mules either, the grass in the U-shaped valley sweet, the benches sandy.

They laid over, giving the mules a chance to recruit; Ty a chance to search out a route to his shelf. He left early, walking along open benches for over an hour, the final one diminishing into a ledge not even Sugar's burros could handle. He worked along it carefully, finding it led to another, then another, each way linking as they narrowed, broke, became giant stairs angling down toward the Kern. Finally he was stopped entirely. A feeder stream pouring from above had split the granite like a cleaver, the chasm dark and slick—walls smooth as marble. Cool lifted from it, a mist veiling sheer walls beyond. The shelf remained above him, its meadows and lakes less visible from here than from the pass—just as Sugar had predicted.

Below him the canyon narrowed, the glacial U giving way to a steep V as the stream cut down toward the Kern. He could see why it was the Kern-Kaweah, the waters rising here, racing for the Kern down a route carved just for them. All of it arranged perfectly, protecting the Kaweah shelf from the steady pull of seasons.

The next day they rode down that canyon, crossing meadows where lakes had been, the timbered lips of moraines, then down once again into meadows. The canyon walls closed as they dropped, and Ty saw the waterfall bursting from the cliffs across the canyon, its spray lifting in misty clouds that offered no hint of the abyss behind them—the rock split by water.

Again they camped on the Kern, sheltered by a stand of Jeffrey pine. The river was swollen from melting snowfields, but in the chill night it lowered and in the morning they forded easily, riding up the the river along falls and tumbling rapids toward its headwaters. At midday they recrossed it, an infant river now, its waters running shallow across granite before starting their run down the great Kern gorge.

They traced up the feeder stream draining Milestone Basin until they were stopped by a rock face. Ty led them away from it to find short rock ledges offering just enough purchase for the mules to gather themselves to push up, push up again until they were into the basin itself, which was wide and gentle with big slabs of granite tilting down smoothly into the grassy bottom.

Ty tied his mules in a stand of lodgepole, let Buck see to the unpacking while he rode alone up the basin, listening for the bells of Sugar's burros. He was as anxious to see Sugar and Nina as he was to look at Milestone Mountain high above him. It still looked like a tombstone to him, quarried square by some quirk of nature, turned on end to become a ghostly marker above the ragged range.

The scattered timber gave way to alpine lakes and high rocky benches, but Sugar was not to be found. Ty returned to the others to find Sugar and Nina by the fire, enjoying Jasper, who had his sherry out and was offering it in hopes someone had something stronger to offer him. To Ty it was as though the world had been put back together, right there in Milestone Basin.

The next morning Nina and Sugar took him to Maria and the rest of the Zumaldis, crossing the creek below Ty's camp and making their way toward a granite fin. Ty had taken it to be one side of the basin itself, but Sugar crossed still another granite slab to make his way around the fin into a smaller bowl. They climbed along a pine-needled game trail to a woodland lake, circled it and went up a granite crevice onto the grassy banks of the loveliest lake Ty had yet seen. The Zumaldi children were already wading, immune to the cold as they fished the freezing water. And Maria was there, lovely and welcoming, completely at home in Sugar's hidden camp.

"What do you call this place?" Ty was feeding Sugar's burros, who had rushed down from some sunny hideaway, sunfishing and farting in their excitement. "I doubt anyone knows it's here."

Sugar was calling each burro by name, making sure each got some sugar. "Because it's not," Sugar said. "At least not on that map of yours. They got the elevation wrong on that fin we come around, missed some of these lakes too, made it look like you got to fly to get here."

"Can I get here again?"

"You can. Buck told me where you been."

"He's not sure where *he's* been," Ty said. "But where am I? If I come back, I'll need to know."

"Ain't got a name. Just a good place for my burros."

"And for me. If I can find it."

"You can. Look from here?" Sugar pointed up at the big slab of Milestone. "Your marker."

Ty saw. It didn't look at all like a tombstone from here.

"A milestone . . . I see it now."

"More clear from here," Sugar said, feeding his last cube to a jenny who nosed at him. He looked at the lake, his sons cleaning fish, Nina getting water from the outlet stream. "Most everything is."

"Let's eat," he said, starting for his camp. "Maria cooked special. Just for you."

C-つ

In its own way, that day established the pattern of Ty's life in the Sierra. He could almost measure the years by the times he saw the milestone from Sugar's basin. But he also came to see that his life was somehow turned on end. He felt at home in mountains only the most daring could visit; he became a visitor in places that were homes to everyone else. Not that he didn't try to bridge that gap. He sought out Norman Clyde in the Valley, finding the old climber as lonely and awkward outside the mountains as he was comfortable in them. He spent time in the Deerlodge, too often drinking more than he should. He taught Otis Johnson's boy to pack, but that part was easy; everything he taught the boy, he taught him in the mountains.

Opie Kittle saw how it was after that first season. And until he died he did what he could to make a place for Ty in the Valley. After that Ty managed as best he could: gentling colts, building fence, doctoring other people's stock.

People liked him. He was always reliable, always on time. They trusted him with any task; it was just that he never seemed happy with any task not in the mountains. If it hadn't been for Angie and Buck—and Cody Jo after Bliss Holliwell died—his winters would have been even more spare, his nights lonelier.

There were women of course. He still loved the dances Cody Jo had taught him. But too often he'd find himself waking with someone who'd only seemed to dance well the night before. The singer didn't come until later. And though everyone knew she was different, few could understand what that difference began to mean to Ty.

But always there was Cody Jo, or the idea of Cody Jo, in his life. They never made love again, but she was part of him always: the way she thought, the music she loved, the concerns that troubled her. After Holliwell was gone she would drive to see him from the retirement community Bliss had joined near Los Angeles. They would talk, go dancing, have dinner with Angie and Buck and Jasper at the Deerlodge. She made sure things stayed alive in him: their times at the pack station; Fenton's unpredictable ways, Horace and Etta Adams—Willie. Cody Jo had a gift for keeping Willie alive in him. And some nights, when the music was just so, the drinks good, and the dancing right, the old Cody Jo would come alive in him as well.

They never talked about their night together. There was no way to talk about it. And no need. They lived with it, each wanting the best for the other. It might even have been a more steady part of her life than Ty's. Certainly she was the one who most wanted something to come of his time with the singer. And certainly she was the one who worried most about his lonely winters, his narrow escapes in the mountains, the times he drank too much.

When the fight with Knots Malloy finally came, it was as much a surprise to her as to the rest of them—its suddenness, its brutality. But what stunned her most was finding she could be the trigger for such terrible violence.

39

Knots

It wasn't that it was over so fast that confused people. It was that what happened was so different from what usually happened when there was a fight in the Deerlodge. There were no threats, hardly any talk at all. It was a Friday night—some people dancing, some gathered around the bowling machine watching a cowboy have a good run. Most of them didn't even know there was a problem until the jukebox went over, the music becoming a screech before the crash. At first everyone thought it was Buck and Ty having the disagreement, not Ty and Knots Malloy. Knots, big as he was, was partly out of sight behind the overturned jukebox, records spilled across him like cards.

It started innocently enough. Ty and Buck had brought a late trip out over Taboose Pass in the big October storm, fighting high drifts to reach the pass then dropping and dropping along the rocky trail until the snow turned to hail, then rain—not letting up until they unpacked. Looking back, they were thankful they'd made it at all, a purple and scarlet sky bleeding into black on the Sierra crest. The blizzard still howling on the pass, six thousand feet above them and under four feet of snow.

They took care of Jasper first, Jasper cold and sore from all that downhill. Everyone knew he was getting too old to be taking trips, but he still found reasons to go. This time he regretted it, his hands so stiff and cold he couldn't unpack his kitchen. They took him to Opie Kittle's with the first load of mules, firing up the stove so he could warm. Ty had taken it over entirely since Opie died, using the barns to store the gear, the pastures to winter the stock.

They hauled the rest back through the night, making three runs—and then still another, the last to get Sugar's burros. Sugar had brought his family out over Goat Pass in the same storm and they knew he was having a harder time than they were—the rain there turning to sleet in the night. Ty went for him as soon as he got word, more worried about Maria than the children, all of them big and strong now and as much help as Sugar could want.

By three in the morning Ty had them all at Opie's. He gave Sugar and Maria his bed and let them settle the kids in the house. He was happy to throw down some saddle pads and sleep out in the barn with Jasper and Buck, happy to let the tension drain away. He knew how lucky they'd been to get everyone out—no frozen fingers or toes; no frostbitten ears.

That morning a foot had already fallen by the time they wrangled the horses. They packed under a high tarp set up to keep off the snow. It was coming hard and getting worse, and they all knew the South Fork of the Kings was no place to be when the snows fell. No way down the canyon at all; the only way out the high passes.

Ty was afraid even the broad saddle of Taboose would be closed when he finally got everything moving, thinking he might have to turn back right there, drop down into the timber, make camp and hope for a melt. The drifts were already deeper than he liked, but the snow was dry, no weight to it. When he hit the first big drift he went right at it, wishing he had Smoky Girl under him again.

Smoky Girl had been long retired by then, the rocky passes too much for her legs. He'd put her into the pastures back of Opie's barns, using different horses until he'd found the black filly—escaped from somewhere to run loose on the desert. It was easy to see she had good blood—easy to see she was wilder than the mustangs she ran with too—until Ty began to work with her, ducking her hooves and naming her Nightmare and running her with his mules until they made her theirs. Calming her until he made her his, his and no one else's—at least according to Buck and Jasper.

She was tough enough, Ty knew that, but he was never sure how desert horses would handle big drifts like these. He was still missing Smoky Girl when Nightmare pushed her way into the drift, hardly hesitating, going at it with such force she almost swam through it, touching down now and then to kick up and plunge ahead, lifting herself above the drift again and then again—finally all the way through it, her legs trembling as she regained the rocky trail, the wind blowing everything off into the drifts still ahead. They came down like that, the mules following Nightmare through, the first few struggling but soon providing passage for the rest. And then they just fought the cold, the trail barely visible, the wind gusting snow into smaller and smaller drifts. And lower down, the hail. The wet.

C—つ

"Thought we might become a Blue Plate Special up there." Buck closed the lantern down. "You got any of those Donner Party recipes, Jasper?" He laughed as he got into his sleeping bag. "Hell, you're so skinny I doubt you'd be tasty."

"Wish you hadn't drank up all that sherry," Jasper said. "My bones could stand a warm."

"We made it." Ty turned over to get comfortable. "I don't want to try that again. We pushed our luck."

"Might have," Buck said. "But we come through. We're here."

Ty was going to answer, but he heard Buck's breathing even out.

Buck had never complained, Ty thought. Neither had Jasper. But Ty knew how close he'd taken them, how much they'd counted on him. He lay there thinking about that until he couldn't think at all, everything in him folding into his own exhaustion.

Cody Jo had written saying she would meet them after Ty's last trip. But he was surprised to find Cody Jo and Angie already there, making breakfast, helping them find clean clothes, deciding with all of them to have a big dinner that night at the Deerlodge.

By late afternoon they had things organized: the tack under cover and feed out for the stock. They were all excited about going to the Deerlodge, excited about Jasper teaming up with Lars to do the cooking. Ty and Sugar were looking forward to a good drink and a chance to compare notes. They counted on that each year after the weather closed down the country they both loved so much.

Lars couldn't have been happier to see them, the big storm being all the news. "Lucky you got down safe, Ty. You deserve a drink. I'll sure buy the first." He pulled tables together and went off to cook with Jasper, liking Jasper's stories about Montana—about Ty's friends, Spec and Fenton; about things that happened at a place called The Bar of Justice.

Everyone was having such a good time Ty hadn't even noticed that Knots Malloy was in the bar, hadn't noticed until Knots came over and put a big boot in the chair they were saving for Jasper.

"Hear you near got yourself froze in up there below Bench Lake."

He leaned on his outsized leg and looked down at Ty. "Doubt old man Kittle would appreciate his mules gettin' in a tight like that."

"Didn't want to come out till I had to. That's pretty country."

"Under snow it ain't. Your ass-man could tell you that."

"Sugar's pretty handy about weather." Ty looked up at Knots. "I believe he's struck an arrangement with whoever makes it."

"Hear you like to get caught up there too," Knots said to Sugar. "Don't sound like such a good arrangement to me."

"My burros got other ways out from where I was," Sugar said. "A little snow's no problem."

Buck and Angie got up to put some music on the jukebox. Sugar and Maria joined them.

"Ain't you askin' me to sit?" Knots said. "Got all them chairs here."

"Taken," Ty said. "When the music stops and everyone comes back."

"I could turn a step or two myself." Knots looked out at the dancers. "With one of your lively ones."

But he didn't do anything about it, walking over to get another beer instead, joining the others to watch the cowboy play the bowling game.

Ty was glad Nina wasn't with them. He didn't want her anywhere around Knots. She had grown up to be as pretty as her mother and so in bloom when she went off to the university that she'd hardly had a chance to think about law school. Ty had trouble keeping up with all the college boys who courted her, both he and Sugar relieved when she finally married a rancher's son from Marysville. The boy had studied ranch management, but Ty doubted he needed to. The family place was so perfectly managed it was hard for Ty to understand how it worked. He'd left the others and looked it all over with Nina the day before the wedding, thinking how little it had to do with the scratchy place he'd known. The Bitterroot seemed another world as he walked through the clean barns, the tidy corrals, liking everything he saw but liking most of all Nina, who'd hardly changed.

"First a family, Ty Hardin. Then law school," she'd said in her serious way as they looked at the machinery. It seemed to Ty there was more machinery around than horses, and no mules at all. Nina watched him, smiling. "And even when I'm in law school," she'd said, "we can still dance. They dance differently now. I like the way you taught me best."

Ty was thinking about what a beautiful bride Nina had been when someone put still another beer in front of him. He didn't know how much he'd had to drink that night, the music too good to keep track. But Buck always claimed he'd been sober, that it was Knots Malloy who had too much to drink. Knots Malloy who had started everything. . . . Ty wasn't clear on that either.

He did remember Knots dancing once with Angie, remembered Buck keeping Angie pretty much to himself after that. And he remembered Maria smiling at Knots and shaking her head to say no, Knots saying something back that rubbed them all the wrong way. But he'd been having such a good time dancing with Cody Jo he couldn't be sure what set things off. All he knew was that Lars had some of Cody Jo's favorites in his jukebox. It was like old times hearing that music, dancing with Cody Jo again.

Cody Jo was nearly sixty then, but she was still Cody Jo, feeling the music, knowing steps that surprised Ty, never missing a beat when she came back into the circle of his arms.

Buck smiled as he watched them. It seemed like old times to him too. Cody Jo was still tall and slender, even if she'd spread a little around the middle. He thought the gray in her hair made her look even prettier. And Ty looked almost the same as he had looked when he came back from the war. Still lean as a rail, still moving to the music in that quiet way, just enough to stay with it, letting Cody Jo do most of the moving for both of them.

Suddenly Buck saw Knots was there, tapping Ty on the shoulder.

"Ain't havin' too much luck with them others." There was a beery grin on Knot's face. "Let's have a spin with your grannie here."

He reached for Cody Jo's hand and was startled to find himself going backward, his weight tipped back so far from the jolt Ty gave him that only the jukebox saved him. And not for long.

"That's Cody Jo." Ty watched Knots stumbling backward, trying to keep his legs under him. "And lay off Sugar." Knots hit the jukebox hard. There was the lifting and falling sound of a needle crossing a record, then the crash—lights popping and smoking, the music stopping altogether.

The screech of the needle, the records spilling out across Knots, Cody Jo standing there beside him—all of it seemed to snap something in Ty. Buck had never seen him look that way. He was afraid Ty was going to kick Knots to death right there behind the jukebox. Before he had time to think he'd jumped on Ty and tried to hold him back. It didn't seem to slow Ty down at all. He kept moving toward Knots, his eyes wild.

Jasper, who'd crouched down beside the bar when the jukebox went, was startled to see Buck up there on Ty's back. Then he saw Knots get up from behind the jukebox, looking desperate as Ty came at him. Knots grabbed a chair and brought it down as hard as he could, the chair splintering over Buck's head as Ty moved in under it and brought the butt of his hand up under Knots's nose so hard blood squirted away as though he'd squashed a tomato.

There was blood coming from Buck's head too, the chair opening a long chunk of his scalp. But he kept clinging to Ty, helped now by the cowboy who'd left his bowling machine and grabbed one of Ty's arms. Lars got hold of the other, the three of them knowing they had to calm Ty before he killed Knots outright.

Years of lifting packs had given Ty a strength even greater than when he'd turned the broom handle on the troop ship. He flung Lars and the cowboy away, shucking Buck like a coat as he drove the butt of his hand into Knots's Adam's apple, cramming it back so far the big man's eyes popped. He drove his hand into Knots again, the noise dense as all the wind left the big body. Knots, clawing at his windpipe, staggered back and fell across the bowling table, drawing his knees up as he fought for air. The bowling table splintered and he rolled away, struggling for the door, going out in a crouch, blood and mucus spewing from him.

The cowboy and Lars had Ty again. It took him a moment to shake free and follow. But only Harvey Kittle was there, his white shirt bluish in the stark light Lars had rigged above the door.

"What's up?" he asked. "Heard you beat that storm . . ."

He saw what was in Ty's face and pointed at the outhouse Lars used when the well-pump wasn't working. "In there," he said. "Crippled some by the looks of him."

The outhouse was framed with four-by-fours and weighted down with boulders. Ty hit it so hard some boulders came free. It went up, rocked back down, and Ty hit it with his shoulder again. It went all the way over and there Knots was, curled at the base of the two seater, bubbles of orangey mucus lifting from his face, eyes bulging. Blood covered his shirt and ran down into his pants. Ty looked at him and felt his anger draining away.

"Shouldn't talk to her that way." He sounded almost thoughtful. "Sugar either. They don't like it."

Harvey Kittle was still trying to make out what had happened. Buck and Lars joined him, Buck holding paper napkins to his head to staunch the blood. Others came out of the bar too.

"Never did put a lock on that door," Lars finally said. "Why'd he have to knock the whole thing over?"

ᑕ−ᓄ

The next morning Ty stopped by to ask Lars about damages. Lars gave him coffee and made up a figure. Ty paid up right there, surprised it wasn't more but too embarrassed to talk about it.

A few days later Lars learned that wouldn't begin to cover the new jukebox, never mind the bowling machine. But he didn't worry. He put a jar out for donations. People dropped a little in when they stopped by to hear about the fight—or to tell their version of it. In less than a month Lars had more than enough to pay for everything.

After Ty left that first morning, Lars got four men to tip the outhouse up so he could get a rope around it. They pulled it upright with a pickup and walked it into place. It was put together so solidly Lars only had to tack a few boards on to keep things straight. They anchored it again with the rocks.

Lars still uses it when his well-pump quits.

40

Fast Water

"Hate to think what would of happened if he'd thought to double up his fist," Harvey Kittle said, putting a few dollars in the jar.

"Did most of it with Buck on his back." Lars wiped at the bar. "Buck's over two hundred pounds. Maybe more. Ty didn't seem to notice."

"Saw him tack a shoe on a rank mule one day." Harvey sipped his beer, remembering. "Mule let Ty hold up a good half of him while he rested up for the next round."

They went out into the sunlight and looked at the outhouse. It was settled back in its place at the edge of the lot.

"Near give us all a hernia gettin' it back," Lars said. "Still don't know why Ty had to knock the whole thing over."

⌒⌒

And so Ty's strength was settled in the minds of all those who knew the Deerlodge, which meant pretty much everyone, those not knowing it getting the story from those who did. The size of Knots Malloy grew in their minds too, partly because Knots was no longer around to prove anyone wrong. After the fight he took up work for a guest ranch in Arizona. It must have satisfied him. No one ever saw him in the valley again.

None of it meant much to Ty. He didn't listen to the talk, and he tried not to think about Knots. He knew something had gone terribly wrong in him that night. He'd seen men get that way with mules, sometimes with horses. To him it was a sickness: no good for the man, a disaster for the animal.

It made him feel more alone than ever—though it might have seemed the opposite. People certainly paid more attention to him— they just began treating him differently, parting to make a place for him at the Deerlodge, wanting to buy his drinks, pay for his coffee. It was better in the mountains, but even there the rangers would stop by his camps for no reason, offer help he didn't need. More and more he felt separate—growing more distant as the years slid by.

Higher roads, lighter gear, fast-talking environmentalists brought more and more hikers into the high country. The regulations that caused drove many of the old packers out, though somehow Ty's business kept improving. Harvey Kittle realized it and pretty much let Ty run everything—despite how choosy Ty seemed to be getting.

Ty even gave up packing for the big Sierra Club trips. "Too damn many people," he told Harvey. "Camping up under the cliffs so they can swing on their ropes. No feed up there for the mules. No room for all their stuff." And if some of the guests brought too many amenities, Ty would back away. "Said I'd show you these mountains," he'd say mildly, returning their deposits. "Not turn them into a trailer park."

Harvey saw no reason to complain. No matter how many people Ty turned away, his pack strings were busy all summer and into the fall. The Haslam family would always take a long trip, sometimes with Jeb Walker, sometimes with others. Their friends seemed to come back too, arranging trips on their own schedules. And when some official from the Park Service or some politician in Washington wanted to see the Sierra, it was Ty they turned to, Ty who picked the routes and chose the horses, decided on the camps.

Angie arranged things on the outside, organized gear and food and people. And after Jasper went to the rest home, it was Angie who found the cooks—cooking herself if she had to or enlisting Nina, one of Nina's friends, or one of the Haslam children—all of them wanting to work with Ty, spend their summers in the Sierra with Ty.

The winters went more slowly, though ranchers from Lone Pine all the way up to Bishop seemed to count on Ty for one thing or another. He knew how to doctor their cattle and straighten their fences and gentle their horses. He even had a way with their children—the boys listening as they could not to their fathers, the girls liking his way with animals. Their parents were different. They didn't have much to say to Ty unless they were asking for help, advice about some problem with a horse or a lame mule or a sickness keeping weight off their cattle. And then they seemed shy about asking, as though they should know what to do themselves.

More and more Ty would find himself drinking too late in the Deerlodge. Many nights hardly talking at all, sometimes talking too much. "No need to tell him you heard that story before," Buck would tell Lars, who was always partial to Montana stories. "It's good for him to do some talkin'."

Most of Ty's stories were about Fenton and Spec. Sometimes they were about Cody Jo, the way she was with Fenton. Sometimes about Etta and Horace or Rosie and Dan Murphy. He didn't need to talk about himself. Or Willie.

Lars was bothered by that, always wanting to learn more about Ty. But it was hard to do. He could only get hints from the secondary roles Ty played in his own stories, or from things Buck and Angie said, or Jasper—before Etta and Horace found him the rest home back in Missoula.

"Fenton knew one thing about that bear," Ty told Lars one night. "To let him go his own way. That bear let Fenton go his too." Ty finished his beer and looked at Lars. "But Spec was interested in more. Where that bear lived. What he needed and ate. Where he slept."

"Jasper told me about Spec in the woods." Lars mopped at his bar. Not mopping down the bar from one conversation to another but sticking with Ty, listening, hoping to get something new for the picture of Ty he carried around in his head.

"It wasn't so much that Spec knew the woods." Ty accepted another beer. "He was part of them. I think he watched that bear," Ty looked across his beer at Lars, "to learn more about himself."

༺ঌ

He didn't need to tell those stories in the summers. And he hardly ever drank too much in the summers. His trips were enough. And more often than not there were emergencies: tracking down horses, finding lost climbers, packing out the sick or the injured, sometimes the dead. They were glad to have Ty handle those things, until the helicopters came. Even then, it was Ty they called on when the weather closed in, when the busy planes couldn't find their way over the passes and down into the canyons.

By then Gretta Haslam was cooking for Ty's trips—had been since high school. She was the first of the Haslam children to work for Ty. And the best. A project at the university had delayed her this time. Nina's friend—the singer Lilly Bird—had taken over until Gretta could cross the snow-choked passes to catch them at Junction Meadows.

"You reckon Gretta can handle that snow?" Buck and Ty were watching the roiling river, the runoff from the snowfields chewing under its banks. "No way we could get here but to ride up the Kern. The trail mostly underwater at that."

"She's got her ice axe. Clyde said she's better than a man with it."

That's just how Norman Clyde had said it, too, Ty thought, missing the hard-bitten mountaineer. His winter cabin had become a ruin only months after he died. The windows broken, the books vandalized, the shade vines dead. It was just what Norman Clyde said would happen. Ty was sad to think he'd been right about that too.

"She'd better show up soon." The amused voice of Lilly Bird startled them. Lilly looked mischievous and pretty all at once. "Singers aren't cut out to be head cooks."

Nina had befriended Lilly Bird in law school, Nina finally getting there after her own children were in school themselves. They'd met on the first day of classes, Nina more than ten years older but the two of them cut from the same cloth. In fact Lilly was so determined to get through law school herself that she'd enrolled before she had enough money, meaning she had to keep singing the old songs with her trio each night so she could study the new laws with Nina each day.

Ty knew Lilly was being funny. Cooking was hardly a chore on this trip. The Haslams did almost everything themselves, and Jeb Walker, still ramrod straight after ten years of retirement, was as considerate of Lilly as any man could be—and as ready to tell his stories to her as he'd once been to Jasper. The truth was that the general was as taken by Lilly Bird as the rest of them, amused that she was so determined to keep Ty in his place.

"You packers," she'd scolded Ty the first morning. "Act like it's a federal case just to find your silly horses."

And she'd just laughed when he asked her to sing by the fire. "Don't be silly. You don't even know the songs I sing." She'd turned away, giving everyone marshmallows and willow sticks, getting Jeb Walker to tell them more stories about the cavalry.

But Ty did know the songs she sang. What he didn't know was how someone so young could sing them the way she did. He'd been won over by her singing the first night he'd heard her.

"Her soul certainly comes up through those lyrics," Cody Jo had said after Lilly Bird's first number. The two of them had driven all the way to Sacramento to listen to Nina's friend sing at the club.

"But how?" Ty wanted to know. "How does she make them hers?"

"Family, maybe. Records around the house. In her blood somehow." Cody Jo looked at Ty. "Apples don't drop far from the tree. Didn't Will and Mary love the country the way you do?"

"No." Ty looked at Cody Jo. "No, they didn't. They fought it. I believe I'm an apple that rolled."

"Maybe." Cody Jo watched Ty's eyes go back to the singer. "You do love this music." She smiled. "Or is it the girl?"

Ty wanted to say something to deflect that look on Cody Jo's face. But he could only say what was true.

"I think it's both. She *is* those words."

Ty took Cody Jo's hand and they went out onto the dance floor.

"Nice combination," he said, the dancing relaxing them. "The girl and the songs."

Lilly was singing ". . . another new day. The mist in the meadow starts fading away . . ." She watched them as she sang, wondering where a packer had learned to dance that way. Then she melted into the lyrics.

It surprised Ty that anyone whose songs came from so deep inside her could taunt him the way Lilly did in the mountains. But he enjoyed it almost as much as the general, liking how happy mocking him made her.

"Will you bring 'em back alive?" She watched him saddle up to look for his horses. "To admire you like we should?"

"Don't want them to go to Siberian Basin and admire that. Thirty miles is a long ride to find out they like grass better than this grain."

She'd laughed, her laughter still with him as he forded the deepening river to pick up tracks, finding them and following them upriver to his horses, comfortable in a little meadow, the grass good, snow holding them from going higher. He gave each some grain and left them—happy in the sun.

He rode back slowly, watching the Kern gather its power as it splashed down the canyon in steps, the mists rising and falling and rising again. He kept an eye out for Gretta as he rode, suspecting she'd be ahead of schedule—Gretta an accomplished mountaineer now, strong and rockwise and tireless. A mile above the ford he picked up her tracks, deciding he should haul her pack across the river, the ford deep and swift, big slick boulders the only footing to be had. He found her there, trying to boulder-hop her way across, poised on a tilted rock and looking wonderful—strong and resilient, her years in the Sierra giving her legs the layered muscles of a runner.

"Can't cross without getting wet," he called above the river's rumble. "I'll haul your pack."

She couldn't hear over the river. She brushed back her kerchief and cupped an ear, the movement pulling her off balance just enough to force her to jump for another rock. Ty saw her laugh as she gave up and pushed off, saw her foot land where the rock was slick from the foaming rapids, saw her go chest deep into an icy pool. He lost her for a moment as the current hit her pack, turning her and sweeping her into still faster water. He saw her slip down a slick between two boulders, the pack floating above as she fought it.

And then—just like that—she was gone.

⌒⌒

Even as he whipped Nightmare across the meadow, Ty regretted the half-second he'd been frozen, watching her slide off the rock. He knew how fast the water would carry her now and didn't skid Nightmare to a stop until they were at the water again, coming off as if he were after a roped calf, running into the water and wishing he'd had that rope, had anything that could hold them from the rapids. He saw the half-second he'd lost was the half-second he needed, reaching now for the pack, needing it to reach Gretta, knowing he had to lift both to free her from the weight of it. He lifted and pulled, felt his boot slide across a rock deep in the river. Then he was in the water with her, pushing the pack away to grasp her, trying to kick the pack free of her with his boots.

Buck had seen Ty bring Nightmare out of the ford, seen him push the mare hard across the meadow, dodging trees as he raced toward the rapids. Buck was running himself when he saw Ty fly from the saddle and splash into the river. By the time he got there Ty was sliding away, struggling with something.

Buck was in the river himself, chest deep and reaching out for Ty, who was clutching at a pack, something under it pulling everything toward the rapids. Buck reached farther and felt the current take him too, sweep him across slippery rocks toward the fast water before he felt a rope across his face. He grasped at it, was pulled by it, felt Thomas Haslam's hand reaching out for him, pulling him now with Lilly pulling too, the two of them clinging to the rope wrapped around a leaning sapling, the three of them holding to one another to keep from being swept away.

They pulled Buck up and out and his legs were already running again, splashing him out of the water to go for the frightened mare. She spun away, left him to circle back to the water's edge where Ty had disappeared. Buck cursed her as he ran back to the ford, ran waist deep through the river and turned down the trail to meet the river again. He was well below the lip of the meadow now, the river running fast and straight, its roar drowning out all sound—but Buck unaware of that, unaware of anything but what his eyes could tell him as he scanned across the river, stumbling up along the serrated and broken bank, crashing through brush and over deadfall as he sought out some sign of the pack, some clothes ripped and hanging from a branch, some signal that would tell him what he didn't want to happen had not happened.

He came back to the ford at last, crossed it and came into camp. Exhausted. Bleeding. . . . Wild.

"We have to find him," he said to Thomas Haslam. "He's down there. In that river. Down there."

"Them," Thomas Haslam said. "It was Gretta . . ." He looked at Buck, his voice not working, his face disintegrating. Buck felt as though something inside Thomas Haslam had torn a hole through both of them.

"They're gone." Haslam had to suck in breath to say it, admit it. Because after he said it there was nothing more he could say.

Lilly reached out, touched him, touched Buck, tears filling her as she reached out for something that made sense.

こ・つ

Ty had pushed the pack ahead, holding the girl as they sluiced through the first rocks. The pack jammed on something and Gretta came free of it, both of them going under it, coming up into foaming water that turned them around and around again. She was behind him now and he tried to push her up, onto something, into air. But the pack came back at them, hitting her, knocking her below him as he struggled to get his legs downstream, bring her up so they could fight toward the shore.

A rush of water more powerful than anything he'd ever felt drove him down and down into rocks deep below the rushing current. He felt Gretta slip from him, her body pulled around a boulder he couldn't see. And then he was on the surface again, gasping. Something hit him from behind and he turned to touch it and felt himself go down again, not knowing what he had touched. He felt for it, felt the dull crack of his head on a rock and was spun around again, lifted, all his body seeming to come free of the water as he went over a ledge and crashed down into a pool where everything was dark and slow as though slow-motion had taken over his life. He felt something brush against him. Then a darkness closed in.

Later he remembered clinging to the branches of a fir, its great roots exposed where the waters that had cut away its life. But he hadn't the strength to hold on, lift himself above the power that flung him there and then reclaimed him, swept him back like a toy. He tried to push off rocks but the river denied him, spun him until he was going headfirst again, his strength no match for the water's power.

After that he remembered only surrendering, becoming no more than the river itself—until it left him on the shallows of a rocky bar, waters pounding past in a darkness that told him nothing. The moon lifted to show him a bank close by. He reached for it, the cold shaking him so violently he had no choice. But the river recaptured him, willows slowing him just enough to find an aspen he could cling to, free himself from the sucking sweep of waters. He crawled onto the flat of a boulder and slept until his own shaking woke him, made him stand, jog, and dance the night away to fight the cold, keep some flame alive in a life he knew had no right to be.

Some time toward morning he fell again, collapsed until a morning sun revived him and he heard the pop-pop-pop of a helicopter going away. He watched it grow smaller as it searched its way down the river. Beyond it clouds were moving in, gray and thick, telling him no helicopter would be back, not soon enough. He sat, his body so sore it was an agony. One boot was gone, his clothes were shredded, heavy with wet, one foot was bloody and raw from the long night's battle.

He still had his knife, used it to cut strips from his shirt. He wrapped the foot, cut thicker strips from his pants and fashioned a sole, made a shoe from the wraps so he could walk—if he could stand.

He looked at the cliffs above him. The crashing river before him. Downriver its banks were choked with growth, huge boulders, more growth. Upriver, cliffs, sheared-off rock—and growth so thick it looked impassable.

The gray sky chilled him. He knew he had to move. Up the river was all he could think of, back to where he'd started. Maybe Gretta was there, cast onto some shoal as he had been. He couldn't think of her dead any more than he could think of himself alive. He couldn't think either of those ways. He just knew he had to go up, that back at Junction Meadows were his horses. Buck. The Haslams. Jeb Walker and Lilly.

He started, each movement uncovering some new pain, something torn and broken in him. But each step bringing him closer to his high country, safety—taking him up against the relentless waters. Every few steps he stopped, let the pain settle as he scanned the banks of the river, looked across it for some sign of Gretta, even a glimpse of the trail that ran along the east bank, provided a way to follow the great river to its source. But he saw nothing: across the river everything was hidden in timber; on his side nothing but cliffs to climb and brush to fight. No sign of Gretta, no sign of anything human.

Mostly he saw the relentless work of the river, its waters taking everything out of the mountains toward the big valley, the sink where a sea had once been, where the great Kern would be swallowed into the earth just as that sea had been.

Sometimes he would fall asleep where he stopped, looking for a way to go on. In his sleep he would see the river rushing down until it became nothing, wasting its great life going nowhere. He would jerk awake with the thought, frightened to think anything would push so hard to rush into the sun-scorched earth, disappear.

❧

In the years that followed, Ty Hardin would take Nightmare down to look across at that place where the river had thrown him on its banks. Had he been airborne, he would think—an eagle seeking food or even a helicopter on a search—he would have seen the bridge scarcely a mile below, seen the hot springs that he could have crossed to in safety, seen the trail that could have returned him safely to his horses, to his people.

But he also understood that what he couldn't see was of no use. What he couldn't conceive, worthless. He'd only known he had to go up—no matter the miles—to what he knew, not down, hoping for something he didn't. And so he'd gone up where no man had gone, crawling and hobbling across a country so broken it seemed more a hundred miles than the ten the Kern had cut in such a breathtaking line that no man could navigate it, walk in its shallows, work with it—survive it.

It had taken him two days and two nights of almost constant movement to do what could not be done. He ate wild onion and miner's lettuce and elderberries—green and sour. He ate currants and serviceberries and the leaves of flowers so bitter he couldn't swallow. When he scraped himself on rocks, he pressed yarrow to his wounds. When he was trapped on cliffs without drink, he dipped his tattered clothes into tiny pools under dripping rock, sucked until he could move on.

He wouldn't rest until he fell asleep, and then only rested until he woke, pulled himself forward again, moved until he could move no more because he was sleeping again, sleeping even as he slowed, collapsed against whatever he could find until he could move again.

It was as though he never rested, as though he had no choice but to keep moving up against everything the river was bringing down, his mind just as determined as his body—but his mind going in no direction he could understand. Things coming back to him and leaving him in no order that made sense. Only Fenton and Cody Jo—and Willie—seemed constant, as though they held the key to what kept him moving.

He saw Otis Johnson's big body at the foot of his bed. "Didn't mean to treat you so rough," he said. And then he was gone and Ty was teaching Walker Johnson to tie a diamond hitch, watching the boy run under a pass at the football game, the pass unbelievably long but the boy running and reaching and balancing the ball until the rest of him caught up with it and he was pulling up in some end zone as quietly as he'd learned to pack Ty's mules, as he'd talked with Jeb Walker around Ty's fires. And then it was Fenton in the fire, his face alive in the fire, worried. "Goddamn it," he said. "Don't get yourself killed." And Fenton turned, held Cody Jo. The two of them looking at Ty from the fire. Cody Jo was crying. And Ty found he was crying too, woke to find himself crying, crying as the Red Cross volunteer dressed his torn leg, crying as he walked the night away after Willie died, crying because the river had taken Gretta—crying when he came over Goat Pass and saw the High Sierra: saw the order, the peace.

⌒⌒

Lilly Bird was the first to see him as he came from where no man could come. "Ty?" she said. "Ty!" And then she was holding him, weeping, taking him to the others. "It's Ty." Her voice broke over the word. "Alive!"

Alice Haslam was there. And Buck. All of them. All but the Search and Rescue teams, far down the Kern by then, searching for Ty's body even below where they'd found Gretta's, searching where the water's power relented, where it finally let you see into it. The helicopters were flying by then, their blades cracking the air as they probed for the dead packer far below where he'd returned to his horses, his people.

"It's all right." Alice Haslam looked at Ty, her throat closing on her words. "It's all right. You're here. You tried."

Ty's mouth worked, but nothing came. He turned to Buck.

"Why'd it take her?" he said, looking up at the Kaweah shelf where he so wanted to take his horses. "Thought of climbing up there. Calling it quits."

"That's not what you'd do, Ty." Buck was kneeling, dressing Ty's mutilated foot. "You don't know what quits is." He hunched a shoulder to clear his eyes. "You never did."

⌐⌐⌐

The helicopters came in with reporters from Bishop and Lone Pine and Sacramento. Thomas Haslam heard one of them radio out that the Park Service had saved the life of a packer.

"No." Haslam stopped him in the midst of his transmittal. "No one rescued Ty Hardin but Ty Hardin. Ty Hardin and maybe that river that could have taken him in a moment. And he wouldn't have needed any rescuing if he hadn't tried to save Gretta. Which there was no way to do. He just had no choice but to try."

Others gathered, took out their pencils, not sure what to write.

"Your Park Service people can take credit for what they did do, but you can't give them credit for saving Ty Hardin. For whatever is in him that made him try to save Gretta." He looked at the reporter with the radio, looked at the others, his voice shaky.

"There aren't people like him anymore," he said. "Maybe you can't say that in your papers, but it's time you heard it." His voice broke as he saw their puzzled looks. "There is no way left to become this man."

They grew uneasy, watched him fight back his tears, not sure he could go on.

"With all these rules and regulations," Thomas Haslam took a breath, "it's a wonder these mountains have any room left for a Ty Hardin."

None of that went into the papers, the reporters embarrassed by Thomas Haslam and confused about what he'd meant. But it made them mindful of what had happened. And that's the way they reported it:

Sierra Packer Survives Kern Rescue Attempt
Fails to Save Girl in Swollen Rapids
Makes Heroic Return to Victim's Family Alone

Ty read the story himself, read it and looked at Lars. "They don't have it right, Lars," he said. "I don't believe they can get it right."

"What in the world do you mean, Ty?" Lars uncapped a beer and put it in front of him. "Surviving them rapids was a miracle. And no one understands how you could get back through that country, alone."

"Just came back to my horses," Ty said, ". . . and I never was alone."

41

Switchbacks

After that Ty knew how much of his own life came from the people he loved. At first he lived it more than he understood it. He would hear Fenton's voice as he tracked horses, watch with Spec as deer picked their way through a glade, feel Cody Jo's despair about people who were bruised, haunted by some darkness. Willie seemed everywhere, in the streams and fires, the moons that helped him through his nights.

It was Lilly Bird who made him understand it, though it took time before he realized her life had made a life of its own somewhere inside him. Before that it was her songs. Not the words so much as what she did with them, her voice giving weight to the simplest line—sometimes cutting into him so sharply he would turn away, gather himself. And he wasn't the only one her voice touched. He would watch Alice and Thomas Haslam come together when she sang, see the general stopped, embarrassed to be moved so—even find Walker Johnson taken by the world she opened with her songs.

Ty had taught Walker Johnson to pack, just as Otis wanted him to—before Walker went on to other things. But Walker returned for trips when he could, helping out, listening by Ty's fires, comforted by Ty's mountains. As a boy he'd packed for Ty each summer, become almost as good a packer as he was a player on his high-school teams. He'd graduated with a shelf full of trophies, but he only looked at them for a week before he sat down and wrote Ty that he wouldn't be packing that year. He was signing up in the army—just as his father had done before him.

Ty missed packing with the boy. He'd liked his quiet ways, his patience with the mules and the comfort he took in the woods. But Ty saw the mountains could never hold him. There was something else he needed. Ty had seen it watching him watch the others around the fires, wanting to know their histories, why they came, chose their work, lived where they lived.

Ty knew there would be no answers in the army and worried when Walker joined. But there was no need. The army saw what he could do with a football. Mostly they wanted him to do that. And when he was discharged the university was waiting, wanting him to do the same for them. Ty and Cody Jo had even gone to see Walker's last game, watched him run under the long pass as drums rolled and students chanted and the players surrounded Walker in the end zone. To Ty Walker seemed the quietest one in the whole stadium. He saw why when they met with Walker and Otis after the game.

"If you don't sign with the football people, what then?" Otis had asked, knowing the boy had few options in this life and not liking it much that being paid to play football was the best.

"More work at the university," Walker said, and Ty knew he'd settled on something. "There's a professor. He wants me to stay. He'll help."

"At what? Reading more damn books?"

"There's more I want to know. Ty . . . he understands."

Walker had looked at Ty just as he'd looked at him across so many campfires, as though Ty had answers to questions he wasn't sure how to ask. Ty had turned to Cody Jo, but she'd looked away. All he could do was look back at Otis. Nod. Say it was all right. Walker should stay. There was nothing else he could think of to do.

⌒⌒

And so Walker had gone on to graduate school in search of his past, and Ty had gone back to the mountains to make sure his past counted. And now Lilly's songs were somehow bridging that difference. Walker was watching Ty's fires again, as moved by the girl's songs as Ty—who did not yet know he'd fallen in love.

That was the year Lilly dropped her last pretensions about lawyering and took the job at the Tahoe lodge, singing each night for an audience as enchanted by the girl as by old songs she sang. After he came out of the mountains Ty caved in to his need to hear her do what she did better than anyone he could imagine. He called Cody Jo and asked her to go to Tahoe with him. But she decided that was a trip she didn't want to make.

"I'm too tired," she said. "And old. Ask her to sing 'Have Mercy.' No one sings it anymore but Lilly . . . and no one should. You'll see why."

So he went alone, arriving late, but the big lodge easy to find on the shore of the silent lake.

"I'll take it, man." A tall boy with lank blond hair opened the pickup's door, as welcoming to Ty as though he'd driven up in a Mercedes.

"Wait'll you hear Lilly." The boy put it in gear, stuck a long arm out the window, and rapped a beat on the roof. "Great pipes!"

Then he was gone. Ty was a little startled by how quickly it had happened. He was more surprised by what he found inside: dark panels and diminished lights, the room hushed to concentrate on Lilly.

He went to the bar and whispered his order. A single light isolated Lilly, crowning her hair, revealing her slenderness. But her singing took her so far beyond that the whole room seemed hers. Nothing about her looks, the moonlight on the lake behind her, the piano, spare and direct, could touch the way she sang.

She finished to applause almost reserved, as though it might break some mood. She sang "It Never Entered My Mind," the room quiet as the lake, and "But Not for Me." Then her eyes found Ty, alone at the bar, as still as the rest, as unable to take his eyes away.

She talked into the microphone as though talking with old friends. "We have a special guest. If this set is longer than usual, I'm sorry." She looked around the room. "I'd like to sing the songs he knows."

Ty thought it must be someone else in the room she was talking about, but he couldn't look away. And then he didn't need to look away. She began singing those songs he would sing a few bars of around the campfire, trying to get her to sing them herself. Wishing she would sing them herself.

She seemed to remember them all. She sang "I Remember You" and "You Go to My Head" and "What's New?" She sang "I Can't Get Started" and "Teach Me Tonight." She sang songs Ty hadn't heard all the way through for years, sang them the same way he'd heard them when he danced with Cody Jo, when he'd stood with Willie watching the snow outside the Helena hotel. It was as though Lilly had some direct line into his life, into the music he loved. Only this time everything came from Lilly.

She finished with "Have Mercy."

⌒⌒

"That's an old song," he said. The bartender slid a glass of soda to Lilly, bubbles rising around a slice of lime. "You make it . . . different."

And it was a different Lilly standing there, her legs long in the flared pants, the blouse white and sheer. Nothing left of the law-school student at all.

"Cody Jo said you'd like it." She turned, thanking people as they stopped, complimented her, asked if she'd recorded this song or that.

"When did she say that?"

"Tonight. She called just before I went on."

The trio was playing, and Lilly led Ty onto the floor. "Cody Jo tells me you aren't at all like a packer when you dance."

"Packers dance," Ty said. "To music like this."

They were playing "Blue Moon," and dancing to it with Lilly was almost like listening to Lilly sing it, the music moving them, connecting them.

They played "Mood Indigo" and "Paper Moon" and "Daybreak," Lilly singing softly ". . . another new day," her cheek on his shoulder.

"Take me home, Ty," she said finally, her breath warm on his neck. "It's time we went home."

The boy with the long hair was playing his radio, rock music loud and insistent, the beat heavy. He turned it down when he saw Lilly.

"Just mine, Tommy," Lilly said to him. "We'll leave Ty's here."

Her Volvo was there in a moment, the motor running as Tommy opened the door for her, looked at Ty.

"Lilly told me about you. Packing up there. I dig that, man. The higher you get, the higher you get." He smiled. "A blast, man."

"Gotta be careful." Ty held out a tip. "Gets cold up there."

Tommy pushed the money away. "It's on me when you're with Lilly." He looked at Ty through the window. "No wheels for me to park without Lilly."

He went to his radio and turned up the volume. "Later, man. Ciao."

Lilly's place, tidy and spare, was high above the lake. Ty felt a little lost being there alone with her.

"I'm going to make drinks," she said. "We're going to sit and talk. Talk all night if we want to."

She put on a tape, Red Garland playing "It Might As Well Be Spring," got drinks and they sat on the couch. She tucked her legs under her and watched him.

"You see it now, Ty. I'm a singer, not a lawyer."

"Yes." Ty was relieved to have the drink. He was shaken by how she moved him. "Anyone who heard you would know."

"It's like what makes you who you are. Your mountains." She brushed his hair from his forehead. "I think I knew it when Gretta died . . . when you lived." She dipped a finger into her bourbon, touched his lips with it. "But it doesn't matter when I knew. . . . It happened."

She leaned forward, her face close to his.

"Didn't it? . . ." Her lips were almost on his as she spoke. "Hasn't it?"

"Yes." Ty tried to collect himself. "And I don't have a notion in the world of what to make of it. What to do."

"Accept it." Her eyes held him. "It's easy."

"It's not that easy. The world you live in . . . is different."

"How?" Lilly touched his hair again. "How different?"

He thought about it. How comfortable she was—with everything. The people in the club. The bartender. The parking-lot boy with his flowing hair and loud music. There was almost too much to say about their differences.

"Your people don't really know my music," he said, hoping to sum it all up somehow. "What it means."

"I do. You know I do." She touched his lips with her finger again, her voice just a whisper as she sang ". . . let's have no controversy, moments like these were meant for kissing, lend your lips to hear. Have mercy, dear."

Then, her voice still low but something sure in it now, "It isn't just that I know your songs, Ty." She watched him. ". . . I know you."

᠔⁓

Lilly had no illusions about Ty. Nina had told her about the nights he would drink too much at the Deerlodge, talking late into the night with Lars, sometimes going home with some woman he'd danced with.

But she knew what he was like in the high country too. He was always steady there. Knew things: where to ford the streams and to free his horses. The peaks first light would reach. Places to camp. How to keep people dry and warm, safe. He was at home in his mountains. That was good enough.

What surprised her was how much Ty wanted her after that night high above the lake. It went beyond making love. He wanted to be a part of her rhythms, her comings and goings, in the flow of her blood. It didn't surprise her how much she wanted to be with him. She'd known that from the moment he showed up, alive, at Junction Meadows.

And she'd understood how hard it was going to be.

"What do you mean the past haunts us?" he would ask. "We'll leave it behind. Start from here. Together."

"We can't. We are our past. Listen to those songs you love."

"I do . . . when you sing them."

"They're all about sadness. How things don't work out." She would hold him, fit herself to him, her head on his chest. "You have it, Ty. Sadness. From a place I can't know. Maybe I have it too."

And she would tell him things about St. Louis, about her father, a church-going lawyer whose practice was filled by the congregation but his heart with the bluesy music from the riverfront. He would take her to the clubs along the river, listen to the jazzmen up from New Orleans. He would drink—listening to the music, talking to the people.

She liked it in those smoky rooms, watching him with his drinks— the drinks that would end all his nights too soon. She liked the music, the words, the rhythms. The singers would make over her and she would sing along with them from her table, taking in their sadness.

"Those songs could be so blue it hurt," she told Ty one night. "All kinds of music came together in those places. Bittersweet songs. All of us in love with some sorrow."

"Maybe it was you." Ty said. "The sadness was in you." When she talked that way, remembered those times, he always found himself wanting to touch the places where she'd lived.

"No." Lilly kissed his neck. "It was in them. It was just there. This piano player told me one night, 'Blues,' he said, 'is about things gone bad. About women . . . and whiskey.'"

"How old were you then?

"Ten. Twelve. I'm not even sure I got it. Not even sure I got it when my father died. After the whiskey got him."

"I think you did." Ty held her.

He held her close for a long time, confused by how much he wanted her in one way, how much he wanted to protect her in another.

Lilly confused him in other ways too, but he loved her so it didn't matter. He thought his heart would break when she talked about growing up, watching her father, the drinking, the singers. And then she could talk another way, so hard and unconsidered it sent a chill through him. She would rail about her agent, a record contract, a cabal she knew was behind the killing of JFK and Bobby and Martin Luther King. She was sure there were powerful people out there who killed.

It didn't make sense to Ty. It was beyond him to imagine anyone out to get anyone. His life was decisions made, consequences lived with. Hard times were like winter storms: You just got through them.

But for Lilly there could be demons everywhere. Sometimes she would go to church, trying to shake them. It didn't help. Nothing did. It wasn't long before Ty saw he couldn't help when she was that way either. That's when he would find his heart breaking not so much because he wanted to touch her as because he couldn't.

But those times would pass. Most of their time together was so easy they seemed to touch each other without touching, hardly needing words. From that first night the lovemaking was right, warm and open and unaffected. She was never afraid to let him know she wanted him, fulfilling him as if she knew the secrets of his body better than he—her fingers rimming the old scar, tracing the ropes of muscle that led from it, liking where they took her.

And from that first night they were in one another's mind and heart steadily, talking often on the telephone and driving long hours to be with one another. Lilly found ways to go into the mountains for at least one trip each summer, and when he could, Ty would find a way to hear her sing, his nights at the Deerlodge fewer and fewer.

Lars and Buck had mixed feelings about that. They were pleased to see Ty happy but sad he wasn't with them, drinking late and explaining why some took to the high country; others found it only something to endure.

"Lilly's what Ty needs," Angie would tell them when they complained. "It's a cold country up there. It never could love him back."

"You and Cody Jo just want him to love some old girl instead of his mountains," Buck would answer. "Want your side to win."

Angie would never take the bait. "All of us worried about him. But we never could see what he needed."

ᴄ-ᴐ

It wasn't long before Lilly signed a contract to make a record with all those tunes Ty loved. The recording people saw what a following she had and began sending her off to sing: San Francisco and Seattle, even St. Louis. Ty joined her when he could. He loved to hear her and needed her closeness in ways that surprised him. . . . And she was glad. She knew she was better when he was in the room.

When they booked her in Sun Valley for the holiday season, she got Ty to drive her there. They even decided to leave early so they could visit Jasper in the rest home in Missoula.

Lilly was as charmed by the stories about Jasper's cooking sherry as she was by Jasper's anxieties about bears. She liked the other stories about Montana too, stories about Spec and Fenton and the way Cody Jo taught Ty to dance up in the Swan, about how he came to take the Haslams on their honeymoon.

"I'm glad we're going," she'd said after her last set at the lodge. "It's where you started. It'll have things to tell you."

"I might not like what it has to say."

"That doesn't matter. You are what it has to say."

"You might not like that."

"I will. That's why you love me. I'm not afraid of your past."

They talked and laughed their way through the high desert, stopping at a hotel in Elko with a huge stuffed bear in the lobby, laughing even more when Lilly played twenty-one for half the night and came away five dollars ahead. Everything seemed funny until they crossed Lost Trail Pass and dropped into the Bitterroot. Ty grew quiet then, watchful, though he almost drove past the Missouri Bar, a grocery store now with a "Special of the Week" sign and paved parking.

But he remembered the country, and when they came to the Hardins' turnoff he drove out across the rutted road to look at the house. He was almost on the site before he realized it was gone, had been for so long that the foundation was hard to find. He tried to remember where the rooms had been, the kitchen and the porch and the cold bedrooms. But it was hard to tell. After awhile he led Lilly down the weed-choked path to the barn. The roof had caved in over the shed, all the shingles blown off by winter storms. The corrals were gone too, the rails collapsed and tangled in the same rusted baling wire that once held them up.

A solemn-looking boy came by on a tractor. Ty learned from him that they'd taken the old house, board by board, up to the big outfit's headquarters, put it back together to use as a saddle shed.

"He says things changed a lot when they started dude ranching," the boy said.

"Who says?"

"Granddad." The boy studied them. "We keep a few cows. To look at."

❧

Missoula had changed too. The outfitters' shops were fly-fishing stores now, with sign-up lists for float trips and llama trips and guided hikes in the Bitterroot. Ty saw hardly any old-timers along the streets or in the stores. Mostly he saw young people, boys in short pants riding bikes, ponytails flying out behind them. Girls in shorts too, or little skirts, coming out of the stores and hurrying along the street with day packs full of books.

Ty wanted to stay in the old Wilma Hotel, right on the river, but it was for students. A girl with her arms full of books sent them off to a motel on the outskirts of town. Ty put their things in and took Lilly to the cemetery. He wanted to show her where Willie was buried right away so it would fade behind whatever else they did. Willie's death, the child's death, might spiral Lilly down into one of her moods.

They put flowers on the grave, on his mother's too, Will buried there with her now. He tried to picture them, but all he could remember was their talking about how to make it through one winter so they could get ready for the next. He even had a hard time picturing Willie, the tombstone blotting out all that energy she brought to life.

Ty was glad to have Lilly holding his arm, and glad to hurry off to find Jasper, both of them amused that the home was called "The Grizzly Den."

Jasper seemed to take it right in stride. "Bout as likely to find a bear here as somethin' to drink." He examined the bottle of sherry Ty had bought him. "Like old times, Ty. Reminds me of when you stayed out in the woods most all night." Jasper turned the bottle in his hands, the past moving in.

"Could have brought a little more." Jasper's eyes got watery. "Buck would of. Or visit more. It's been almost a year."

Jasper was well into his nineties, but confusion about the years—and being cold most of the time—were the only sure signs of it. It was more like fifteen years since Ty had seen him, and that was back in the Deerlodge when they had to get him drunk so he'd get on the bus for Missoula. Jasper unwrapped the scarf around his neck, wrapped it still tighter.

"Truth is it ain't so bad, Ty." He patted the scarf to get it settled. "She does right good for me. Pours me a glass or two each night." He looked around his little room, only one chair there, pulled close to a tiny and silent television set where a host with perfectly combed hair talked with two earnest-looking teenagers. "Sometimes she even takes me down to the Elkhorn. Some of them boys still bend an elbow."

"Who's she?"

"Her." Jasper motioned at a round woman who'd suddenly appeared in the doorway. Ty thought she might actually be as wide as she was tall.

"Ty Hardin!" the woman exclaimed. "Ain't you a sight."

She was across the room in a moment, hugging him and making over him, the sweetness of her powder telling him what his eyes had not.

"Beth," he said. "It's you."

"I've growed." She laughed, her bracelets jangling.

"I sure didn't expect to see you here."

"Who else could run this place, honey?" She turned to Lilly, whose smile seemed frozen on her face, and gave her a hug. "And you're Ty's sweetie." She patted Lilly, admired her. "You take care of him, hon. We been awful fond of him—since he was a boy."

They all went out for dinner at the Elkhorn. Jasper kept trying to tell them stories about bears but he had a hard time outtalking Beth, who seemed to have the history of Missoula tucked away in her head. Most of the history of the Swan as well. She talked about Bob Ring going off to Seattle and finally just disappearing. About Gus Wilson coming into town to pry his brothers free from The Bar of Justice and falling in love with Loretta, taking her off to Canada to open a government sawmill. She even talked about Bernard's parents coming out to put flowers on his grave, how the Forest Service stuck with Ring's story, always calling Bernard's death an accident. She talked about Spec and Tommy Yellowtail too. And about how Horace and Etta left all their money to the church, making sure the church took care of Jasper first. She talked about other people too, most of them dead—just still alive to her.

In the morning Ty set out for the Swan, wanting to see Fenton's big house before they started back for Sun Valley. Lilly, quiet during the long dinner, had decided to stay in Missoula. "Beth says the Catholic church is still the way it was. I'd like to see it. I'd like to be in church today."

Ty drove out alone, surprised to find houses and little pastures where he remembered only lodgepole and aspen and bear grass. There were almost twice as many stores along the road at Seeley Lake. Even the pack station looked different, all the logs of the big house varnished and a lawn running out to the barn, everything manicured as though for a calendar picture.

"Bed and breakfast now," the woman cleaning up inside told him. "They do a nice business. Hire some boys to take folks for rides up to the lake and back. The owners go south in the winter. Works out all right."

The Murphys had left too. A young couple was running the store. They weren't even sure the Murphys were still alive.

"What do you do with the cabins?" Ty saw that a few new ones had been built. "I knew the people who lived in that old one."

"Rent them to the writers." The young woman looked at Ty. "Not many like you around anymore. But there's always a writer or two. They like a cabin in the woods."

They started back early the next day, hardly talking as they drove along the Bitterroot and crossed the pass to drop down along the Salmon toward Ketchum.

"They say they got hunting camps all through the mountains now. Even down in Lost Bird Canyon."

"Why didn't you tell me?" Lilly said. "You should have told me about Bernard and Willie. About what happened. What that did to her." That edge was coming into her voice, as though something were threatening her.

"Hard to think I got myself lost up there." Ty spoke softly, reaching over with his free hand and massaging Lilly's neck, her shoulders.

"Don't even try that. You've never been lost in your life."

"In that snowstorm I was. If Spec hadn't put the lodgepole up in that tree, I believe I'd still be wandering around back there."

"What do you mean in a tree?"

"Like a signpost." Ty eased her head onto his shoulder. "Saved me." They were widening the road that wound down from the mountains. Ty had to slow to get by all the equipment.

"You've been kind of like that, Lilly. Outside the mountains. Kept me from getting lost."

"You learned something back there." Lilly looked at him. "That country told you something. Didn't it?"

"It did." Ty picked up speed as the construction dropped away behind them. "I learned it's gone."

"What's gone?"

"Where I grew up. It isn't there anymore."

42

The Highest Pass

They came in over Goat Pass, Ty free-herding his mules and so happy to have Lilly with him that Thomas Haslam saw his smile from three switchbacks below. Lilly saw it too, and when they reached the basin she dropped back to ride with him.

"Haven't felt so happy since that first night in Sun Valley," Ty said, tying his his mules back into their long string.

"You were *happy*? I'd never seen you look so sad."

"Your songs filled me with all those places along the river. The people. Your father. Those singers. I felt like you. . . . Is it possible to be so sad you're happy?"

"Yes, I think so. Or the reverse. Maybe that's what I am now."

⌒⁀

Lilly's career was in full flower. After singing for the skiers and snowboarders and all the people in their bright clothes at Sun Valley, she'd gone back to Tahoe and done the same for them there. In the spring she'd sung at the top of the hotel in San Francisco. And after Ty's trip she was off to Chicago to sing at a supper club in the Loop.

But it was Ty's trip that pleased her. She'd set aside time, refused to let anyone talk her out of it. He was taking the Haslams into the Upper Kern, the country that had taken Gretta but that they still loved as no other. He brought them there a different way, taking the high trail south, hugging the spine of the Sierra to cross Pinchot and Glen passes, camping in Ty's hidden places, and finally crossing towering Forester Pass—if the snow would let them—to drop into the Upper Kern.

"Will we cross the Kern where it's just a stream?" Lilly asked. "Go into Milestone?"

"If snow doesn't stop us. And later camp right under Whitney. The country on the way there just as pretty as Whitney too. Only thing prettier is the Kaweahs. Under them there's that high shelf. Lakes. Meadows. I want you to see it."

"Will we go onto the shelf?"

"We can look. No way to get there. Except ropes."

"No Ty Hardin route we can use?"

"Just cliffs. Can't even sneak Sugar's burros up there."

She was looking back at him as she rode, her hat hanging behind her, her hair moving in the wind, picking up light from the sun.

"It's a short list of people I'd take there, Lilly. You'd be at the top."

"Yes . . . I think I know that," she said.

The trip went so wonderfully Ty hardly missed Buck, who was helping Angie out in the valley. The camps good. The feed rich. The weather clear. The Haslams were so much help each camp seemed set up by magic. And he was taking Lilly along a route she'd never traveled, the country meaning all the more to him because she was in it. He liked the smell of her, the touch. He liked it that she was never edgy in the mountains, would lie on the warm rocks and talk with him after her baths. He loved the songs she sang around his fires, her visits in the night.

His one worry was the snow on Forester, and it was a worry he couldn't shake. He and Buck had crossed snow there once, taking their whole party over a treacherous cornice. He had no stomach for trying that again. Lars hadn't believed Jasper when Jasper told him what they'd done—not until Jasper brought in a photograph a guest had taken. Lars was so impressed he'd had it blown up, framed to hang behind his bar. Each time Ty looked at it he wondered why he'd ever tried to cross in the first place.

His worries grew as they closed on Forester. They wound down into Vidette Meadows and climbed again along the creek, riding late through upper meadows, up still higher to finally drop from the trail to the creek again, camping in the last timber just below the highest meadow. Sugar had shown him the spot, a huge rock dropped by glaciers and split by ice, half of it on its back, a giant table made by some god of housekeeping.

It was a fine place for a layover, which Ty needed to check the pass. He was on Nightmare and gone by first light, the camp shovel slung under his leg like a rifle. He rode under cirques and cliffs scooped so clear he wondered how old Josiah Whitney could think of anything but glaciers. At the high lake, before the trail moved onto the long moraine stretching down from the pass, he saw it—blinding white and rising almost to the pass itself. The pass looked open, blown free of everything by winter storms. But there was at least a mile of gleaming snow below it.

He rode on, knowing the snow would be firm, that the hard part was not the snowfield but getting his mules across the rocks and onto it, how steep it was when you got there, how much ice lurked under the surface, how to come down from the cornice left at the top.

Nightmare had become such a part of him, he let her make her own way. She scrambled onto the snow without hesitating, working hard to pull up the first pitch and then moving easily across the blanket of white—like a deer crossing a divide to find better feed. She found crude switchbacks left by shifting winds, worked her way along them, used deep sun pockets for purchase. He rode it out easily, thinking of that chaos of cliffs and tumbled boulders fifty feet below them, knowing he was riding across a country made safe—for now—by the leveling powers of winter.

"Use the cold to get to the warm," Fenton had told him. "Old snow, packed snow," Fenton's voice seemed alive in the chill lifting from the snowfield, "can solve your problems. Don't need to know where you are so much as where you want to go."

And Ty knew where he wanted to go. He could see the pass; in his mind he could even see down into the Upper Kern. He wondered if it weren't Fenton who was somehow getting him there, the past still alive in him getting him there. The place where he'd grown up might be gone, but there was still the past that place had given him.

The snow took him almost as high as the pass before he saw the trail. It was snaking out from under the snow thirty feet below him, the snowfield ending abruptly in a sheer face, just as smooth as though carved by the same god who had leveled the rock table back in camp. He felt a little sick by the finality of it. It seemed much higher than the one he and Buck had crossed. But he also saw it was south-facing, that the sun had been hitting it all morning. He pulled his shovel from under his leg and was off Nightmare and at work, the mare's reins on the snow all she needed to hold her.

He shoveled for three hours before he had a trough Nightmare could start down, helped by four rough steps he'd hacked high in the passage. He eased her down them, slid her the last ten feet to come down safely on the trail, the pass just ahead. He led her up to the pass, the other side of it just dizzying granite cliffs, the trail a dropped thread winding down and down—a thousand feet into the basin below. But it was clear. . . . It would do.

He turned back, still leading Nightmare, wanting to get across the snowfield before it got still softer. They had to make three runs at the chute before they made it up, Ty scrambling ahead on the last try without even looking back, hearing the mare struggle behind him, struggling himself until he was on the snowfield, moving without stopping to cross it, jogging when he could, sliding and slipping when he couldn't jog, making his way down and down to the point where they'd left the trail that morning, a hard day's work and a mile of softening snow behind them.

C-ɔ

They were out of camp before dawn, across the broad snowfield only a few hours after the sun had begun its work.

"Are we riding into heaven?" Lilly had to squint to see, the snow dazzling under the early sun.

"Only one trail higher." Ty had them leading their horses now, sliding them down the chute and leading them up onto the pass. He rode Nightmare down himself, rode her up onto the pass where Lilly waited. They looked back at Jug, the big mule all the others followed and the mule who needed Nightmare as a colt needs his mother. Jug picked his way down the chute, nose to it to make sure. "The highest is Trail Crest, over the Whitney ridge. Nearly fourteen thousand feet there. So many folks running up and down that trail, they've closed it to stock."

"This one will do." Lilly held her hat on her head with one hand, the wind whipping hair across her face. "Just us and the sky." She laughed, looking out at the country ahead. "We *are* on our way to heaven."

"We might be." All Ty's worries fell away as he watched his mules slide down the trough, each inching into it carefully before sitting back, sliding down, shaking off the snow and moving onto the pass. He was watching the mules but his mind was on Lilly.

"If you come visit tonight," he looked at her, "I'll know that's where we are."

"Told you an hour in the morning's worth two at night," Ty told Thomas Haslam. They had crossed the pass so efficiently that they were unpacking in Milestone Basin in time for a late lunch.

"You did," Haslam said. "Told me it's hard to beat a tight rope too, which must apply to a lot of things. I'd just rather not get up the night before to find out what."

"We got started a little late." Ty was coiling a lash cinch.

"That's why it took me two years to recover from my honeymoon. I'm surprised you let us sleep till four."

"I've softened."

"Alice is right. You're more like Fenton each day."

"There's worse things." Ty wound the last loop around the coil, threaded it through the cinch ring, hung it on a snag. "If you think about it."

The next day Ty put a lunch in a day pack and hiked with Lilly into the smaller basin where Sugar had camped, where Maria and Nina had fed him so many years ago, Sugar calling his burros in from the shelves above.

"I can't imagine how he got those burros here," Lilly said. They'd been out for almost an hour, following a faint game trail through woods and above willows and up the rocky drainage to the high lake. "It doesn't look as if it's been touched." She stood on a rock by the lake, shooting stars and monkey flowers and Indian paintbrush rimming it. "Ever."

"Sugar hardly leaves a track," Ty said, thinking she looked pretty as a wildflower herself.

They bathed, Ty staying in the icy water longer than he thought he could just to be with Lilly. When they came out they needed sun, flattened themselves naked on the granite, let it warm them as they talked lazily about the lunch, happy to be with each other in this high country that embraced them completely.

"Sometimes you scare me, Lilly." Ty wasn't afraid to talk with her about anything here.

"You don't scare at all, Ty Hardin." Lilly held herself still, collecting the sun's warmth.

"When you feel threatened, I scare." He rolled onto his side, kissed the wet of her hair. "You don't get that way here, do you?"

She turned her head toward him, found his hand. "No, I don't . . . up here you take care of everything."

"You think it's real up here?" Ty's voice was such a part of them it seemed a breeze lifting from the lake.

"It makes me sure I love you, up here. It makes you . . . possible. Is that real?"

She sat up, wet hair falling over her shoulders in strands, beads of water drying on her arms, her breasts.

Ty sat up too, feeling whatever she was going to say was in him already, as though he were she, she were he. They had this thing to say to themselves, were sorting out how to make it count.

"I want in me . . ." She searched his face, wanting to touch him with her need, ". . . your child."

She watched everything about him shift, as though a cloud had moved in.

"Shush." She put a finger to his lips. "Not now. Just know I want to carry in me . . . you." And then she held him to her, let her hair fall across him, her wetness become his.

⌒⌒

Ty was still bewildered when they made camp two days later at Crabtree, the great hump of Whitney's western flank lifting above them, the meadow alive with spring flowers that in the Sierra must wait for summer.

She hadn't let him talk about it at all after she'd said it, not even as they came down from the lake. She had come to him in the night but again hadn't let him say a word. And when he'd stopped his string as they made their way to Whitney, pointing out the high shelf below the Kaweahs, showing her the lakes and meadows, she had just looked at him, smiled at him.

"Ty's dream," Thomas Haslam had said to them both. "Guess it's good to have a dream. Even a crazy one."

"When I find a way onto that shelf, you may not get an invite."

"Oh I'll get one. And I'll probably be fool enough to accept. Watch you fight the bogs and mosquitoes and deadfall to stay alive over there."

Lilly had just laughed, loving Ty in his high country, Ty with his friends and his animals. His peace with himself.

After dinner Ty took her onto the ridge behind camp to watch the last light on the Kaweahs, far out across Kern Canyon. He leaned against a boulder, Lilly leaning against him, pulling his arms around her against the cool.

"I never expected," he said, "after Willie and the baby, after Montana, that anyone could want such a thing. With me."

"I do." Lilly didn't bother to turn her head, her voice low but the two of them so complete there was no need. "I never thought there'd be a 'you' in my life. Never thought there could be . . . this."

The last light slanted up from behind the Kaweahs, purple and pink shafts lifting into low clouds, the Kaweah shelf dropping into night.

"Be careful, Lilly. Up here you can forget about out there." He kissed her hair. "That's what the doc says."

"Tell him not to worry." Lilly turned and held him. "I *am* careful. I think about out there."

C-♥

Clouds had gathered by the time they got back to camp. Ty busied himself setting up shelters. But he didn't move his things under one, helping the others move theirs but leaving his sleeping bag at the base of a big lodgepole.

"You've forgotten," he told them, smiling. "It doesn't rain at night up here." Then he walked out into the meadow to listen for the bells. He took comfort in their sound at night.

Lilly came to him before dawn, slipping away from the shelter and with him in a moment, loving him, holding him, whispering nonsense until he wanted her completely, emptied himself in her completely, her hand over his mouth to silence his cry. Then she was gone, gone as silently as she'd come.

Emptied as he was, he lay there wanting her still, wanting her even more as he watched the clouds skitter by, liking the gaps between them—the cool blue of the stars when they broke through.

C-♥

No rain, but clouds, low and solid, by morning; the new Crabtree ranger there too, filling his notebook with whatever Thomas Haslam was saying to him, turning to look at Ty anxiously when Ty came back from checking his horses.

"Ty Hardin." The ranger, earnest and young, introduced himself. "They tell all of us about you."

Ty looked at Haslam, who was looking up at the gray sky.

"There's a pretty sick boy below Timberline Lake, Ty." He was already getting his medical satchel from the pannier where Lilly stored it each night. "Sounds like edema."

"No helicopters today." Ty looked at the massive shoulder of Whitney, the cliffs lifting up into the gray ceiling, hiding the ridges and peaks.

He knew what was coming.

"The dispatcher told me you would help." The ranger's eyes followed Ty's up toward the hidden crest. "Didn't know you had a doctor. Said you could bring the patient out over Trail Crest."

"If I could keep those hikers from spooking my mule I might. But he's likely to be all right. I'll get horses. Let Doc take a look."

In half an hour Ty had them in. He saddled Lilly's gelding so she could come with them, putting the ranger on Jug, as good a saddle mule as he was a pack animal. And just right if there were trouble. He would follow Nightmare into hell, if that's where Nightmare decided to go.

They crossed the big meadow and rode up Whitney Creek, stopping at the ranger cabin for oxygen and then riding higher to the stand of whitebark where the boy was huddled in the ranger's sleeping bags.

Ty knew: Pulmonary edema requires lower elevation. The fastest way out was over the Whitney crest to Lone Pine, to the hospital where the mountain-sickness doctors prowled the halls waiting for such cases. He knew who would have to take him, too. Knew even more surely than that that he didn't want to do it. Not now. Not after wanting Lilly the way he had in the night, needing her to know that, understand that he was ready to face a new life with her.

"Think that oxygen might work?" He turned in his saddle so he could watch Thomas Haslam's face.

"Might," Haslam said. "A little. Maybe."

Ty heard the coughing even before he saw the boy, the cough rattling, deep and raw. The boy was pale, almost bluish, dank hair hanging to his shoulders. Ty wasn't sure he knew they were there.

"Tommy!" Lilly was off her gelding already. "Tommy! What have you done!"

Only then did Ty recognize him, remember the music in the parking lot, the carefree face, the lank hair. The boy offered a weak smile as Haslam pulled his shirt away, listened to his chest, peered at his gums, his fingernails. Ty already knew. He didn't need Haslam's stethoscope. The oxygen might make the boy's eyes focus, but it wouldn't clear his lungs of that gurgle.

For a moment the boy did focus, looking over Haslam's shoulder at Ty and Lilly. "Told you. No big deal, man," he said. "Made it up in five. Got high up high." His smile would have frightened Lilly even without the residue of the coughing smeared across the pale face. The cough started in again. Orange spittle coming up, streaking his face, his chin. "Didn't even need to rest." The cough racked him again. He took some of the oxygen the ranger held to his mouth. "Till here."

His eyes rolled back even as the oxygen helped and the cough subsided.

"Get him out of here." Thomas Haslam seemed disgusted as he put his stethoscope away. "Pulmonary. Blood in his lungs—worse from whatever he's been using, whatever makes him think the world's all rosy. Get him low, Ty. The hospital."

The boy flopped around as Ty heaved him up onto Jug, not so much heavy as disjointed, a misshapen sack. Ty didn't like to tie the boy's feet under Jug's belly, but he did it anyway. Jug might get a little jumpy if the boy slid under him, but that was better than dropping him off a switchback—sometimes a thousand feet before things began to slow.

"Hoped this wouldn't happen." Ty tightened Nightmare's cinch and looked at Thomas Haslam. "Wanted to talk with Lilly."

"I noticed." Thomas Haslam put an awkward arm around Ty, touched by what he saw in Ty's face. "First things first. I guess."

"Search and Rescue will be at the trailhead," the ranger said. "The dispatcher promised."

Lilly said nothing, but Ty felt the wet on her cheek as she hugged him.

"Back tomorrow night," he said. "We got things to talk about." He pulled her closer. "To do."

He climbed on Nightmare and looked at Lilly. "Look after the horses. They wander off in these high meadows."

He looked back from high above them, saw the ranger busy at his radio, Thomas Haslam and Lilly looking up before turning back to camp. Then he was into the climb for certain, the switchbacks cutting back onto themselves again and then again, the boy's cough rattling in bursts. Ty tried not to hear it, tried not to think of the foolishness, the boy's rush into the mountains as though they were some amusement park.

They were almost into the clouds when he looked back and saw rays of sun filtering through and catching the expanse of the Kaweah shelf, bringing light to the blue lakes and green meadows. It wasn't a bad dream to have, he thought—a safe place. He could take Lilly there and tell her everything—about Willie and the baby, about Cody Jo. Maybe he could tell those things to Thomas Haslam and Alice too, Buck and Angie. Even to Walker Johnson, if Walker Johnson would quit being so pensive. They could even live with the red bear there, watch him with Spec and Fenton, learn from him.

Then he was into the cloud itself. It was thick, the visibility bad and getting worse. A wind picked up. Not strong but cold. Ty thought they might be closing on the crest, but there was no way to tell. He couldn't see anything now, couldn't tell if they were going up or down. Jug was lost in the mist behind him, only the wracking cough to tell him what was back there, following Ty, counting on Ty.

When the rain began he dismounted, feeling for the trail as Nightmare followed. He took off his jacket, untied his slicker from behind his cantle, worked his way back to the coughing boy, wrapped him in the jacket, covered him with the slicker. He worked his way forward again, unsnapping Jug's lead, setting Jug and Nightmare free to make their own way. He needed his hands to feel his way, touch the rocks along the trail. Now and then he would see the trail, but mostly there was no way to see at all.

The wind kicked up, and he was sure they were on top. He knew there was a long traverse there. It took them above the glacier and then turned back, turning away from it into switchbacks again, switchbacks that turned and turned again down to parallel the long glacier and cross below it, below the moraine the glacier had deposited through the centuries. He thought the moraine must be older than the mountain, at least the mountain he knew—the one still heaving itself up, growing even as the glacier tore away its flank.

He was not surprised when he heard the distant rumble. It was the kind of day that could call up a thunderstorm. But he wasn't worried. The rain was still light, the weather just getting ready. All Ty wanted to do was see. He hoped at least that would be given him by the time he had to drop down through the switchbacks.

ᥴ᷏ᗒ

When it came he heard nothing. It was too late for him to hear. But the boy, Nightmare and Jug, were jolted upright by the flash, deafened by the crash. They waited in the silence, Nightmare quiet as the cloud they were in. The boy's cough rattled, once, twice. Then stillness. A hush.

Finally Nightmare began to move. Jug sensed it, moved along behind her. Nightmare seemed to be looking for something, but moving on with an instinct for the trail as sure as Smoky Girl had had before her, an instinct as sure as Ty Hardin's—the man she was seeking, the man who had taught them both, learned from them both.

But Ty Hardin was gone.

43

Requiem

The *Los Angeles Times* headline read:

Two Die As Lightning Hits Hikers
Struck on Mt. Whitney in Freak Storm
Fourteen Hikers Struck While Taking Shelter in Summit Hut:
Two Dead, Six Others Injured

The story named each hiker, describing the background of the dead and the injured. At the end it noted that Ty Hardin, a Sierra packer, had died at about the same time.

> Few details can be confirmed. All that is known is that Ty Hardin's horse, followed by a mule carrying a hiker suffering altitude sickness, made its way to the Whitney trailhead. They were discovered there by Norman "Buck" Conner, a colleague of Hardin, and two Forest Service paramedics.
>
> After the hiker was evacuated, Conner returned up the trail to recover the body of Hardin, which he found on the boulder field below the Whitney glacier.
>
> At this time it is not known whether Hardin fell from the trail because of poor visibility or was dislodged by the force of a lightning strike.

The people in the valley paid little attention to the falling part, knowing Ty Hardin would never fall off a trail—not on the blackest night. But they paid much attention to his being gone, stories about him growing even as the news spread, most concluding that only lightning could separate Ty Hardin from his mountains.

Lilly and the Haslams learned Ty was gone the same day it happened, the young ranger coming to their camp at dusk with the dispatcher's report. Lilly had not accepted it, everything in her going numb, staying numb through a sleepless night. It was not until the next day, when Buck—riding through the night to find them—took her into his arms, held her against his big body, and wept uncontrollably, that the loss washed through her.

⌒⌒

On the day of the service they gathered in the chapel yard, warming under a weak fall sun. Lilly held Buck's arm and talked with Angie, worrying about what this day would do to Buck. When the doors opened they filed in and filled the second row, awkward as they settled into their own thoughts. Cody Jo came down the aisle, helped by a gentleman friend who had driven her, her cane clicking on the wooden floor. She motioned them to join her in the front and sent her friend away, nodding to the Haslams, who were filling the row across the aisle. Then she sent Buck up the aisle to get Sugar and Maria Zumaldi, wanting them to sit with her too.

They sang a hymn the minister had chosen, the piano loud, the voices ragged. There was a prayer. Then the minister spoke about Ty. Lilly tried to listen, but her mind drifted to their day at the lake, the last camp at Crabtree, Ty leading the mule and the crumpled boy up into the cloud. The minister was brief and she was thankful, paying more attention to the prayer about "lifting thine eyes unto the hills."

There was another song. Then it was over, Lilly walking up the aisle with the Haslams and Cody Jo and realizing the chapel was full—cowboys from up and down the valley, rangers and trail-crew workers, young packers, Harvey Kittle standing at the back with Cody Jo's driver friend.

Lars had invited everyone to the Deerlodge, and most went there directly. At first they were quiet, reflective; but Lars was generous, and soon they were telling and retelling stories about Ty. Lars liked it when they began to relax. He knew Ty would like it too.

Alice Haslam had kept in touch with Walker Johnson. She went over to Lilly and Cody Jo by the bowling machine and read them a letter from him. It was about all the things Ty had done for Walker, meant to Walker. Lilly, sensing the rhythms of the south in Walker's words, grew even more blue as the letter went on.

When Alice finished she turned to Lilly and pressed something into her hand. "His music box," she said. "He'd want you to have it."

Lilly knew the box, had listened to the tinkle of "Red River Valley." She turned it in her hands, feeling the frayed corners, the leather worn away—wishing it were Ty she were feeling, Ty she were touching.

Someone was rapping a jackknife against a bottle. Lilly looked up and saw it was Buck.

"Like to thank Lars for having us." Buck looked around the room, his beer high.

Lilly turned the music box over and over in her hands, unable to worry about Buck anymore.

"There's Ty to thank, too." Buck hesitated, made sure he could go on. "Just for being Ty." He stood there, unable to say anything at all for a few minutes, the room waiting, the young packers awkward in their best clothes, the styles they had taken on—high-crowned hats, kerchiefs tied just so, pants tucked into high boots.

"He always found our horses," Buck finally said, his voice shaky, "when they run off."

The quiet held, the packers thinking how seldom horses ran off these days, all of them tying their horses up so there would be no need to seek tracks in the morning.

The talk picked up again. There were more toasts, more drinking, more thanking Lars for his generosity. But they didn't quiet for those toasts as they had for Buck's, weren't as interested as they'd been in Buck's—as though Buck was part of something that might be slipping away forever.

"Well, it figures," Harvey Kittle said, coming over to where Thomas Haslam and Lilly stood, still talking with Cody Jo. "Him loving them glaciers so. 'Let time heal the wounds those glaciers make,' he'd always say. 'Leaves the prettiest country of all.'"

"You think that glacier was telling us something?" Thomas Haslam said. "Or what those glaciers left was? Think that country doesn't want us up there?"

"That's the thing," Harvey Kittle said. "It don't like you too close. It liked to killed my old man. Crippled me. Now it's done Ty in."

"Ty didn't see it that way," Thomas Haslam said. "Thought he was part of it. That if he could get Lilly up on that Kaweah shelf of his, he could have it forever."

"Well he should of thought twice," Harvey Kittle said. "No way up on that shelf for one thing. For another, he never could of run off with just one person. Too damn many backpackers up there now. Climbers."

Cody Jo saw the blood rising in Lilly's face.

"You don't know anything," Lilly blurted. "Ty had things in him he couldn't explain. Can't you see what the mountains were to him? They were . . . his music."

Thomas Haslam saw her begin to shake, clutching hard at the music box.

"Harvey's just wondering," he said, calming her, "why it was the boy who was saved. By Ty's mare. Ty's mule."

"We should have waited." Lilly's anger dissolved into tears. "It would have cleared. You should never have told him to go. We could have waited."

"If we'd waited, Lilly, that boy wouldn't be alive."

"Don't you see?" Lilly cried, Cody Jo holding her now. "We gave him no choice. He *had* no choice. He's worth ten Tommies. A hundred . . ."

Cody Jo led her away, soothing her, listening to her, touching her.

�csᴐ

"Never seen anything like that," Cody Jo's friend said, pointing the car down the long reach of Owens Valley. "All those toasts. Sometimes I couldn't tell if they were about Ty Hardin or that husband you talk about."

"They came to be a lot alike over the years," Cody Jo said. "I get them mixed up myself." She thought she'd had more to drink than she should have, but so had everyone else, even the singer, who'd taken her aside when she was leaving, tried to tell her something.

It troubled her that she couldn't remember what Lilly had said. She liked her, liked her music, liked it that she'd tried to give Ty what she'd been unable to give him herself.

"Only I think Ty was more haunted." She looked at the long stretch of highway ahead. "Afraid he might run out of those high meadows."

She rested her head on the window and tried to sleep, watching the mountains, dozing a little, watching the mountains again.

The sun had dropped behind the crest, the eastern escarpment fading into that half-light of a day's end. A glow remained on Whitney— high and lonely. She watched the shadows lifting toward it, wondering what Lilly had wanted to say, liking it that the singer had given Ty more comfort than he'd ever known, thinking about the mountains taking him at last.

Maybe it *was* time, she thought. Maybe Harvey was right: there was no place for a Ty Hardin up there any more.

The light was gone from Whitney now, only the darkening mass outlined above the crest.

And suddenly Cody Jo was with Fenton again. They were at White River. "People might get you," Fenton was saying. "But not these mountains." He was watching her, loving her there on that big rock that tilted down into the currents of White River.

"The high country doesn't want to get you—or anybody else." He said it as though he could see into the night, unsparing as the moon.

"It's too big to care."

Acknowledgments

This book was a long time in coming. It was conceived along countless miles of Montana and Sierra trails, and through countless winter nights contemplating those miles. The writing took over four years, the revisions as many. Thanks to friends who have shared my camps—and to others who have relished the stories about those camps—it is finally done.

My thanks for helping it find sunlight go to many. I owe much to the rangers and trail crew members with whom I have shared humor and wisdom and high country routes. To my sons, Bill and Jed, and to the many who have come on my trips, traded tales and shared passages of this book around my fires, I owe more. Whole families have read drafts and chapters as they came to life: the Mosers and the Polhemi, the Ponds and the Hastorfs, the Pennypackers and the Bests—especially Craig, gone now in fact but not in spirit. There have been wonderful cheerleaders too: Betty and Ruth, Gaye and Danny, Brad, Kathy, Will, and Sarah—even Annie. I thank Cam Schryver, Ike Livermore, and David Buschena for their technical advice, particularly David, whose wife Maire urged more talk about cooking while constituting one half of an extraordinary set of high country twins. To the other half, Fiona O'Neill, I owe even more, not only for her delicate sketches of the Sierra ranges but for her wise humor and unflagging encouragement.

To Nancy Flowers I am indebted for intelligent readings and steady optimism about where this work was going. And I owe deep thanks to those sure readers kind enough to take on the entire text and beard me with its problems: Stacey-Lee Caminker, Dorothy Ingebretsen, Lois Miller, Trish Hooper.

I am also grateful to the writers and critics kind enough to nudge my work along: Willie and JoAnne Morris, who were among the first to tell me I'd written something of value. Steve Pyne, my old student and the gifted writer about fire and life who told me it was my characters, not my mountains, who made this story. Robert "Ace" Parker, my old friend and that master of dialogue who admitted that I "might" even know what I was doing. Toby Wolff who brought warmth to my campfires, to my life, and to my work. Chris Ames, who claims he'd never understood the mountains until I brought them to him. Jim Houston, who declared this work "authentic"—and meant it. John Sweney, who suffered a bruising pack trip only to return and go through my text with new understanding and intelligence—and the thoughtfulness to bring it to the attention of Joe Martin of Cornell's EPOCH, who in turn helped me reshape a long passage into the story, "Fenton's Cut-off."

Not quite finally, but almost, I am forever grateful to two kind readers and steadfast supporters who somehow provided both practical help and almost poetic hope: John Hessler and Tom Haydon, each of them so unassuming they have no way to understand their importance to the completion of this novel.

It is hard to think of a way to thank my Oklahoma Press editors: Bill Kittredge, for having the courage to take this book on, Karen Wieder and Sarah Nestor, who had the patience of Job and the wisdom of Solomon as they pruned my excesses and tolerated my crudities, and Marian Stewart, who brought us all together on the printed page. They were cheerful and generous, good-spirited and smart. I am deeply in their debt for their work, their generosity, their friendship.

Finally there is Jane to thank. No one could have suffered through so much so gracefully. She has somehow managed to be at once the most hawkeyed and kindest critic of all. Her good sense was a gift to this novel. It is irreplaceable.